"SUTHIN INTERESTIN"
—*The Heritage of Dedlow Marsh*

"ARGONAUT EDITION" OF
THE WORKS OF BRET HARTE

# A WARD
# OF THE GOLDEN GATE

## THE HERITAGE OF DEDLOW MARSH

BY

## BRET HARTE

*ILLUSTRATED*

VIGILANS ET AUDAX

P. F. COLLIER & SON
NEW YORK

*Published under special arrangement with
the Houghton Mifflin Company*

# A WARD OF THE GOLDEN GATE.

## PROLOGUE.

IN San Francisco the "rainy season" had been making itself a reality to the wondering Eastern immigrant. There were short days of drifting clouds and flying sunshine, and long succeeding nights of incessant downpour, when the rain rattled on the thin shingles or drummed on the resounding zinc of pioneer roofs. The shifting sand-dunes on the outskirts were beaten motionless and sodden by the onslaught of consecutive storms; the southeast trades brought the saline breath of the outlying Pacific even to the busy haunts of Commercial and Kearney streets; the low-lying Mission road was a quagmire; along the City Front, despite of piles and pier and wharf, the Pacific tides still asserted themselves in mud and ooze as far as Sansome Street;

the wooden sidewalks of Clay and Montgomery streets were mere floating bridges or buoyant pontoons superposed on elastic bogs; Battery Street was the Silurian beach of that early period on which tin cans, packing-boxes, freight, household furniture, and even the runaway crews of deserted ships had been cast away. There were dangerous and unknown depths in Montgomery Street and on the Plaza, and the wheels of a passing carriage hopelessly mired had to be lifted by the volunteer hands of a half dozen high-booted wayfarers, whose wearers were sufficiently content to believe that a woman, a child, or an invalid was behind its closed windows, without troubling themselves or the occupant by looking through the glass.

It was a carriage that, thus released, eventually drew up before the superior public edifice known as the City Hall. From it a woman, closely veiled, alighted, and quickly entered the building. A few passers-by turned to look at her, partly from the rarity of the female figure at that period, and partly from the greater rarity of its being well formed and even ladylike.

As she kept her way along the corridor

and ascended an iron staircase, she was passed by others more preoccupied in business at the various public offices. One of these visitors, however, stopped as if struck by some fancied resemblance in her appearance, turned, and followed her. But when she halted before a door marked " Mayor's Office," he paused also, and, with a look of half humorous bewilderment and a slight glance around him as if seeking for some one to whom to impart his arch fancy, he turned away. The woman then entered a large anteroom with a certain quick feminine gesture of relief, and, finding it empty of other callers, summoned the porter, and asked him some question in a voice so suppressed by the official severity of the apartment as to be hardly audible. The attendant replied by entering another room marked " Mayor's Secretary," and reappeared with a stripling of seventeen or eighteen, whose singularly bright eyes were all that was youthful in his composed features. After a slight scrutiny of the woman — half boyish, half official — he desired her to be seated, with a certain exaggerated gravity as if he was over-acting a grown-up part, and, taking a card from her, reëntered his

office.  Here, however, he did *not* stand on
his head or call out a confederate youth
from a closet, as the woman might have expected.  To the left was a green baize door,
outlined with brass-studded rivets like a
cheerful coffin-lid, and bearing the mortuary
inscription, " Private." This he pushed
open, and entered the Mayor's private
office.

The municipal dignitary of San Francisco,
although an erect, soldier-like man of strong
middle age, was seated with his official chair
tilted back against the wall and kept in position by his feet on the rungs of another,
which in turn acted as a support for a second man, who was seated a few feet from
him in an easy-chair.  Both were lazily
smoking.

The Mayor took the card from his secretary, glanced at it, said " Hullo ! " and
handed it to his companion, who read aloud
" Kate Howard," and gave a prolonged
whistle.

" Where is she ? " asked the Mayor.

" In the anteroom, sir."

" Any one else there ? "

" No, sir."

" Did you say I was engaged ? "

" Yes, sir ; but it appears she asked Sam who was with you, and when he told her, she said, All right, she wanted to see Colonel Pendleton too."

The men glanced interrogatively at each other, but Colonel Pendleton, abruptly anticipating the Mayor's functions, said, " Have her in," and settled himself back in his chair.

A moment later the door opened, and the stranger appeared. As she closed the door behind her she removed her heavy veil, and displayed the face of a very handsome woman of past thirty. It is only necessary to add that it was a face known to the two men, and all San Francisco.

" Well, Kate," said the Mayor, motioning to a chair, but without rising or changing his attitude. " Here I am, and here is Colonel Pendleton, and these are office hours. What can we do for you?"

If he had received her with magisterial formality, or even politely, she would have been embarrassed, in spite of a certain boldness of her dark eyes and an ever present consciousness of her power. It is possible that his own ease and that of his companion was part of their instinctive good nature and perception. She accepted it as such, took the chair familiarly, and seated herself sideways upon it, her right arm half encircling its back and hanging over it; altogether an easy and not ungraceful pose.

" Thank you, Jack — I mean, Mr. Mayor — and you, too, Harry. I came on business. I want you two men to act as guardians for my little daughter."

" Your what ? " asked the two men simultaneously.

" My daughter," she repeated, with a short laugh, which, however, ended with a note of defiance. " Of course you don't know. Well," she added half aggressively, and yet with the air of hurrying over a compromising and inexplicable weakness, " the long and short of it is I've got a little girl down at the Convent of Santa Clara, and have had — there! I've been taking care of her — *good* care, too, boys — for some time. And now I want to put things square for her for the future. See? I want to make over to her all my property — it's nigh on to seventy-five thousand dollars, for Bob Snelling put me up to getting those water lots a year ago — and, you see, I'll have to have regular guardians, trustees, or

whatever you call 'em, to take care of the
money for her."

"Who's her father?" asked the Mayor.

"What's that to do with it?" she said
impetuously.

"Everything — because he's her natural
guardian."

"Suppose he isn't known? Say dead,
for instance."

"Dead will do," said the Mayor gravely.
"Yes, dead will do," repeated Colonel Pendleton. After a pause, in which the two
men seemed to have buried this vague relative, the Mayor looked keenly at the
woman.

"Kate, have you and Bob Ridley had a
quarrel?"

"Bob Ridley knows too much to quarrel
with me," she said briefly.

"Then you are doing this for no motive
other than that which you tell me?"

"Certainly. That's motive enough —
ain't it?"

"Yes." The Mayor took his feet off his
companion's chair and sat upright. Colonel Pendleton did the same, also removing
his cigar from his lips. "I suppose you'll
think this thing over?" he added.

" No — I want it done *now* — right here — in this office."

" But you know it will be irrevocable."

" That's what I want it — something might happen afterwards."

" But you are leaving nothing for yourself, and if you are going to devote everything to this daughter and lead a different life, you 'll " —

" Who said I was?"

The two men paused, and looked at her.

" Look here, boys, you don't understand. From the day that paper is signed, I 've nothing to do with the child. She passes out of my hands into yours, to be schooled, educated, and made a rich girl out of — and never to know who or what or where *I* am. She does n't know now. I have n't given her and myself away in that style — you bet! She thinks I 'm only a friend. She has n't seen me more than once or twice, and not to know me again. Why, I was down there the other day, and passed her walking out with the Sisters and the other scholars, and she did n't know me — though one of the Sisters did. But they 're mum — *they* are, and don't let on. Why, now I think of it, *you* were down there,

Jack, presiding in big style as Mr. Mayor at the exercises. You must have noticed her. Little thing, about nine — lot of hair, the same color as mine, and brown eyes. White and yellow sash. Had a necklace on of real pearls I gave her. *I bought them,* you understand, myself at Tucker's — gave two hundred and fifty dollars for them — and a big bouquet of white rosebuds and lilacs I sent her."

"I remember her now on the platform," said the Mayor gravely. "So that is your child?"

"You bet — no slouch either. But that's neither here nor there. What I want now is you and Harry to look after her and her property the same as if I did n't live. More than that, as if I had *never lived.* I've come to you two boys, because I reckon you're square men and won't give me away. But I want to fix it even firmer than that. I want you to take hold of this trust not as Jack Hammersley, but as the *Mayor of San Francisco!* And when you make way for a new Mayor, *he* takes up the trust by virtue of his office, you see, so there's a trustee all along. I reckon there'll always be a San Francisco and always a Mayor — at least till

the child's of age ; and it gives her from the
start a father, and a pretty big one too.   Of
course the new man is n't to know the why
and wherefore of this.   It's enough for him
to take on that duty with his others, without asking questions.   And he's only got to
invest that money and pay it out as it's
wanted, and consult Harry at times."

The two men looked at each other with
approving intelligence.   "But have you
thought of a successor for *me*, in case somebody shoots me on sight any time in the
next ten years?" asked Pendleton, with a
gravity equal to her own.

"I reckon, as you're President of the
El Dorado Bank, you'll make that a part
of every president's duty too.   You'll get
the directors to agree to it, just as Jack
here will get the Common Council to make
it the Mayor's business."

The two men had risen to their feet, and,
after exchanging glances, gazed at her silently.   Presently the Mayor said : —

"It can be done, Kate, and we'll do it
for you — eh, Harry ? "

" Count me in," said Pendleton, nodding.

" But you'll want a third man."

"What's that for ? "

"The casting vote in case of any difficulty."

The woman's face fell. "I reckoned to
keep it a secret with only you two," she
said half bitterly.

"No matter. We'll find some one to
act, or you'll think of somebody and let us
know."

"But I wanted to finish this thing right
here," she said impatiently. She was silent
for a moment, with her arched black brows
knitted. Then she said abruptly, "Who's
that smart little chap that let me in? He
looks as if he might be trusted."

"That's Paul Hathaway, my secretary.
He's sensible, but too young. Stop! I
don't know about that. There's no legal
age necessary, and he's got an awfully old
head on him," said the Mayor thoughtfully.

"And *I* say his youth's in his favor,"
said Colonel Pendleton, promptly. "He's
been brought up in San Francisco, and he's
got no d—d old-fashioned Eastern notions
to get rid of, and will drop into this as a
matter of business, without prying about or
wondering. *I'll* serve with him."

"Call him in!" said the woman.

He came. Very luminous of eye, and

composed of lip and brow. Yet with the
same suggestion of " making believe " very
much, as if to offset the possible munching
of forbidden cakes and apples in his own
room, or the hidden presence of some still
in his pocket.

The Mayor explained the case briefly, but
with business-like precision. " Your duty,
Mr. Hathaway," he concluded, " at present
will be merely nominal and, above all, confidential. Colonel Pendleton and myself
will set the thing going." As the youth —
who had apparently taken in and " illuminated " the whole subject with a single
bright-eyed glance — bowed and was about
to retire, as if to relieve himself of his real
feelings behind the door, the woman stopped
him with a gesture.

" Let 's have this thing over now," she
said to the Mayor. " You draw up something that we can all sign at once." She
fixed her eyes on Paul, partly to satisfy her
curiosity and justify her predilection for
him, and partly to detect him in any overt
act of boyishness. But the youth simply
returned her glance with a cheerful, easy
prescience, as if her past lay clearly open
before him. For some minutes there was

only the rapid scratching of the Mayor's
pen over the paper. Suddenly he stopped
and looked up.

" What's her name ? "

" She must n't have mine," said the woman quickly. " That's a part of my idea.
I give that up with the rest. She must
take a new name that gives no hint of me.
Think of one, can't you, you two men?
Something that would kind of show that she
was the daughter of the city, you know."

" You could n't call her ' Santa Francisca,'
eh ? " said Colonel Pendleton, doubtingly.

" Not much," said the woman, with a seriousness that defied any ulterior insinuation.

" Nor Chrysopolinia ? " said the Mayor,
musingly.

" But that's only a *first* name. She must
have a family name," said the woman impatiently.

" Can *you* think of something, Paul ? "
said the Mayor, appealing to Hathaway.
" You 're a great reader, and later from
your classics than I am." The Mayor,
albeit practical and Western, liked to be
ostentatiously forgetful of his old Alma
Mater, Harvard, on occasions.

" How would *Yerba Buena* do, sir ? " re-

sponded the youth gravely. "It's the old
Spanish title of the first settlement here. It
comes from the name that Father Junipero
Serra gave to the pretty little vine that
grows wild over the sandhills, and means
'good herb.' He called it 'A balm for the
wounded and sore.'"

"For the wounded and sore?" repeated
the woman slowly.

"That's what they say," responded Hathaway.

"You ain't playing us, eh?" she said,
with a half laugh that, however, scarcely
curved the open mouth with which she had
been regarding the young secretary.

"No," said the Mayor, hurriedly. "It's
true. I've often heard it. And a capital
name it would be for her too. *Yerba* the
first name. *Buena* the second. She could
be called Miss Buena when she grows up."

"Yerba Buena it is," she said suddenly.
Then, indicating the youth with a slight toss
of her handsome head, "His head's level
—you can see that."

There was a silence again, and the scratching of the Mayor's pen continued. Colonel
Pendleton buttoned up his coat, pulled his
long moustache into shape, slightly arranged

his collar, and walked to the window without looking at the woman. Presently the Mayor arose from his seat, and, with a certain formal courtesy that had been wanting in his previous manner, handed her his pen and arranged his chair for her at the desk. She took the pen, and rapidly appended her signature to the paper. The others followed ; and, obedient to a sign from him, the porter was summoned from the outer office to witness the signatures. When this was over, the Mayor turned to his secretary. " That 's all just now, Paul."

Accepting this implied dismissal with undisturbed gravity, the newly made youthful guardian bowed and retired. When the green baize door had closed upon him, the Mayor turned abruptly to the woman with the paper in his hand.

"Look here, Kate ; there is still time for you to reconsider your action, and tear up this solitary record of it. If you choose to do so, say so, and I promise you that this interview, and all you have told us, shall never pass beyond these walls. No one will be the wiser for it, and we will give you full credit for having attempted something that was too much for you to perform."

She had half risen from her chair when he began, but fell back again in her former position and looked impatiently from him to his companion, who was also regarding her earnestly.

"What are you talking about?" she said sharply.

"*You*, Kate," said the Mayor. "You have given everything you possess to this child. What provision have you made for yourself?"

"Do I look played out?" she said, facing them.

She certainly did not look like anything but a strong, handsome, resolute woman, but the men did not reply.

"That is not all, Kate," continued the Mayor, folding his arms and looking down upon her. "Have you thought what this means? It is the complete renunciation not only of any claim but any interest in your child. That is what you have just signed, and what it will be our duty now to keep you to. From this moment we stand between you and her, as we stand between her and the world. Are you ready to see her grow up away from you, losing even the little recollection she has had of your kindness

— passing you in the street without knowing you, perhaps even having you pointed out to her as a person she should avoid? Are you prepared to shut your eyes and ears henceforth to all that you may hear of her new life, when she is happy, rich, respectable, a courted heiress — perhaps the wife of some great man? Are you ready to accept that she will never know — that no one will ever know — that you had any share in making her so, and that if you should ever breathe it abroad we shall hold it our duty to deny it, and brand the man who takes it up for you as a liar and the slanderer of an honest girl?"

"That's what I came here for," she said curtly, then, regarding them curiously, and running her ringed hand up and down the railed back of her chair, she added, with a half laugh, "What are you playin' me for, boys?"

"But," said Colonel Pendleton, without heeding her, "are you ready to know that in sickness or affliction you will be powerless to help her; that a stranger will take your place at her bedside; that as she has lived without knowing you she will die without that knowledge, or that if through any weakness of yours it came to her then, it would embitter her last thoughts of earth and, dying, she would curse you?"

The smile upon her half-open mouth still fluttered around it, and her curved fingers still ran up and down the rails of the chair-back as if they were the cords of some mute instrument, to which she was trying to give voice. Her rings once or twice grated upon them as if she had at times gripped them closely. But she rose quickly when he paused, said "Yes," sharply, and put the chair back against the wall.

"Then I will send you copies of this to-morrow, and take an assignment of the property."

"I 've got the check here for it now," she said, drawing it from her pocket and laying it upon the desk. "There, I reckon that 's finished. Good-by!"

The Mayor took up his hat, Colonel Pendleton did the same; both men preceded her to the door, and held it open with grave politeness for her to pass.

"Where are you boys going?" she asked, glancing from the one to the other.

"To see you to your carriage, Mrs. Howard," said the Mayor, in a voice that had become somewhat deeper.

"Through the whole building? Past all the people in the hall and on the stairs? Why, I passed Dan Stewart as I came in."

"If you will allow us?" he said, turning half appealing to Colonel Pendleton, who, without speaking, made a low bow of assent.

A slight flush rose to her face — the first and only change in the even healthy color she had shown during the interview.

"I reckon I won't trouble you, boys, if it's all the same to you," she said, with her half-strident laugh. "*You* might n't mind being seen — but *I* would — Good-by."

She held out a hand to each of the men, who remained for an instant silently holding them. Then she passed out of the door, slipping on her close black veil as she did so with a half-funereal suggestion, and they saw her tall, handsome figure fade into the shadows of the long corridor.

"Paul," said the Mayor, reëntering the office and turning to his secretary, "do you know who that woman is?"

"Yes, sir."

"She's one in a million! And now forget that you have ever seen her."

# CHAPTER I.

THE principal parlor of the New Golden Gate Hotel in San Francisco, fairly reported by the local press as being " truly palatial " in its appointments, and unrivaled in its upholstery, was, nevertheless, on August 5, 1860, of that startling newness that checked any familiarity, and evidently had produced some embarrassment on the limbs of four visitors who had just been ushered into its glories. After hesitating before one or two gorgeous fawn-colored brocaded easy-chairs of appalling and spotless virginity, one of them seated himself despairingly on a tête-à-tête sofa in marked and painful isolation, while another sat uncomfortably upright on a sofa. The two others remained standing, vaguely gazing at the ceiling, and exchanging ostentatiously admiring but hollow remarks about the furniture in unnecessary whispers. Yet they were apparently men of a certain habit of importance and small authority, with more or less critical attitude in their speech.

To them presently entered a young man
of about five-and-twenty, with remarkably
bright and singularly sympathetic eyes.
Having swept the group in a smiling glance,
he singled out the lonely occupier of the
tête-à-tête, and moved pleasantly towards
him. The man rose instantly with an eager
gratified look.

"Well, Paul, I did n't allow you'd remember me. It's a matter of four years
since we met at Marysville. And now you're
bein' a great man you've " —

No one could have known from the young
man's smiling face that he really had not
recognized his visitor at first, and that his
greeting was only an exhibition of one of
those happy instincts for which he was remarkable. But, following the clew suggested
by his visitor, he was able to say promptly
and gayly : —

"I don't know why I should forget Tony
Shear or the Marysville boys," turning with
a half-confiding smile to the other visitors,
who, after the human fashion, were beginning to be resentfully impatient of this special attention.

"Well, no, — for I've allus said that you
took your first start from Marysville. But

I 've brought a few friends of our party that
I reckoned to introduce to you.   Cap'n
Stidger, Chairman of our Central Committee, Mr. Henry J. Hoskins, of the firm of
Hoskins and Bloomer, and Joe Slate, of the
' Union Press,' one of our most promising
journalists.   Gentlemen," he continued, suddenly and without warning lifting his voice
to an oratorical plane in startling contrast
to his previous unaffected utterance, " I
need n't say that this is the Honorable Paul
Hathaway, the youngest state senator in the
Legislature.   You know his record ! "  Then,
recovering the ordinary accents of humanity,
he added, " We read of your departure last
night from Sacramento, and I thought we 'd
come early, afore the crowd."

" Proud to know you, sir," said Captain
Stidger, suddenly lifting the conversation to
the platform again.   " I have followed your
career, sir.   I 've read your speech, Mr.
Hathaway, and, as I was telling our mutual
friend, Mr. Shear, as we came along, I don't
know any man that could state the real party
issues as squarely.   Your castigating exposition of so-called Jeffersonian principles, and
your relentless indictment of the resolutions
of '98, were — were " — coughed the cap-

tain, dropping into conversation again —
" were the biggest thing out. You have only
to signify the day, sir, that you will address
us, and I can promise you the largest audience in San Francisco."

" I 'm instructed by the proprietor of the
' Union Press,' " said Mr. Slate, feeling for
his notebook and pencil, " to offer you its
columns for any explanations you may desire to make in the form of a personal letter
or an editorial in reply to the ' Advertiser's'
strictures on your speech, or to take any information you may have for the benefit of
our readers and the party."

" If you are ever down my way, Mr.
Hathaway," said Mr. Hoskins, placing a
large business card in Hathaway's hand,
" and will drop in as a friend, I can show
you about the largest business in the way of
canned provisions and domestic groceries in
the State, and give you a look around Battery Street generally. Or if you 'll name
your day, I 've got a pair of 2.35 Blue Grass
horses that 'll spin you out to the Cliff House
to dinner and back. I 've had Governor
Fiske, and Senator Doolan, and that big
English capitalist who was here last year,
and they — well, sir, — they were *pleased!*

Or if you'd like to see the town — if this is your first visit — I'm a hand to show you."

Nothing could exceed Mr. Hathaway's sympathetic acceptance of their courtesies, nor was there the least affectation in it. Thoroughly enjoying his fellowmen, even in their foibles, they found him irresistibly attractive. "I lived here seven years ago," he said, smiling, to the last speaker.

"When the water came up to Montgomery Street," interposed Mr. Shear, in a hoarse but admiring aside.

"When Mr. Hammersley was mayor," continued Hathaway.

"Had an official position — private secretary — afore he was twenty," explained Shear, in perfectly audible confidence.

"Since then the city has made great strides, leaping full-grown, sir, in a single night," said Captain Stidger, hastily ascending the rostrum again with a mixed metaphor, to the apparent concern of a party of handsomely dressed young ladies who had recently entered the parlor. "Stretching from South Park to Black Point, and running back to the Mission Dolores and the Presidio, we are building up a metropolis,

sir, worthy to be placed beside the Golden
Gate that opens to the broad Pacific and the
shores of far Cathay! When the Pacific
Railroad is built we shall be the natural
terminus of the Pathway of Nations!"

Mr. Hathaway's face betrayed no consciousness that he had heard something like
this eight years before, and that much of it
had come true, as he again sympathetically
responded. Neither was his attention attracted by a singular similarity which the
attitude of the group of ladies on the other
side of the parlor bore to that of his own
party. They were clustered around one of
their own number — a striking-looking girl
— who was apparently receiving their mingled flatteries and caresses with a youthful
yet critical sympathy, which, singularly
enough, was not unlike his own. It was evident also that an odd sort of rivalry seemed
to spring up between the two parties, and
that, in proportion as Hathaway's admirers
became more marked and ostentatious in
their attentions, the supporters of the young
girl were equally effusive and enthusiastic
in their devotion. As usual in such cases,
the real contest was between the partisans
themselves; each successive demonstration

on either side was provocative or retaliatory, and when they were apparently rendering homage to their idols they were really distracted by and listening to each other. At last, Hathaway's party being reinforced by fresh visitors, a tall brunette of the opposition remarked in a professedly confidential but perfectly audible tone : —

"Well, my dear, as I don't suppose you want to take part in a political caucus, perhaps we 'd better return to the Ladies' Boudoir, unless there 's a committee sitting there too."

"I know how valuable your time must be, as you are all business men," said Hathaway, turning to his party, in an equally audible tone ; " but before you go, gentlemen, you must let me offer you a little refreshment in a private room," and he moved naturally towards the door. The rival fair, who had already risen at their commander's suggestion, here paused awkwardly over an embarrassing victory. Should they go or stay ? The object of their devotion, however, turned curiously towards Hathaway. For an instant their eyes met. The young girl turned carelessly to her companions and said, " No ; stay here — it 's the public parlor ; " and her followers, evidently accustomed to her authority, sat down again.

"A galaxy of young ladies from the Convent of Santa Clara, Mr. Hathaway," explained Captain Stidger, naively oblivious of any discourtesy on their part, as he followed Hathaway's glance and took his arm as they moved away. "Not the least of our treasures, sir. Most of them daughters of pioneers — and all Californian bred and educated. Connoisseurs have awarded them the palm, and declare that for Grace, Intelligence, and Woman's Highest Charms the East cannot furnish their equal!" Having delivered this Parthian compliment in an oratorical passage through the doorway, the captain descended, outside, into familiar speech. "But I suppose you will find that out for yourself if you stay here long. San Francisco might furnish a fitting bride to California's youngest senator."

"I am afraid that my stay here must be brief, and limited to business," said Hathaway, who had merely noticed that the principal girl was handsome and original-looking. "In fact, I am here partly to see an old acquaintance — Colonel Pendleton."

The three men looked at each other cu'

riously. "Oh! Harry Pendleton," said Mr. Hoskins, incredulously. "You don't know *him?*"

"An old pioneeer — of course," interposed Shear, explanatorily and apologetically. "Why, in Paul's time the colonel was a big man here."

"I understand the colonel has been unfortunate," said Hathaway, gravely; "but in *my* time he was President of the El Dorado Bank."

"And the bank has n't got through its settlement yet," said Hoskins. "I hope *you* ain't expecting to get anything out of it?"

"No," said Hathaway, smiling; "I was a boy at that time, and lived up to my salary. I know nothing of his bank difficulties, but it always struck me that Colonel Pendleton was himself an honorable man."

"It ain't that," said Captain Stidger, energetically, "but the trouble with Harry Pendleton is that he has n't grown with the State, and never adjusted himself to it. And he won't. He thinks the Millennium was between the fall of '49 and the spring of '50, and after that everything dropped. He belongs to the old days, when a man's simple *word* was good for any amount if **you** knew him; and they say that the old bank had n't a scrap of paper for half that was owing to it. That was all very well, sir, in '49 and '50, and — Luck; but it won't do for '59 and '60, and — Business! And the old man can't see it."

" But he is ready to fight for it now, as in the old time," said Mr. Slate, " and that's another trouble with his chronology. He's done more to keep up dueling than any other man in the State, and don't know the whole spirit of progress and civilization is against it."

It was impossible to tell from Paul Hathaway's face whether his sympathy with Colonel Pendleton's foibles or his assent to the criticisms of his visitors was the truer. Both' were no doubt equally sincere. But the party was presently engaged in the absorption of refreshment, which, being of a purely spirituous and exhilarating quality, tended to increase their good humor with the host till they parted. Even then a gratuitous advertisement of his virtues and their own intentions in calling upon him was oratorically voiced from available platforms and landings, in the halls and stairways, until it was pretty well known throughout the

Golden Gate Hotel that the Hon. Mr. Paul
Hathaway had arrived from Sacramento and
had received a "spontaneous ovation."

Meantime the object of it had dropped
into an easy-chair by the window of his
room, and was endeavoring to recall a less
profitable memory. The process of human
forgetfulness is not a difficult one between
the ages of eighteen and twenty-six, and
Paul Hathaway had not only fulfilled the
Mayor's request by forgetting the particulars
of a certain transfer that he had witnessed
in the Mayor's office, but in the year succeeding that request, being about to try his
fortunes in the mountains, he had formally
constituted Colonel Pendleton to act as his
proxy in the administration of Mrs. Howard's singular Trust, in which, however, he
had never participated except yearly to sign
his name. He was, consequently, somewhat
astonished to have received a letter a few
days before from Colonel Pendleton, asking
him to call and see him regarding it.

He vaguely remembered that it was eight
years ago, and eight years had worked considerable change in the original trustees,
greatest of all in his superior officer, the
Mayor, who had died the year following,

leaving his trusteeship to his successor in
office, whom Paul Hathaway had never seen.
The Bank of El Dorado, despite Mrs. Howard's sanguine belief, had long been in
bankruptcy, and, although Colonel Pendleton still survived it, it was certain that no
other president would succeed to his office
as trustee, and that the function would lapse
with him. Paul himself, a soldier of fortune, although habitually lucky, had only
lately succeeded to a profession — if his political functions could be so described. Even
with his luck, energy, and ambition, while
everything was possible, nothing was secure.
It seemed, therefore, as if the soulless official must eventually assume the duties of
the two sympathizing friends who had origi-
nated them, and had stood *in loco parentis*
to the constructive orphan. The mother,
Mrs. Howard, had disappeared a year after
the Trust had been made — it was charita-
bly presumed in order to prevent any complications that might arise from her presence
in the country. With these facts before
him, Paul Hathaway was more concerned in
wondering what Pendleton could want with
him than, I fear, any direct sympathy with
the situation. On the contrary, it appeared

to him more favorable for keeping the secret
of Mrs. Howard's relationship, which would
now die with Colonel Pendleton and himself; and there was no danger of any emo-
tional betrayal of it in the cold official administration of a man who had received the
Trust through the formal hands of successive predecessors. He had forgotten the
time limited for the guardianship, but the
girl must soon be of age and off their hands.
If there had ever been any romantic or
chivalrous impression left upon his memory
by the scene in the mayor's office, I fear he
had put it away with various other foolish
illusions of his youth, to which he now believed he was superior.

Nevertheless, he would see the colonel,
and at once, and settle the question. He
looked at the address, " St. Charles Hotel."
He remembered an old hostelry of that
name, near the Plaza. Could it be possible
that it had survived the alterations and improvements of the city? It was an easy
walk through remembered streets, yet with
changed shops and houses and faces. When
he reached the Plaza, scarce recognizable in
its later frontages of brick and stone, he
found the old wooden building still intact,

v. 3                            Bret Harte I

with its villa-like galleries and verandas incongruously and ostentatiously overlooked by two new and aspiring erections on either side. For an instant he tried to recall the glamour of old days. He remembered when his boyish eyes regarded it as the crowning work of opulence and distinction; he remembered a ball given there on some public occasion, which was to him the acme of social brilliancy and display. How tawdry and trivial it looked beside those later and more solid structures! How inconsistent were those long latticed verandas and balconies, pathetic record of that first illusion of the pioneers that their climate was a tropical one! A restaurant and billiard-saloon had aggrandized all of the lower story; but there was still the fanlight, over which the remembered title of " St. Charles," in gilded letters, was now reinforced by the too demonstrative legend, " Apartments and Board, by the Day or Week." Was it possible that this narrow, creaking staircase had once seemed to him the broad steps of Fame and Fortune? On the first landing, a preoccupied Irish servant-girl, with a mop, directed him to a door at the end of the passage, at which he knocked. The door was

opened by a grizzled negro servant, who was
still holding a piece of oily chamois-leather
in his hand ; and the contents of a dueling-
case, scattered upon a table in the centre of
the room, showed what had been his occupation.   Admitting Hathaway with great
courtesy, he said : —

"Marse Harry bin havin' his ole trubble,
sah, and bin engaged just dis momen' on
his toylet ; ef yo'll accommodate yo'self on de
sofa, I inform him yo' is heah."

As the negro passed into the next room,
Paul cast a hasty glance around the apartment.   The furniture, originally rich and
elegant, was now worn threadbare and lustreless.   A book - case, containing, among
other volumes, a few law books — there being a vague tradition, as Paul remembered,
that Colonel Pendleton had once been connected with the law — a few French chairs
of tarnished gilt, a rifle in the corner, a
presentation sword in a mahogany case, a
few classical prints on the walls, and one or
two iron deed-boxes marked "El Dorado
Bank," were the principal objects.   A mild
flavor of dry decay and methylated spirits
pervaded the apartment.   Yet it was scrupulously clean and well kept, and a few

clothes neatly brushed and folded on a chair
bore witness to the servant's care. As Paul,
however, glanced behind the sofa, he was
concerned to see a coat, which had evidently
been thrust hurriedly in a corner, with the
sleeve lining inside out, and a needle and
thread still sticking in the seam. It struck
him instantly that this had been the negro's
occupation, and that the pistol-cleaning was
a polite fiction.

"Yo' 'll have to skuse Marse Harry seein'
yo in bed, but his laig 's pow'ful bad to-day,
and he can't stand," said the servant reëntering the room. "Skuse me, sah," he
added in a dignified confidential whisper,
half closing the door with his hand, " but if
yo' would n't mind avoidin' 'xcitin' or con-
troversical topics in yo' conversation, it would
be de better fo' him."

Paul smilingly assented, and the black retainer, with even more than the usual solemn ceremonious exaggeration of his race,
ushered him into the bedroom. It was furnished in the same faded glory as the sitting-room, with the exception of a low, iron
camp-bedstead, in which the tall, soldierly
figure of Colonel Pendleton, clad in threadbare silk dressing-gown, was stretched. He

had changed in eight years : his hair had
become gray, and was thinned over the
sunken temples, but his iron-gray moustache
was still particularly long and well pointed.
His face bore marks of illness and care;
there were deep lines down the angle of the
nostril that spoke of alternate savage out-
break and repression, and gave his smile a
sardonic rigidity.  His dark eyes, that shone
with the exaltation of fever, fixed Paul's on
entering, and with the tyranny of an invalid
never left them.

" Well, Hathaway ? "

With the sound of that voice Paul felt
the years slip away, and he was again a boy,
looking up admiringly to the strong man,
who now lay helpless before him.  He had
entered the room with a faint sense of sympathizing superiority and a consciousness of
having had experience in controlling men.
But all this fled before Colonel Pendleton's
authoritative voice ; even its broken tones
carried the old dominant spirit of the man,
and Paul found himself admiring a quality
in his old acquaintance that he missed in
his newer friends.

" I have n't seen you for eight years,
Hathaway.  Come here and let me look at
you."

Paul approached the bedside with boyish obedience. Pendleton took his hand and gazed at him critically.

"I should have recognized you, sir, for all your moustache and your inches. The last time I saw you was in Jack Hammersley's office. Well, Jack's dead, and here *I* am, little better, I reckon. You remember Hammersley's house?"

"Yes," said Paul, albeit wondering at the question.

"Something like this, Swiss villa style. I remember when Jack put it up. Well, the last time I was out, I passed there. And what do you think they've done to it?"

Paul could not imagine.

"Well, sir," said the colonel gravely, "they've changed it into a church missionary shop and young men's Christian reading-room! But that's 'progress' and 'improvement'!" He paused, and, slowly withdrawing his hand from Paul's, added with grim apology, "You're young, and belong to the new school, perhaps. Well, sir, I've read your speech; I don't belong to your party — mine died ten years ago — but I congratulate you. George! Confound it! where's that boy gone?"

The negro indicated by this youthful title, although he must have been ten years older than his master, after a hurried shuffling in the sitting-room eventually appeared at the door.

" George, champagne and materials for cocktails for the gentleman. The *best*, you understand. No new-fangled notions from that new barkeeper."

Paul, who thought he observed a troubled blinking in George's eyelid, and referred it to a fear of possible excitement for his patient, here begged his host not to trouble himself — that he seldom took anything in the morning.

"Possibly not, sir ; possibly not," returned the colonel, hastily. " I know the new ideas are prohibitive, and some other blank thing, but you 're safe here from your constituents, and by gad, sir, I shan't force you to take it ! It 's *my* custom, Hathaway — an old one — played out, perhaps, like all the others, but a custom nevertheless, and I 'm only surprised that George, who knows it, should have forgotten it."

" Fack is, Marse Harry," said George, with feverish apology, " it bin gone 'scaped my mind dis mo'nin' in de prerogation ob

business, but I 'm goin' now, shuah ! " and
he disappeared.

" A good boy, sir, but beginning to be
contaminated. Brought him here from
Nashville over ten years ago. Eight years
ago they proved to him that he was no longer
a slave, and made him d—d unhappy until
I promised him it should make no difference
to him and he could stay. I had to send for
his wife and child — of course, a dead loss
of eighteen hundred dollars when they set
foot in the State — but I 'm blanked if he
is n't just as miserable with them here, for
he has to take two hours in the morning and
three in the afternoon every day to be with
'em. I tried to get him to take his family
to the mines and make his fortune, like those
fellows they call bankers and operators and
stockbrokers nowadays ; or to go to Oregon
where they 'll make him some kind of a mayor
or sheriff — but he won't. He collects my
rents on some little property I have left, and
pays my bills, sir, and, if this blank civilization would only leave him alone, he 'd be a
good enough boy."

Paul could n't help thinking that the rents
George collected were somewhat inconsistent
with those he was evidently mending when

he arrived, but at that moment the jingle of glasses was heard in the sitting-room, and the old negro reappeared at the door. Drawing himself up with ceremonious courtesy, he addressed Paul. " Wo'd yo' mind, sah, taking a glance at de wine for yo' choice?" Paul rose, and followed him into the sitting-room, when George carefully closed the door. To his surprise Hathaway beheld a tray with two glasses of whiskey and bitters, but no wine. " Skuse me, sah," said the old man with dignified apology, " but de Kernel won't have any but de best champagne for hono'ble gemmen like yo'self, and I 'se despaired to say it can't be got in de house or de suburbs. De best champagne dat we gives visitors is de Widder Glencoe. Wo'd yo' mind, sah, for de sake o' not 'xcitin' de Kernel wid triflin' culinary matter, to say dat yo' don' take but de one brand?"

" Certainly," said Paul, smiling. " I really don't care for anything so early;" then, returning to the bedroom, he said carelessly, " You 'll excuse me taking the liberty, colonel, of sending away the champagne and contenting myself with whiskey. Even the best brand — the Widow Cliquot "— with a glance at the gratified George — " I find rather trying so early in the morning."

"As you please, Hathaway," said the colonel, somewhat stiffly. "I dare say there's a new fashion in drinks now, and a gentleman's stomach is a thing of the past. Then, I suppose, we can spare the boy, as this is his time for going home. Put that tin box with the Trust papers on the bed, George, and Mr. Hathaway will excuse your waiting." As the old servant made an exaggerated obeisance to each, Paul remarked, as the door closed upon him, "George certainly keeps his style, colonel, in the face of the progress you deplore."

"He was always a 'dandy nigger,'" returned Pendleton, his face slightly relaxing as he glanced after his grizzled henchman, "but his exaggeration of courtesy is a blank sight more natural and manly than the exaggeration of discourtesy which your superior civilized 'helps' think is self-respect. The excuse of servitude of any kind is its spontaneity and affection. When you know a man hates you and serves you from interest, you know he's a cur and you're a tyrant. It's your blank progress that's made menial service degrading by teaching men to

avoid it.  Why, sir, when I first arrived here,
Jack Hammersley and myself took turns as
cook to the party.  I did n't consider myself
any the worse master for it.  But enough of
this."  He paused, and, raising himself on
his elbow, gazed for some seconds half cautiously, half doubtfully, upon his companion.
" I 've got something to tell you, Hathaway,"
he said, slowly.  " You 've had an easy time
with this Trust; your share of the work
has n't worried you, kept you awake nights,
or interfered with your career.  I understand
perfectly," he continued, in reply to Hathaway's deprecating gesture.  " I accepted to
act as your proxy, and I *have*.  I 'm not
complaining.  But it is time that you should
know what I 've done, and what you may
still have to do.  Here is the record.  On
the day after that interview in the Mayor's
office, the El Dorado Bank, of which I was,
and still am, president, received seventy-five
thousand dollars in trust from Mrs. Howard.
Two years afterwards, on that same day, the
bank had, by lucky speculations, increased
that sum to the credit of the trust one hundred and fifty thousand dollars, or double
the original capital.  In the following year
the bank suspended payment."

# CHAPTER II.

IN an instant the whole situation and his relations to it flashed upon Paul with a terrible, but almost grotesque, completeness. Here he was, at the outset of his career, responsible for the wasted fortune of the daughter of a social outcast, and saddled with her support! He now knew why Colonel Pendleton had wished to see him; for one shameful moment he believed he also knew why he had been content to take his proxy! The questionable character of the whole transaction, his own carelessness, which sprang from that very confidence and trust that Pendleton had lately extolled — what *would*, what *could* not be made of it! He already heard himself abused by his opponents — perhaps, more terrible still, faintly excused by his friends. All this was visible in his pale face and flashing eyes as he turned them on the helpless invalid.

Colonel Pendleton received his look with the same critical, half-curious scrutiny that

had accompanied his speech. At last his
face changed slightly, a faint look of disappointment crossed his eyes, and a sardonic
smile deepened the lines of his mouth.

"There, sir," he said hurriedly, as if dis-
missing an unpleasant revelation; "don't
alarm yourself! Take a drink of that whiskey. You look pale. Well; turn your eyes
on those walls. You don't see any of that
money laid out here — do you? Look at me.
I don't look like a man enriched with other
people's money — do I? Well, let that content you. Every dollar of that Trust fund,
Hathaway, with all the interests and profits
that have accrued to it, is *safe!* Every cent
of it is locked up in government bonds with
Rothschild's agent. There are the receipts,
dated a week before the bank suspended.
But enough of *that* — *that* is n't what I asked
you to come and see me for."

The blood had rushed back to Paul's
cheeks uncomfortably. He saw now, as impulsively as he had previously suspected his
co-trustee, that the man had probably ruined
himself to save the Trust. He stammered
that he had not questioned the management
of the fund nor asked to withdraw his proxy.

"No matter, sir," said the colonel, impa-

tiently; "you had the right, and I suppose,"
he added with half-concealed scorn, "it was
your duty. But let that pass. The money
is safe enough; but, Mr. Hathaway, — and
this is the point I want to discuss with you,
— it begins to look as if the *secret* was safe
no longer!" He had raised himself with
some pain and difficulty to draw nearer to
Paul, and had again fixed his eyes eagerly
upon him. But Paul's responsive glance
was so vague that he added quickly, "You
understand, sir; I believe that there are
hounds — I say hounds! — who would be
able to blurt out at any moment that that
girl at Santa Clara is Kate Howard's
daughter."

At any other moment Paul might have
questioned the gravity of any such contin-
gency, but the terrible earnestness of the
speaker, his dominant tone, and a certain
respect which had lately sprung up in his
breast for him, checked him, and he only
asked with as much concern as he could
master for the moment: —

"What makes you think so?"

"That's what I want to tell you, Hathaway, and how I, and I alone, am responsible
for it. When the bank was in difficulty and

I made up my mind to guard the Trust with
my own personal and private capital, I knew
that there might be some comment on my
action. It was a delicate matter to show
any preference or exclusion at such a moment,,and I took two or three of my brother
directors whom I thought I could trust into
my confidence. I told them the whole story,
' and how the Trust was sacred. I made a
mistake, sir," continued Pendleton sardon-
ically, " a grave mistake. I did not take
into account that even in three years civilization and religion had gained ground here.
There was a hound there — a blank Judas
in the Trust. Well; he did n't see it. I
think he talked Scripture and morality. He
said something about the wages of sin being
infamous, and only worthy of confiscation.
He talked about the sins of the father being visited upon the children, and justly. I
stopped him. Well! Do you know what's
the matter with my ankle ? Look!" He
stopped and, with some difficulty and invincible gravity, throwing aside his dressing-
gown, turned down his stocking, and exposed
to Paul's gaze the healed cicatrix of an old
bullet-wound. " Troubled me damnably near
a year. Where I hit *him* — has n't troubled
him at all since !

"I think," continued the colonel, falling
back upon the pillow with an air of relief,
"that he told others — of his own kidney,
sir, — though it was a secret among gentlemen. But they have preferred to be silent
now — than *afterwards*. They know that
I'm ready. But I can't keep this up long ;
some time, you know, they're bound to im-
prove in practice and hit higher up ! As
far as I'm concerned," he added, with a
grim glance around the faded walls and
threadbare furniture, "it don't mind ; but
mine isn't the mouth to be stopped." He
paused, and then abruptly, yet with a sudden
and pathetic dropping of his dominant note,
said : "Hathaway, you're young, and Hammersley liked you — what's to be done? I
thought of passing over my tools to you.
You can shoot, and I hear you *have*. But
the h—l of it is that if you dropped a man
or two people would ask *why*, and want to
know what it was about ; while, when I do,
nobody here thinks it anything but *my way !*
I don't mean that it would hurt you with
the crowd to wipe out one or two of these
hounds during the canvass, but the trouble
is that they belong to *your party*, and," he
added grimly, "that wouldn't help your
career."

"But," said Paul, ignoring the sarcasm,
"are you not magnifying the effect of a disclosure? The girl is an heiress, excellently
brought up. Who will bother about the
antecedents of the mother, who has disappeared, whom she never knew, and who is
legally dead to her?"

"In my day, sir, no one who knew the
circumstances," returned the colonel, quickly.
"But we are living in a blessed era of Christian retribution and civilized propriety, and
I believe there are a lot of men and women
about who have no other way of showing
their own virtue than by showing up another's vice. We're in a reaction of reform.
It's the old drunkards who are always more
clamorous for total abstinence than the mod-
erately temperate. I tell you, Hathaway,
there couldn't be an unluckier moment for
our secret coming out."

"But she will be of age soon."

"In two months."

"And sure to marry."

"Marry!" repeated Pendleton, with grim
irony. "Would *you* marry her?"

"That's another question," said the young
man, promptly, "and one of individual taste;
but it does not affect my general belief that

she could easily find a husband as good and better."

"Suppose she found one *before* the secret is out. Ought he be told?"

"Certainly."

"And that would imply telling *her?*"

"Yes," said Paul, but not so promptly.

"And you consider *that* fulfilling the promise of the Trust — the pledges exchanged with that woman?" continued Pendleton, with glittering eyes and a return to his own dominant tone.

"My dear colonel," said Paul, somewhat less positively, but still smiling, "you have made a romantic, almost impossible compact with Mrs. Howard that, you yourself are now obliged to admit, circumstances may prevent your carrying out substantially. You forget, also, that you have just told me that you have already broken your pledge — under circumstances, it is true, that do you honor — and that now your desperate attempts to retrieve it have failed. Now, I really see nothing wrong in your telling to a presumptive well-wisher of the girl what you have told to her enemy."

There was a dead silence. The prostrate man uttered a slight groan, as if in pain, and drew up his leg to change his position. After a pause, he said, in a restrained voice, "I differ from you, Mr. Hathaway; but enough of this for the present. I have something else to say. It will be necessary for one of us to go at once to Santa Clara and see Miss Yerba Buena."

"Good heavens!" said Paul, quickly. "Do you call her *that*?"

"Certainly, sir. *You* gave her the name. Have you forgotten?"

"I only suggested it," returned Paul, hopelessly; "but no matter — go on."

"*I* cannot go there, as you see," continued Pendleton, with a weary gesture towards his crippled ankle; "and I should particularly like you to see her before we make the joint disposition of her affairs with the Mayor, two months hence. I have some papers you can show her, and I have already written a letter introducing you to the Lady Superior at the convent, and to her. You have never seen her?"

"No," said Paul. "But of course you have?"

"Not for three years."

Paul's eyes evidently expressed some wonder, for a moment after the colonel added,

" I believe, Hathaway, I am looked upon as a queer survival of a rather lawless and improper past. At least, I have thought it better not socially to compromise her by my presence. The Mayor goes there — at the examinations and exercises, I believe, sir; they make a sort of reception for him — with a — a — banquet — lemonade and speeches."

" I had intended to leave for Sacramento, to-morrow night," said Paul, glancing curiously at the helpless man; " but I will go there if you wish."

" Thank you. It will be better."

There were a few words of further explanation of the papers, and Pendleton placed the packet in his visitor's hands. Paul rose. Somehow, it appeared to him that the room looked more faded and forgotten than when he entered it, and the figure of the man before him more lonely, helpless, and abandoned. With one of his sympathetic impulses he said : —

" I don't like to leave you here alone. Are you sure you can help yourself without George? Can I do anything before I go?"

" I am quite accustomed to it," said Pendleton, quietly. " It happens once or twice a year, and when I go out — well — I miss more than I do here."

He took Paul's proffered hand mechanically, with a slight return of the critical, doubting look he had cast upon him when he entered. His voice, too, had quite recovered its old dominance, as he said, with half-patronizing conventionality, "You'll have to find your way out alone. Let me know how you have sped at Santa Clara, will you? Good-by."

The staircase and passage seemed to have grown shabbier and meaner as Paul, slowly and hesitatingly, descended to the street. At the foot of the stairs he paused irresolutely, and loitered with a vague idea of turning back on some pretense, only that he might relieve himself of the sense of desertion. He had already determined upon making that inquiry into the colonel's personal and pecuniary affairs which he had not dared to offer personally, and had a half-formed plan of testing his own power and popularity in a certain line of relief that at once satisfied his sympathies and ambitions. Nevertheless, after reaching the street, he lingered a moment, when an odd idea of temporizing with his inclinations struck him. At the farther end of the hotel — one of the parasites living on its decayed fortunes — was a small barber's shop. By having his hair trimmed and his clothes brushed he could linger a little longer beneath the same roof with the helpless solitary, and perhaps come to some conclusion. He entered the clean but scantily furnished shop, and threw himself into one of the nearest chairs, hardly noting that there were no other customers, and that a single assistant, stropping a razor behind a glass door, was the only occupant. But there was a familiar note of exaggerated politeness about the voice of this man as he opened the door and came towards the back of the chair with the formula : —

" Mo'nin', sah ! Shall we hab de pleshure of shavin' or hah-cuttin' dis mo'nin' ? " Paul raised his eyes quickly to the mirror before him. It reflected the black face and grizzled hair of George.

More relieved at finding the old servant still near his master than caring to comprehend the reason, Hathaway said pleasantly, " Well, George, is this the way you look after your family ? "

The old man started ; for an instant his full red lips seemed to become dry and ashen, the whites of his eyes were suffused and staring, as he met Paul's smiling face in the glass. But almost as quickly he recovered himself, and, with a polite but deprecating bow, said, — "For God sake, sah! I admit de sarkumstances is agin me, but de simple fack is dat I'm temper'ly occupyin' de place of an ole frien', sah, who is called round de cornah."

"And I'm devilish glad of any fact, George, that gives me a chance of having my hair cut by Colonel Pendleton's right-hand man. So fire away!"

The gratified smile which now suddenly overspread the whole of the old man's face, and seemed to quickly stiffen the rugged and wrinkled fingers that had at first trembled in drawing a pair of shears from a ragged pocket, appeared to satisfy Paul's curiosity for the present. But after a few moments' silent snipping, during which he could detect in the mirror some traces of agitation still twitching the negro's face, he said with an air of conviction : —

"Look here, George — why don't you regularly use your leisure moments in this trade? You'd make your fortune by your taste and skill at it."

For the next half minute the old man's frame shook with silent childlike laughter

behind Paul's chair. "Well, Marse Hathaway, yo's an ole frien' o' my massa, and a
gemman yo'self, sah, and a senetah, and I
do'an mind tellin' yo' — dat 's jess what I
bin gone done! It makes a little ready
money for de ole woman and de chilleren.
But de Kernel don' no'. Ah, sah! de Kernel kill me or hisself if he so much as 'spi-
cioned me. De Kernel is high-toned, sah!
— bein' a gemman yo'self, yo' understand.
He would n't heah ob his niggah worken' for
two massas — for all he 's willen' to lemme
go and help myse'f. But, Lord bless yo',
sah, dat ain't in de category! De Kernel
could n't get along widout me."

"You collect his rents, don't you?" said
Paul, quietly.

"Yes, sah."

"Much?"

"Well, no, sah; not so much as fom'ly,
sah! Yo' see, de Kernel's prop'ty lies in de
ole parts ob de town, where de po' white folks
lib, and dey ain't reg'lar. De Kernel dat
sof' in his heart, he dare n' press 'em; some
of 'em is ole fo'ty-niners, like hisself, sah;
and some is Spanish, sah, and dey is sof'
too, and ain't no more gumption dan chilleren, and tink it 's ole time come ag'in, and

dey 's in de ole places like afo' de Mexican wah! and dey don' bin payin' noffin'. But we gets along, sah, — we gets along, — not in de *prima facie* style, sah! mebbe not in de modden way dut de Kernel don't like; but we keeps ourse'f, sah, and has wine fo' our friends. When yo' come again, sah, yo' 'll find de Widder Glencoe on de sideboard."

"Has the colonel many friends here?"

"Mos' de ole ones bin done gone, sah, and de Kernel don' cotton to de new. He don' mix much in sassiety till de bank settlements bin gone done. Skuse me, sah! — but you don' happen to know when dat is? It would be a pow'ful heap off de Kernel's mind if it was done. Bein' a high and mighty man in committees up dah in Sacramento, sah, I did n't know but what yo' might know as it might come befo' yo'."

"I 'll see about it," said Paul, with an odd, abstracted smile.

"Shampoo dis mornen', sah?"

"Nothing more in this line," said Paul, rising from his chair, "but something more, perhaps, in the line of your other duties. You 're a good barber for the public, George, and I don't take back what I said about your future; but *just now* I think the colonel wants all your service. He's not at all well. Take this," he said, putting a twenty-dollar gold piece in the astonished servant's hand, "and for the next three or four days drop the shop, and under some pretext or another arrange to be with him. That money will cover what you lose here, and as soon as the colonel's all right again you can come back to work. But are you not afraid of being recognized by some one?"

"No, sah, dat's just it. On'y strangers dat don't know no better come yere."

"But suppose your master should drop in? It's quite convenient to his rooms."

"Marse Harry in a barber-shop!" said the old man with a silent laugh. "Skuse me, sah," he added, with an apologetic mixture of respect and dignity, "but fo' twenty years no man hez touched de Kernel's chin but myself. When Marse Harry hez to go to a barber's shop, it won't make no matter who's dar."

"Let's hope he will not," said Paul gayly; then, anxious to evade the gratitude which, since his munificence, he had seen beaming in the old negro's eye and evidently trying to find polysyllabic and elevated expression on his lips, he said hurriedly, "I shall expect to find you with the colonel when I call again in a day or two," and smilingly departed.

At the end of two hours George's barber-employer returned to relieve his assistant, and, on receiving from him an account and a certain percentage of the afternoon's fees (minus the gift from Paul), was informed by George that he should pretermit his attendance for a few days.   " Udder private and personal affairs," explained the old negro, who made no social distinction in his vocabulary, "peroccupyin' dis niggah's time." The head barber, unwilling to lose a really good assistant, endeavored to dissuade him by the offer of increased emolument, but George was firm.

As he entered the sitting-room the colonel detected his step, and called him in.

" Another time, George, never allow a guest of mine to send away wine.   If he don't care for it, put it on the sideboard."

" Yes, sah ; but as yo' did n't like it yo'self, Marse Harry, and de wine was de most 'xpensive quality ob Glencoe " —

" D—n the expense ! "   He paused, and gazed searchingly at his old retainer.

"George," he said suddenly, yet in a gentle voice, "don't lie to me, or "— in a still kinder voice — " I 'll flog the black skin off you! Listen to me. *Have* you got any money left?"

" 'Deed, sah, dere *is*," said the negro earnestly. "I 'll jist fetch it wid de accounts."

"Hold on! I 've been thinking, lying here, that if the Widow Molloy can't pay because she sold out, and that tobacconist is ruined, and we 've had to pay the water tax for old Bill Soames, the rent last week don't amount to much, while there 's the month's bill for the restaurant and that blank druggist's account for lotions and medicines to come out of it. It strikes me we 're pretty near touching bottom. I 've everything I want here, but, by God, sir, if I find *you* skimping yourself or lying to me or borrowing money " —

"Yes, Marse Harry, but the Widder Molloy done gone and paid up dis afernoon. I 'll bring de books and money to prove it;" and he hurriedly reëntered the sitting-room.

Then with trembling hands he emptied his pockets on the table, including Paul's gift and the fees he had just received, and opening a desk-drawer took from it a striped cotton handkerchief, such as negro women wear on their heads, containing a small quantity of silver tied up in a hard knot, and a boy's purse. This he emptied on the table with his own money.

They were the only rents of Colonel Henry Pendleton! They were contributed by "George Washington Thomson;" his wife, otherwise known as "Aunt Dinah," washerwoman; and "Scipio Thomson," their son, aged fourteen, bootblack. It did not amount to much. But in that happy moisture that dimmed the old man's eyes, God knows it looked large enough.

# CHAPTER III.

ALTHOUGH the rays of an unclouded sun were hot in the Santa Clara roads and by-ways, and the dry, bleached dust had become an impalpable powder, the perspiring and parched pedestrian who rashly sought relief in the shade of the wayside oak was speedily chilled to the bone by the northwest trade-winds that on those August afternoons swept through the defiles of the Coast Range, and even penetrated the pastoral valley of San José. The anomaly of straw hats and over-coats with the occupants of buggies and station wagons was thus accounted for, and even in the sheltered garden of " El Rosario " two young girls in light summer dresses had thrown wraps over their shoulders as they lounged down a broad rose-alley at right angles with the deep, long veranda of the *casa*. Yet, in spite of the chill, the old Spanish house and gardens presented a lux-urious, almost tropical, picture from the roadside. Banks, beds, and bowers of roses

lent their name and color to the grounds;
tree-like clusters of hanging fuchsias, mound-
like masses of variegated verbena, and
tangled thickets of ceanothus and spreading
heliotrope were set in boundaries of venerable olive, fig, and pear trees.   The old
house itself, a picturesque relief to the glaring
newness of the painted villas along the road,
had been tastefully modified to suit the
needs and habits of a later civilization; the
galleries of the inner courtyard, or *patio*,
had been transferred to the outside walls in
the form of deep verandas, while the old
adobe walls themselves were hidden beneath
flowing Cape jessamine or bestarred passion
vines, and topped by roofs of cylindrical red
tiles.

"Miss Yerba!" said a dry, masculine
voice from the veranda.

The taller young girl started, and drew
herself suddenly behind a large Castilian
rose-tree, dragging her companion with her,
and putting her finger imperatively upon a
pretty but somewhat passionate mouth.   The
other girl checked a laugh, and remained
watching her friend's wickedly leveled brows
in amused surprise.

The call was repeated from the veranda.

After a moment's pause there was the sound of retreating footsteps, and all was quiet again.

"Why, for goodness' sake, did n't you answer, Yerba?" asked the shorter girl.

"Oh, I hate him!" responded Yerba. "He only wanted to bore me with his stupid, formal, sham-parental talk. Because he's my official guardian he thinks it necessary to assume this manner towards me when we meet, and treats me as if I were something between his stepdaughter and an almshouse orphan or a police board. It's perfectly ridiculous, for it 's only put on while he is in office, and he knows it, and I know it, and I 'm tired of making believe. Why, my dear, they change every election; I 've had seven of them, all more or less of this kind, since I can remember."

"But I thought there were two others, dear, that were not official," said her companion, coaxingly.

Yerba sighed. "No; there was another, who was president of a bank, but that was also to be official if he died. I used to like him, he seemed to be the only gentleman among them; but it appears that he is dreadfully improper; shoots people now and then

for nothing at all, and burst up his bank —
and, of course, he's impossible, and, as
there's no more bank, when he dies there'll
be no more trustee."

"And there's the third, you know — a
stranger, who never appears?" suggested
the younger girl.

"And who do you suppose *he* turns out to
be? Do you remember that conceited little
wretch — that 'Baby Senator,' I think they
called him — who was in the parlor of the
Golden Gate the other morning surrounded
by his idiotic worshipers and toadies and
ballot-box stuffers? Well, if you please,
*that's* Mr. Paul Hathaway — the Honorable
Paul Hathaway, who washed his hands of
me, my dear, at the beginning!"

"But really, Yerba, I thought that he
looked and acted"—

"You thought of nothing at all, Milly,"
returned Yerba, with authority. "I tell
you he's a mass of conceit. What else
can you expect of a Man — toadied and
fawned upon to that extent? It made me
sick! I could have just shaken them!"

As if to emphasize her statement, she
grasped one of the long willowy branches of
the enormous rose-bush where she stood, and

shook it lightly. The action detached a few of the maturer blossoms, and sent down a shower of faded pink petals on her dark hair and yellow dress. " I can't bear conceit," she added.

" Oh, Yerba, just stand as you are! I do wish the girls could see you. You make the *loveliest* picture! "

She certainly did look very pretty as she stood there — a few leaves lodged in her hair, clinging to her dress, and suggesting by reflection the color that her delicate satin skin would have resented in its own texture. But she turned impatiently away — perhaps not before she had allowed this passing vision to impress the mind of her devoted adherent — and said, " Come along, or that dreadful man will be out on the veranda again."

" But, if you dislike him so, why did you accept the invitation to meet him here at luncheon? " said the curious Milly.

" *I* did n't accept; the Mother Superior did for me, because he 's the Mayor of San Francisco visiting your uncle, and she 's always anxious to placate the powers that be. And I thought he might have some information that I could get out of him. And it was better than being in the convent all day.

And I thought I could stand *him* if you were here."

Milly gratefully accepted this doubtful proof of affection by squeezing her companion's arm. "And you didn't get any information, dear?"

"Of course not! The idiot knows only the old tradition of his office — that I was a mysterious Trust left in Mayor Hammersley's hands. He actually informed me that 'Buena' meant 'Good'; that it was likely the name of the captain of some whaler, that put into San Francisco in the early days, whose child I was, and that, if I chose to call myself 'Miss Good,' he would allow it, and get a bill passed in the Legislature to legalize it. Think of it, my dear! 'Miss Good,' like one of Mrs. Barbauld's stories, or a moral governess in the 'Primary Reader.'"

"'Miss Good,'" repeated Milly, innocently. "Yes, you might put an *e* at the end — G-double-o-d-e. There are Goodes in Philadelphia. And then you won't have to sacrifice that sweet pretty 'Yerba,' that's so stylish and musical, for you'd still be 'Yerba Good.' But," she added, as Yerba made an impatient gesture, "why do you worry your-

self about *that*? You would n't keep your
own name long, whatever it was. An heiress
like you, dear, — lovely and accomplished, —
would have the best names as well as the
best men in America to choose from."

"Now please don't repeat that idiot's
words. That's what *he* says; that's what
they *all* say!" returned Yerba, pettishly.
"One would really think it was necessary
for me to get married to become anybody at
all, or have any standing whatever. And,
whatever you do, don't go talking of me as
if I were named after a vegetable. 'Yerba
Buena' is the name of an island in the bay
just off San Francisco. I'm named after
that."

"But I don't see the difference, dear.
The island was named after the vine that
grows on it."

"*You* don't see the difference?" said
Yerba, darkly. "Well, *I* do. But what
are you looking at?"

Her companion had caught her arm, and
was gazing intently at the house.

"Yerba," she said quickly, "there's the
Mayor, and uncle, and a strange gentleman
coming down the walk. They're looking
for us. And, as I live, Yerb! the strange

gentleman is that young senator, Mr. Hath
away ! "

" Mr. Hathaway ?    Nonsense ! "

" Look for yourself."

Yerba glanced at the three gentlemen,
who, a hundred yards distant, were slowly
advancing in the direction of the ceanothus-
hedge, behind which the girls had instinctively strayed during their conversation.

" What are you going to do ? " said Milly,
eagerly.    " They 're coming straight this
way.    Shall we stay here and let them pass,
or make a run for the house ? "

" No," said Yerba, to Milly's great surprise.    " That would look as if we cared.
Besides, I don't know that Mr. Hathaway
has come to see *me*.   We'll stroll out and
meet them accidentally."

Milly was still more astonished.  However,
she said, " Wait a moment, dear ! " and, with
the instinctive deftness of her sex, in three
small tugs and a gentle hitch, shook Yerba's
gown into perfect folds, passed her fingers
across her forehead and over her ears, securing, however, with a hairpin on their passage
three of the rose petals where they had
fallen.    Then, discharging their faces of any
previous expression, these two charming

hypocrites sallied out innocently into the walk. Nothing could be more natural than their manner : if a criticism might be ventured upon, it was that their elbows were slightly drawn inwards and before them, leaving their hands gracefully advanced in the line of their figures, an attitude accepted throughout the civilized world of deportment as indicating fastidious refinement not unmingled with permissible hauteur.

The three gentlemen lifted their hats at this ravishing apparition, and halted. The Mayor advanced with great politeness.

" I feared you did n't hear me call you, Miss Yerba, so we ventured to seek you." As the two girls exchanged almost infantile glances of surprise, he continued : " Mr. Paul Hathaway has done us the honor of seeking you here, as he did not find you at the convent. You may have forgotten that Mr. Hathaway is the third one of your trustees."

" And so inefficient and worthless that I fear he does n't count," said Paul, " but," raising his eyes to Yerba's, " I fancy that I have already had the pleasure of seeing you, and, I fear, the mortification of having dis-

turbed you and your friends in the parlor of
the Golden Gate Hotel yesterday."

The two girls looked at each other with
the same childlike surprise. Yerba broke
the silence by suddenly turning to Milly.
" Certainly, you remember how greatly interested we were in the conversation of a party
of gentlemen who were there when we came
in. I am afraid our foolish prattle must
have disturbed *you.* I know that we were
struck with the intelligent and eloquent devotion of your friends."

" Oh, perfectly," chimed in the loyal but
somewhat infelix Milly ; " and it was so
kind and thoughtful of Mr. Hathaway to
take them away as he did."

" I felt the more embarrassed," continued
Hathaway, smiling, but still critically examining Yerba for an indication of something
characteristic, beyond this palpable conventionality, " as I unfortunately must present
my credentials from a gentleman as much of
a stranger as myself — Colonel Pendleton."

The trade-wind was evidently making itself
felt even in this pastoral retreat, for the two
gentlemen appeared to shrink slightly within
themselves, and a chill seemed to have passed
over the group. The Mayor coughed. The

avuncular Woods gazed abstractedly at a
large cactus. Even Paul, prepared by previous experience, stopped short.

" Colonel Pendleton ! Oh, do tell me all
about him ! " flashed out Yerba, suddenly,
with clasped hands and eager girlish breath.

Paul cast a quick grateful glance at the
girl. Whether assumed or not, her enthusiastic outburst was effective. The Mayor
looked uneasily at Woods, and turned to
Paul.

" Ah, yes ! You and he are original co-
trustees. I believe Pendleton is in reduced
circumstances. Never quite got over that
bank trouble."

" That is only a question of legislative
investigation and relief," said Paul lightly,
yet with purposely vague official mystery of·
manner. Then, turning quickly to Yerba,
as if replying to the only real question at
issue, he continued pointedly, " I am sorry
to say the colonel's health is so poor that it
keeps him quite a recluse. I have a letter
from him and a message for you." His
bright eyes added plainly — " as soon as we
can get rid of those people."

" Then you think that a bill " — began
the Mayor, eagerly.

" I think, my dear sir," said Paul plaintively, " that I and my friends have already tried the patience of these two young ladies quite enough yesterday with politics and law-making. I have to catch the six-o'clock train to San Francisco this evening, and have already lost the time I hoped to spend with Miss Yerba by missing her at the convent. Let me stroll on here, if you like, and if I venture to monopolize the attention of this young lady for half an hour, you, my dear Mr. Mayor, who have more frequent access to her, I know, will not begrudge it to me."

He placed himself beside Yerba and Milly, and began an entertaining, although, I fear, slightly exaggerated, account of his reception by the Lady Superior, and her evident doubts of his identity with the trustee mentioned in Pendleton's letter of introduction. " I confess she frightened me," he continued, " when she remarked that, according to my statement, I could have been only eighteen years old when I became your guardian, and as much in want of one as you were. I think that only her belief that Mr. Woods and the Mayor would detect me as an impostor provoked her at last to tell me your whereabouts."

" But why *did* they ever make you a trustee, for goodness' sake ? " said Milly, naïvely. " Was there no one grown up at that time that they could have called upon ? "

" Those were the *early* days of California," responded Paul, with great gravity, although he was conscious that Yerba was regarding him narrowly, " and I probably looked older and more intelligent than I really was. For, candidly," with the consciousness of Yerba's eyes still upon him, " I remember very little about it. I dare say I was selected, as you kindly suggest, ' for goodness' sake.' "

" After all," said the volatile Milly, who seemed inclined, as chaperone, to direct the conversation, " there was something pretty and romantic about it. You two poor young things taking care of each other, for of course there were no women here in those days."

" Of course there *were* women here," interrupted Yerba, quickly, with a half-meaning, half-interrogative glance at Paul that made him instinctively uneasy. " You later comers "— to Milly — " always seem to think that there was nothing here before you ! " She paused, and then added, with a naïve mixture of reproach and coquetry that was as charming as it was unexpected, " As to taking care of each other, Mr. Hathaway very quickly got rid of me, I believe."

" But I left you in better hands, Miss Yerba; and let me thank you now," he added in a lower tone, " for recognizing it as you did a moment ago. I 'm glad that you instinctively liked Colonel Pendleton. Had you known him better, you would have seen how truthful that instinct was. His chief fault in the eyes of our worthy friends is that he reminds them of a great deal they can't perpetuate and much they would like to forget." He checked himself abruptly. "But here is your letter," he resumed, drawing Colonel Pendleton's missive from his pocket, " perhaps you would like to read it now, in case you have any message to return by me. Miss Woods and I will excuse you."

They had reached the end of the rose-alley, where a summer-house that was in itself a rose-bower partly disclosed itself. The other gentlemen had lagged behind. " I will amuse *myself*, and console your other guardian, dear," said the vivacious Milly, with a rapid exchange of glances with Yerba, " until this horrid business is over. Besides," she added with cheerful vague-

ness, " after so long a separation you must
have a great deal to say to each other."

Paul smiled as she rustled away, and
Yerba, entering the summer-house, sat down
and opened the letter. The young man remained leaning against the rustic archway,
occasionally glancing at her and at the moving figures in the gardens. He was conscious of an odd excitement which he could
trace to no particular cause. It was true
that he had been annoyed at not finding the
young girl at the convent, and at having to
justify himself to the Lady Superior for
what he conceived to be an act of gratuitous
kindness; nor was he blind to the fact that
his persistence in following her was more
an act of aggression against the enemies of
Pendleton than of concern for Yerba. She
was certainly pretty; he could not remember her mother sufficiently to trace any likeness, and he had never admired the mother's
pronounced beauty. She had flashed out
for an instant into what seemed originality
and feeling. But it had passed, and she
had asked no further questions in regard to
the colonel.

She had hurriedly skimmed through the
letter, which seemed to be composed of cer-

tain figures and accounts. " I suppose it 's all right," she said ; " at least you can say so if he asks you. It 's only an explanation why he has transferred my money from the bank to Rothschild's agent years ago. I don't see why it should interest me *now*."

Paul made no doubt that it was the same transfer that had shipwrecked the colonel's fortune and alienated his friends, and could not help replying somewhat pointedly, " But I think it should, Miss Yerba. I don't know what the colonel explained to you — doubtless, not the whole truth, for he is not a man to praise himself ; but, the fact is, the bank was in difficulties at the time of that transfer, and, to make it, he sacrificed his personal fortune, and, I think, awakened some of that ill-feeling you have just noticed." He checked himself too late : he had again lost not only his tact and self-control, but had nearly betrayed himself. He was surprised that the girl's justifiable ignorance should have irritated him. Yet she had evidently not noticed, or misunderstood it, for she said, with a certain precision that was almost studied : —

" Yes, I suppose it would have been a terrible thing to him to have been suspected of

misappropriating a Trust confided to him by
parties who had already paid him the high
compliment of confiding to his care a secret
and a fortune."

Paul glanced at her quickly with astonishment. Was this ignorance, or suspicion?
Her manner, however, suddenly changed,
with the charming capriciousness of youth
and conscious beauty. " He speaks of you
in this letter," she said, letting her dark eyes
rest on him provokingly.

" That accounts for your lack of interest
then," said Paul gayly, relieved to turn a
conversation fraught with so much danger.

" But he speaks very flatteringly," she
went on. " He seems to be another one of
your admirers. I 'm sure, Mr. Hathaway,
after that scene in the hotel parlor yesterday, *you*, at least, cannot complain of having been misrepresented before *me*. To tell
you the truth, I think I hated you a little
for it."

" You were quite right," returned Paul.
" I must have been insufferable! And I
admit that I was slightly piqued against *you*
for the idolatries showered upon you at the
same moment by your friends."

Usually, when two young people have

reached the point of confidingly exchanging
their first impressions of each other, some
progress has been made in first acquaintance. But it did not strike Paul in that
way, and Yerba's next remark was discour-
aging.

"But I'm rather disappointed, for all
·that. Colonel Pendleton tells me you know
nothing of my family or of the secret."

Paul was this time quite prepared, and
withstood the girl's scrutiny calmly. "Do
you think," he asked lightly, "that even *he*
knows?"

"Of course he does," she returned quickly.
"Do you suppose he would have taken all
that trouble you have just talked about if
he didn't know it? And feared the consequences, perhaps?" she added, with a slight
return of her previous expressive manner.

Again Paul was puzzled and irritated, he
knew not why. But he only said pleasantly,
"I differ from you there. I am afraid that
such a thing as fear never entered into Colonel
Pendleton's calculations on any subject. I
think he would act the same towards the highest and the lowest, the powerful or the most
weak." As she glanced at him quickly and
mischievously, he added, "I am quite will-

ing to believe that his knowledge of you
made his duty pleasanter."

He was again quite sincere, and his slight
sympathy had that irresistible quality of
tone and look which made him so dangerous.
For he was struck with the pretty, soothed
self-complacency that had shone in her face
since he had spoken of Pendleton's equal
disinterestedness. It seemed, too, as if what
he had taken for passion or petulance in her
manner had been only a resistance to some
continual aggression of condition. With
that remainder held in check, a certain la-
tent nobility was apparent, as of her true
self. In this moment of pleased abstraction she had drawn through the lattice-work
of one of the windows a spray of roses
clinging to the vine, and with her graceful
head a little on one side, was softly caressing
her cheek with it. She certainly was very
pretty. From the crown of her dark little
head to the narrow rosetted slippers that
had been idly tapping the ground, but now
seemed to press it more proudly, with arched
insteps and small ankles, she was pleasant
to look upon.

"But you surely have something else to
think about, Miss Yerba ?" said the young

man, with conviction. "In a few months
you will be of age, and rid of those dreadfully stupid guardians ; with your " —

The loosened rose-spray flew from her
hand out of the window as she made a gesture, half real, half assumed, of imploring
supplication. "Oh, please, Mr. Hathaway,
for Heaven's sake don't *you* begin too! You
are going to say that, with my wealth, my
accomplishments, my beauty, my friends,
what more can I want? What do I care
about a secret that can neither add to them
nor take them away? Yes, you were! It's
the regular thing to say — everybody says
it. Why, I should have thought ' the youngest senator ' could afford to have been more
original."

"I plead guilty to *all* the weaknesses of
humanity," said Paul, warmly, again beginning to believe that he had been most unjust
to her independence.

"Well, I forgive you, because you have
forgotten to say that, if I don't like the
name of Yerba Buena, I could *so* easily
change that too."

"But you *do* like it," said Paul, touched
with this first hearing of her name in her
own musical accents, " or would like it if

you heard yourself pronounce it." It suddenly recurred to him, with a strange thrill of pleasure, that he himself had given it to her. It was as if he had created some musical instrument to which she had just given voice. In his enthusiasm he had thrown himself on the bench beside her in an attitude that, I fear, was not as dignified as became his elderly office.

"But you don't think that is my *name*," said the girl, quickly.

"I beg your pardon?" said Paul, hesitatingly.

"You don't think that anybody would have been so utterly idiotic as to call me after a ground-vine — a vegetable?" she continued petulantly.

"Eh?" stammered Paul.

"A name that could be so easily translated," she went on, half scornfully, "and when translated, was no possible title for anybody? Think of it — Miss Good Herb! It is too ridiculous for anything."

Paul was not usually wanting in self-possession in an emergency, or in skill to meet attack. But he was so convinced of the truth of the girl's accusation, and now recalled so vividly his own consternation on hearing the result of his youthful and romantic sponsorship for the first time from Pendleton, that he was struck with confusion.

"But what do you suppose it was intended for?" he said at last, vaguely. "It was certainly 'Yerba Buena' in the Trust. At least, I suppose so," he corrected himself hurriedly.

"It is only a supposition," she said quietly, "for you know it cannot be proved. The Trust was never recorded, and the only copy could not be found among Mr. Hammersley's papers. It is only part of the name, of which the first is lost."

"Part of the name?" repeated Paul, uneasily.

"Part of it. It is a corruption of *de la Yerba Buena*, — of the Yerba Buena, — and refers to the island of Yerba Buena in the bay, and not to the plant. That island was part of the property of my family — the Arguellos — you will find it so recorded in the Spanish grants. My name is Arguello de la Yerba Buena."

It is impossible to describe the timid yet triumphant, the half-appealing yet complacent, conviction of the girl's utterance. A

moment before, Paul would have believed
it impossible for him to have kept his gravity and his respect for his companion under
this egregious illusion. But he kept both.
For a sudden conviction that she suspected
the truth, and had taken this audacious and
original plan of crushing it, overpowered all
other sense. The Arguellos, it flashed upon
him, were an old Spanish family, former
owners of Yerba Buena Island, who had in
the last years become extinct. There had
been a story that one of them had eloped
with an American ship captain's wife at
Monterey. The legendary history of early
Spanish California was filled with more remarkable incidents, corroborated with little
difficulty from Spanish authorities, who, it
was alleged, lent themselves readily to any
fabrication or forgery. There was no racial
pride: on the contrary, they had shown an
eager alacrity to ally themselves with their
conquerors. The friends of the Arguellos
would be proud to recognize and remember
in the American heiress the descendant of
their countrymen. All this passed rapidly
through his mind after the first moment of
surprise; all this must have been the deliberate reasoning of this girl of seventeen,

whose dark eyes were bent upon him. Whether she was seeking corroboration or complicity he could not tell.

" Have you found this out yourself? " he asked, after a pause.

" Yes. One of my friends at the convent was Josita Castro; she knew all the history of the Arguellos. She is perfectly satisfied."

For an instant Paul wondered if it was a joint conception of the two schoolgirls. But, on reflection, he was persuaded that Yerba would commit herself to no accomplice — of her own sex. She might have dominated the girl, and would make her a firm partisan, while the girl would be convinced of it herself, and believe herself a free agent. He had had such experience with men himself.

" But why have you not spoken of it before — and to Colonel Pendleton? "

" He did not choose to tell *me*," said Yerba, with feminine dexterity. " I have preferred to keep it myself a secret till I am of age."

" When Colonel Pendleton and some of the other trustees have no right to say anything," thought Paul quickly. She had evidently trusted him. Yet, fascinated as he had been by her audacity, he did not know whether to be pleased, or the reverse. He would have preferred to be placed on an equal footing with Josita Castro. She anticipated his thoughts by saying, with half-raised eyelids : —

" What do *you* think of it ? "

" It seems to be so natural and obvious an explanation of the mystery that I only wonder it was not thought of before," said Paul, with that perfect sincerity that made his sympathy so effective.

" You see," — still under her pretty eyelids, and the tender promise of a smile parting her little mouth, — " I 'm believing that you tell the truth when you say you don't know anything about it."

It was a desperate moment with Paul, but his sympathetic instincts, and possibly his luck, triumphed. His momentary hesitation easily simulated the caution of a conscientious man ; his knit eyebrows and bright eyes, lowered in an effort of memory, did the rest. " I remember it all so indistinctly," he said, with literal truthfulness ; " there was a veiled lady present, tall and dark, to whom Mayor Hammersley and the colonel

showed a singular, and, it struck me, as an
almost superstitious, respect. I remember
now, distinctly, I was impressed with the
reverential way they both accompanied her
to the door at the end of the interview."
He raised his eyes slightly; the young girl's
red lips were parted; that illumination of
the skin, which was her nearest approach to
color, had quite transfigured her face. He
felt, suddenly, that she believed it, yet he
had no sense of remorse. He half believed
it himself; at least, he remembered the nobility of the mother's self-renunciation and
its effect upon the two men. Why should
not the daughter preserve this truthful picture of her mother's momentary exaltation?
Which was the most truthful — that, or the
degrading facts? "You speak of a secret,"
he added. " I can remember little more
than that the Mayor asked me to forget
from that moment the whole occurrence. I
did not know at the time how completely I
should fulfill his request. You must remember, Miss Yerba, as your Lady Superior
has, that I was absurdly young at the time.
I don't know but that I may have thought,
in my youthful inexperience, that this sort
of thing was of common occurrence. And

then, I had my own future to make — and youth is brutally selfish. I was quite friendless and unknown when I left San Francisco for the mines, at the time you entered the convent as Yerba Buena."

She smiled, and made a slight impulsive gesture, as if she would have drawn nearer to him, but checked herself, still smiling, and without embarrassment. It may have been a movement of youthful *camaraderie*, and that occasional maternal rather than sisterly instinct which sometimes influences a young girl's masculine friendship, and elevates the favored friend to the plane of the doll she has outgrown. As he turned towards her, however, she rose, shook out her yellow dress, and said with pretty petulance : —

"Then you must go so soon — and this your first and last visit as my guardian?"

"No one could regret that more than I," looking at her with undefined meaning.

"Yes," she said, with a tantalizing coquetry that might have suggested an underlying seriousness. "I think you *have* lost a good deal. Perhaps, so have I. We might have been good friends in all these years. But that is past."

"Why? Surely, I hope, my shortcomings with Miss Yerba Buena will not be remembered by Miss Arguello?" said Paul, earnestly.

"Ah! *She* may be a very different person."

"I hope not," said the young man, warmly. "But *how* different?"

"Well, she may not put herself in the way of receiving such point-blank compliments as that," said the young girl, demurely.

"Not from her guardian?"

"She will have no guardian then." She said this gravely, but almost at the same moment turned and sat down again, throwing her linked hands over her knee, and looked at him mischievously. "You see what you have lost, sir."

"I see," said Paul, but with all the gravity that she had dropped.

"No; but you don't see all. I had no brother — no friend. You might have been both. You might have made me what you liked. You might have educated me far better than these teachers, or, at least given me some pride in my studies. There were so many things I wanted to know that they

could n't teach me ; so many times I wanted
advice from some one that I could trust.
Colonel Pendleton was very good to me
when he came ; he always treated me like a
princess even when I wore short frocks. It
was his manner that first made me think he
knew my family ; but I never felt as if I
could tell him anything, and I don't think,
with all his chivalrous respect, he ever understood me. As to the others — the Mayors — well, you may judge from Mr. Henderson. It is a wonder that I did not run
away or do something desperate. Now, are
you not a *little* sorry ? "

Her voice, which had as many capricious
changes as her manner, had been alternately
coquettish, petulant, and serious, had now
become playful again. But, like the rest of
her sex, she was evidently more alert to her
surroundings at such a moment than her
companion, for before he could make any
reply, she said, without apparently looking,
" But there is a deputation coming for you,
Mr. Hathaway. You see, the case is hopeless. You never would be able to give to
one what is claimed by the many."

Paul glanced down the rose-alley, and
saw that the deputation in question was com-

posed of the Mayor, Mr. Woods, a thin,
delicate - looking woman, — evidently Mrs.
Woods, — and Milly.   The latter managed
to reach the summer-house first, with apparently youthful alacrity, but really to exchange, in a single glance, some mysterious
feminine signal with Yerba.   Then she said
with breathless infelicity : —

"Before you two get bored with each other
now, I must tell you there's a chance of you
having more time.   Aunty has promised to
send off a note excusing you to the Reverend
Mother, if she can persuade Mr. Hathaway
to stay over to-night.   But here they are.
[To Yerba] Aunty is most anxious, and
won't hear of his going."

Indeed, it seemed as if Mrs. Woods was,
after a refined fashion, most concerned that
a distinguished visitor like Mr. Hathaway
should have to use her house as a mere accidental meeting-place with his ward, without
deigning to accept her hospitality.   She was
reinforced by Mr. Woods, who enunciated
the same idea with more masculine vigor;
and by the Mayor, who expressed his conviction that a slight of this kind to Rosario
would be felt in the Santa Clara valley.
"After dinner, my dear Hathaway," con-

cluded Mr. Woods, "a few of our neighbors may drop in, who would be glad to shake you by the hand — no formal meeting, my boy — but, hang it! *they* expect it."

Paul looked around for Yerba. There was really no reason why he should n't accept, although an hour ago the idea had never entered his mind. Yet, if he did, he would like the girl to know that it was for *her* sake. Unfortunately, far from exhibiting any concern in the matter, she seemed to be preoccupied with Milly, and only the charming back of her head was visible behind Mrs. Woods. He accepted, however, with a hesitation that took some of the graciousness from his yielding, and a sense that he was giving a strange importance to a trivial circumstance.

The necessity of attaching himself to his hostess, and making a more extended tour of the grounds, for a while diverted him from an uneasy consideration of his past interview. Mrs. Woods had known Yerba through the school friendship of Milly, and, as far as the religious rules of the convent would allow, had always been delighted to show her any hospitality. She was a beautiful girl — did not Mr. Hathaway think so?

— and a girl of great character. It was a pity, of course, that she had never known a mother's care, and that the present routine of a boarding-school had usurped the tender influences of home. She believed, too, that the singular rotation of guardianship had left the girl practically without a counseling friend to rely upon, except, perhaps, Colonel Pendleton; and while she, Mrs. Woods, did not for a moment doubt that the colonel might be a good friend and a pleasant companion of *men*, really he, Mr. Hathaway, must admit that, with his reputation and habits, he was hardly a fit associate for a young lady. Indeed, Mr. Woods would have never allowed Milly to invite Yerba here if Colonel Pendleton was to have been her escort. Of course, the poor girl could not choose her own guardian, but Mr. Woods said *he* had a right to choose who should be his niece's company. Perhaps Mr. Woods was prejudiced, — most men were, — yet surely Mr. Hathaway, although a loyal friend of Colonel Pendleton's, must admit that when it was an open scandal that the colonel had fought a duel about a notoriously common woman, and even blasphemously defended her before a party of gentlemen,

it was high time, as Mr. Woods said, that
he should be remanded to their company
exclusively. No; Mrs. Woods could not
admit that this was owing to the injustice of
her own sex! Men are really the ones who
make the fuss over those things, just as they,
as Mr. Hathaway well knew, made the laws!
No; it was a great pity, as she and her husband had just agreed, that Mr. Hathaway,
of all the guardians, could not have been
always the help and counselor — in fact,
the elder brother — of poor Yerba! Paul
was conscious that he winced slightly, consistently and conscientiously, at the recollection of certain passages of his youth; in-
consistently and meanly, at this suggestion
of a joint relationship with Yerba's mother.

"I think, too," continued Mrs. Woods,
"she has worried foolishly about this ridiculous mystery of her parentage — as if it
could make the slightest difference to a girl
with a quarter of a million, or as if that
did n't show quite conclusively that she *was*
somebody!"

"Certainly," said Paul, quickly, with a
relief that he nevertheless felt was ridiculous.

"And, of course, I dare say it will all

come out when she is of age. I suppose
you know if any of the family are still living?"

"I really do not."

"I beg your pardon," said Mrs. Woods,
with a smile. "I forgot it's a profound
secret until then. But here we are at the
house; I see the girls have walked over to
our neighbors'. Perhaps you would like to
have a few moments to yourself before you
dress for dinner, and your portmanteau,
which has been sent for, comes from your
hotel. You must be tired of seeing so many
people."

Paul was glad to accept any excuse for
being alone, and, thanking his hostess, followed a servant to his room — a low-ceil-
inged but luxuriously furnished apartment
on the first floor. Here he threw himself
on a cushioned lounge that filled the angle
of the deep embrasure — the thickness of
the old adobe walls — that formed a part
of the wooden-latticed window. A Cape
jessamine climbing beside it filled the room
with its subtle, intoxicating perfume. It
was so strong, and he felt himself so irresistibly overpowered and impelled towards
a merely idle reverie, that, in order to think

more clearly and shut out some strange and unreasoning enthrallment of his senses, he rose and sharply closed the window. Then he sat down and reflected.

What was he doing here? and what was the meaning of all this? He had come simply to fulfill a duty to his past, and please a helpless and misunderstood old acquaintance. He had performed that duty. But he had incidentally learned a certain fact that might be important to this friend, and clearly his duty was simply to go back and report it. He would gain nothing more in the way of corroboration of it by staying now, if further corroboration were required. Colonel Pendleton had already been uselessly and absurdly perplexed about the possible discovery of the girl's parentage, and its effect upon her fortunes and herself. She had just settled that of her own accord, and, without committing herself or others, had suggested a really sensible plan by which all trouble would be avoided in future. That was the common-sense way of looking at it. He would lay the plan before the colonel, have him judge of its expediency and its ethics — and even the question whether she already knew the real truth, or was self-de-

ceived. That done, he would return to his
own affairs in Sacramento. There was nothing difficult in this, or that need worry him,
only he could have done it just as well an
hour ago.

He opened the window again. The scent
of the jessamine came in as before, but mingled with the cooler breath of the roses.
There was nothing intoxicating or unreal in
it now; rather it seemed a gentle aromatic
stimulant — of thought. Long shadows of
unseen poplars beyond barred the garden
lanes and alleys with bands of black and
yellow. A slanting pencil of sunshine
through the trees was for a moment focussed
on a bed of waxen callas before a hedge of
ceanothus, and struck into dazzling relief
the cold white chalices of the flowers and
the vivid shining green of their background.
Presently it slid beyond to a tiny fountain,
before invisible, and wrought a blinding
miracle out of its flashing and leaping spray.
Yet even as he gazed the fountain seemed
to vanish slowly, the sunbeam slipped on,
and beyond it moved the shimmer of white
and yellow dresses. It was Yerba and Milly
returning to the house. Well, he would
not interrupt his reflections by idly watching

them ; he would, probably, see a great deal
of Yerba that evening, and by that time he
would have come to some conclusion in regard to her.

But he had not taken into consideration
her voice, which, always musical in its
Southern intonation and quite audible in the
quiet garden, struck him now as being full
of joyous sweetness. Well, she was certainly
very happy — or very thoughtless. She
was actually romping with Milly, and was
now evidently being chased down the rose-
alley by that volatile young woman. Then
these swift Camillas apparently neared the
house, there was the rapid rustle of skirts,
the skurrying of little feet on the veranda,
a stumble, a mouse-like shriek from Milly,
and *her* voice, exhausted, dying, happy,
broken with half-hushed laughter, rose to
him on the breath of the jessamine and
rose.

Surely she *was* a child, and, if a child,
how he had misjudged her ! What if all
that he had believed was mature deliberation
was only the innocent imaginings of a romantic girl, all that he had taken seriously
only a school-girl's foolish dream ! Instead
of combating it, instead of reasoning with

v. 3

4

her, instead of trying to interest her in other
things, he had even helped on her illusions.
He had treated her as if the taint of her
mother's worldliness and knowledge of evil
was in her pure young flesh.  He had recognized her as the daughter of an adventuress,
and not as his ward, appealing to his chivalry
through her very ignorance — it might be
her very childish vanity.  He had brought
to a question of tender and pathetic interest
only his selfish opinion of the world and the
weaknesses of mankind.  The blood came to
his cheeks — with all his experienced self-
control, he had not lost the youthful trick
of blushing — and he turned away from the
window as if it had breathed a reproach.

But ought he have even contented himself
with destroying her illusions — ought he not
have gone farther and told her the whole
truth?  Ought he not first have won her
confidence — he remembered bitterly, now,
how she had intimated that she had no one
to confide in — and, after revealing her
mother's history, have still pledged himself
to keep the secret from all others, and assisted
her in her plan?  It would not have altered
the state of affairs, except so far as she was
concerned; they could have combined to-

gether; his ready wit would have helped him; and his sympathy would have sustained her; but —

How and in what way could he have told her? Leaving out the delicate and difficult periphrase by which her mother's shame would have to be explained to an innocent school-girl — what right could he have assumed to tell it? As the guardian who had never counseled or protected her? As an acquaintance of hardly an hour ago? Who would have such a right? A lover — on whose lips it would only seem a tacit appeal to her gratitude or her fears, and whom no sensitive girl could accept thereafter? No. A husband? Yes! He remembered, with a sudden start, what Pendleton had said to him. Good Heavens! Had Pendleton that idea in his mind? And yet — it seemed the only solution.

A knock at his door was followed by the appearance of Mr. Woods. Mr. Hathaway's portmanteau had come, and Mrs. Woods had sent a message, saying that in view of the limited time that Mr. Hathaway would have with his ward, Mrs. Woods would forego her right to keep him at her side at dinner, and yield her place to Yerba. Paul thanked him with a grave inward smile. What if he made his dramatic disclosure to her confidentially over the soup and fish? Yet, in his constantly recurring conviction of the girl's independence, he made no doubt she would have met his brutality with unflinching pride and self-possession. He began to dress slowly, at times almost forgetting himself in a new kind of pleasant apathy, which he attributed to the odor of the flowers, and the softer hush of twilight that had come on with the dying away of the trade winds, and the restful spice of the bay-trees near his window. He presently found himself not so much thinking of Yerba as of *seeing* her. A picture of her in the summer-house caressing her cheek with the roses seemed to stand out from the shadows of the blank wall opposite him. When he passed into the dressing-room beyond, it was not his own face he saw in the glass, but hers. It was with a start, as if he had heard *her* voice, that he found upon his dressing-table a small vase containing a flower for his coat, with the penciled words on a card in a school-girl's hand, "From Yerba, with thanks for staying." It must have been placed there by a servant while he was musing at the window.

Half a dozen people were already in the drawing-room when Paul descended. It appeared that Mr. Woods had invited certain of his neighbors — among them a Judge Baker and his wife, and Don Cæsar Briones, of the adjacent Rancho of Los Pajaros, and his sister, the Doña Anna. Milly and Yerba had not yet appeared. Don Cæsar, a young man of a toreador build, roundly bland in face and murky in eye, seemed to notice their absence, and kept his glances towards the door, while Paul engaged in conversation with Doña Anna — if that word could convey an impression of a conventionality which that good-humored young lady converted into an animated flirtation at the second sentence with a single glance and two shakes of her fan. And then Milly fluttered in — a vision of school-girl freshness and white tulle, and a moment later — with a pause of expectation — a tall, graceful figure, that at first Paul scarcely recognized.

It is a popular conceit of our sex that we are superior to any effect of feminine adornment, and that a pretty girl is equally pretty in the simplest frock. Yet there was not a man in the room who did not believe that Yerba in her present attire was not only far

prettier than before, but that she indicated
a new and more delicate form of beauty. It
was not the mere revelation of contour and
color of an ordinary *décolleté* dress, it was a
perfect presentment of pure symmetry and
carriage. In this black grenadine dress,
trimmed with jet, not only was the delicate
satin sheen of her skin made clearer by contrast, but she looked every inch her full
height, with an ideal exaltation of breeding
and culture. She wore no jewelry except a
small necklace of pearls — so small it might
have been a child's — that fitted her slender
throat so tightly that it could scarcely be
told from the flesh that it clasped. Paul
did not know that it was the gift of the
mother to the child that she had forsworn
only a few weeks before she parted from her
forever ; but he had a vague feeling that, in
that sable dress that seemed like mourning,
she walked at the funeral of her mother's
past. A few white flowers in her corsage,
the companions of the solitary one in his
button-hole, were the only relief.

Their eyes met for a single moment, the
look of admiration in Paul's being answered
by the naïve consciousness in Yerba's of a
woman looking her best ; but the next mo-

ment she appeared preoccupied with the others, and the eager advances of Don Cæsar.

"Your brother seems to admire Miss Yerba," said Paul.

"Ah, ye — es," returned Doña Anna. "And you?"

"Oh!" said Paul, gayly, "*I? I* am her guardian — with me it is simple egotism, you know."

"Ah!" returned the arch Doña Anna, "you are then already *so* certain of her? Good! I shall warn him."

A precaution that did seem necessary; as later, when Paul, at a signal from his hostess, offered his arm to Yerba, the young Spaniard regarded him with a look of startled curiosity.

"I thank you for selecting me to wear your colors," said Paul with a glance at the flowers in her corsage, as they sat at table, "and I think I deserve them, since, but for you, I should have been on my way to San Francisco at this moment. Shall I have an opportunity of talking to you a few minutes later in the evening?" he added, in a lower tone.

"Why not now?" returned Yerba, mis-

chievously. " We are set here expressly
for that purpose."

" Surely not to talk of our own business
— I should say, of our *family* affairs," said
Paul, looking at her with equal playfulness ;
" though I believe your friend Don Cæsar,
opposite, would be more pleased if he were
sure that was all we did."

" And you think his sister would share in
that pleasure ? " retorted Yerba. " I warn
you, Mr. Hathaway, that you have been
quite justifying the Reverend Mother's
doubts about your venerable pretensions.
Everybody is staring at you now."

Paul looked up mechanically. It was
true. Whether from some occult sympathy,
from a human tendency to admire obvious
fitness and symmetry, or the innocent love
with which the world regards innocent lovers,
they were all observing Yerba and himself
with undisguised attention. A good talker,
he quickly led the conversation to other
topics. It was then that he discovered that
Yerba was not only accomplished, but that
this convent-bred girl had acquired a singular breadth of knowledge apart from the
ordinary routine of the school curriculum.
She spoke and thought with independent

perceptions and clearness, yet without the
tactlessness and masculine abruptness that
is apt to detract from feminine originality
of reflection. By some tacit understanding
that had the charm of mutual confidence,
they both exerted themselves to please the
company rather than each other, and Paul,
in the interchange of sallies with Doña
Anna, had a certain pleasure in hearing
Yerba converse in Spanish with Don Cæsar.
But in a few moments he observed, with
some uneasiness, that they were talking ol
the old Spanish occupation, and presently of
the old Spanish families. Would she prematurely expose an ignorance that might be
hereafter remembered against her, or invite
some dreadful genealogical reminiscence that
would destroy her hopes and raze her Spanish castles? Or was she simply collecting
information? He admired the dexterity
with which, without committing herself, she
made Don Cæsar openly and even confidentially communicative. And yet he was on
thorns; at times it seemed as if he himself
were playing a part in this imposture of
Yerba's. He was aware that his wandering
attention was noticed by the quick-witted
Doña Anna, when he regained his self-pos-

session by what appeared to be a happy
diversion. It was the voice of Mrs. Judge
Baker calling across the table to Yerba. By
one of the peculiar accidents of general conversation, it was the one apparently trivial
remark that in a pause challenged the ears
of all.

"We were admiring your necklace, Miss
Yerba."

Every eye was turned upon the slender
throat of the handsome girl. The excuse
was so natural.

Yerba put her hand to her neck with a
smile. "You are joking, Mrs. Baker. I
know it is ridiculously small, but it is a
child's necklace, and I wear it because it
was a gift from my mother."

Paul's heart sank again with consternation. It was the first time he had heard the
girl distinctly connect herself with her actual
mother, and for an instant he felt as startled
as if the forgotten Outcast herself had returned and taken a seat at the board.

"I told you it could n't be so?" remarked
Mrs. Baker, to her husband.

Everybody naturally looked inquiringly
upon the couple, and Mrs. Baker explained
with a smile: "Bob thinks he's seen it before; men are so obstinate."

" Pardon me, Miss Yerba," said the Judge, blandly, " would you mind showing it to me, if it is not too much trouble ? "

" Not at all," said Yerba, smiling, and detaching the circlet from her neck. " I 'm afraid you 'll find it rather old-fashioned."

" That 's just what I hope to find it," said Judge Baker, with a triumphant glance at his wife. " It was eight years ago when I saw it in Tucker's jewelry shop. I wanted to buy it for my little Minnie, but as the price was steep I hesitated, and when I did make up my mind he had disposed of it to another customer. Yes," he added, examining the necklace which Yerba had handed to him. " I am certain it is the same : it was unique, like this. Odd, is n't it ? "

Everybody said it *was* odd, and looked upon the occurrence with that unreasoning satisfaction with which average humanity receives the most trivial and unmeaning coincidences. It was left to Don Cæsar to give it a gallant application.

" I have not-a the pleasure of knowing-a the Miss Minnie, but the jewelry, when she arrives, to the throat-a of Miss Yerba, she has not lost the value — the beauty — the charm."

"No," said Woods, cheerily. "The fact is, Baker, you were too slow. Miss Yerba's folks gobbled up the necklace while you were thinking. You were a new - comer. Old 'forty-niners' did not hesitate over a thing they wanted."

"You never knew who was your successful rival, eh?" said Doña Anna, turning to Judge Baker with a curious glance at Paul's pale face in passing.

"No," said Baker, "but" — he stopped with a hesitating laugh and some little confusion. "No, I've mixed it up with something else. It's so long ago. I never knew, or if I did I've forgotten. But the necklace I remember." He handed it back to Yerba with a bow, and the incident ended.

Paul had not looked at Yerba during this conversation, an unreasoning instinct that he might confuse her, an equally unreasoning dread that he might see her confused by others, possessing him. And when he did glance at her calm, untroubled face, that seemed only a little surprised at his own singular coldness, he was by no means relieved. He was only convinced of one thing. In the last five minutes he had settled upon

the irrevocable determination that his present relations with the girl could exist no
longer. He must either tell her everything,
or see her no more. There was no middle
course. She was on the brink of an exposure
at any moment, either through her ignorance
or her unhappy pretension. In his intolerable position, he was equally unable to con-
template her peril, accept her ·defense, or
himself defend her.

As if, with some feminine instinct, she
had attributed his silence to some jealousy
of Don Cæsar's attentions, she more than
once turned from the Spaniard to Paul with
an assuring smile. In his anxiety, he half
accepted the rather humiliating suggestion,
and managed to say to her, in a lower tone :

"On this last visit of your American
guardian, one would think, you need not
already anticipate your Spanish relations."

He was thrilled with the mischievous yet
faintly tender pleasure that sparkled in her
eyes as she said, —

" You forget it is my American guardian's
*first* visit, as well as his last."

"And as your guardian," he went on,
with half - veiled seriousness, "I protest
against your allowing your treasures, the

property of the Trust," he gazed directly into her beautiful eyes, " being handled and commented upon by everybody."

When the ladies had left the table, he was, for a moment, relieved. But only for a moment. Judge Baker drew his chair beside Paul's, and, taking his cigar from his lips, said, with a perfunctory laugh : —

"I say, Hathaway, I pulled up just in time to save myself from making an awful speech, just now, to your ward."

Paul looked at him with cold curiosity.

"Yes. Gad! Do you know *who* was my rival in that necklace transaction?"

"No," said Paul, with frigid carelessness.

"Why, Kate Howard! Fact, sir. She bought it right under my nose — and overbid me, too."

Paul did not lose his self-possession. Thanks to the fact that Yerba was not present, and that Don Cæsar, who had overheard the speech, moved forward with a suggestive and unpleasant smile, his agitation congealed into a coldly placid fury.

"And I suppose," he returned, with perfect calmness, " that, after the usual habit of this class of women, the necklace very soon found its way back, through the pawnbroker,

to the jeweler again. It's a common
fate."

"Yes, of course," said Judge Baker,
cheerfully. "You're quite right. That's
undoubtedly the solution of it. But," with
a laugh, "I had a narrow escape from saying something — eh?"

"A very narrow escape from an apparently gratuitous insult," said Paul, gravely,
but fixing his eyes, now more luminous than
ever with anger, not on the speaker, but on
the face of Don Cæsar, who was standing at
his side. "You were about to say," —

"Eh — oh — ah! this Kate Howard?
So! I have heard of her — yees! And
Miss Yerba — ah — she is of my country
— I think. Yes — we shall claim her — of
a truth — yes."

"Your countrymen, I believe, are in the
habit of making claims that are more often
founded on profit than verity," said Paul,
with smileless and insulting deliberation.
He knew perfectly what he was saying, and
the result he expected. Only twenty-four
hours before he had smiled at Pendleton's
idea of averting scandal and discovery by
fighting, yet he was endeavoring to pick a
quarrel with a man, merely on suspicion, for

the same purpose, and he saw nothing strange in it. A vague idea, too, that this would irrevocably confirm him in opposition to Yerba's illusions probably determined him.

But Don Cæsar, albeit smiling lividly, did not seem inclined to pick up the gauntlet, and Woods interfered hastily. "Don Cæsar means that your ward has some idea herself that she is of Spanish origin — at least, Milly says so. But of course, as one of the oldest trustees, *you* know the facts."

In another moment Paul would have committed himself. "I think we'll leave Miss Yerba out of the question," he said, coldly. "My remark was a general one, although, of course, I am responsible for any personal application of it."

"Spoken like a politician, Hathaway," said Judge Baker, with an effusive enthusiasm, which he hoped would atone for the alarming results of his infelicitous speech. "That's right, gentlemen! You can't get the facts from him before he is ready to give them. Keep your secret, Mr. Hathaway, the court is with you."

Nevertheless, as they passed out of the room to join the ladies, the Mayor lingered a little behind with Woods. "It's easy to see the influence of that Pendleton on our young friend," he said, significantly. "Somebody ought to tell him that it's played out down here — as Pendleton is. It's quite enough to ruin his career."

Paul was too observant not to notice this, but it brought him no sense of remorse; and his youthful belief in himself and his power kept him from concern. He felt as if he had done something, if only to show Don Cæsar that the girl's weakness or ignorance could not be traded upon with impunity. But he was still undecided as to the course he should pursue. But he should determine that to-night. At present there seemed no chance of talking to her alone — she was unconcernedly conversing with Milly and Mrs. Woods, and already the visitors who had been invited to this hurried *levée* in his honor were arriving. In view of his late indiscretion, he nervously exerted his fullest powers, and in a very few minutes was surrounded by a breathless and admiring group of worshipers. A ludicrous resemblance to the scene in the Golden Gate Hotel passed through his mind; he involuntarily turned his eyes to seek Yerba in the half-fear, half-expectation of meeting her mischievous smile.

Their glances met; to his surprise hers was smileless, and instantly withdrawn, but not until he had been thrilled by an unconscious prepossession in its luminous depths that he scarcely dared to dwell upon. What mattered now this passage with Don Cæsar or the plaudits of his friends? *She* was proud of him!

Yet, after that glance, she was shy, preoccupying herself with Milly, or even listening sweetly to Judge Baker's somewhat practical and unromantic reminiscences of the deprivations and the hardships of California early days, as if to condone his past infelicity. She was pleasantly unaffected with Don Cæsar, although she managed to draw Doña Anna into the conversation; she was unconventional, Paul fancied, to all but himself. Once or twice, when he had artfully drawn her towards the open French window that led to the moonlit garden and shadowed veranda, she had managed to link Milly's arm in her own, and he was confident that a suggestion to stroll with him in the open air would be followed by her invitation to Milly to accompany them. Disappointed and mortified as he was, he found some solace in her manner, which he still

believed suggested the hope that she might
be made accessible to his persuasions. Persuasions to what? He did not know.

The last guest had departed; he lingered
on the veranda with a cigar, begging his
host and hostess not to trouble themselves to
keep him company. Milly and Yerba had
retired to the former's boudoir, but, as they
had not yet formally bade him good night,
there was a chance of their returning. He
still stayed on in this hope for half an hour,
and then, accepting Yerba's continued absence as a tacit refusal of his request, he
turned abruptly away. But as he glanced
around the garden before reëntering the
house, he was struck by a singular circumstance — a white patch, like a forgotten
shawl, which he had observed on the distant
ceanothus hedge, and which had at first
thrilled him with expectation, had certainly
*changed its position.* Before, it seemed to
be near the summer-house; now it was, undoubtedly, farther away. Could they, or
*she* alone, have slipped from the house and
be awaiting him there? With a muttered
exclamation at his stupidity he stepped hastily from the veranda and walked towards it.
But he had scarcely proceeded a dozen yards

before it disappeared. He reached the summer-house — it was empty; he followed the line of hedge — no one was there. It could not have been her, or she would have waited, unless he were the victim of a practical joke. He turned impatiently back to the house, reëntered the drawing-room by the French window, and was crossing the half-lit apartment, when he heard a slight rustle in the shadow of the window. He looked around quickly, and saw that it was Yerba, in a white, loose gown, for which she had already exchanged her black evening dress, leaning back composedly on the sofa, her hands clasped behind her shapely head.

" I am waiting for Milly," she said, with a faint smile on her lips. He fancied, in the moonlight that streamed upon her, that her beautiful face was pale. " She has gone to the other wing to see one of the servants who is ill. We thought you were on the veranda smoking and I should have company, until I saw you start off, and rush up and down the hedge like mad."

Paul felt that he was losing his self-possession, and becoming nervous in her presence. " I thought it was *you*," he stammered.

" Me ! Out in the garden at this hour,

alone, and in the broad moonlight? What
are you thinking of, Mr. Hathaway? Do
you know anything of convent rules, or is
that your idea of your ward's education?"

He fancied that, though she smiled faintly,
her voice was as tremulous as his own.

"I want to speak with you," he said, with
awkward directness. "I even thought of
asking you to stroll with me in the garden."

"Why not talk here?" she returned,
changing her position, pointing to the other
end of the sofa, and drawing the whole over-
flow of her skirt to one side. "It is not so
very late, and Milly will return in a few moments."

Her face was in shadow now, but there
was a glow-worm light in her beautiful eyes
that seemed faintly to illuminate her whole
face. He sank down on the sofa at her side,
no longer the brilliant and ambitious politician, but, it seemed to him, as hopelessly a
dreaming, inexperienced boy as when he had
given her the name that now was all he
could think of, and the only word that rose
to his feverish lips.

"Yerba!"

"I like to hear you say it," she said
quickly, as if to gloss over his first omission

of her formal prefix, and leaning a little forward, with her eyes on his. "One would think you had created it. You almost make me regret to lose it."

He stopped. He felt that the last sentence had saved him. "It is of that I want to speak," he broke out suddenly and almost rudely. "Are you satisfied that it means nothing, and can mean nothing, to you? Does it awaken no memory in your mind — recall nothing you care to know? Think! I beg you, I implore you to be frank with me!"

She looked at him with surprise.

"I have told you already that my present name must be some absurd blunder, or some intentional concealment. But why do you want to know *now*?" she continued, adding her faint smile to the emphasis.

"To help you!" he said, eagerly. "For that alone! To do all I can to assist you, if you really believe, and want to believe, that you have another. To ask you to confide in me; to tell me all you have been told, all that you know, think you know, or *want* to know about your relationship to the Arguellos — or to — any one. And then to devote myself entirely to proving what you shall

say is your desire. You see, I am frank
with you, Yerba. I only ask you to be as
frank with me ; to let me know your doubts,
that I may counsel you ; your fears, that I
may give you courage."

" Is that all you came here to tell me ? "
she asked quietly.

"No, Yerba," he said, eagerly, taking her
unresisting but indifferent hand, "not all ;
but all that I must say, all that I have the
right to say, all that you, Yerba, would per-
mit me to tell you *now*. But let me hope
that the day is not far distant when I can
tell you *all*, when you will understand that
this silence has been the hardest sacrifice of
the man who now speaks to you."

" And yet not unworthy of a rising politician," she added, quickly withdrawing her
hand. " 1 agree," she went on, looking towards the door, yet without appearing to
avoid his eager eyes, " and when I have settled upon ' a local habitation and a name '
we shall renew this interesting conversation.
Until then, as my fourth official guardian
used to say — he was a lawyer, Mr. Hathaway, like yourself — when he was winding
up his conjectures on the subject — all that
has passed is to be considered ' without pre-
judice.' "

" But Yerba " — began Paul, bitterly.

She slightly raised her hand as if to check him with a warning gesture. "Yes, dear," she said suddenly, lifting her musical voice, with a mischievous side-glance at Paul, as if to indicate her conception of the irony of a possible application, " this way. Here we are waiting for you." Her listening ear 'had detected Milly's step in the passage, and in another moment that cheerful young woman discreetly stopped on the threshold of the room, with every expression of apologetic indiscretion in her face.

" We have finished our talk, and Mr. Hathaway has been so concerned about my having no real name that he has been promising me everything, but his own, for a suitable one. Have n't you, Mr. Hathaway?" She rose slowly and, going over to Milly, put her arm around her waist and stood for one instant gazing at him between the curtains of the doorway. " Good night. My very proper chaperon is dreadfully shocked at this midnight interview, and is taking me away. Only think of it, Milly ; he actually proposed to me to walk in the garden with him ! Good night, or, as my ancestors — don't forget, *my ancestors* — used to say:

' *Buena noche — hasta mañana!* ' " She lingered over the Spanish syllables with an imitation of Doña Anna's lisp, and with another smile, but more faint and more ghost-like than before, vanished with her companion.

At eight o'clock the next morning Paul was standing beside his portmanteau on the veranda.

" But this is a sudden resolution of yours, Hathaway," said Mr. Woods. " Can you not possibly wait for the next train ? The girls will be down then, and you can breakfast comfortably."

" I have much to do — more than I imagined — in San Francisco before I return," said Paul, quickly. " You must make my excuses to them and to your wife."

" I hope," said Woods, with an uneasy laugh, " you have had no more words with Don Cæsar, or he with you ? "

" No," said Paul, with a reassuring smile, " nothing more, I assure you."

" For you know you 're a devilish quick fellow, Hathaway," continued Woods, " quite as quick as your friend Pendleton. And, by the way, Baker is awfully cut up about that absurd speech of his, you know. Came to me last night and wondered if anybody could think it was intentional. I told him it was d—d stupid, that was all. I guess his wife had been at him. Ha! ha! You see, he remembers the old times, when everybody talked of these things, and that woman Howard was quite a character. I 'm told she went off to the States years ago."

"Possibly," said Paul, carelessly. After a pause, as the carriage drove up to the door, he turned to his host. "By the way, Woods, have you a ghost here?"

"The house is old enough for one. But no. Why?"

"I 'll swear I saw a figure moving yonder, in the shrubbery, late last evening; and when I came up to it, it most unaccountably disappeared."

"One of Don Cæsar's servants, I dare say. There is one of them, an Indian, prowling about here, I 've been told, at all hours. I 'll put a stop to it. Well, you must go then? Dreadfully sorry you could n't stop longer! Good-by!"

# CHAPTER IV.

It was two months later that Mr. Tony Shear, of Marysville, but lately confidential clerk to the Hon. Paul Hathaway, entered his employer's chambers in Sacramento, and handed the latter a letter.

" I only got back from San Francisco this morning; but Mr. Slate said I was to give you that, and if it satisfied you, and was what you wanted, you would send it back to him."

Paul took the envelope and opened it. It contained a printer's proof - slip, which he hurriedly glanced over. It read as follows:

" Those of our readers who are familiar with the early history of San Francisco will be interested to know that an eccentric and irregular trusteeship, vested for the last eight years in the Mayor of San Francisco and two of our oldest citizens, was terminated yesterday by the majority of a beautiful and accomplished young lady, a pupil of the convent of Santa Clara. Very few, except the original trustees, were cognizant of the fact that the administration of the trustees has been a recognized function of the successive Mayors of San Francisco during this period; and the mystery surrounding it has been only lately divulged. It offers a touching and romantic instance of a survival of the old patriarchal duties of the former *Alcaldes* and the simplicity of pioneer days. It seems that, in the unsettled conditions of the Mexican land-titles that followed the American occupation, the consumptive widow of a scion of one of the oldest Californian families intrusted her property and the custody of her infant daughter virtually to the city of San Francisco, as represented by the trustees specified, until the girl should become of age. Within a year, the invalid mother died. With what loyalty, sagacity, and prudence these gentlemen fulfilled their trust may be gathered from the fact that the property left in their charge has not only been secured and protected, but increased a hundredfold in value; and that the young lady, who yesterday attained her majority, is not only one of the richest landed heiresses on the Pacific Slope, but one of the most accomplished and thoroughly educated of her sex. It is now no secret that this favored child of Chrysopolis is the Doña Maria Concepcion de Arguello de la Yerba Buena, so called from her ancestral property on the island, now owned by the Federal government. But it is an affecting and poetic tribute to the parent of her adoption that she has preferred to pass under the old, quaintly typical name of the city, and has been known to her friends simply as ' Miss Yerba Buena.' It is a no less pleasant and suggestive circumstance that our ' youngest senator,' the Honorable Paul Hathaway, formerly private secretary to Mayor Hammersley, is one of the original unofficial trustees; while the chivalry of the older days is perpetuated in the person of Colonel Harry Pendleton, the remaining trustee."

As soon as he had finished, Paul took a pencil and crossed out the last sentence; but instead of laying the proof aside, or returning it to the waiting secretary, he remained with it in his hand, his silent, set face turned towards the window. Whether the merely human secretary was tired of waiting, or the devoted partisan saw something on his young chief's face that disturbed him, he turned to Paul with that exaggerated respect which his functions as secretary had grafted upon his affection for his old associate, and said : —

"I hope nothing's wrong, sir. Not another of those scurrilous attacks on you for putting that bill through to relieve Colonel Pendleton? Yet it was a risky thing for you, sir."

Paul started, recovered himself as if from some remote abstraction, and, with a smile, said : "No, — nothing. Quite the reverse. Write to Mr. Slate, thank him, and say that it will do very well — with the exception of the lines I have marked out. Then bring me the letter, and I will add this inclosure. Did you call on Colonel Pendleton?"

"Yes, sir. He was at Santa Clara, and had not yet returned, — at least, that's what that dandy nigger of his told me. The airs and graces that that creature puts on since the colonel's affairs have been straightened out is a little too much for a white man to stand. Why, sir! d—d if he did n't want to patronize *you*, and allowed to me that 'de Kernel' had a 'fah ideah' of you, 'and thought you a promisin' young man.' The fact is, sir, the party is making a big mistake trying to give votes to that kind of cattle — it would only be giving two votes to the other side, for, slave or free, they 're the chattels of their old masters. And as to the masters' gratitude for what you 've done affecting a single vote of their party — you 're mistaken."

" Colonel Pendleton belongs to no party," said Paul, curtly; " but if his old constituents ever try to get into power again, they 've lost their only independent martyr."

He presently became abstracted again, and Shear produced from his overcoat pocket a series of official-looking documents.

" I 've brought the reports, sir."

" Eh ? " said Paul, absently.

The secretary stared. " The reports of the San Francisco Chief of Police that you asked me to get." His employer was certainly very forgetful to-day.

" Oh, yes; thank you. You can lay them on my desk. I 'll look them over in Committee. You can go now, and if any one calls to see me say I 'm busy."

The secretary disappeared in the adjoining room, and Paul leaned back in his chair, thinking. He had, at last, effected the work he had resolved upon when he left Rosario two months ago; the article he had just read, and which would appear as an editorial

in the San Francisco paper the day after to-
morrow, was the culmination of quietly persistent labor, inquiry, and deduction, and
would be accepted, hereafter, as authentic
history, which, if not thoroughly established,
at least could not be gainsaid. Immediately
on arriving at San Francisco, he had hastened to Pendleton's bedside, and laid the
facts and his plan before him. To his mingled astonishment and chagrin, the colonel
had objected vehemently to this "saddling
of anybody's offspring on a gentleman who
could n't defend himself," and even Paul's
explanation that the putative father was a
myth scarcely appeased him. But Paul's
timely demonstration, by relating the scene
he had witnessed of Judge Baker's infelicitous memory, that the secret was likely to be
revealed at any moment, and that if the girl
continued to cling to her theory, as he feared
she would, even to the parting with her fortune, they would be forced to accept it, or
be placed in the hideous position of publish-
ing her disgrace, at last convinced him. On
the other hand, there was less danger of her
*positive* imposition being discovered than of
the *vague and impositive* truth. The real
danger lay in the present uncertainty and

mystery, which courted surmise and invited discovery. Paul, himself, was willing to take all the responsibility, and at last extracted from the colonel a promise of passive assent. The only revelation he feared was from the interference of the mother, but Pendleton was strong in the belief that she had not only utterly abandoned the girl to the care of her guardians, but that she would never rescind her resolution to disclaim her relationship; that she had gone into self-exile for that purpose ; and that if she *had* changed her mind, he would be the first to know of it. On this day they had parted. Meantime, Paul had not forgotten another resolution he had formed on his first visit to the colonel, and had actually succeeded in getting legislative relief for the Golden Gate Bank, and restoring to the colonel some of his private property that had been in the hands of a receiver.

This had been the background of Paul's meditation, which only threw into stronger relief the face and figure that moved before him as persistently as it had once before in the twilight of his room at Rosario. There were times when her moonlit face, with its faint, strange smile, stood out before him as it had stood out of the shadows of the half-darkened drawing-rooom that night ; as he had seen it — he believed for the last time — framed for an instant in the parted curtains of the doorway, when she bade him " Good-night." For he had never visited her since, and, on the attainment of her majority, had delegated his passing functions to Pendleton, whom he had induced to accompany the Mayor to Santa Clara for the final and formal ceremony. For the present she need not know how much she had been indebted to him for the accomplishment of her wishes.

With a sigh he at last recalled himself to his duty, and, drawing the pile of reports which Shear had handed him, he began to examine them. These, again, bore reference to his silent, unobtrusive inquiries. In his function as Chairman of Committee he had taken advantage of a kind of advanced moral legislation then in vogue, and particularly in reference to a certain social reform, to examine statistics, authorities, and witnesses, and in this indirect but exhaustive manner had satisfied himself that the woman " Kate Howard," alias " Beverly," alias " Durfree," had long passed beyond the ken of local police supervision, and that in the record there

was no trace or indication of her child. He
was going over those infelix records of early
transgressions with the eye of trained experience, making notes from time to time for
his official use, and yet always watchful of
his secret quest, when suddenly he stopped
with a quickened pulse. In the record of
an affray at a gambling-house, one of the
parties had sought refuge in the rooms of
"Kate Howard," who was represented before the magistrate by *her protector, Juan
de Arguello.* The date given was contem-
porary with the beginning of the Trust, but
that proved nothing. But the name — had
it any significance, or was it a grim coincidence, that spoke even more terribly and
hopelessly of the woman's promiscuous
frailty? He again attacked the entire report, but there was no other record of her
name. Even that would have passed any
eye less eager and watchful than his own.

He laid the reports aside, and took up the
proof-slip again. Was there any man living
but himself and Pendleton who would connect these two statements? That her relations with this Arguello were brief and not
generally known was evident from Pendleton's ignorance of the fact. But he must

see him again, and at once. Perhaps he
might have acquired some information from
Yerba; the young girl might have given to
his age that confidence she had withheld
from the younger man; indeed, he remembered with a flush it was partly in that hope
he had induced the colonel to go to Santa
Clara. He put the proof-slip in his pocket
and stepped to the door of the next room.

" You need not write that letter to Slate,
Tony. I will see him myself. I am going
to San Francisco to-night."

" And do you want anything copied from
the reports, sir ? "

Paul quickly swept them from the table
into his drawer, and locked it. " Not now,
thank you. I 'll finish my notes later."

The next morning Paul was in San Francisco, and had again crossed the portals
of the Golden Gate Hotel. He had been
already told that the doom of that palatial
edifice was sealed by the laying of the corner-
stone of a new erection in the next square
that should utterly eclipse it; he even fancied that it had already lost its freshness, and
its meretricious glitter had been tarnished.
But when he had ordered his breakfast he
made his way to the public parlor, happily

deserted at that early hour. It was here
that he had first seen her. She was standing there, by that mirror, when their eyes
first met in a sudden instinctive sympathy.
She herself had remembered and confessed
it. He recalled the pleased yet conscious,
girlish superiority with which she had received the adulation of her friends; his
memory of her was broad enough now even
to identify Milly, as it repeopled the vacant
and silent room.

An hour later he was making his way to
Colonel Pendleton's lodgings, and half expecting to find the St. Charles Hotel itself
transformed by the eager spirit of improvement. But it was still there in all its bar-
baric and provincial incongruity. Public
opinion had evidently recognized that nothing save the absolute razing of its warped
and flimsy walls could effect a change, and
waited for it to collapse suddenly like the
house of cards it resembled. Paul wondered
for a moment if it were not ominous of its
lodgers' hopeless inability to accept changed
conditions, and it was with a feeling of
doubt that he even now ascended the creaking staircase. But it was instantly dissipated
on the threshold of the colonel's sitting-room

by the appearance of George and his reception of his master's guest.

The grizzled negro was arrayed in a surprisingly new suit of blue cloth with a portentous white waistcoat and an enormous crumpled white cravat, that gave him the appearance of suffering from a glandular swelling. His manner had, it seemed to Paul, advanced in exaggeration with his clothes. Dusting a chair and offering it to the visitor, he remained gracefully posed with 'his hand on the back of another.

"Yo' finds us heah yet, Marse Hathaway," he began, elegantly toying with an enormous silver watch-chain, "fo' de Kernel he don' bin find contagious apartments dat at all approximate, and he don' build, for his mind's not dat settled dat he ain't goin' to trabbel. De place is low down, sah, and de fo'ks is low down, and dah's a heap o' white trash dat has congested under de roof ob de hotel since we came. But we uses it temper'ly, sah, fo' de present, and in a dissolutory fashion."

It struck Paul that the contiguity of a certain barber's shop and its dangerous reminiscences had something to do with George's lofty depreciation of his surroundings, and he could not help saying : —

"Then you don't find it necessary to have it convenient to the barber's shop any more? I am glad of that, George."

The shot told. The unfortunate George, after an endeavor to collect himself by altering his pose two or three times in rapid succession, finally collapsed, and, with an air of mingled pain and dignity, but without losing his ceremonious politeness or unique vocabulary, said : —

"Yo' got me dah, sah! Yo' got me dah! De infirmities o' human natcheh, sah, is de common p'operty ob man, and a gemplum like yo'self, sah, a legislato' and a pow'ful speakah, is de lass one to hol' it agin de individal pusson. I confess, sah, de circumstances was propiskuous, de fees fahly good, and de risks inferior. De gemplum who kept de shop was an artess hisself, and had been niggah to Kernel Henderson of Tennessee, and de gemplum I relieved was a Mr. Johnson. But de Kernel, he wouldn't see it in dat light, sah, and if yo' don' mind, sah " —

"I have n't the slightest idea of telling the colonel or anybody, George," said Paul, smiling ; "and I am glad to find on your own account that you are able to put aside any work beyond your duty here."

"Thank yo', sah. If yo' 'll let me introduce yo' to de refreshment, yo' 'll find it all right now. De Glencoe is dah. De Kernel will be here soon, but he would be pow'ful mo'tified, sah, if yo' did n't hab something afo' he come." He opened a well-filled sideboard as he spoke. It was the first evidence Paul had seen of the colonel's restored fortunes. He would willingly have contented himself with this mere outward manifestation, but in his desire to soothe the ruffled dignity of the old man he consented to partake of a small glass of spirits. George at once became radiant and communicative. "De Kernel bin gone to Santa Clara to see de young lady dat 's finished her edercation dah — de Kernel's only ward, sah. She 's one o' dose million-heiresses and highly connected, sah, wid de old Mexican Gobbermen, I understand. And I reckon dey 's bin big goin's on doun dar, foh de Mayer kem hisself fo' de Kernel. Looks like des might bin a proceshon, sah. Yo' don' know of a young lady bin hab a title, sah? I won't be shuah, his Honah de Mayer or de Kernel did n't say someting about a 'Donna.' "

"Very likely," said Paul, turning away with a faint smile. So it was already in the air! Setting aside the old negro's characteristic exaggeration, there had already been some conversation between the colonel and the Mayor, which George had vaguely overheard. He might be too late, the alternative might be no longer in his hands. But his discomposure was heightened a moment later by the actual apparition of the returning Pendleton.

He was dressed in a tightly buttoned blue frock-coat, which fairly accented his tall, thin military figure, although the top lappel was thrown far enough back to show a fine ruffled cambric shirt and checked gingham necktie, and was itself adorned with a white rosebud in the button-hole. Fawn-colored trousers strapped over narrow patent-leather boots, and a tall white hat, whose broad mourning-band was a perpetual memory of his mother, who had died in his boyhood, completed his festal transformation. Yet his erect carriage, high aquiline nose, and long gray drooping moustache lent a distinguishing grace to this survival of a bygone fashion, and over-rode any irreverent comment. Even his slight limp seemed to give a peculiar character to his massive gold-headed stick, and made it a part of his formal elegance.

Handing George his stick and a military cape he carried easily over his left arm, he greeted Paul warmly, yet with a return of his old dominant manner.

"Glad to see you, Hathaway, and glad to see the boy has served you better than the last time. If I had known you were coming, I would have tried to get back in time to have breakfast with you. But your friends at ' Rosario ' — I think they call it ; in my time it was owned by Colonel Briones, and *he* called it ' The Devil's Little Cañon ' — detained me with some d—d civilities. Let's see — his name is Woods, is n't it ? Used to sell rum to runaway sailors on Long Wharf, and take stores in exchange? Or was it Baker? — Judge Baker ? I forget which. Well, sir, they wished to be remembered."

It struck Paul, perhaps unreasonably, that the colonel's indifference and digression were both a little assumed, and he asked abruptly, —

"And you fulfilled your mission ? "

"I made the formal transfer, with the Mayor, of the property to Miss Arguello."

"To Miss Arguello ? "

"To the Doña Maria Concepcion de Arguello de la Yerba Buena — to speak precisely, " said the colonel, slowly. " George, you can take that hat to that blank hatter — what's his blanked name? I read it only yesterday in a list of the prominent citizens here — and tell him, with my compliments, that I want a *gentleman's* mourning band around my hat, and not a child's shoelace. It may be *his* idea of the value of his own parents — if he ever had any — but I don't care for him to appraise mine. Go!"

As the door closed upon George, Paul turned to the colonel —

"Then am I to understand that you have agreed to her story?"

The colonel rose, picked up the decanter, poured out a glass of whiskey, and holding it in his hand, said : —

"My dear Hathaway, let us understand each other. As a gentleman, I have made a point through life never to question the age, name, or family of any lady of my acquaintance. Miss Yerba Buena came of age yesterday, and, as she is no longer my ward, she is certainly entitled to the consideration I have just mentioned. If she, therefore, chooses to tack to her name the whole Spanish directory, I don't see why I should n't accept it."

Characteristic as this speech appeared to be of the colonel's ordinary manner, it struck Paul as being only an imitation of his usual frank independence, and made him uneasily conscious of some vague desertion on Pendleton's part. He fixed his bright eyes on his host, who was ostentatiously sipping his liquor, and said : —

" Am I to understand that you have heard nothing more from Miss Yerba, either for or against her story? That you still do not know whether she has deceived herself, has been deceived by others, or is deceiving us?"

" After what I have just told you, Mr. Hathaway," said the colonel, with an increased exaggeration of manner which Paul thought must be apparent even to himself, " I should have but one way of dealing with questions of that kind from anybody but yourself."

This culminating extravagance — taken in connection with Pendleton's passing doubts — actually forced a laugh from Paul in spite of his bitterness.

Colonel Pendleton's face flushed quickly. Like most positive one-idea'd men, he was restricted from any possible humorous combination, and only felt a mysterious sense of being detected in some weakness. He put down his glass.

" Mr. Hathaway," he began, with a slight vibration in his usual dominant accents, " you have lately put me under a sense of personal obligation for a favor which I felt I could accept without derogation from a younger man, because it seemed to be one not only of youthful generosity but of justice, and was not unworthy the exalted ambition of a young man like yourself or the simple deserts of an old man such as I am. I accepted it, sir, the more readily, because it was entirely unsolicited by me, and seemed to be the spontaneous offering of your own heart. If I have presumed upon it to express myself freely on other matters in a way that only excites your ridicule, I can but offer you an apology, sir. If I have accepted a favor I can neither renounce nor return, I must take the consequences to myself, and even beg *you*, sir, to put up with them."

Remorseful as Paul felt, there was a singular resemblance between the previous reproachful pose of George and this present attitude of his master, as if the mere propinquity of personal sacrifice had made them alike, that struck him with a mingled pathos

and ludicrousness. But he said warmly,
" It is I who must apologize, my dear colonel. I am not laughing at your conclusions,
but at this singular coincidence with a discovery I have made."

" As how, sir ? "

" I find in the report of the Chief of the
Police for the year 1850 that Kate Howard
was under the protection of a man named
Arguello."

The colonel's exaggeration instantly left
him. He stared blankly at Paul. " And
you call this a laughing matter, sir ? " he
said sternly, but in his more natural manner.

" Perhaps not, but I don't think, if you
will allow me to say so, my dear colonel,
that *you* have been treating the whole affair
very seriously. I left you two months ago
utterly opposed to views which you are now
treating as of no importance. And yet you
wish me to believe that nothing has happened, and that you have no further information than you had then. That this is so,
and that you are really no nearer the *facts*,
I am willing to believe from your ignorance
of what I have just told you, and your concern at it. But that you have not been influenced in your *judgment* of what you do

know, I cannot believe?" He drew nearer
Pendleton, and laid his hand upon his arm.
"I beg you to be frank with me, for the
sake of the person whose interests I see you
have at heart. In what way will the discovery I have just made affect them? You
are not so far prejudiced as to be blind to
the fact that it may be dangerous because it
seems corroborative."

Pendleton coughed, rose, took his stick,
and limped up and down the room, finally
dropping into an armchair by the window,
with his cane between his knees, and the
drooping gray silken threads of his long
moustache curled nervously between his
fingers.

"Mr. Hathaway, I *will* be frank with you.
I know nothing of this blank affair — blank
it all! — but what I 've told you. Your discovery may be a coincidence, nothing more.
But I *have* been influenced, sir, — influenced
by one of the most perfect goddess-like —
yes, sir; one of the most simple girlish creatures that God ever sent upon earth. A
woman that I should be proud to claim as
my daughter, a woman that would always
be the superior of any man who dare aspire
to be her husband! A young lady as peer-

less in her beauty as she is in her accomplishments, and whose equal don't walk this planet! I know, sir, *you* don't follow me; I know, Mr. Hathaway, your Puritan prejudices; your Church proclivities, your worldly sense of propriety; and, above all, sir, the blanked hypocritical Pharisaic doctrines of your party — I mean no offense to *you*, sir, personally — blind you to that girl's perfections. She, poor child, herself has seen it and felt it, but never, in her blameless innocence and purity, suspecting the cause. 'There is,' she said to me last night, confidentially, 'something strangely antagonistic and repellent in our natures, some undefined and nameless barrier between our ever understanding each other.' You comprehend, Mr. Hathaway, she does full justice to your intentions and your unquestioned abilities. 'I am not blind,' she said, 'to Mr. Hathaway's gifts, and it is very possible the fault lies with me.' Her very words, sir."

"Then you believe she is perfectly ignorant of her real mother?" asked Paul, with a steady voice, but a whitening face.

"As an unborn child," said the colonel, emphatically. "The snow on the Sierras is

not more spotlessly pure of any trace or con-
tamination of the mud of the mining ditches,
than she of her mother and her past. The
knowledge of it, the mere breath of suspicion
of it, in her presence would be a profanation,
sir! Look at her eye — open as the sky
and as clear; look at her face and figure —
as clean, sir, as a Blue-Grass thoroughbred!
Look at the way she carries herself, whether
in those white frillings of her simple school-
gown, or that black evening dress that makes
her look like a princess! And, blank me, if
she is n't one! There 's no poor stock there
— no white trash — no mixed blood, sir.
Blank it all, sir, if it comes to *that* — the
Arguellos — if there 's a hound of them living — might go down on their knees to have
their name borne by such a creature! By
the Eternal, sir, if one of them dared to cross
her path with a word that was n't abject —
yes, sir, *abject*, I 'd wipe his dust off the
earth and send it back to his ancestors before he knew where he was, or my name is n't
Harry Pendleton! "

Hopeless and inconsistent as all this was,
it was a wonderful sight to see the colonel,
his dark stern face illuminated with a zeal-
ot's enthusiasm, his eyes on fire, the ends of

his gray moustache curling around his set jaw, his head thrown back, his legs astride, and his gold-headed stick held in the hollow of his elbow, like a lance at rest ? Paul saw it, and knew that this Quixotic transformation was part of *her* triumph, and yet had a miserable consciousness that the charms of this Dulcinea del Toboso had scarcely been exaggerated. He turned his eyes away, and said quietly, —

"Then you don't think this coincidence will ever awaken any suspicion in regard to her real mother?"

"Not in the least, sir — not in the least," said the colonel, yet, perhaps, with more doggedness than conviction of accent. "Nobody but yourself would ever notice that police report, and the connection of that woman's name with his was not notorious, or I should have known it."

"And you believe," continued Paul hopelessly, "that Miss Yerba's selection of the name was purely accidental?"

"Purely — a school-girl's fancy. Fancy, did I say? No, sir; by Jove, an inspiration!"

"And," continued Paul, almost mechanically, "you do not think it may be some insidious suggestion of an enemy who knew of this transient relation that no one suspected?"

To his final amazement Pendleton's brow cleared! "An enemy? Gad! you may be right. I'll look into it; and, if that is the case, which I scarcely dare hope for, Mr. Hathaway, you can safely leave him to *me.*"

He looked so supremely confident in his fatuous heroism that Paul could say no more. He rose and, with a faint smile upon his pale face, held out his hand. "I think that is all I have to say. When you see Miss Yerba again, — as you will, no doubt, — you may tell her that I am conscious of no misunderstanding on my part, except, perhaps, as to the best way I could serve her, and that, but for what she has told *you*, I should certainly have carried away no remembrance of any misunderstanding of *hers.*"

"Certainly," said the colonel, with cheerful philosophy, "I will carry your message with pleasure. You understand how it is, Mr. Hathaway. There is no accounting for these instincts — we can only accept them as they are. But I believe that your intentions, sir, were strictly according to what you conceived to be your duty. You won't take something before you go? Well, then — good-by."

Two weeks later Paul found among his morning letters an envelope addressed in Colonel Pendleton's boyish scrawling hand. He opened it with an eagerness that no studied self-control nor rigid preoccupation of his duties had yet been able to subdue, and glanced hurriedly at its contents : —

DEAR SIR, — As I am on the point of sailing to Europe to-morrow to escort Miss Arguello and Miss Woods on an extended visit to England and the Continent, I am desirous of informing you that I have thus far been unable to find any foundation for the suggestions thrown out by you in our last interview. Miss Arguello's Spanish acquaintances have been very select, and limited to a few school friends and Don Cæsar and Doña Anna Briones, tried friends, who are also fellow-passengers with us to Europe. Miss Arguello suggests that some political difference between you and Don Cæsar, which occurred during your visit to Rosario three months ago, may have, perhaps, given rise to your supposition. She joins me in best wishes for your public career, which even in the distraction of foreign travel and the obligations of her position she will follow from time to time with the greatest interest.

Very respectfully yours,

HARRY PENDLETON.

# CHAPTER V.

It was on the 3d of August, 1863, that Paul Hathaway resigned himself and his luggage to the care of the gold-laced, ostensible porter of the Strudle Bad Hof, not without some uncertainty, in a land of uniforms, whether he would be eventually conducted to the barracks, the police office, or the Conservatoire. He was relieved when the omnibus drove into the courtyard of the Bad Hof, and the gold-chained chamberlain, flanked by two green tubs of oleanders, received him with a gravity calculated to check any preconceived idea he might have that traveling was a trifling affair, or that an arrival at the Bad Hof was not of serious moment. His letters had not yet arrived, for he had, in a fit of restlessness, shortened his route, and he strolled listlessly into the reading-room. Two or three English guests were evidently occupied in eminently respectable reading and writing; two were sitting by the window engaged in sub-

dued but profitable conversation; and two
Americans from Boston were contentedly
imitating them on the other side of the
room. A decent restraint, as of people who
were not for a moment to be led into any
foreign idea of social gayety at a watering-
place, was visible everywhere. A specta-
cled Prussian officer in full uniform passed
along the hall, halted for a moment at the
doorway as if contemplating an armed invasion, thought better of it, and took his uniform away into the sunlight of the open
square, where it was joined by other uniforms, and became by contrast a miracle of
unbraced levity. Paul stood the Polar silence for a few moments, until one of the
readers arose and, taking his book — a Mur-
ray — in his hand, walked slowly across the
room to a companion, mutely pointed to a
passage in the book, remained silent until
the other had dumbly perused it, and then
walked back again to his seat, having
achieved the incident without a word. At
which Paul, convinced of his own incongruity, softly withdrew with his hat in his hand,
and his eyes fixed devotionally upon it.

It was good after that to get into the
slanting sunlight and checkered linden

shadows of the *Allée;* to see even a tightly
jacketed cavalryman naturally walking with
Clärchen and her two round-faced and drab-
haired young charges; to watch the returning invalid procession, very real and very
human, each individual intensely involved
in the atmosphere of his own symptoms;
and very good after that to turn into the
Thiergarten, where the animals, were, however, chiefly of his own species, and shame-
lessly and openly amusing themselves. It
was pleasant to contrast it with his first
visit to the place three months before, and
correct his crude impressions. And it was
still more pleasant suddenly to recognize,
under the round flat cap of a general officer,
a former traveler who was fond of talking
with him about America with an intelligence and understanding of it that Paul
had often missed among his own traveled
countrymen. It was pleasant to hear his
unaffected and simple greeting, to renew
their old acquaintance, and to saunter back
to the hotel together through the long twilight.

They were only a few squares from the
hotel, when Paul's attention was attracted
by the curiosity and delight of two or three

children before him, who appeared to be following a quaint-looking figure that was evidently not unfamiliar to them. It appeared to be a servant in a striking livery of green with yellow facings and crested silver buttons, but still more remarkable for the indescribable mingling of jaunty ease and conscious dignity with which he carried off his finery. There was something so singular and yet so vaguely reminiscent in his peculiar walk and the exaggerated swing of his light bamboo cane that Paul could not only understand the childish wonder of the passers-by, who turned to look after him, but was stirred with a deeper curiosity. He quickened his pace, but was unable to distinguish anything of the face or features of the stranger, except that his hair under his cocked hat appeared to be tightly curled and powdered. Paul's companion, who was amused at what seemed to be the American's national curiosity, had seen the figure before. "A servant in the suite of some Eastern *Altesse* visiting the baths. You will see stranger things, my friend, in the Strudle Bad. *Par example*, your own countrymen, too; the one who has enriched himself by that pork of Chicago, or that soap, or this candle, in a carriage with the crest of the title he has bought in Italy with his dollars, and his beautiful daughters, who are seeking more titles with possible matrimonial contingencies."

After an early dinner, Paul found his way to the little theatre. He had already been struck by a highly colored poster near the *Bahnhof*, purporting that a distinguished German company would give a representation of "Uncle Tom's Cabin," and certain peculiarities in the pictorial advertisement of the tableaux gave promise of some entertainment. He found the theatre fairly full; there was the usual contingent of *abonnirte* officers, a fair sprinkling of English and German travelers, but apparently none of his own countrymen. He had no time to examine the house more closely, for the play, commencing with simple punctuality, not only far exceeded the promise of the posters, but of any previous performance of the play he had witnessed. Transported at once to a gorgeous tropical region — the slave States of America — resplendent with the fruits and palms of Mauritius, and peopled exclusively with Paul and Virginia's companions in striped cotton, Hathaway

managed to keep a composed face, until the
arrival of the good Southern planter St.
Clair as one of the earlier portraits of Goe-
the, in top boots, light kerseymere breeches,
redingote and loose Byron collar, compelled
him to shrink into the upper corner of the
box with his handkerchief to his face.
Luckily, the action passed as the natural
effect upon a highly sympathetic nature of
religious interviews between a round-faced
flaxen-haired "Kleine Eva" and "Onkeel
Tome," occasionally assisted by a Dissent-
ing clergyman in Geneva bands; of exces-
sive brutality with a cattle whip by a Zamiel-
like Legree; of the sufferings of a runaway
negro *Zimmermädchen* with a child three
shades lighter than herself; and of a painted
canvas "man-hunt," where apparently four
well known German composers on horseback, with flowing hair, top boots, and a
*Cor de chasse*, were pursuing, with the aid
of a pack of fox hounds, "the much too
deeply abused and yet spiritually elevated
Onkeel Tome." Paul did not wait for the
final apotheosis of "der Kleine Eva," but,
in the silence of a hushed audience, made
his way into the corridor and down the staircase. He was passing an open door marked

"Direction," when his attention was sharply attracted by a small gathering around it and the sounds of indignant declamation. It was the voice of a countryman — more than that, it was a familiar voice, that he had not heard for three years — the voice of Colonel Harry Pendleton!

"Tell him," said Pendleton, in scathing tones, to some invisible interpreter, — "tell, him, sir, that a more infamous caricature of the blankest caricature that ever maligned a free people, sir, I never before had the honor of witnessing. Tell him that *I*, sir — I, Harry Pendleton, of Kentucky, a Southerner, sir — an old slaveholder, sir, declare it to be a tissue of falsehoods unworthy the credence of a Christian civilization like this — unworthy the attention of the distinguished ladies and gentlemen that are gathered here to-night. Tell him, sir, he has been imposed upon. Tell him I am responsible — give him my card and address — personally responsible for what I say. If he wants proofs — blank it all! — tell him you yourself have been a slave — *my* slave, sir! Take off your hat, sir! Ask him to look at you — ask him if he thinks you ever looked or could look like that lop-

eared, psalm-singing, white-headed hypocrite
on the stage! Ask him, sir, if he thinks
that blank ringmaster they call St. Clair
looks like *Me!*"

At this astounding exordium Paul eagerly
pressed forward and entered the bureau.
There certainly was Colonel Pendleton, in
spotless evening dress; erect, flashing, and
indignant; his aquiline nose lifted like a
hawk's beak over his quarry, his iron-gray
moustache, now white and waxed, parted
like a swallow's tail over his handsome
mouth, and between him and the astounded
"Direction" stood the apparition of the
*Allée* — George! There was no mistaking
him now. What Paul had thought was a
curled wig or powder was the old negro's
own white knotted wool, and the astounding
livery he wore was carried off as no one but
George could carry it.

But he was still more amazed when the
old servant, in a German as exaggerated, as
incoherent, but still as fluent and persuasive
as his own native speech, began an extravagant but perfectly dignified and diplomatic
translation of his master's protests. Where
and when, by what instinct, he had assimi-
lated and made his own the grotesque inver-

sions and ponderous sentimentalities of Teutonic phrasing, Paul could not guess; but it was with breathless wonder that he presently became aware that, so perfect and convincing was the old man's style and deportment, not only the simple officials but even the bystanders were profoundly impressed by this farrago of absurdity. A happy word here and there, the full title and rank given, even with a slight exaggeration, to each individual, brought a deep and guttural "So!" from lips that would have found it difficult to repeat a line of his ceremonious idiocy.

In their preoccupation neither the colonel nor George had perceived Paul's entrance, but, as the old servant turned with magnificent courtesy towards the bystanders, his eyes fell upon Paul. A flash of surprise, triumph, and satisfaction lit up his rolling eyes. Paul instantly knew that he not only recognized him, but that he had already heard of and thoroughly appreciated a certain distinguished position that Paul had lately held, and was quick to apply it. Intensifying for a moment the grandiloquence of his manner, he called upon his master's most distinguished and happily arrived old friend, the Lord Lieutenant Governor of

the Golden Californias, to corroborate his
statement. Colonel Pendleton started, and
grasped Paul's hand warmly. Paul turned
to the already half-mollified Director with
the diplomatic suggestion that the vivid and
realistic acting of the admirable company
which he himself had witnessed had perhaps
unduly excited his old friend, even as it had
undoubtedly thrown into greater relief the
usual exaggerations of dramatic representation, and the incident terminated with a
profusion of apologies, and the most cordial
expressions of international good feeling on
both sides.

Yet, as they turned away from the theatre together, Paul could not help noticing
that, although the colonel's first greeting
had been spontaneous and unaffected, it was
succeeded by an uneasy reserve. Paul made
no attempt to break it, and confined himself to a few general inquiries, ending by
inviting the colonel to sup with him at the
hotel. Pendleton hesitated. "At any other
time, Mr. Hathaway, I should have insisted
upon you, as the stranger, supping with me;
but since the absence of — of — the rest of
my party — I have given up my suite of
rooms at the Bad Hof, and have taken

smaller lodgings for myself and the boy at the Schwartze Adler. Miss Woods and Miss Arguello have accepted an invitation to spend a few days at the villa of the Baron and Baroness von Schilprecht — an hour or two from here." He lingered over the title with an odd mingling of impressiveness and inquiry, and glanced at Paul. But Hathaway exhibiting neither emotion nor surprise at the mention of Yerba's name or the title of her host, he continued, " Miss Arguello, I suppose you know, is immensely admired : she has been, sir, the acknowledged belle of Strudle Bad."

"I can readily believe it," said Paul, simply.

" And has taken the position — the position, sir, to which she is entitled."

Without appearing to notice the slight challenge in Pendleton's tone, Paul returned, " I am glad to hear it. The more particularly as, I believe, the Germans are great sticklers for position and pedigree."

" You are right, sir — quite right : they are," said the colonel, proudly — " although " — with a certain premeditated deliberation — " I have been credibly informed that the King can, in certain cases, if he chooses,

supply — yes, sir — *supply* a favored person
with ancestors — yes, sir, with *ancestors!*"

Paul cast a quick glance at his companion.

"Yes, sir — that is, we will say, in the
case of a lady of inferior rank — or even
birth, the King of these parts can, on her
marriage with a nobleman — blank it all! —
ennoble her father and mother, and their
fathers and mothers, though they've been
dead, or as good as dead, for years."

"I am afraid that's a slight exaggeration
of the rare custom of granting 'noble lands,'
or estates that carry hereditary titles with
them," said Paul, more emphatically, perhaps, than the occasion demanded.

"Fact, sir — George there knows it all,"
said Pendleton. "He gets it from the
other servants. I don't speak the language,
sir, but *he* does. Picked it up in a year."

"I must compliment him on his fluency,
certainly," said Paul, looking at George.

The old servant smiled, and not without a
certain condescension. "Yes, sah; I don'
say to a scholar like yo'self, sah, dat I 'se
got de grandmatical presichion; but as fah,
sah — as fah as de *idiotisms* ob de language
goes. Sah — it's gen'lly allowed I 'm dar!

As to what Marse Harry says ob de igno-
bling ob predecessors, I 've had it, sah, from
de best autority, sah — de furst, I may say,
sah — de real *prima facie* men — de gemplum ob his Serene Highness, in de korse
eb ordinary conversashun, sah."

"That 'll do, George," said Pendleton,
with paternal brusqueness. "Run on ahead
and tell that blank chamberlain that Mr.
Hathaway is one of my friends — and have
supper accordingly." As the negro hastened away he turned to Paul: "What he
says is true: he 's the most popular man or
boy in all Strudle Bad — a devilish sight
more than his master — and goes anywhere
where *I* can't go. Princes and princesses
stop and talk to him in the street; the
Grand Duke asked permission to have him
up in his carriage at the races the other day;
and, by the Eternal, sir, he gives the style
to all the flunkeys in town!"

"And I see, he dresses the character,"
observed Paul.

"His own idea — entirely. And, by
Jove! he proves to be right. You can't do
anything here without a uniform. And
they tell me he 's got everything correct,
down to the crest on the buttons."

They walked on in silence for a few moments, Pendleton retaining a certain rigidity of step and bearing which Paul had come to recognize as indicating some uneasiness or mental disturbance on his part. Hathaway had no intention of precipitating the confidence of his companion. Perhaps experience had told him it would come soon enough. So he spoke carelessly of himself. How the need of a year's relaxation and change had brought him abroad, his journeyings, and, finally, how he had been advised by his German physician to spend a few weeks at Strudle Bad preparatory to the voyage home. Yet he was perfectly aware that the colonel from time to time cast a furtive glance at his face. " And *you*," he said in conclusion — " when do you intend to return to California ?"

The colonel hesitated slightly. " I shall remain in Europe until Miss Arguello is — settled — I mean," he added hurriedly, " until she has — ahem ! — completed her education in foreign ways and customs. You see, Hathaway, I have constituted myself, after a certain fashion, I may say — still, her guardian. I am an old man, with neither kith nor kin myself, sir — I 'm a

little too old-fashioned for the boys over
there " — with a vague gesture towards the
west, which, however, told Paul how near
it still was to him. "But then, among the
old fogys here — blank it all! — it is n't
noticed. So I look after her, you see, or
rather make myself responsible for her generally — although, of course, she has other
friends and associates, you understand, more
of her own age and tastes."

"And I 've no doubt she 's perfectly satisfied," said Paul in a tone of conviction.

"Well, yes, sir, I presume so," said the
colonel slowly; "but I 've sometimes
thought, Mr. Hathaway, that it would have
been better if she 'd have had a woman's
care — the protection you understand, of an
elderly woman of society. That seems to
be the style here, you know — a chaperon,
they call it. Now, Milly Woods, you see,
is about the same age, and the Doña Anna,
of course, is older, but — blank it! — she 's
as big a flirt as the rest — I mean," he
added, correcting himself sharply, "she
lacks balance, sir, and — what shall I call
it? — self-abnegation."

"Then Doña Anna is still of your party?"
asked Paul.

"She is, sir, and her brother, Don Cæsar. I have thought it advisable, on Yerba's account, to keep up as much as possible the suggestion of her Spanish relationship — although by reason of their absurd ignorance of geography and political divisions out here, there is a prevailing impression that she is a South American. A fact, sir. I have myself been mistaken for the Dictator of one of these infernal Republics, and I have been pointed out as ruling over a million or two of niggers like George!"

There was no trace of any conception of humor in the colonel's face, although he uttered a short laugh, as if in polite acceptance of the possibility that Paul might have one. Far from that, his companion, looking at the striking profile and erect figure at his side — at the long white moustache which drooped from his dark cheeks, and remembering his own sensations at first seeing George — thought the popular belief not so wonderful. He was even forced to admit that the perfect unconsciousness on the part of master and man of any incongruity or peculiarity in themselves assisted the public misconception. And it was, I fear, with a feeling of wicked delight that, on entering

the hotel, he hailed the evident consternation of those correct fellow-countrymen from
whom he had lately fled, at what they apparently regarded as a national scandal. He
overheard their hurried assurance to their
English friends that his companions were
*not* from Boston, and enjoyed their mortification that this explanation did not seem to
detract from the interest and relief with
which the Britons surveyed them, or the
open admiration of the Germans.

Although Pendleton somewhat unbent
during supper, he did not allude to the secret of Yerba's parentage, nor of any tardy
confidence of hers. To all appearance the
situation remained as it was three years ago.
He spoke of her great popularity as an
heiress and a beautiful woman, and the
marked attentions she received. He doubted
not that she had rejected very distinguished
offers, but she kept that to herself. She
was perfectly competent to do so. She was
no giddy girl, to be flattered or deceived;
on the contrary, he had never known a
cooler or more sensible woman. She knew
her own worth. When she met the man
who satisfied her ambition and understanding, she would marry, and not before. He

did not know what that ambition was; it was something exalted, of course. He could only say, of his own knowledge, that last year, when they were on the Italian lakes, there was a certain prince — Mr. Hathaway would understand why he did not mention names — who was not only attentive to her, but attentive to *him*, sir, by Jove! and most significant in his inquiries. It was the only occasion when he, the colonel, had ever spoken to her on such subjects; and, knowing that she was not indifferent to the fellow, who was not bad of his kind, he had asked her why she had not encouraged his suit. She had said, with a laugh, that he couldn't marry her unless he gave up his claim of succession to a certain reigning house; and she wouldn't accept him *without it*. Those were her words, sir, and he could only say that the prince left a few days afterwards, and they had never seen him since. As to the princelings and counts and barons, she knew to a day the date of their patents of nobility, and what privileges they were entitled to; she could tell to a dot the value of their estates, the amount of their debts, and, by Jove! sir, the amount of mortgages she was expected

to pay off before she married them. She
knew the amount of income she had to
bring to the Prussian Army, from the general to the lieutenant. She understood her
own value and her rights. There was a
young English lordling she met on the
Rhine, whose boyish ways and simplicity
seemed to please her. They were great
friends; but he wanted him — the colonel
— to induce her to accept an invitation for
both to visit his mother's home in England,
that his people might see her. But she declined, sir! She declined to pass in review
before his mother. She said it was for *him*
to pass in review before *her* mother.

"Did she say that?" interrupted Paul,
fixing his bright eyes upon the colonel.

"If she had one, if she had one," corrected the colonel, hastily. "Of course it
was only an illustration. That she is an
orphan is generally known, sir."

There was a dead silence for a few moments. The colonel leaned back in his chair
and pulled his moustache. Paul turned
away his eyes, and seemed absorbed in reflection. After a moment the colonel
coughed, pushed aside his glass, and, leaning across the table, said, "I have a favor
to ask of you, Mr. Hathaway."

There was such a singular change in the tone of his voice, an unexpected relaxation of some artificial tension, — a relaxation which struck Paul so pathetically as being as much physical as mental, as if he had suddenly been overtaken in some exertion by the weakness of age, — that he looked up quickly. Certainly, although still erect and lightly grasping his moustache, the colonel looked older.

"By all means, my dear colonel," said Paul warmly.

"During the time you remain here you can hardly help meeting Miss Arguello, perhaps frequently. It would be strange if you did not; it would appear to everybody still stranger. Give me your word as a gentleman that you will not make the least allusion to her of the past — nor reopen the subject."

Paul looked fixedly at the colonel. "I certainly had no intention of doing so," he said after a pause, "for I thought it was already settled by you beyond disturbance or discussion. But do I understand you, that *she* has shown any uneasiness regarding it? From what you have just told me of her plans and ambition, I can scarcely imagine that she has any suspicion of the real facts."

"Certainly not," said the colonel hurriedly. "But I have your promise."

"I promise you," said Paul, after a pause, "that I shall neither introduce nor refer to the subject myself, and that if *she* should question me again regarding it, which is hardly possible, I will reveal nothing without your consent."

"Thank you," said Pendleton, without, however, exhibiting much relief in his face. "She will return here to-morrow."

"I thought you said she was absent for some days," said Paul.

"Yes; but she is coming back to say good-by to Doña Anna, who arrives here with her brother the same day, on their way to Paris."

It flashed through Paul's mind that the last time he had seen her was in the company of the Briones. It was not a pleasant coincidence. Yet he was not aware that it had affected him, until he saw the colonel watching him.

"I believe you don't fancy the brother," said Pendleton.

For an instant Paul was strongly tempted

to avow his old vague suspicions of Don Cæsar, but the utter hopelessness of reopening the whole subject again, and his recollection of the passage in Pendleton's letter that purported to be Yerba's own theory of his dislike, checked him in time. He only said, " I don't remember whether I had any cause for disliking Don Cæsar; I can tell better when I see him again," and changed the subject. A few moments later the colonel summoned George from some lower region of the hotel, and rose to take his leave. " Miss Arguello, with her maid and courier, will occupy her old suite of rooms here," he remarked, with a return of his old imperiousness. " George has given the orders for her. *I* shall not change my present lodgings, but of course will call every day. Goodnight! "

## CHAPTER VI.

THE next morning Paul could not help
noticing an increased and even exaggerated
respect paid him by the hotel attendants.
He was asked if his *Exeellency* would be
served with breakfast in a private room,
and his condescension in selecting the public coffee-room struck the obsequious chamberlain, but did not prevent him from preceding Paul backwards to the table, and
summoning a waiter to attend specially upon
" milor." Surmising that George and the
colonel might be in some way connected
with this extravagance, he postponed an investigation till he should have seen them
again. And, although he hardly dared to
confess it to himself, the unexpected prospect of meeting Yerba again fully preoccupied his thoughts. He had believed that
he would eventually see her in Europe, in
some vague and indefinite way and hour:
it had been in his mind when he started
from California. That it would be so soon,

and in such a simple and natural manner,
he had never conceived.

" He had returned from his morning walk
to the *Brunnen*, and was sitting idly in his
room, when there was a knock at the door.
It opened to a servant bearing a salver with
a card. Paul lifted it with a slight tremor,
not at the engraved name of " Maria Concepcion de Arguellos de la Yerba Buena,"
but at the remembered school-girl hand that
had penciled underneath the words, " wishes
the favor of an audience with his Excellency
the Lord Lieutenant-Governor of the Californias."

Paul looked inquiringly at the servant.
" The *gnädige Fräulein* was in her own
salon. Would *Excellency* walk that way ?
It was but a step; in effect, the next apartment."

Paul followed him into the hall with wondering steps. The door of the next room
was open, and disclosed a handsomely furnished salon. A tall graceful figure rose
quickly from behind a writing-table, and
advanced with outstretched hands and a
frank yet mischievous smile. It was Yerba.

Standing there in a grayish hat, mantle,
and traveling dress, all of one subdued yet

alluring tone, she looked as beautiful as
when he had last seen her — and yet — unlike. For a brief bitter moment his instincts
revolted at this familiar yielding up in his
fair countrywomen of all that was distinc-
tively original in them to alien tastes and
habits, and he resented the plastic yet char-
acterless mobility which made Yerba's Pari-
sian dress and European manner fit her so
charmingly and yet express so little. For
a brief critical moment he remembered the
placid, unchanging simplicity of German,
and the inflexible and ingrained reserve of
English, girlhood, in opposition to this indis-
tinctive cosmopolitan grace. But only for
a moment. As soon as she spoke, a certain
flavor of individuality seemed to return to
her speech.

" Confess," she said, " it was a courageous
thing for me to do. You might have been
somebody else — a real Excellency — or
Heaven knows what! Or, what is worse in
your new magnificence, you might have forgotten one of your oldest, most humble, but
faithful subjects." She drew back and made
him a mock ceremonious curtsy, that even
in its charming exaggeration suggested to
Paul, however, that she had already made
it somewhere seriously.

"But what does it all mean?" he asked, smiling, feeling not only his doubts and uneasiness vanish, but even the years of separation melt away in her presence. "I know I went to bed last night a very humble individual, and yet I seem to awaken this morning a very exalted personage. Am I really Commander of the Faithful, or am I dreaming? Might I trouble you, as my predecessor Abou Hassan did Sweetlips, to bite my little finger?"

"Do you mean to say you have not seen the 'Anzeiger?'" she returned, taking a small German printed sheet from the table and pointing to a paragraph. Paul took the paper. Certainly there was the plain announcement among the arrivals of "His Excellency Paul Hathaway, Lord Lieutenant-Governor of the Californias." A light flashed upon him.

"This is George's work. He and Colonel Pendleton were here with me last night."

"Then you have seen the colonel already?" she said, with a scarcely perceptible alteration of expression, which, however, struck Paul.

"Yes. I met him at the theatre last evening." He was about to plunge into an animated description of the colonel's indignation, but checked himself, he knew not why. But he was thankful the next moment that he had.

"That accounts for everything," she said, lifting her pretty shoulders with a slight shrug of weariness. "I had to put a stop to George's talking about *me* three months ago, — his extravagance is something *too* awful. And the colonel, who is completely in his hands, — trusting him for everything, even the language, — does n't see it."

"But he is extravagant in the praise of his friends only, and you certainly justify all he can say."

She was taking off her hat, and stopped for a moment to look at him thoughtfully, with the soft tendrils of her hair clinging to her forehead. "Did the colonel talk much about me?"

"A great deal. In fact, I think we talked of nothing else. He has told me of your triumphs and your victims ; of your various campaigns and your conquests. And yet I dare say he has not told me all — and I am dying to hear more."

She had laid down her hat and unloosed a large bow of her mantle, but stopped sud-

denly in the midst of it and sat down
again.

"I wish you'd do something for me."

"You have only to name it."

"Well, drop all this kind of talk! Try
to think of me as if I had just come from
California — or, better, as if you had never
known anything of me at all — and we met
for the first time. You could, I dare say,
make yourself very agreeable to such a
young lady who was willing to be pleased —
why not to me? I venture to say you have
not ever troubled yourself about me since
we last met. No — hear me through —
why, then, should you wish to talk over
what did n't concern you at the time?
Promise me you will stop this reminiscent
gossip, and I promise you *I* will not only
not bore you with it, but take care that it is
not intruded upon you by others. Make
yourself pleasant to me by talking about
yourself and your prospects — anything but
*me* — and I will throw over those princes
and barons that the colonel has raved about
and devote myself to you while you are
here. Does that suit your Excellency?"
She had crossed her knees, and, with her
hands clasped over them, and the toe of her

small boot advanced beyond her skirt, leaned forward in the attitude he remembered to have seen her take in the summer-house at Rosario.

" Perfectly," he said.

" How long will you be here ? "

" About three weeks : that, I believe, is the time allotted for my cure."

" Are you really ill," she said quietly, " or imagine yourself so ? "

" It amounts to about the same thing. But my cure may not take so long," he added, fixing his bright eyes upon her.

She returned his gaze thoughtfully, and they remained looking at each other silently.

" Then you are stronger than you give yourself credit for. That is very often the case," she said quietly. " There," she added in another tone, " it is settled. You will come and go as you like, using this salon as your own. Stay, we can do something to-day. What do you say to a ride in the forest this afternoon ? Milly is n't here yet, but it will be quite proper for you to accompany me on horseback, though, of course, we could n't walk a hundred yards down the *Allée* together unless we were *verlobt*."

" But," said Paul, " you are expecting

company this afternoon. Don Cæsar — I mean Miss Briones and her brother are coming here to say good-by."

She regarded him curiously, but without emotion.

"Colonel Pendleton should have added that they were to remain here overnight as my guests," she said composedly. And of course we shall be back in time for dinner. But that is nothing to you. You have only to be ready at three o'clock. I will see that the horses are ordered. I often ride here, and the people know my tastes and habits. We will have a pleasant ride and a good long talk together, and I 'll show you a ruin and a distant view of the villa where I have been staying." She held out her hand with a frank girlish smile, and even a girlish anticipation of pleasure in her brown eyes. He bent over her slim fingers for a moment, and withdrew.

When he was in his own room again, he was conscious only of a strong desire to avoid the colonel until after his ride with Yerba. He would keep his word so far as to abstain from allusion to her family or her past : indeed, he had his own opinion of its futility. But it would be strange if, with

his past experience, he could not find some
other way to determine her convictions or
win her confidence during those two hours
of companionship.  He would accept her
terms fairly; if she had any ulterior design
in her advances, he would detect it; if she
had the least concern for him, she could not
continue long an artificial friendship.  But
he must not think of that!

By absenting himself from the hotel he
managed to keep clear of Pendleton until
the hour arrived.  He was gratified to find
Yerba in the simplest and most sensible of
habits, as if she had already divined his
tastes and had wished to avoid attracting
undue attention.  Nevertheless, it very pret-
tily accented her tall graceful figure, and
Paul, albeit, like most artistic admirers of
the sex, not recognizing a woman on a horse
as a particularly harmonious spectacle, was
forced to admire her.  Both rode well, and
naturally — having been brought up in the
same Western school — the horses recognized it, and instinctively obeyed them, and
their conversation had the easy deliberation
and inflection of a *tête-à-tête*.  Paul, in view
of her previous hint, talked to her of himself and his fortunes, of which she ap-

peared, however, to have some knowledge.
His health had obliged him lately to abandon
politics and office ; he had been successful
in some ventures, and had become a junior
partner in a bank with foreign correspon-
dence. She listened to him for some time
with interest and attention, but at last her
face became abstracted and thoughtful. "I
wish I were a man!" she said suddenly.

Paul looked at her quickly. For the first
time he detected in the ring of her voice
something of the passionate quality he fancied he had always seen in her face.

"Except that it might give you better
control of your horse, I don't see why," said
Paul. "And I don't entirely believe you."

"Why?"

"Because no woman really wishes to be a
man unless she is conscious of her failure as
a woman."

"And how do you know I'm not?" she
said, checking her horse and looking in his
face. A quick conviction that she was on
the point of some confession sprang into his
mind, but unfortunately showed in his face.
She beat back his eager look with a short
laugh. "There, don't speak, and don't
look like that. That remark was worthy

the usual artless maiden's invitation to a compliment, was n't it? Let us keep to the subject of yourself. Why, with your political influence, don't you get yourself appointed to some diplomatic position over here?"

"There are none in our service. You would n't want me to sink myself in some absurd social functions, which are called by that name, merely to become the envy and hatred of a few rich republicans, like your friends who haunt foreign courts?"

"That's not a pretty speech — but I suppose I invited *that* too. Don't apologize. I'd rather see you flare out like that than pay compliments. Yet I fancy you're a diplomatist, for all that."

"You did me the honor to believe I was one once, when I was simply the most palpable ass and bungler living," said Paul bitterly.

She was still sweetly silent, apparently preoccupied in smoothing out the mane of her walking horse. "Did I?" she said softly. He drew close beside her.

"How different the vegetation is here from what it is with us!" she said with nervous quickness, directing his attention to the grass road beneath them, without lifting her eyes. "I don't mean what is cultivated, — for I suppose it takes centuries to make the lawns they have in England, — but even here the blades of grass seem to press closer together, as if they were crowded or over-populated, like the country; and this forest, which has been always wild and was a hunting park, has a *blasé* look, as if it was already tired of the unchanging traditions and monotony around it. I think over there Nature affects and influences us: here, I fancy, it is itself affected by the people."

"I think a good deal of Nature comes over from America for that purpose," he said dryly.

"And I think you are breaking your promise — besides being a goose!" she retorted smartly. Nevertheless, for some occult reason they both seemed relieved by this exquisite witticism, and trotted on amicably together. When Paul lifted his eyes to hers he could see that they were suffused with a tender mischief, as of a reproving yet secretly admiring sister, and her strangely delicate complexion had taken on itself that faint Alpine glow that was more of an illumination than a color. "There," she said gayly, pointing with her whip as the wood opened upon a glade through which the parted trees showed a long blue curvature of distant hills, "you see that white thing lying like a snowdrift on the hills?"

"Or the family washing on a hedge."

"As you please. Well, that is the villa."

"And you were very happy there?" said Paul, watching her girlishly animated face.

"Yes; and as you don't ask questions, I'll tell you why. There is one of the sweetest old ladies there that I ever met — the perfection of old-time courtliness with all the motherishness of a German woman. She was very kind to me, and, as she had no daughter of her own, I think she treated me as if I was one. At least, I can imagine how one would feel to her, and what a woman like that could make of any girl. You laugh, Mr. Hathaway, you don't understand — but you don't know what an advantage it would be to a girl to have a mother like that, and know that she could fall back on her and hold her own against anybody. She's equipped from the start, instead of being handicapped. It's all very well to talk about the value of money. It can give you everything but one thing — the power to do without it."

"I think its purchasing value would include even the *gnädige Frau*," said Paul, who had laughed only to hide the uneasiness that Yerba's approach to the tabooed subject had revived in him. She shook her head ; then, recovering her tone of gentle banter, said, "There — I 've made a confession. If the colonel talks to you again about my conquests, you will know that at present my affections are centred on the Baron's mother. I admit it's a strong point in his — in *anybody's* — favor, who can show an unblemished maternal pedigree. What a pity it is you are an orphan, like myself, Mr. Hathaway ! For I fancy your mother must have been a very perfect woman. A great deal of her tact and propriety has descended to you. Only it would have been nicer if she had given it to you, like pocket money, as occasion required — which you might have shared with me — than leaving it to you in one thumping legacy."

It was impossible to tell how far the playfulness of her brown eyes suggested any ulterior meaning, for as Paul again eagerly drew towards her, she sent her horse into a rapid canter before him. When he was

at her side again, she said, "There is still
the ruin to see on our way home. It is just
off here to the right. But if you wish to
go over it we will have to dismount at the
foot of the slope and walk up. It has n't
any story or legend that I know of; I
looked over the guide-book to cram for it
before you came, but there was nothing. So
you can invent what you like."

They dismounted at the beginning of a
gentle acclivity, where an ancient wagon-
road, now grass-grown, rose smooth as a
glacis. Tying their horses to two moplike
bushes, they climbed the slope hand in hand
like children. There were a few winding
broken steps, part of a fallen archway, a
few feet of vaulted corridor, a sudden breach
— the sky beyond — and that was all! Not
all; for before them, overlooked at first,
lay a chasm covering half an acre, in which
the whole of the original edifice — tower
turrets, walls, and battlements — had been
apparently cast, inextricably mixed and mingled at different depths and angles, with
here and there, like mushrooms from a dust-
heap, a score of trees upspringing.

"This is not Time — but gunpowder,"
said Paul, leaning over a parapet of the

wall and gazing at the abyss, with a slight grimace.

"It don't look very romantic, certainly," said Yerba. "I only saw it from the road before. I'm dreadfully sorry," she added, with mock penitence. "I suppose, however, *something* must have happened here."

"There may have been nobody in the house at the time," said Paul gravely. "The family may have been at the baths."

They stood close together, their elbows resting upon the broken wall, and almost touching. Beyond the abyss and darker forest they could see the more vivid green and regular lines of the plane-trees of Strudle Bad, the glitter of a spire, or the flash of a dome. From the abyss itself arose a cool odor of moist green leaves, the scent of some unseen blossoms, and around the baking vines on the hot wall the hum of apparently taskless and disappointed bees. There was nobody in sight in the forest road, no one working in the bordering fields, and no suggestion of the present. There might have been three or four centuries between them and Strudle Bad.

"The legend of this place," said Paul, glancing at the long brown lashes and oval

outline of the cheek so near his own, " is
simple, yet affecting. A cruel, remorse-
less, but fascinating Hexie was once loved
by a simple shepherd. He had never dared
to syllable his hopeless affection, or claim
from her a syllabled — perhaps I should
say a one-syllabled — reply. He had followed her from remote lands, dumbly wor-
shiping her, building in his foolish brain
an air-castle of happiness, which by reason
of her magic power she could always see
plainly in his eyes. And one day, beguil-
ing him in the depths of the forest, she led
him to a fair-seeming castle, and, bidding
him enter its portals, offered to show him a
realization of his dream. But, lo! even as
he entered the stately corridor it seemed to
crumble away before him, and disclosed a
hideous abyss beyond, in which the whole
of that goodly palace lay in heaped and
tangled ruins — the fitting symbol of his
wrecked and shattered hopes."

She drew back a little way from him, but
still holding on to the top of the broken
wall with one slim gauntleted hand, and
swung herself to one side, while she surveyed him with smiling, parted lips and conscious eyelids. He promptly covered her

hand with his own, but she did not seem to notice it.

"That is not the story," she said, in a faint voice that even her struggling sauciness could not make steadier. "The true story is called 'The Legend of the Goose-Girl of Strudle Bad, and the enterprising Gosling.' There was once a goose-girl of the plain who tried honestly to drive her geese to market, but one eccentric and willful gosling — Mr. Hathaway! Stop — please — I beg you let me go!'"

He had caught her in his arms — the one encircling her waist, the other hand still grasping hers. She struggled, half laughing; yielded for a breathless moment as his lips brushed her cheek, and — threw him off. "There!" she said, "that will do: the story was not illustrated."

"But, Yerba," he said, with passionate eagerness, "hear me — it is all God's truth. — I love you!"

She drew back farther, shaking the dust of the wall from the folds of her habit. Then, with a lower voice and a paler cheek, as if his lips had sent her blood and utterance back to her heart, she said, "Come, let us go."

" But not until you 've heard me, Yerba."

" Well, then — I believe you — there ! "
she said, looking at him.

" You believe me ? " he repeated eagerly,
attempting to take her hand again.

She drew back still farther. " Yes," she
said, " or I should n't be here now. There!
that must suffice you. And if you wish me
still to believe you, you will not speak of
this again while we are out together. Come,
let us go back to the horses."

He looked at her with all his soul. She
was pale, but composed, and — he could see
— determined. He followed her without a
word. She accepted his hand to support
her again down the slope without embarrassment or reminiscent emotion. The whole
scene through which she had just passed
might have been buried in the abyss and
ruins behind her. As she placed her foot
in his hand to remount, and for a moment
rested her weight on his shoulder, her brown
eyes met his frankly and without a tremor.

Nor was she content with this. As Paul
at first rode on silently, his heart filled with
unsatisfied yearning, she rallied him mischievously. Was it kind in him on this,
their first day together, to sulk in this fash-

ion? Was it a promise for their future
excursions? Did he intend to carry this
lugubrious visage through the *Allée* and up
to the courtyard of the hotel to proclaim
his sentimental condition to the world? At
least, she trusted he would not show it to
Milly, who might remember that this was
only the *second time* they had met each
other. There was something so sweetly
reasonable in this, and withal not without
a certain hopefulness for the future, to say
nothing of the half - mischievous, half - reproachful smile that accompanied it, that
Paul exerted himself, and eventually recovered his lost gayety. When they at last
drew up in the courtyard, with the flush of
youth and exercise in their faces, Paul felt
he was the object of envy to the loungers,
and of fresh gossip to Strudle Bad. It
struck him less pleasantly that two dark
faces, which had been previously regarding
him in the gloom of the corridor and vanished as he approached, reappeared some
moments later in Yerba's salon as Don
Cæsar and Doña Anna, with a benignly different expression. Doña Anna especially
greeted him with so much of the ostentatious
archness of a confident and forgiving woman

to a momentarily recreant lover, that he felt
absurdly embarrassed in Yerba's presence.
He was thinking how he could excuse himself, when he noticed a beautiful basket of
flowers on the table and a tiny note bearing
a baron's crest.    Yerba had put it aside
with — as it seemed to him at the moment
— an almost too pronounced indifference
— and an indifference that was strongly
contrasted to Doña Anna's eagerly expressed
enthusiasm over the offering, and her ultimate supplications to Paul and her brother
to admire its beauties and the wonderful
taste of the donor.

All this seemed so incongruous with Paul's
feelings, and above all with the recollection
of his scene with Yerba, that he excused
himself from dining with the party, alleging
an engagement with his old fellow-traveler
the German officer, whose acquaintance he
had renewed.  Yerba did not press him ; he
even fancied she looked relieved.  Colonel
Pendleton was coming ; Paul was not loath,
in his present frame of mind, to dispense
with his company.  A conviction that the
colonel's counsel was not the best guide for
Yerba, and that in some vague way their interests were antagonistic, had begun to

force itself upon him. He had no intention of being disloyal to her old guardian, but he felt that Pendleton had not been frank with him since his return from Rosario. Had he ever been so with *her?* He sometimes doubted his disclaimer.

He was lucky in finding the General disengaged, and together they dined at a restaurant and spent the evening at the *Kursaal.* Later, at the Residenz Club, the General leaned over his beer-glass and smilingly addressed his companion.

"So I hear you, too, are a conquest of the beautiful South American."

For an instant Paul, recognizing only Doña Anna under that epithet, looked puzzled.

"Come, my friend," said the General regarding him with some amusement, "I am an older man than you, yet I hardly think I could have ridden out with such a goddess without becoming her slave."

Paul felt his face flush in spite of himself. "Ah! you mean Miss Arguello," he said hurriedly, his color increasing at his own mention of that name as if he were imposing it upon his honest companion. "She is an old acquaintance of mine — from my own State — California."

7

"Ah, so," said the General, lifting his eyebrows in profound apology. "A thousand pardons."

"Surely," said Paul, with a desperate attempt to recover his equanimity, "*you* ought to know our geography better.'

"So, I am wrong. But still the name — Arguello — surely that is not American? Still, they say she has no accent, and does not look like a Mexican."

For an instant Paul was superstitiously struck with the fatal infelicity of Yerba's selection of a foreign name, that now seemed only to invite that comment and criticism which she should have avoided. Nor could he explain it at length to the General without assisting and accenting the deception, which he was always hoping in some vague way to bring to an end. He was sorry he had corrected the General; he was furious that he had allowed himself to be confused.

Happily his companion had misinterpreted his annoyance, and with impulsive German friendship threw himself into what he believed to be Paul's feelings. "*Donnerwetter!* Your beautiful countrywoman is made the subject of curiosity just because that stupid baron is persistent in his serious at-

tentions. That is quite enough, my good
friend, to make *Klatschen* here among those
animals who do not understand the freedom
of an American girl, or that an heiress may
have something else to do with her money
than to expend it on the Baron's mortgages.
But " — he stopped, and his simple, honest
face assumed an air of profound and saga-
cious cunning — " I am glad to talk about
it with you, who of course are perfectly
familiar with the affair. I shall now be
able to know what to say. My word, my
friend, has some weight here, and I shall
use it. And now you shall tell me *who* is
our lovely friend, and *who* were her parents
and her kindred in her own home. Her
associates here, you possibly know, are an
impossible colonel and his never-before-ap-
proached valet, with some South American
Indian planters, and, I believe, a pork-
butcher's daughter. But of *them* — it makes
nothing. Tell me of *her* people."

With his kindly serious face within a few
inches of Paul's, and sympathizing curiosity
beaming from his pince-nez, he obliged the
wretched and conscience-stricken Hathaway
to respond with a detailed account of
Yerba's parentage as projected by herself

and indorsed by Colonel Pendleton. He
dwelt somewhat particularly on the romantic character of the Trust, hoping to draw
the General's attention away from the question of relationship, but he was chagrined
to find that the honest warrior evidently
confounded the Trust with some eleemosy-
nary institution and sympathetically glossed
it over. " Of course," he said, " the Mexican Minister at Berlin would know all about
the Arguello family : so there would be no
question there."

Paul was not sorry when the time came
to take leave of his friend ; but once again
in the clear moonlight and fresh, balmy air
of the *Allée*, he forgot the unpleasantness
of the interview. He found himself thinking only of his ride with Yerba. Well ! he
had told her that he loved her. She knew
it now, and although she had forbidden him
to speak further, she had not wholly rejected
it. It must be her morbid consciousness of
the mystery of her birth that withheld a return of her affections, — some half-know-
ledge, perhaps, that she would not divulge,
yet that kept her unduly sensitive of accepting his love. He was satisfied there was no
entanglement ; her heart was virgin. He

even dared to hope that she had *always* cared for him. It was for *him* to remove all obstacles — to prevail upon her to leave this place and return to America with him as her husband, the guardian of her good name, and the custodian of her secret. At times the strains of a dreamy German waltz, played in the distance, brought back to him the brief moment that his arm had encircled her waist by the crumbling wall, and his pulses grew languid, only to leap firmer the next moment with more desperate resolve. He would win her, come what may! He could never have been in earnest before : he loathed and hated himself for his previous passive acquiescence to her fate. He had been a weak tool of the colonel's from the first : he was even now handicapped by a preposterous promise he had given him! Yes, she was right to hesitate — to question his ability to make her happy! He had found her here, surrounded by stupidity and cupidity — to give it no other name — so patent that she was the common gossip, and had offered nothing but a boyish declaration! As he strode into the hotel that night it was well that he did not meet the unfortunate colonel on the staircase!

It was very late, although there was still visible a light in Yerba's salon, shining on her balcony, which extended before and included his own window. From time to time he could hear the murmur of voices. It was too late to avail himself of the invitation to join them, even if his frame of mind had permitted it. He was too nervous and excited to go to bed, and, without lighting his candle, he opened the French window that gave upon the balcony, drew a chair in the recess behind the curtain, and gazed upon the night. It was very quiet; the moon was high, the square was sleeping in a trance of checkered shadows, like a gigantic chessboard, with black foreshortened trees for pawns. The click of a cavalry sabre, the sound of a footfall on the pavement of the distant Königsstrasse, were distinctly audible; a far-off railway whistle was startling in its abruptness. In the midst of this calm the opening of the door of the salon, with the sudden uplifting of voices in the hall, told Paul that Yerba's guests were leaving. He heard Doña Anna's arch accents — arch even to Colonel Pendleton's monotonous baritone! — Milly's high, rapid utterances, the suave falsetto of Don Cæsar, and *her* voice, he thought a trifle wearied, — the sound of retiring footsteps, and all was still again.

So still that the rhythmic beat of the distant waltz returned to him, with a distinctiveness that he could idly follow. He thought of Rosario and the rose-breath of the open windows with a strange longing, and remembered the half-stifled sweetness of her happy voice rising with it from the veranda. Why had he ever let it pass from him then and waft its fragrance elsewhere? Why — What was that?

The slight turning of a latch! The creaking of the French window of the salon, and somebody had slipped softly half out on the balcony. His heart stopped beating. From his position in the recess of his own window, with his back to the partition of the salon, he could see nothing. Yet he did not dare to move. For with the quickened senses of a lover he felt the diffused and perfumed aura of *her* presence, of *her* garments, of *her* flesh, flow in upon him through the open window, and possess his whole breathless being! It was *she!* Like him, perhaps, longing to enjoy the perfect night — like him, perhaps, thinking of —

" So you ar-range to get rid of me — ha!

lik thees ? To tur-rn me off from your heels like a dog who have follow you — but without a word — without a — a — thanks — without a 'ope! Ah! — we have ser-rved you — me and my sister ; we are the or-range dry — now we can go! Like the old shoe, we are to be flung away! Good! But I am here again — you see. I shall speak, and you shall hear-r."

Don Cæsar's voice — alone with her! Paul gripped his chair and sat upright.

"Stop! Stay where you are! How dared you return here?" It was Yerba's voice, on the balcony, low and distinct.

"Shut the window! I shall speak with you what you will not the world to hear."

"I prefer to keep where I am, since you have crept into this room like a thief!"

"A thief! Good!" He broke out in Spanish, and, as if no l)nger fearful of being overheard, had evidently drawn nearer to the window. "A thief. Ha! *muy bueno* — but it is not *I*, you understand — I, Cæsar Briones, who am the thief! No! It is that swaggering *espadachin* — that *fanfarron* of a Colonel Pendleton — that pattern of an official, Mr. Hathaway — that most beautiful heiress of the Californias,

Miss *Arguello* — that are thieves! Yes —
of a *name* — Miss Arguello — of a *name!*
The name of Arguello!"

Paul rose to his feet.

"Ah, so! You start — you turn pale —
you flash your eyes, señora, but you think
you have deceived me all these years. You
think I did not see your game at Rosario —
yes, even when that foolish Castro *mucha-
cha* first put that idea in your head. Who
furnished you the facts you wanted? I —
Mother of God! *such facts!* — I, who knew
the Arguello pedigree — I, who know it was
as impossible for you to be a daughter of
them as — what? let me think — as — as it
is impossible for you to be the wife of that
baron whom you would deceive with the
rest! Ah, yes; it was a high flight for you,
Mees — Mees — Doña Fulana — a noble
game for you to bring down!"

Why did she not speak? What was she
doing? If she had but uttered a single
word of protest, of angry dismissal, Paul
would have flown to her side. It could not
be the paralysis of personal fear: the balcony was wide; she could easily pass to the
end; she could even see his open window.

"Why did I do this? Because I loved

you, señora — and you knew it! Ah! you
can turn your face away now; you can pre-
tend to misunderstand me, as you did a moment ago; you can part from me now like a
mere acquaintance — but it was not always
so! No, it was *you* who brought me here;
your eyes that smiled into mine — and drove
home the colonel's request that I and my
sister should accompany you. God! I was
weak then! You smile, señora; you think
you have succeeded — you and your pom-
pous colonel and your clever governor!
You think you have compromised me, and
perjured *me*, because of this. You are
wrong! You think I dare not speak to this
puppet of a baron, and that I have no
proofs. You are wrong!"

"And even if you can produce them,
what care I?" said Yerba unexpectedly,
yet in a voice so free from excitement and
passion that the weariness which Paul had
at first noticed seemed to be the only dominant tone. "Suppose you prove that I am
not an Arguello. Good! you have yet to
show that a connection with any of your
race would be anything but a disgrace."

"Ah! you defy me, little one! *Caramba!*
Listen, then! You do not know all! When

you thought I was only helping you to fabricate your claim to the Arguellos' name, I was finding out *who you really were!* Ah! It was not so difficult as you fondly hope, señora. We were not all brutes and fools in the early days, though we stood aside to let your people run their vulgar course. It was your hired bully — your respected guardian — this dog of an *espadachin,* who let out a hint of the secret — with a prick of his blade — and a scandal. One of my *peon* women was a servant at the convent when you were a child, and recognized the woman who put you there and came to see you as a friend. She overheard the Mother Superior say it was your mother, and saw a necklace that was left for you to wear. Ah! you begin to believe! When I had put this and that together I found that Pepita could not identify you with the child that she had seen. But you, señora, you *yourself* supplied the missing proof! Yes! you supplied it with the *necklace* that you wore that evening at Rosario, when you wished to do honor to this young Hathaway — the guardian who had always thrown you off! Ah! — you now suspect why, perhaps! It was your mother's necklace that you wore, and you said so! That night I sent the good Pepita to identify it; to watch through the window from the garden when you were wearing it; to make it sure as the Creed. I sent her to your room late that night when you had changed your dress, that she might examine it among your jewels. And she did and will swear — look you! — *swear* that it is the one given you as a child by the woman at the convent, who was your mother! And who was that woman — eh? Who was the mother of the Arguello de la Yerba Buena? — who this noble ancestress?"

"Excuse me — but perhaps you are not aware that you are raising your voice in a lady's drawing-room, and that although you are speaking a language no one here understands, you are disturbing the hotel."

It was Paul, quiet, pale in the moonlight, erect on the balcony before the window. As Yerba, with a start, retreated quickly into the room, Don Cæsar stepped forward angrily and suspiciously towards the window. He had his hand reached forward towards the handle as if to close the swinging sash against the intruder, when in an instant he was seized by Paul, tightly locked in a desperate grip, and whirled out on the balcony. Before he could gain breath to utter a cry, Hathaway had passed his right arm around the Mexican's throat, effectively stopping his utterance, and, with a supreme effort of strength, dragged him along the wall, falling with him into the open window of his own room. As he did so, to his inexpres-sible relief he heard the sash closed and the bolt drawn of the salon window, and re-gained his feet, collected, quiet, and trium-phant.

"I am sorry," he said, coolly dusting his clothes, " to have been obliged to change the scene of this discussion so roughly, but you will observe that you can speak more freely *here*, and that any altercation *we* may have in this room will be less likely to at-tract comment."

"Assassin!" said Don Cæsar chokingly, as he struggled to his feet.

"Thank you. Relieve your feelings as much as you like here; in fact, if you would speak a little louder you would oblige me. The guests are beginning to be awake," con-tinued Paul, with a wicked smile, indicat-ing the noise of an opening door and foot-steps in the passage, " and are now able to locate without difficulty the scene of the disturbance."

Briones apparently understood his meaning and the success of his stratagem. "You think you have saved *her* from disgrace," he said, with a livid smile, in a lower tone and a desperate attempt to imitate Paul's coolness. "For the present — ah — yees! perhaps in this hotel and this evening. But you have not stop my mouth for — a — tomorrow — and the whole world, Mr. Hathaway."

"Well," said Paul, looking at him critically, "I don't know about that. Of course, there's the equal chance that you may kill me — but that's a question for to-morrow, too."

The Mexican cast a quick glance at the door and window. Paul, as if carelessly, changed the key of the former from one pocket to the other, and stepped before the window.

"So this is a plot to murder me! Have a care! You are not in your own brigand California!"

"If you think so, alarm the house. They will find us quarreling, and you will only precipitate matters by receiving the insult that will make you fight — before them."

"I am r-ready, sir, when and where you will," said Briones, with a swaggering air but a shifting, furtive eye. "Open — a — the door."

"Pardon me. We will leave this room *together* in an hour for the station. We will board the night express that will take us in three hours beyond the frontier, where we can each find a friend."

"But my affairs here — my sister — I must see her."

"You shall write a note to her at that table, saying that important business — a dispatch — has called you away, and we will leave it with the porter to be delivered *in the morning*. Or — I do not restrict you — you can say what you like, provided she don't get it until we have left."

"And you make of me a prisoner, sir?"

"No; a visitor, Don Cæsar — a visitor whose conversation is so interesting that I am forced to detain him to hear more. You can pass the time pleasantly by finishing the story I was obliged to interrupt a moment ago. Do you know this mother of Miss Yerba, of whom you spoke?"

"That's m — my affair."

"That means you don't know her. If

you did, you'd have had her within **call.**
And, as she is the only person who is **able**
to say that Miss Yerba is *not* an Arguello,
you have been very remiss."

"Ah, bah! I am not one of your — a —
lawyers."

"No; or you would know that, with **no**
better evidence than you have, you might **be**
sued for slander."

"Ah! Why does not Miss **Yer**ba sue,
then?"

"Because she probably expects that somebody will shoot you."

"As *you* for instance?"

"Perhaps."

"And if you do *not* — eh? — you **have**
not stop my mouth, but your own. And if
you *do*, you help her to marry the Baron,
your rival. You are not wise, friend Hathaway."

"May I remind you that you have not
yet written to your sister, and you may prefer to do it carefully and deliberately?"

Don Cæsar arose with a vindictive glance
at Paul, and pulled a chair before the table,
as the latter placed pen, ink, and paper before him. "Take your time," he added,
folding his arms and walking towards the

window. "Say what you like, and don't let
my presence restrain you."

The Mexican began to write furiously,
then spasmodically, then slowly and reluctantly. "I war-r-n you, I shall expose all,"
he said suddenly.

"As you please."

"And shall say that if I disappear, you
are my murderer — you understand — my
*murderer !* "

"Don't consult me on a question of epi-
thets, but go on."

Don Cæsar recommenced his writing with
a malign smile. There was a sudden sharp
rap at the door.

Don Cæsar leaped to his feet, grasped his
papers, and rushed to the door; but Paul
was before him. "Who is there?" he demanded.

"Pendleton."

At the sound of the colonel's voice Don
Cæsar fell back. Paul opened the door, admitted the tall figure of the colonel, and
was about to turn the key again. But Pendleton lifted his hand in grim deprecation.

"That will do, Mr. Hathaway. I know
all. But I wish to speak with Briones elsewhere, alone."

" Excuse me, Colonel Pendleton," said Paul firmly, " but I have the prior claim. Words have passed between this gentleman and myself which we are now on our way to the station and the frontier to settle. If you are willing to accompany us, I shall give you every opportunity to converse with him alone, and arrange whatever business you may have with him, provided it does not interfere with mine."

" My business," said Pendleton, " is of a personal nature, that will not interfere with any claim of yours that Mr. Briones may choose to admit, but is of a private quality that must be transacted between us now." His face was pale, and his voice, although steady and self-controlled, had that same strange suggestion of sudden age in it which Paul had before noticed. Whether Don Cæsar detected it, or whether he had some other instinctive appreciation of greater security, Paul could not tell. He seemed to recover his swagger again, as he said, —

" I shall hear what Colonel Pendleton has to say first. But I shall hold myself in readiness to meet you afterwards — you shall not fear, sir ! "

Paul remained looking from the one to

the other without speaking. It was Don
Cæsar who returned his glance boldly and
defiantly, Colonel Pendleton who, with thin
white fingers pulling his moustache, evaded
it. Then Paul unlocked the door, and said
slowly, " In five minutes I leave this house
for the station. I shall wait there until the
train arrives. If this gentleman does not
join me, I shall be better able to understand
all this and take measures accordingly."

"And I tell to you, Meester Hathaway,
sir," said Don Cæsar, striking an attitude
in the doorway, " you shall do as *I* please —
*Caramba!* — and shall beg" —

"Hold your tongue, sir — or, by the
Eternal!" — burst out Pendleton suddenly,
bringing down his thin hand on the Mexican's shoulder. He stopped as suddenly.
"Gentlemen, this is childish. Go, sir!"
to Don Cæsar, pointing with a gaunt white
finger into the darkened hall. "I will follow you. Mr. Hathaway, as an older man,
and one who has seen a good deal of foolish
altercation, I regret, sir, deeply regret, to
be a witness to this belligerent quality in a
law-maker and a public man; and I must
deprecate, sir — deprecate, your demand on
that gentleman for what, in the folly of

youth, you are pleased to call personal satisfaction."

As he moved with dignity out of the
room, Paul remained blankly staring after
him. Was it all a dream? — or was this
Colonel Pendleton the duelist? Had the
old man gone crazy, or was he merely acting
to veil some wild purpose? His sudden arrival showed that Yerba must have sent for
him and told him of Don Cæsar's threats;
would he be wild enough to attempt to
strangle the man in some remote room or in
the darkness of the passage? He stepped
softly into the hall: he could still hear the
double tread of the two men: they had
reached the staircase — they were *descend-
ing!* He heard the drowsy accents of the
night porter and the swinging of the door —
they were in the street!

Wherever they were going, or for what
purpose, *he* must be at the station, as he
had warned them he would be. He hastily
threw a few things into his valise, and prepared to follow them. When he went downstairs he informed the porter that owing to
an urgent call of business he should try to
catch the through express at three o'clock,
but they must retain his room and luggage

until they heard from him. He remembered Don Cæsar's letter. Had either of the gentlemen, his friends who had just gone out, left a letter or message? No, Excellency; the gentlemen were talking earnestly — he believed, in the South American language — and had not spoken to him.

Perhaps it was this that reminded Paul, as he crossed the square again, that he had made no preparation for any possible fatal issue to himself in this adventure. *She* would know it, however, and why he had undertaken it. He tried to think that perhaps some interest in himself had prompted her to send the colonel to him. Yet, mingled with this was an odd sense of a certain ridiculousness in his position: there was the absurdity of his prospective antagonist being even now in confidential consultation with his own friend and ally, whose functions he had usurped, and in whose interests he was about to risk his life. And as he walked away through the silent streets, the conviction more than once was forced upon him that he was going to an appointment that would not be kept.

He reached the station some ten minutes before the train was due. Two or three

half-drowsy, wrapped-up passengers were
already on the platform; but neither Don
Cæsar nor Colonel Pendleton was among
them. He explored the waiting-rooms and
even the half-lit buffet, but with no better
success. Telling the *Bahnhof Inspector*
that his passage was only contingent upon
the arrival of one or two companions, and
describing them minutely to prevent mis-
takes, he began gloomily to pace before the
ticket-office. Five minutes passed — the
number of passengers did not increase; ten
minutes; a distant shriek — the hoarse inquiry of the inspector — had the Herr's
companions yet *gekommt?* the sudden glare
of a Cyclopean eye in the darkness, the on-
gliding of the long-jointed and gleaming
spotted serpent, the train — a hurried glance
around the platform, one or two guttural
orders, the slamming of doors, the remount-
ing of black uniformed figures like caryati-
des along the *marchepieds*, a puff of vapor,
and the train had come and gone without
them.

Yet he would give his adversary fifteen
minutes more to allow for accident or delay, or the possible arrival of the colonel
with an explanation, and recommenced his

gloomy pacing, as the *Bahnhof* sank back
into half-lit repose. At the end of five minutes there was another shriek. Paul turned
quickly to the inspector. Ah, then, there
was another train? No; it was only the *up
express* for Basle, going the other way and
stopping at the *Nord Station*, half a mile
away. It would not stop here, but the Herr
would see it pass in a few moments at full
speed.

It came presently, with a prolonged despairing shriek, out of the darkness; a flash,
a rush and roar at his side, a plunge into
the darkness again with the same despairing
cry; a flutter of something white from one
of the windows, like a loosened curtain, that
at last seemed to detach itself, and, after a
wild attempt to follow, suddenly soared
aloft, whirled over and over, dropped, and
drifted slowly, slantwise, to the ground.

The inspector had seen it, ran down the
line, and picked it up. Then he returned
with it to Paul with a look of sympathizing
concern. It was a lady's handkerchief, evidently some signal waved to the well-born
Herr, who was the only passenger on the
platform. So, possibly, it might be from
his friends, who by some stupid mischance

had gone to the wrong station, and — *Gott
im Himmel!* — it was hideously stupid, yet
possible, got on the wrong train!

The Herr, a little pale, but composed,
thought it *was* possible. No; he would not
telegraph to the next station — not yet — he
would inquire.

He walked quickly away, reaching the
hotel breathlessly, yet in a space that
seemed all too brief for his disconnected
thought. There were signs of animation in
the hall, and an empty carriage was just
reëntering the courtyard. The hall-porter
met him with demonstrative concern and
apology. Ah! if he had only understood
his Excellency better, he could have saved
him all this trouble. Evidently his Excellency was going with the Arguello party,
who had ordered a carriage, doubtless, for
the same important journey, an hour before,
yet had left only a few moments after his
Excellency, and his Excellency, it would appear, had gone to the wrong station.

Paul pushed hurriedly past the man and
ascended to his room. Both windows were
open, and in the faint moonlight he could
see that something white was pinned to his
pillow. With nervous fingers he relit his

candles, and found it was a note in Yerba's handwriting. As he opened it, a tiny spray of the vine that had grown on the crumbling wall fell at his feet. He picked it up, pressed it to his lips, and read, with dim eyes, as follows: —

You know now why I spoke to you as I did to-day, and why the other half of this precious spray is the only memory I care to carry with me out of this crumbling ruin of all my hopes. You were right, Paul: my taking you there *was an omen* — not to you, who can never be anything but proud, beloved, and true — but to *me* of all the shame and misery. Thank you for all you have done — for all you would do, my friend, and don't think me ungrateful, only because I am unworthy of it. Try to forgive me, but don't forget me, even if you must hate me. Perhaps, if you knew all — you might still love a little the poor girl to whom you have already given the only name she can ever take from you — YERBA BUENA!

# CHAPTER VII.

IT was already autumn, and in the city of New York an early Sunday morning breeze was sweeping up the leaves that had fallen from the regularly planted ailantus trees before the brown-stone frontage of a row of monotonously alike five-storied houses on one of the principal avenues. The Pastor of the Third Presbyterian Church, that uplifted its double towers on the corner, stopped before one of these dwellings, ran up the dozen broad steps, and rang the bell. He was presently admittted to the sombre richness of a hall and drawing-room with high-backed furniture of dark carved woods, like cathedral stalls, and, hat in hand, somewhat impatiently awaited the arrival of his hostess and parishioner. The door opened to a tall, white-haired woman in lustreless black silk. She was regular and resolute in features, of fine but unbending presence, and, though somewhat past middle age, showed no signs of either the weakness or mellowness of years.

"I am sorry to disturb your Sabbath morning meditations, Sister Argalls, nor would I if it were not in the line of Christian duty; but Sister Robbins is unable to-day to make her usual Sabbath hospital visit, and I thought if you were excused from the Foreign Missionary class and Bible instruction at three you might undertake her functions. I know, my dear old friend," he continued, with bland deprecation of her hard-set eyes, "how distasteful this promiscuous mingling with the rough and ungodly has always been to you, and how reluctant you are to be placed in the position of being liable to hear coarse, vulgar, or irreverent speech. I think, too, in our long and pleasant pastoral relations, you have always found me mindful of it. I admit I have sometimes regretted that your late husband had not more generally familiarized you with the ways of the world. But so it is — we all have our weaknesses. If not one thing, another. And as Envy and Uncharitableness sometimes find their way in even Christian hearts, I should like you to undertake this office for the sake of example. There are some, dear Sister Argalls, who think that the rich widow who is most lib-

eral in the endowment of the goods that
Providence has intrusted to her hands claims
therefore to be exempt from labor in the
Christian vineyard. Let us teach them how
unjust they are."

"I am willing," said the lady, with a dry,
determined air. "I suppose these patients
are not professedly bad characters?"

"By no means. A few, perhaps; but the
majority are unfortunates — dependent either
upon public charity or some small provision
made by their friends."

"Very well."

"And you understand that though they
have the privilege of rejecting your Christian
ministrations, dear Sister Argalls, you are
free to judge when you may be patient or
importunate with them?"

"I understand."

The Pastor was not an unkindly man,
and, as he glanced at the uncompromising
look in Mrs. Argalls's eyes, felt for a moment some inconsistency between his hu-
mane instincts and his Christian duty.
"Some of them may require, and be benefited by, a stern monitress, and Sister Robbins, I fear, was weak," he said consolingly
to himself, as he descended the steps again.

At three o'clock Mrs. Argalls, with a reticule and a few tracts, was at the door of St. John's Hospital. As she displayed her testimonials and announced that she had taken Mrs. Robbins's place, the officials received her respectfully, and gave some instructions to the attendants, which, however, did not stop some individual comments.

"I say, Jim, it does n't seem the square thing to let that grim old girl loose among them poor convalescents."

"Well, I don't know: they say she's rich and gives a lot o' money away, but if she tackles that swearing old Kentuckian in No. 3, she 'll have her hands full."

However, the criticism was scarcely fair, for Mrs. Argalls, although moving rigidly along from bed to bed of the ward, equipped with a certain formula of phrases, nevertheless dropped from time to time some practical common-sense questions that showed an almost masculine intuition of the patients' needs and requirements. Nor did she betray any of that over-sensitive shrinking from coarseness which the good Pastor had feared, albeit she was quick to correct its exhibition. The languid men listened to her with half-aggressive, half-amused inter-

est, and some of the satisfaction of taking a
bitter but wholesome tonic. It was not until she reached the bed at the farther end of
the ward that she seemed to meet with any
check.

It was occupied by a haggard man, with
a long white moustache and features that
seemed wasted by inward struggle and fever.
At the first sound of her voice he turned
quickly towards her, lifted himself on his
elbow, and gazed fixedly in her face.

"Kate Howard — by the Eternal!" he
said, in a low voice.

Despite her rigid self-possession the woman started, glanced hurriedly around, and
drew nearer to him.

"Pendleton!" she said, in an equally
suppressed voice. "What, in God's name,
are you doing here?"

"Dying, I reckon — sooner or later," he
said grimly, "that's what they do here."

"But — what," she went on hurriedly,
still glancing over her shoulder as if she
suspected some trick — "what has brought
you to this?"

"*You!*" said the colonel, dropping back
exhaustedly on his pillow. "You and your
daughter."

"I don't understand you," she said quickly, yet regarding him with stern rigidity. "You know perfectly well I have *no* daughter. You know perfectly well that I've kept the word I gave you ten years ago, and that I have been dead to her as she has been to me."

"I know," said the colonel, "that within the last three months I have paid away my last cent to keep the mouth of an infernal scoundrel shut who *knows* that you are her mother, and threatens to expose her to her friends. I know that I'm dying here of an old wound that I got when I shut the mouth of another hound who was ready to bark at her two years after you disappeared. I know that between you and her I've let my old nigger die of a broken heart, because I could n't keep him to suffer with me, and I know that I'm here a pauper on the State. I know that, Kate, and when I say it I don't regret it. I've kept my word to *you*, and, by the Eternal, your daughter's worth it! For if there ever was a fair and peerless creature — it's your child!"

"And she — a rich woman — unless she squandered the fortune I gave her — lets you lie here!" said the woman grimly.

" She don't know it."

" She *should* know it! Have you quarreled ? " She was looking at him keenly.

" She distrusts me, because she half suspects the secret, and I had n't the heart to tell her all."

" All ? What does she know ? What does this man know ? What has been told her ? " she said rapidly.

" She only knows that the name she has taken she has no right to."

" Right to ? Why, it was written on the Trust — Yerba Buena."

" No, not that. She thought it was a mistake. She took the name of Arguello."

" What ? " said Mrs. Argalls, suddenly grasping the invalid's wrist with both hands. " What name ? " Her eyes were startled from their rigid coldness, her lips were colorless.

" Arguello! It was some foolish schoolgirl fancy which that hound helped to foster in her. Why — what 's the matter, Kate ? "

The woman dropped the helpless man's wrist, then, with an effort, recovered herself sufficiently to rise, and, with an air of increased decorum, as if the spiritual character of their interview excluded worldly intrusion, adjusted the screen around his bed, so as partly to hide her own face and Pendleton's. Then, dropping into the chair beside him, she said, in her old voice, from which the burden of ten long years seemed to have been lifted, —

"Harry, what's that you're playing on me?"

"I don't understand you," said Pendleton amazedly.

"Do you mean to say you don't know it, and didn't tell her yourself?" she said curtly.

"What? Tell her what?" he repeated impatiently.

"That Arguello *was* her father!"

"Her father?" He tried to struggle to his elbow again, but she laid her hand masterfully upon his shoulder and forced him back. "Her father!" he repeated hurriedly. "José Arguello! Great God! — are you sure?"

Quietly and yet mechanically gathering the scattered tracts from the coverlet, and putting them back, one by one in her reticule, she closed it and her lips with a snap as she uttered — "Yes."

Pendleton remained staring at her silently, " Yes," he muttered, " it may have been some instinct of the child's, or some diabolical fancy of Briones'. But," he said bitterly, "true or not, she has no right to his name."

" And I say she *has.*"

She had risen to her feet, with her arms folded across her breast, in an attitude of such Puritan composure that the distant spectators might have thought she was delivering an exordium to the prostrate man.

" I met José Arguello, for the second time, in New Orleans," she said slowly, " eight years ago. He was still rich, but ruined in health by dissipation. I was tired of my way of life. He proposed that I should marry him to take care of him and legitimatize our child. I was forced to tell him what I had done with her, and that the Trust could not be disturbed until she was of age and her own mistress. He assented. We married, but he died within a year. He died, leaving with me his acknowledgment of her as his child, and the right to claim her if I chose."

" And ? " — interrupted the colonel with sparkling eyes.

" *I don't choose.*

"Hear me!" she continued firmly. "With his name and my own mistress, and the girl, as I believed, properly provided for and ignorant of my existence, I saw no necessity for reopening the past. I resolved to lead a new life as his widow. I came north. In the little New England town where I first stopped, the country people contracted my name to Mrs. Argalls. I let it stand so. I came to New York and entered the service of the Lord and the bonds of the Church, Henry Pendleton, as Mrs. Argalls, and have remained so ever since."

"But you would not object to Yerba knowing that you lived, and rightly bore her father's name?" said Pendleton eagerly.

The woman looked at him with compressed lips. "I should. I have buried all my past, and all its consequences. Let me not seek to reopen it or recall them."

"But if you knew that she was as proud as yourself, and that this very uncertainty as to her name and parentage, although she has never known the whole truth, kept her from taking the name and becoming the wife of a man whom she loves?"

"Whom she loves!"

"Yes; one of her guardians — Hathaway

— to whom you intrusted her when she was a child."

"Paul Hathaway — but *he* knew it."

"Yes. But *she* does not know he does. He has kept the secret faithfully, even when she refused him."

She was silent for a moment, and then said, —

"So be it. I consent."

"And you 'll write to her?" said the colonel eagerly.

"No. But *you* may, and if you want them I will furnish you with such proofs as you may require."

"Thank you." He held out his hand with such a happy yet childish gratitude upon his worn face that her own trembled slightly as she took it. "Good-by!"

"I shall see you soon," she said.

"I shall be here," he said grimly.

"I think not," she returned, with the first relaxation of her smileless face, and moved away.

As she passed out she asked to see the house surgeon. How soon did he think the patient she had been conversing with could be removed from the hospital with safety? Did Mrs. Argalls mean "far?" Mrs. Ar-

galls meant as far as *that* — tendering her
card and eminently respectable address.
Ah! — perhaps in a week. Not before?
Perhaps before, unless complications ensued; the patient had been much run down
physically, though, as Mrs. Argalls had
probably noticed, he was singularly strong
in nervous will force. Mrs. Argalls *had*
noticed it, and considered it an extraordinary case of conviction — worthy of the
closest watching and care. When he was
able to be moved she would send her own
carriage and her own physician to superin-
tend his transfer. In the mean time he was
to want for nothing. Certainly, he had
given very little trouble, and, in fact, wanted
very little. Just now he had only asked for
paper, pens, and ink.

## CHAPTER VIII.

As Mrs. Argalls's carriage rolled into Fifth Avenue, it for a moment narrowly grazed another carriage, loaded with luggage, driving up to a hotel. The abstracted traveler within it was Paul Hathaway, who had returned from Europe that morning.

Paul entered the hotel, and, going to the register mechanically, turned its leaves for the previous arrivals, with the same hopeless patience that had for the last six weeks accompanied this habitual preliminary performance on his arrival at the principal European hotels. For he had lost all trace of Yerba, Pendleton, Milly, and the Briones from the day of their departure. The entire party seemed to have separated at Basle, and, in that eight-hours' start they had of him, to have disappeared to the four cardinal points. He had lingered a few days in London to transact some business; he would linger a few days longer in New York before returning to San Francisco.

The daily papers already contained his name in the list of the steamer passengers who arrived that morning. It might meet *her* eye, although he had been haunted during the voyage by a terrible fancy that she was still in Europe, and had either hidden herself in some obscure provincial town with the half-crazy Pendleton, or had entered a convent, or even, in reckless despair, had accepted the name and title of some penniless nobleman. It was this miserable doubt that had made his homeward journey at times seem like a cruel desertion of her, while at other moments the conviction that Milly's Californian relatives might give him some clew to her whereabouts made him feverishly fearful of delaying an hour on his way to San Francisco. He did not believe that she had tolerated the company of Briones a single moment after the scene at the Bad Hof, and yet he had no confidence in the colonel's attitude towards the Mexican. Hopeless of the future as her letter seemed, still its naïve and tacit confession of her feelings at the moment was all that sustained him.

Two days passed, and he still lingered aimlessly in New York. In two days more

the Panama steamer would sail — yet in his
hesitation he had put off securing his passage.  He visited the offices of the different
European steamer lines, and examined the
recent passenger lists, but there was no record of any of the party.  What made his
quest seem the more hopeless was his belief
that, after Briones' revelation, she had cast
off the name of Arguello and taken some
other.  She might even be in New York
under that new name now.

On the morning of the third day, among
his letters was one that bore the postmark
of a noted suburban settlement of wealthy
villa-owners on the Hudson River.  It was
from Milly Woods, stating that her father
had read of his arrival in the papers, and
begged he would dine and stay the next
night with them at "Under Cliff," if he
" still had any interest in the fortunes of
old friends.  Of course," added the peren-
nially incoherent Milly, " if it bores you we
sha'n't expect you."  The quick color came
to Paul's careworn cheek.  He telegraphed
assent, and at sunset that afternoon stepped
off the train at a little private woodland
station — so abnormally rustic and picturesque in its brown-bark walls covered with

scarlet Virginia creepers that it looked like
a theatrical erection.

Mr. Woods's station wagon was in waiting, but Paul, handing the driver his valise,
and ascertaining the general direction of
the house, and that it was not far distant,
told him to go on and he would follow
afoot. The tremor of vague anticipation
had already come upon him; something that
he knew not whether he feared or longed
for, only that it was inevitable, had begun
to possess him. He would soon recover himself in the flaring glory of this woodland,
and the invigoration of this hale October
air.

It was a beautiful and brilliant sunset,
yet not so beautiful and brilliant but that
the whole opulent forest around him seemed
to challenge and repeat its richest as well as
its most delicate dyes. The reddening west,
seen through an opening of scarlet maples,
was no longer red; the golden glory of the
sun, sinking over a promontory of gleaming
yellow sumach that jutted out into the noble
river, was shorn of its intense radiance; at
times in the thickest woods he seemed surrounded by a yellow nimbus; at times so
luminous was the glow of these translucent

leaves that the position of the sun itself seemed changed, or the shadows cast in defiance of its glory. As he walked on, long reaches of the lordly placid stream at his side were visible, as far as the terraces of the opposite shore, lifted on basaltic columns, themselves streaked and veined with gold and fire. Paul had seen nothing like this since his boyhood; for an instant the great heroics of the Sierran landscape were forgotten in this magnificent harlequinade.

A dim footpath crossed the road in the direction of the house, which for the last few moments had been slowly etching itself as a soft vignette in a tinted aureole of walnut and maple upon the steel blue of the river. He was hesitating whether to take this short cut or continue on by the road, when he heard the rustling of quick footsteps among the fallen leaves of the variegated thicket through which it stole. He stopped short, the leafy screen shivered and parted, and a tall graceful figure, like a draped and hidden Columbine, burst through its painted foliage. It was Yerba!

She ran quickly towards him, with parted lips, shining eyes, and a few scarlet leaves clinging to the stuff of her worsted dress in a way that recalled the pink petals of Rosario.

"When I saw you were not in the wagon and knew you were walking I slipped out to intercept you, as I had something to tell you before you saw the others. I thought you would n't mind." She stopped, and suddenly hesitated.

What was this new strange shyness that seemed to droop her eyelids, her proud head, and even the slim hand that had been so impulsively and frankly outstretched towards him? And he — Paul — what was he doing? Where was this passionate outburst that had filled his heart for nights and days? Where this eager tumultuous questioning that his feverish lips had rehearsed hour by hour? Where this desperate courage that would sweep the whole world away if it stood between them? Where, indeed? He was standing only a few feet from her — cold, silent, and tremulous!

She drew back a step, lifted her head with a quick toss that seemed to condense the moisture in her shining eyes, and sent what might have been a glittering dew-drop flying into the loosed tendrils of her hair. Calm and erect again, she put her little hand to her jacket pocket.

"I only wanted you to read a letter I got yesterday," she said, taking out an envelope.

The spell was broken. Paul caught eagerly at the hand that held the letter, and would have drawn her to him; but she put him aside gravely but sweetly.

"Read that letter!"

"Tell me of *yourself* first!" he broke out passionately. "Why you fled from me, and why I now find you here, by the merest chance, without a word of summons from yourself, Yerba? Tell me who is with you? Are you free and your own mistress — free to act for yourself and me? Speak, darling — don't be cruel! Since that night I have longed for you, sought for you, and suffered for you every day and hour. Tell me if I find you the same Yerba who wrote" —

"Read that letter!"

"I care for none but the one you left me. I have read and reread it, Yerba — carried it always with me. See! I have it here!" He was in the act of withdrawing it from his breast-pocket, when she put up her hand piteously.

"Please, Paul, please — read this letter first!"

There was something in her new suppli-
cating grace, still retaining the faintest suggestion of her old girlish archness, that
struck him. He took the letter and opened
it. It was from Colonel Pendleton.

Plainly, concisely, and formally, without
giving the name of his authority or suggesting his interview with Mrs. Argalls, he had
informed Yerba that he had documentary
testimony that she was the daughter of the
late José de Arguello, and legally entitled
to bear his name. A copy of the instructions given to his wife, recognizing Yerba
Buena, the ward of the San Francisco Trust,
as his child and hers, and leaving to the
mother the choice of making it known to
her and others, was inclosed.

Paul turned an unchanged face upon
Yerba, who was watching him eagerly, uneasily, almost breathlessly.

"And you think this concerns *me!*" he
said bitterly. "You think only of this,
when I speak of the precious letter that
bade me hope, and brought me to you?"

"Paul," said the girl, with wondering
eyes and hesitating lips; "do you mean to
say that — that — this is — nothing to you?"

"Yes — but forgive me, darling!" he

broke out again, with a sudden vague re-
morsefulness, as he once more sought her
elusive hand. " I am a brute — an egotist!
I forgot that it might be something to *you*."

" Paul," continued the girl, her voice quiv-
ering with a strange joy, " do you say that
you — *you* yourself, care nothing for this ? "

" Nothing," he answered, gazing at her
transfigured face with admiring wonder.

" And " — more timidly, as a faint aurora
kindled in her cheeks — " that you don't
care — that — that — I am coming to you
*with a name*, to give you in — exchange ? "

He started.

" Yerba, you are not mocking me ? You
will be my wife ? "

She smiled, yet moving softly backwards
with the grave stateliness of a vanishing yet
beckoning goddess, until she reached the
sumach-bush from which she had emerged.
He followed. Another backward step, and
it yielded to let her through; but even as it
did so she caught him in her arms, and for
a single moment it closed upon them both,
and hid them in its glory. A still lingering
song-bird, possibly convinced that he had
mistaken the season, and that spring had
really come, flew out with a little cry to

carry the message south; but even then Paul and Yerba emerged with such innocent, childlike gravity, and, side by side, walked so composedly towards the house, that he thought better of it.

# CHAPTER IX.

IT was only the *third* time they had ever met — did Paul consider that when he thought her cold? Did he know now why she had not understood him at Rosario? Did he understand now how calculating and selfish he had seemed to her that night? Could he look her in the face now — no, he must be quiet — they were so near the house, and everybody could see them! — and say that he had ever believed her capable of making up that story of the Arguellos? Could he not have guessed that she had some memory of that name in her childish recollections, how or where she knew not? Was it strange that a daughter should have an instinct of her father? Was it kind to her to know all this himself and yet reveal nothing? Because her mother and father had quarreled, and her mother had run away with somebody and left her a ward to strangers — was that to be concealed from her, and she left without a name?

This, and much more, tenderly reproachful, bewildering and sweetly illogical, yet inexpressibly dear to Paul, as they walked on in the gloaming.

More to the purpose, however, the fact that Briones, as far as she knew, did not know her mother, and never before the night at Strudle Bad had ever spoken of her. Still more to the purpose, that he had disappeared after an interview with the colonel that night, and that she believed always that the colonel had bought him off. It was not with *her* money. She had sometimes thought that the colonel and he were in confidence, and that was why she had lately distrusted Pendleton. But she had refused to take the name of Arguello again after that scene, and had called herself only by the name he had given her — would he forgive her for ever speaking of it as she had? — Yerba Buena. But on shipboard, at Milly's suggestion, and to keep away from Briones, her name had appeared on the passenger list as Miss Good, and they had come, not to New York, but Boston.

It was possible that the colonel had extracted the information he sent her *from* Briones. They had parted from Pendleton

in London, as he was grumpy and queer,
and, as Milly thought, becoming very mi-
serly and avaricious as he grew older, for he
was always quarreling over the hotel bills.
But he had Mrs. Woods's New York address
at Under Cliff, and, of course, guessed where
she was.   There was no address on his letter: he had said he would write again.

Thus much until they reached the steps
of the veranda, and Milly, flying down, was
ostentatiously overwhelmed with the unexpected appearance of Mr. Paul Hathaway
and Yerba, whom she had been watching
from the window for the last ten minutes.
Then the appearance of Mr. Woods, Californian and reminiscent, and Mrs. Woods,
metropolitan, languid, and forgetful, and
the sudden and formal retirement of the
girls.   An arch and indefinable mystery in
the air whenever Paul and Yerba appeared
together — of which even the servants were
discreetly conscious.

At dinner Mr. Woods again became ret-
rospective and Californian, and dwelt upon
the changes he had noticed.   It appeared
the old pioneers had in few cases attained a
comfortable fortune for their old age.   "I
know," he added, "that your friend Colonel

Pendleton has dropped a good deal of money over in Europe. Somebody told me that he actually was reduced to take a steerage passage home. It looks as if he might gamble — it's an old Californian complaint." As Paul, who had become suddenly grave again, did not speak, Mrs. Woods reminded them that she had always doubted the colonel's moral principles. Old as he was, he had never got over that freedom of life and social opinion which he had imbibed in early days. For her part, she was very glad he had not returned from Europe with the girls, though, of course, the presence of Don Cæsar and his sister during their European sojourn was a corrective. As Paul's face grew darker during this languid criticism, Yerba, who had been watching it with a new and absorbing sympathy, seized the first moment when they left the table to interrogate him with heartbreaking eyes.

"You don't think, Paul, that the colonel is really poor?"

"God only knows," said Paul. "I tremble to think how that scoundrel may have bled him."

"And all for me! Paul, dear, you know you were saying in the woods that you would

never, never touch my money. What " —
exultingly — " if we gave it to him ? "

What answer Paul made did not transpire, for it seemed to have been indicated
by an interval of profound silence.

But the next morning, as he and Mr.
Woods were closeted in the library, Yerba
broke in upon them with a pathetic face
and a telegram in her hand. " Oh, Paul —
Mr. Hathaway — *it's true !* "

Paul seized the telegram quickly : it had
no signature, only the line : " Colonel Pendleton is dangerously ill at St. John's Hospital."

" I must go at once," said Paul, rising.

" Oh, Paul " — imploringly — " let me go
with you ! I should never forgive myself
if — *and it's addressed to me,* and what
would he think if I didn't come ? "

Paul hesitated. " Mrs. Woods will let
Milly go with us — and she can stay at the
hotel. Say yes," she continued, seeking his
eyes eagerly.

He consented, and in half an hour they
were in the train for New York. Leaving
Milly at the hotel, ostensibly in deference
to the Woods's prejudices, but really to
save the presence of a third party at this

meeting, Paul drove with Yerba rapidly to the hospital. They were admitted to an anteroom. The house surgeon received them respectfully, but doubtingly. The patient was a little better this morning, but very weak. There was a lady now with him — a member of a religious and charitable guild, who had taken the greatest interest in him — indeed, she had wished to take him to her own home — but he had declined at first, and now he was too weak to be removed.

"But I received this telegram : it must have been sent at his request," protested Yerba.

The house surgeon looked at the beautiful face. He was mortal. He would see if the patient was able to stand another interview ; possibly the regular visitor might withdraw.

When he had gone, an attendant volunteered the information that the old gentleman was perhaps a little excited at times. He was a wonderful man ; he had seen a great deal ; he talked much of California and the early days ; he was very interesting. Ah, it would be all right now if the doctor found him well enough, for the lady was already going — that was she, coming through the hall.

She came slowly towards them — erect, gray, grim — a still handsome apparition. Paul started. To his horror, Yerba ran impulsively forward, and said eagerly : " Is he better ? Can he see us now ? "

The woman halted an instant, seemed to gather the prayer-book and reticule she was carrying closer to her breast, but was otherwise unchanged. Replying to Paul rather than the young girl, she said rigidly : " The patient is able to see Mr. Hathaway and Miss Yerba Buena," and passed slowly on. But as she reached the door she unloosed her black mourning veil from her bonnet, and seemed to drop it across her face with the gesture that Paul remembered she had used twelve years ago.

" She frightens me ! " said Yerba, turning a suddenly startled face on Paul. " Oh, Paul, I hope it is n't an omen, but she looked like some one from the grave ! "

" Hush ! " said Paul, turning away a face that was whiter than her own. " They are coming now."

The house surgeon had returned a trifle graver. They might see him now, but they

must be warned that he wandered at times
a little; and, if he might suggest, if it was
anything of family importance, they had
better make the most of their time and his
lucid intervals. Perhaps if they were old
friends — *very* old friends — he would recognize them. He was wandering much in
the past — always in the past.

They found him in the end of the ward,
but so carefully protected and partitioned
off by screens that the space around his cot
had all the privacy and security of an apartment. He was very much changed; they
would scarcely have known him, but for the
delicately curved aquiline profile and the
long white moustache — now so faint and
etherealized as to seem a mere spirit wing
that rested on his pillow. To their surprise
he opened his eyes with a smile of perfect
recognition, and, with thin fingers beyond
the coverlid, beckoned to them to approach.
Yet there was still a shadow of his old reserve in his reception of Paul, and, although
one hand interlocked the fingers of Yerba —
who had at first rushed impulsively forward
and fallen on her knees beside the bed —
and the other softly placed itself upon her
head, his eyes were fixed upon the young

man's with the ceremoniousness due to a stranger.

" I am glad to see, sir," he began in a slow, broken, but perfectly audible voice, " that now you are — satisfied with the right — of this young lady — to bear the name of — Arguello — and her relationship — sir — to one of the oldest " —

" But, my dear old friend," broke out Paul, earnestly, " I *never* cared for that — I beg you to believe " —

" He never — never — cared for it — dear, dear colonel," sobbed Yerba, passionately : " it was all my fault — he thought only of me — you wrong him ! "

" *I* think otherwise," said the colonel, with grim and relentless deliberation. " I have a vivid — impression — sir — of an — interview I had with you — at the St. Charles — where you said " — He was silent for a moment, and then in a quite different voice called faintly —

" George ! "

Paul and Yerba glanced quickly at each other.

" George, set out some refreshment for the Honorable Paul Hathaway. The best, sir — you understand. . . . A good nigger, sir — a good boy; and he never leaves me, sir. Only, by gad! sir, he will starve himself and his family to be with me. I brought him with me to California away back in the fall of 'forty-nine. Those were the early days, sir — the early days."

His head had fallen back quite easily on the pillow now; but a slight film seemed to be closing over his dark eyes, like the inner lid of an eagle when it gazes upon the sun.

" They were the old days, sir — the days of Men — when a man's *word* was enough for anything, and his trigger-finger settled any doubt. When the Trust that he took from Man, Woman, or Child was never broken. When the tide, sir, that swept through the Golden Gate came up as far as Montgomery Street."

He did not speak again. But they who stood beside him knew that the tide had once more come up to Montgomery Street, and was carrying Harry Pendleton away with it.

# THE HERITAGE OF DEDLOW MARSH
## AND OTHER TALES

# CONTENTS.

————◆————

# THE HERITAGE OF DEDLOW
# MARSH.

## I.

THE sun was going down on the Dedlow
Marshes. The tide was following it fast as
if to meet the reddening lines of sky and
water in the west, leaving the foreground to
grow blacker and blacker every moment, and
to bring out in startling contrast the few
half-filled and half-lit pools left behind and
forgotten. The strong breath of the Pacific
fanning their surfaces at times kindled them
into a dull glow like dying embers. A
cloud of sand-pipers rose white from one of
the nearer lagoons, swept in a long eddying
ring against the sunset, and became a black
and dropping rain to seaward. The long
sinuous line of channel, fading with the light
and ebbing with the tide, began to give off
here and there light puffs of gray-winged
birds like sudden exhalations. High in the
darkening sky the long arrow-headed lines

of geese and ' brant ' pointed towards the upland. As the light grew more uncertain the
air at times was filled with the rush of view-
less and melancholy wings, or became plain-
tive with far-off cries and lamentations. As
the Marshes grew blacker the far-scattered
tussocks and accretions on its level surface
began to loom in exaggerated outline, and
two human figures, suddenly emerging erect
on the bank of the hidden channel, assumed
the proportion of giants.

When they had moored their unseen boat,
they still appeared for some moments to be
moving vaguely and aimlessly round the
spot where they had disembarked. But as
the eye became familiar with the darkness it
was seen that they were really advancing inland, yet with a slowness of progression and
deviousness of course that appeared inexplicable to the distant spectator. Presently it
was evident that this seemingly even, vast,
black expanse was traversed and intersected
by inky creeks and small channels, which
made human progression difficult and dangerous. As they appeared nearer and their
figures took more natural proportions, it
could be seen that each carried a gun; that
one was a young girl, although dressed so

like her companion in shaggy pea-jacket and
sou'wester as to be scarcely distinguished
from him above the short skirt that came
halfway down her high india-rubber fishing-
boots. By the time they had reached firmer
ground, and turned to look back at the sunset, it could be also seen that the likeness
between their faces was remarkable. Both,
had crisp, black, tightly curling hair; both
had dark eyes and heavy eyebrows; both
had quick vivid complexions, slightly heightened by the sea and wind. But more striking than their similarity of coloring was the
likeness of expression and bearing. Both
wore the same air of picturesque energy;
both bore themselves with a like graceful
effrontery and self-possession.

The young man continued his way. The
young girl lingered for a moment looking
seaward, with her small brown hand lifted
to shade her eyes, — a precaution which her
heavy eyebrows and long lashes seemed to
render utterly gratuitous.

"Come along, Mag. What are ye waitin'
for?" said the young man impatiently.

"Nothin'. Lookin' at that boat from the
Fort." Her clear eyes were watching a small
skiff, invisible to less keen-sighted observers,

aground upon a flat near the mouth of the channel. "Them chaps will have a high ole time gunnin' thar, stuck in the mud, and the tide goin' out like sixty!"

"Never you mind the sodgers," returned her companion, aggressively, "they kin take care o' their own precious skins, or Uncle Sam will do it for 'em, I reckon. Anyhow the people — that's you and me, Mag — is expected to pay for their foolishness. That's what they're sent yer for. Ye oughter to be satisfied with that," he added with deep sarcasm.

"I reckon they ain't expected to do much off o' dry land, and they can't help bein' queer on the water," returned the young girl with a reflecting sense of justice.

"Then they ain't no call to go gunnin', and wastin' Guv'nment powder on ducks instead o' Injins."

"Thet's so," said the girl thoughtfully. "Wonder ef Guv'nment pays for them frocks the Kernel's girls went cavortin' round Logport in last Sunday — they looked like a cirkis."

"Like ez not the old Kernel gets it outer contracts — one way or another. *We* pay for it all the same," he added gloomily.

" Jest the same ez if they were *my* clothes,"
said the girl, with a quick, fiery, little laugh,
" ain't it ? Wonder how they 'd like my
sayin' that to 'em when they was prancin'
round, eh, Jim ? "

But her companion was evidently unpre-
pared for this sweeping feminine deduction,
and stopped it with masculine promptitude.

" Look yer — instead o' botherin' your
head about what the Fort girls wear, you 'd
better trot along a little more lively. It 's
late enough now."

" But these darned boots hurt like pizen,"
said the girl, limping. " They swallowed a
lot o' water over the tops while I was wadin'
down there, and my feet go swashin' around
like in a churn every step."

" Lean on me, baby," he returned, passing
his arm around her waist, and dropping her
head smartly on his shoulder. "Thar !" The
act was brotherly and slightly contemptuous,
but it was sufficient to at once establish their
kinship.

They continued on thus for some moments
in silence, the girl, I fear, after the fashion
of her sex, taking the fullest advantage of
this slightly sentimental and caressing attitude. They were moving now along the

edge of the Marsh, parallel with the line of rapidly fading horizon, following some trail only known to their keen youthful eyes. It was growing darker and darker. The cries of the sea-birds had ceased; even the call of a belated plover had died away inland; the hush of death lay over the black funereal pall of marsh at their side. The tide had run out with the day. Even the sea-breeze had lulled in this dead slack-water of all nature, as if waiting outside the bar with the ocean, the stars, and the night.

Suddenly the girl stopped and halted her companion. The faint far sound of a bugle broke the silence, if the idea of interruption could have been conveyed by the two or three exquisite vibrations that seemed born of that silence itself, and to fade and die in it without break or discord. Yet it was only the 'retreat' call from the Fort two miles distant and invisible.

The young girl's face had become irradiated, and her small mouth half opened as she listened. " Do you know, Jim," she said with a confidential sigh, " I allus put words to that when I hear it — it's so pow'ful pretty. It allus goes to me like this : ' Goes the day, Far away, With the light, And the night Comes along — Comes along — Comes along — Like a-a so-o-ong.' " She here lifted her voice, a sweet, fresh, boyish contralto, in such an admirable imitation of the bugle that her brother, after the fashion of more select auditors, was for a moment quite convinced that the words meant something. Nevertheless, as a brother, it was his duty to crush this weakness. " Yes; and it says : ' Shut your head, Go to bed,' " he returned irascibly; "and *you 'd* better come along, if we 're goin' to hev any supper. There 's Yeller Bob hez got ahead of us over there with the game already."

The girl glanced towards a slouching burdened figure that now appeared to be preceding them, straightened herself suddenly, and then looked attentively towards the Marsh.

" Not the sodgers again ? " said her brother impatiently.

" No," she said quickly; " but if that don't beat anythin' ! I 'd hev sworn, Jim, that Yeller Bob was somewhere behind us. I saw him only jest now when ' Taps ' sounded, somewhere over thar." She pointed with a half-uneasy expression in quite another direction from that in which the slouching Yellow Bob had just loomed.

"Tell ye what, Mag, makin' poetry outer bugle calls hez kinder muddled ye. *That's* Yeller Bob ahead, and ye orter know Injins well enuff by this time to remember that they allus crop up jest when ye don't expect them. And there's the bresh jest afore us. Come!"

The 'bresh,' or low bushes, was really a line of stunted willows and alders that seemed to have gradually sunk into the level of the plain, but increased in size farther inland, until they grew to the height and density of a wood. Seen from the channel it had the appearance of a green cape or promontory thrust upon the Marsh. Passing through its tangled recesses, with the aid of some unerring instinct, the two companions emerged upon another and much larger level that seemed as illimitable as the bay. The strong breath of the ocean lying just beyond the bar and estuary they were now facing came to them salt and humid as another tide. The nearer expanse of open water reflected the after-glow, and lightened the landscape. And between the two wayfarers and the horizon rose, bleak and startling, the strange outlines of their home.

At first it seemed a ruined colonnade of

many pillars, whose base and pediment were buried in the earth, supporting a long parallelogram of entablature and cornices. But a second glance showed it to be a one-storied building, upheld above the Marsh by numberless piles placed at regular distances; some of them sunken or inclined from the perpendicular, increasing the first illusion. Between these pillars, which permitted a free circulation of air, and, at extraordinary tides, even the waters of the bay itself, the level waste of marsh, the bay, the surges of the bar, and finally the red horizon line, were distinctly visible. A railed gallery or platform, supported also on piles, and reached by steps from the Marsh, ran around the building, and gave access to the several rooms and offices.

But if the appearance of this lacustrine and amphibious dwelling was striking, and not without a certain rude and massive grandeur, its grounds and possessions, through which the brother and sister were still picking their way, were even more grotesque and remarkable. Over a space of half a dozen acres the flotsam and jetsam of years of tidal offerings were collected, and even guarded with a certain care. The blackened hulks of huge uprooted trees, scarcely distinguishable from the fragments of genuine wrecks beside them, were securely fastened by chains to stakes and piles driven in the marsh, while heaps of broken and disjointed bamboo orange crates, held together by ropes of fibre, glistened like ligamented bones heaped in the dead valley. Masts, spars, fragments of shell-encrusted boats, binnacles, round-houses and galleys, and part of the after-deck of a coasting schooner, had ceased their wanderings and found rest in this vast cemetery of the sea. The legend on a wheel-house, the lettering on a stern or bow, served for mortuary inscription. Wailed over by the trade winds, mourned by lamenting sea-birds, once every year the tide visited its lost dead and left them wet with its tears.

To such a spot and its surroundings the atmosphere of tradition and mystery was not wanting. Six years ago Boone Culpepper had built the house, and brought to it his wife — variously believed to be a gypsy, a Mexican, a bright mulatto, a Digger Indian, a South Sea princess from Tahiti, somebody else's wife — but in reality a little Creole woman from New Orleans, with whom he had contracted a marriage, with other

gambling debts, during a winter's vacation
from his home in Virginia. At the end of
two years she had died, succumbing, as dif-
ferently stated, from perpetual wet feet, or
the misanthropic idiosyncrasies of her husband, and leaving behind her a girl of
twelve and a boy of sixteen to console him.
How futile was this bequest may be guessed
from a brief summary of Mr. Culpepper's
peculiarities. They were the development
of a singular form of aggrandizement and
misanthropy. On his arrival at Logport he
had bought a part of the apparently value-
less Dedlow Marsh from the Government at
less than a dollar an acre, continuing his
singular investment year by year until he
was the owner of three leagues of amphibious domain. It was then discovered that
this property carried with it the *water front*
of divers valuable and convenient sites for
manufactures and the commercial ports of a
noble bay, as well as the natural *embarcade-
ros* of some 'lumbering' inland settlements.
Boone Culpepper would not sell. Boone
Culpepper would not rent or lease. Boone
Culpepper held an invincible blockade of his
neighbors, and the progress and improvement he despised — granting only, after a

royal fashion, occasional license, revocable
at pleasure, in the shape of tolls, which
amply supported him, with the game he
shot in his kingfisher's eyrie on the Marsh.
Even the Government that had made him
powerful was obliged to ' condemn ' a part
of his property at an equitable price for the
purposes of Fort Redwood, in which the
adjacent town of Logport shared.   And
Boone Culpepper, unable to resist the act,
refused to receive the compensation or quit-
claim the town.   In his scant intercourse
with his neighbors he always alluded to it
as his own, showed it to his children as part
of their strange inheritance, and exhibited
the starry flag that floated from the Fort as
a flaunting insult to their youthful eyes.
Hated, feared, and superstitiously shunned
by some, regarded as a madman by others,
familiarly known as ' The Kingfisher of Dedlow,' Boone Culpepper was one day found
floating dead in his skiff, with a charge of
shot through his head and shoulders.   The
shot-gun lying at his feet at the bottom of
the boat indicated the ' accident ' as recorded
in the verdict of the coroner's jury — but
not by the people.   A thousand rumors of
murder or suicide prevailed, but always with

the universal rider, 'Served him right.' So
invincible was this feeling that but few
attended his last rites, which took place at
high water. The delay of the officiating
clergyman lost the tide; the homely cata-
falque — his own boat — was left aground
on the Marsh, and deserted by all mourners
except the two children. Whatever he had
instilled into them by precept and example,
whatever took place that night in their
lonely watch by his bier on the black marshes,
it was certain that those who confidently
looked for any change in the administration
of the Dedlow Marsh were cruelly mistaken.
The old Kingfisher was dead, but he had
left in the nest two young birds, more beautiful and graceful, it was true, yet as fierce
and tenacious of beak and talon.

## II.

ARRIVING at the house, the young people
ascended the outer flight of wooden steps,
which bore an odd likeness to the compan-
ion-way of a vessel, and the gallery, or
' deck,' as it was called — where a number
of nets, floats, and buoys thrown over the
railing completed the nautical resemblance.

This part of the building was evidently devoted to kitchen, dining-room, and domestic
offices; the principal room in the centre
serving as hall or living-room, and communicating on the other side with two sleeping
apartments. It was of considerable size,
with heavy lateral beams across the ceiling
— built, like the rest of the house, with a
certain maritime strength — and looked not
unlike a saloon cabin. An enormous open
Franklin stove between the windows, as
large as a chimney, blazing with drift-wood,
gave light and heat to the apartment, and
brought into flickering relief the boarded
walls hung with the spoils of sea and shore,
and glittering with gun-barrels. Fowling-
pieces of all sizes, from the long ducking-
gun mounted on a swivel for boat use to the
light single-barrel or carbine, stood in racks
against the walls; game-bags, revolvers in
their holsters, hunting and fishing knives in
their sheaths, depended from hooks above
them. In one corner stood a harpoon; in
another, two or three Indian spears for
salmon. The carpetless floor and rude chairs
and settles were covered with otter, mink,
beaver, and a quantity of valuable seal-skins,
with a few larger pelts of the bear and elk.

The only attempt at decoration was the displayed wings and breasts of the wood and harlequin duck, the muir, the cormorant, the gull, the gannet, and the femininely delicate half-mourning of petrel and plover, nailed against the wall. The influence of the sea was dominant above all, and asserted its saline odors even through the spice of the curling drift-wood smoke that half veiled the ceiling.

A berry-eyed old Indian woman with the complexion of dried salmon ; her daughter, also with berry eyes, and with a face that seemed wholly made of a moist laugh ; 'Yellow Bob,' a Digger 'buck,' so called from the prevailing ochre markings of his cheek, and 'Washooh,' an ex-chief ; a nondescript in a blanket, looking like a cheap and dirty doll whose fibrous hair was badly nailed on his carved wooden head, composed the Culpepper household. While the two former were preparing supper in the adjacent dining-room, Yellow Bob, relieved of his burden of game, appeared on the gallery and beckoned mysteriously to his master through the window. James Culpepper went out, returned quickly, and after a minute's hesitation and an uneasy glance towards his sister, who had meantime pushed back her sou'-wester from her forehead, and without taking off her jacket had dropped into a chair before the fire with her back towards him, took his gun noiselessly from the rack, and saying carelessly that he would be back in a moment, disappeared.

Left to herself, Maggie coolly pulled off her long boots and stockings, and comfortably opposed to the fire two very pretty feet and ankles, whose delicate purity was slightly blue-bleached by confinement in the tepid sea-water. The contrast of their waxen whiteness with her blue woolen skirt, and with even the skin of her sunburnt hands and wrists, apparently amused her, and she sat for some moments with her elbows on her knees, her skirts slightly raised, contemplating them, and curling her toes with evident satisfaction. The firelight playing upon the rich coloring of her face, the fringe of jet-black curls that almost met the thick sweep of eyebrows, and left her only a white strip of forehead, her short upper lip and small chin, rounded but resolute, completed a piquant and striking figure. The rich brown shadows on the smoke-stained walls and ceiling, the occasional starting into relief of the scutcheons of brilliant plumage, and the momentary glitter of the steel barrels, made a quaint background to this charming picture. Sitting there, and following some lingering memory of her tramp on the Marsh, she hummed to herself a few notes of the bugle call that had impressed her — at first softly, and finally with the full pitch of her voice.

Suddenly she stopped.

There was a faint and unmistakable rapping on the floor beneath her. It was distinct, but cautiously given, as if intended to be audible to her alone. For a moment she stood upright, her feet still bare and glistening, on the otter skin that served as a rug. There were two doors to the room, one from which her brother had disappeared, which led to the steps, the other giving on the back gallery, looking inland. With a quick instinct she caught up her gun and ran to that one, but not before a rapid scramble near the railing was followed by a cautious opening of the door. She was just in time to shut it on the extended arm and light blue sleeve of an army overcoat that protruded through the opening, and for a moment threw her whole weight against it.

" A dhrop of whiskey, Miss, for the love of God."

She retained her hold, cocked her weapon, and stepped back a pace from the door. The blue sleeve was followed by the rest of the overcoat, and a blue cap with the infantry blazoning, and the letter H on its peak. They were for the moment more distinguishable than the man beneath them — grimed and blackened with the slime of the Marsh. But what could be seen of his mud-stained face was more grotesque than terrifying. A combination of weakness and audacity, insinuation and timidity struggled through the dirt for expression. His small blue eyes were not ill-natured, and even the intruding arm trembled more from exhaustion than passion.

" On'y a dhrop, Miss," he repeated piteously, "and av ye pleeze, quick! afore I'm stharved with the cold entoirely."

She looked at him intently — without lowering her gun.

" Who are you ? "

" Thin, it's the truth I'll tell ye, Miss — whisth then ! " he said in a half-whisper; " l'm a desarter ! "

" Then it was *you* that was doggin' us on the Marsh ? "

"It was the sarjint I was lavin', Miss."

She looked at him hesitatingly.

"Stay outside there; if you move a step into the room, I'll blow you out of it."

He stepped back on the gallery. She closed the door, bolted it, and still holding the gun, opened a cupboard, poured out a glass of whiskey, and returning to the door, opened it and handed him the liquor.

She watched him drain it eagerly, saw the fiery stimulant put life into his shivering frame, trembling hands, and kindle his dull eye — and — quietly raised her gun again.

"Ah, put it down, Miss, put it down! Fwhot's the use? Sure the bullets yee carry in them oiyes of yours is more deadly! It's out here oi'll sthand, glory be to God, all night, without movin' a fut till the sarjint comes to take me, av ye won't levil them oiyes at me like that. Ah, whirra! look at that now! but it's a gooddess she is — the livin' Jaynus of warr, standin' there like a statoo, wid her alybaster fut put forward."

In her pride and conscious superiority, any suggestion of shame at thus appearing before a common man and a mendicant was as impossible to her nature as it would have been to a queen or the goddess of his simile.

His presence and his compliment alike passed her calm modesty unchallenged. The wretched scamp recognized the fact and felt its power, and it was with a superstitious reverence asserting itself through his native extravagance that he raised his grimy hand to his cap in military salute and became respectfully rigid.

" Then the sodgers were huntin' *you?* " she said thoughtfully, lowering her weapon.

" Thrue for you, Miss — they worr, and it 's meself that was lyin' flat in the ditch wid me faytures makin' an illigant cast in the mud — more betoken, as ye see even now — and the sarjint and his daytail thrampin' round me. It was thin that the mortial cold sthruck thro' me mouth, and made me wake for the whiskey that would resthore me."

" What did you desert fer ? "

" Ah, list to that now! Fwhat did I desart fer? Shure ev there was the ghost of an inemy round, it 's meself that would be in the front now! But it was the letthers from me ould mother, Miss, that is sthruck wid a mortial illness — long life to her! — in County Clare, and me sisthers in Ninth Avenue in New York, fornint the daypo, that is brekken their harruts over me listin' in the Fourth Infanthry to do duty in a hay-then wilderness. Av it was the cavalry — and it's me own father that was in the In-nishkillen Dthragoons, Miss — oi would n't moind. Wid a horse betune me legs, it's on parade oi 'd be now, Miss, and not wan-dhering over the bare flure of the Marsh, stharved wid the cold, the thirst, and hun-ger, wid the mud and the moire thick on me; facin' an illigant young leddy as is the ekal ov a Fayld Marshal's darter — not to sphake ov Kernal Preston's — ez could n't hold a candle to her."

Brought up on the Spanish frontier, Mag-gie Culpepper was one of the few American girls who was not familiar with the Irish race. The rare smile that momentarily lit up her petulant mouth seemed to justify the intruder's praise. But it passed quickly, and she returned dryly:

" That means you want more drink, suthin' to eat, and clothes. Suppose my brother comes back and ketches you here ? "

" Shure, Miss, he's just now hunten me, along wid his two haythen Diggers, beyond the laygoon there. It worr the yellar one that sphotted me lyin' there in the ditch; it worr only your own oiyes, Miss — more

power to their beauty for that! — that saw
me folly him unbeknownst here; and that
desaved them, ye see!"

The young girl remained for an instant
silent and thoughtful.

"We're no friends of the Fort," she said
finally, "but I don't reckon for that reason
my brother will cotton to *you*. Stay out
thar where ye are, till I come to ye. If you
hear me singin' again, you'll know he's
come back, and ye'd better scoot with what
you've already got, and be thankful."

She shut the door again and locked it,
went into the dining-room, returned with
some provisions wrapped in paper, took a
common wicker flask from the wall, passed
into her brother's bedroom, and came out
with a flannel shirt, overalls, and a coarse
Indian blanket, and, reopening the door,
placed them before the astonished and delighted vagabond. His eye glistened; he
began, " Glory be to God," but for once his
habitual extravagance failed him. Nature
triumphed with a more eloquent silence over
his well-worn art. He hurriedly wiped his
begrimed face and eyes with the shirt she
had given him, and catching the sleeve of
her rough pea-jacket in his dirty hand,
raised it to his lips.

"Go!" she said imperiously. "Get away while you can."

"Av it vas me last words — it's speechless oi am," he stammered, and disappeared over the railing.

She remained for a moment holding the door half open, and gazing into the darkness that seemed to flow in like a tide. Then she shut it, and going into her bedroom resumed her interrupted toilette. When she emerged again she was smartly stockinged and slippered, and even the blue serge skirt was exchanged for a bright print, with a white fichu tied around her throat. An attempt to subdue her rebellious curls had resulted in the construction from their ruins of a low Norman arch across her forehead with pillared abutments of ringlets. When her brother returned a few moments later she did not look up, but remained, perhaps a little ostentatiously, bending over the fire.

"Bob allowed that the Fort boat was huntin' *men* — deserters, I reckon," said Jim aggrievedly. "Wanted me to believe that he *saw* one on the Marsh hidin'. On'y an Injin lie, I reckon, to git a little extra fire-water, for toting me out to the bresh on a fool's errand."

" Oh, *that's* where you went ! " said Maggie, addressing the fire. " Since when hev you tuk partnership with the Guv'nment and Kernel Preston to hunt up and take keer of their property ? "

" Well, I ain't goin' to hev such wreckage as they pick up and enlist set adrift on our marshes, Mag," said Jim decidedly.

" What would you hev done had you ketched him ? " said Maggie, looking suddenly into her brother's face.

" Given him a dose of snipe-shot that he'd remember, and be thankful it wasn't slugs," said Jim promptly. Observing a deeper seriousness in her attitude, he added, " Why, if it was in war-time he'd get a *ball* from them sodgers on sight."

" Yes; but *you* ain't got no call to interfere," said Maggie.

" Ain't I ? Why, he's no better than an outlaw. I ain't sure that he hasn't been stealin' or killin' somebody over theer."

" Not *that* man ! " said Maggie impulsively.

" Not what man ? " said her brother, facing her quickly.

" Why," returned Maggie, repairing her indiscretion with feminine dexterity, " not *any* man who might have knocked you and me over on the marshes in the dusk, and grabbed our guns."

"Wish he'd hev tried it," said the brother, with a superior smile, but a quickly rising color. "Where d'ye suppose *I*'d hev been all the while?"

Maggie saw her mistake, and for the first time in her life resolved to keep a secret from her brother — overnight. "Supper's gettin' cold," she said, rising.

They went into the dining-room — an apartment as plainly furnished as the one they had quitted, but in its shelves, cupboards, and closely fitting boarding bearing out the general nautical suggestion of the house — and seated themselves before a small table on which their frugal meal was spread. In this *tête-à-tête* position Jim suddenly laid down his knife and fork and stared at his sister.

"Hello!"

"What's the matter?" said Maggie, starting slightly. "How you do skeer one."

"Who's been prinkin', eh?"

"My ha'r was in kinks all along o' that hat," said Maggie, with a return of higher

color, " and I had to straighten it. It's a
boy's hat, not a girl's."

" But that necktie and that gown — and
all those frills and tuckers ? " continued Jim
generalizing, with a rapid twirling of his
fingers over her. " Are you expectin' Judge
Martin, or the Expressman, this evening ? "

Judge Martin was the lawyer of Logport, who had proven her father's will, and
had since raved about his single interview
with the Kingfisher's beautiful daughter ; the
Expressman was a young fellow who was
popularly supposed to have left his heart
while delivering another valuable package
on Maggie in person, and had " never been
the same man since." It was a well-worn
fraternal pleasantry that had done duty
many a winter's evening, as a happy combination of moral admonition and cheerfulness. Maggie usually paid it the tribute of
a quick little laugh and a sisterly pinch, but
that evening those marks of approbation
were withheld.

" Jim dear," said she, when their Spartan
repast was concluded and they were reëstab-
lished before the living-room fire. " What
was it the Redwood Mill Kempany offered
you for that piece near Dead Man's
Slough ? "

Jim took his pipe from his lips long enough to say, " Ten thousand dollars," and put it back again.

" And what do ye kalkilate all our property, letting alone this yer house, and the driftwood front, is worth all together ? "

" Includin' wot the Gov'nment owes us ? — for that's all ours, ye know ? " said Jim quickly.

" No — leavin' that out — jest for greens, you know," suggested Maggie.

" Well nigh onter a hundred and seventy-five thousand dollars, I reckon, by and large."

" That's a heap o' money, Jim ! I reckon old Kernel Preston would n't raise that in a hundred years," continued Maggie, warming her knees by the fire.

" In five million years," said Jim, promptly sweeping away further discussion. After a pause he added, " You and me, Mag, kin see anybody's pile, and go 'em fifty thousand better."

There were a few moments of complete silence, in which Maggie smoothed her knees, and Jim's pipe, which seemed to have become gorged and apoplectic with its owner's wealth, snored unctuously.

"Jim dear, what if — it's on'y an idea of mine, you know — what if you sold that piece to the Redwood Mill, and we jest tuk that money and — and — and jest lifted the ha'r offer them folks at Logport? Jest astonished 'em! Jest tuk the best rooms in that new hotel, got a hoss and buggy, dressed ourselves, you and me, fit to kill, and made them Fort people take a back seat in the Lord's Tabernacle, oncet for all. You see what I mean, Jim," she said hastily, as her brother seemed to be succumbing, like his pipe, in apoplectic astonishment, "jest on'y to *show* 'em what we *could* do if we keerd. Lord! when we done it and spent the money we'd jest snap our fingers and skip back yer ez nat'ral ez life! Ye don't think, Jim," she said, suddenly turning half fiercely upon him, "that I'd allow to *live* among 'em — to stay a menet after that!"

Jim laid down his pipe and gazed at his sister with stony deliberation. "And — what — do — you — kalkilate — to make by all that?" he said with scornful distinctness.

"Why, jest to show 'em we *have* got money, and could buy 'em all up if we wanted to," returned Maggie, sticking boldly to her guns, albeit with a vague conviction that her fire was weakened through elevation, and somewhat alarmed at the deliberation of the enemy.

"And you mean to say they don't know it now," he continued with slow derision.

"No," said Maggie. "Why, theer's that new school-marm over at Logport, you know, Jim, the one that wanted to take your picter in your boat for a young smuggler or fancy pirate or Eyetalian fisherman, and allowed that you'r handsomed some, and offered to pay you for sittin' — do you reckon *she'd* believe you owned the land her schoolhouse was built on. No! Lots of 'em don't. Lots of 'em thinks we're poor and low down — and them ez does n't, thinks " —

"What?" asked her brother sharply.

"That we're *mean.*"

The quick color came to Jim's cheek. "So," he said, facing her quickly, "for the sake of a lot of riff-raff and scum that's drifted here around us — jest for the sake of cuttin' a swell before them — you'll go out among the hounds ez allowed your mother was a Spanish nigger or a kanaka, ez called your father a pirate and landgrabber, ez much as allowed he was shot by some one or killed himself a purpose, ez said you was a heathen and a looney because you did n't go to school or church along with their trash, ez kept away from Maw's sickness ez if it was smallpox, and Dad's fun'ral ez if he was a hoss-thief, and left you and me to watch his coffin on the marshes all night till the tide kem back. And now you — *you* that jined hands with me that night over our father lyin' there cold and despised — ez if he was a dead dog thrown up by the tide — and swore that ez long ez that tide ebbed and flowed it could n't bring you to them, or them to you agin! You now want — what? What? Why, to go and cast your lot among 'em, and live among 'em, and join in their God-forsaken holler foolishness, and — and — and " —

"Stop! It's a lie! I *did n't* say that. Don't you dare to say it!" said the girl, springing to her feet, and facing her brother in turn, with flashing eyes.

For a moment the two stared at each other — it might have been as in a mirror, so perfectly were their passions reflected in each line, shade, and color of the other's face. It was as if they had each confronted their own

passionate and willful souls, and were frightened. It had often occurred before, always
with the same invariable ending. The
young man's eyes lowered first; the girl's
filled with tears.

"Well, ef ye did n't mean that, what did
ye mean?" said Jim, sinking, with sullen
apology, back into his chair.

"I — only — meant it — for — for — revenge!" sobbed Maggie.

"Oh!" said Jim, as if allowing his higher
nature to be touched by this noble instinct.
"But I did n't jest see where the revenge
kem in."

"No? But, never mind now, Jim," said
Maggie, ostentatiously ignoring, after the
fashion of her sex, the trouble she had provoked; "but to think — that — that — you
thought" — (sobbing).

"But I did n't, Mag" — (caressingly).

With this very vague and impotent conclusion, Maggie permitted herself to be
drawn beside her brother, and for a few moments they plumed each other's ruffled feathers, and smoothed each other's lifted crests,
like two beautiful young specimens of that
halcyon genus to which they were popularly
supposed to belong. At the end of half an

hour Jim rose, and, yawning slightly, said in a perfunctory way:

" Where 's the book ? "

The book in question was the Bible. It had been the self-imposed custom of these two young people to read aloud a chapter every night as their one vague formula of literary and religious discipline. When it was produced, Maggie, presuming on his affectionate and penitential condition, suggested that to-night he should pick out "suthin' interestin'." But this unorthodox frivolity was sternly put aside by Jim — albeit, by way of compromise, he agreed to " chance it," *i. e.*, open its pages at random.

He did so. Generally he allowed himself a moment's judicious pause for a certain chaste preliminary inspection necessary before reading aloud to a girl. To-night he omitted that modest precaution, and in a pleasant voice, which in reading was singularly free from colloquial infelicities of pronunciation, began at once:

"' Curse ye Meroz, said the angel of the Lord, curse ye bitterly the inhabitants thereof; because they came not to the help of the Lord, to the help of the Lord against the mighty.' "

"Oh, you looked first," said Maggie.

"I did n't now — honest Injin! I just opened."

"Go on," said Maggie, eagerly shoving him and interposing her neck over his shoulder.

And Jim continued Deborah's wonderful song of Jael and Sisera to the bitter end of its strong monosyllabic climax.

"There," he said, closing the volume, "that's what *I* call revenge. That's the real Scripture thing — no fancy frills theer."

"Yes; but, Jim dear, don't you see that she treated him first — sorter got round him with free milk and butter, and reg'larly blandished him," argued Maggie earnestly.

But Jim declined to accept this feminine suggestion, or to pursue the subject further, and after a fraternal embrace they separated for the night. Jim lingered long enough to look after the fastening of the door and windows, and Maggie remained for some moments at her casement, looking across the gallery to the Marsh beyond.

The moon had risen, the tide was half up. Whatever sign or trace of alien footprint or occupation had been there was already smoothly obliterated; even the configuration of the land had changed. A black cape had disappeared, a level line of shore had been eaten into by teeth of glistening silver. The whole dark surface of the Marsh was beginning to be streaked with shining veins as if a new life was coursing through it. Part of the open bay before the Fort, encroaching upon the shore, seemed in the moonlight to be reaching a white and outstretched arm towards the nest of the Kingfisher.

## III.

THE reveille at Fort Redwood had been supplemented full five minutes by the voice of Lieutenant George Calvert's servant, before that young officer struggled from his bed. His head was splitting, his tongue and lips were dry and feverish, his bloodshot eyes were shrinking from the insufferable light of the day, his mind a confused medley of the past night and the present morning, of cards and wild revelry, and the vision of a reproachfully trim orderly standing at his door with reports and orders which he now held composedly in his hand. For Lieutenant Calvert had been enjoying a symposium

variously known as " Stag Feed " and " A
Wild Stormy Night " with several of his
brother officers, and a sickening conviction
that it was not the first or the last time he
had indulged in these festivities. At that
moment he loathed himself, and then after
the usual derelict fashion cursed the fate
that had sent him, after graduating, to a
frontier garrison — the dull monotony of
whose duties made the Border horse-play of
dissipation a relief. Already he had reached
the miserable point of envying the veteran
capacities of his superiors and equals. " If
I could drink like Kirby or Crowninshield,
or if there was any other cursed thing a man
could do in this hole," he had wretchedly repeated to himself, after each misspent occasion, and yet already he was looking forward to them as part of a ' sub's ' duty and
worthy his emulation. Already the dream of
social recreation fostered by West Point had
been rudely dispelled. Beyond the garrison circle of Colonel Preston's family and
two officers' wives, there was no society. The
vague distrust and civil jealousy with which
some frontier communities regard the Federal power, heightened in this instance by
the uncompromising attitude the Government

had taken towards the settlers' severe Indian policy, had kept the people of Logport aloof from the Fort. The regimental band might pipe to them on Saturdays, but they would not dance.

Howbeit, Lieutenant Calvert dressed himself with uncertain hands but mechanical regularity and neatness, and, under the automatic training of discipline and duty, managed to button his tunic tightly over his feelings, to pull himself together with his sword-belt, compressing a still cadet-like waist, and to present that indescribable combination of precision and jauntiness which his brother officers too often allowed to lapse into frontier carelessness. His closely clipped light hair, yet dripping from a plunge in the cold water, had been brushed and parted with military exactitude, and when surmounted by his cap, with the peak in an artful suggestion of extra smartness tipped forward over his eyes, only his pale face — a shade lighter than his little blonde moustache — showed his last night's excesses. He was mechanically reaching for his sword and staring confusedly at the papers on his table when his servant interrupted :

" Major Bromley arranged that Lieutenant Kirby takes your sash this morning, as you 're not well, sir; and you 're to report for special to the colonel," he added, pointing discreetly to the envelope.

Touched by this consideration of his superior, Major Bromley, who had been one of the veterans of last night's engagement, Calvert mastered the contents of the envelope without the customary anathema of specials, said, "Thank you, Parks," and passed out on the veranda.

The glare of the quiet sunlit quadrangle, clean as a well-swept floor, the whitewashed walls and galleries of the barrack buildings beyond, the white and green palisade of officers' cottages on either side, and the glitter of a sentry's bayonet, were for a moment intolerable to him. Yet, by a kind of subtle irony, never before had the genius and spirit of the vocation he had chosen seemed to be as incarnate as in the scene before him. Seclusion, self-restraint, cleanliness, regularity, sobriety, the atmosphere of a wholesome life, the austere reserve of a monastery without its mysterious or pensive meditation, were all there. To escape which, he had of his own free will successively accepted a fool's distraction, the inevitable result of which was,

the viewing of them the next morning with
tremulous nerves and aching eyeballs.

An hour later, Lieutenant George Calvert
had received his final instructions from Colonel Preston to take charge of a small detachment to recover and bring back certain
deserters, but notably one, Dennis M'Caffrey of Company H, charged additionally
with mutinous solicitation and example. As
Calvert stood before his superior, that distinguished officer, whose oratorical powers had
been considerably stimulated through a long
course of " returning thanks for the Army,"
slightly expanded his chest and said pater-
nally :

" I am aware, Mr. Calvert, that duties
of this kind are somewhat distasteful to
young officers, and are apt to be considered
in the light of police detail; but I must remind you that no one part of a soldier's
duty can be held more important or honorable than another, and that the fulfilment of
any one, however trifling, must, with honor
to himself and security to his comrades, receive his fullest devotion. A sergeant and a
file of men might perform your duty, but I
require, in addition, the discretion, courtesy,
and consideration of a gentleman who will

command an equal respect from those with whom his duty brings him in contact. The unhappy prejudices which the settlers show to the military authority here render this, as you are aware, a difficult service, but I believe that you will, without forgetting the respect due to yourself and the Government you represent, avoid arousing these prejudices by any harshness, or inviting any conflict with the civil authority. The limits of their authority you will find in your written instructions; but you might gain their confidence, and impress them, Mr. Calvert, with the idea of your being their *auxiliary* in the interests of justice — you understand. Even if you are unsuccessful in bringing back the men, you will do your best to ascertain if their escape has been due to the sympathy of the settlers, or even with their preliminary connivance. They may not be aware that inciting enlisted men to desert is a criminal offence ; you will use your own discretion in informing them of the fact or not, as occasion may serve you. I have only to add, that while you are on the waters of this bay and the land covered by its tides, you have no opposition of authority, and are responsible to no one but your military superiors.

Good-bye, Mr. Calvert. Let me hear a good account of you."

Considerably moved by Colonel Preston's manner, which was as paternal and real as his rhetoric was somewhat perfunctory, Calvert half forgot his woes as he stepped from the commandant's piazza. But he had to face a group of his brother officers, who were awaiting him.

"Good-bye, Calvert," said Major Bromley; "a day or two out on grass won't hurt you — and a change from commissary whiskey will put you all right. By the way, if you hear of any better stuff at Westport than they're giving us here, sample it and let us know. Take care of yourself. Give your men a chance to talk to you now and then, and you may get something from them, especially Donovan. Keep your eye on Ramon. You can trust your sergeant straight along."

"Good-bye, George," said Kirby. "I suppose the old man told you that, although no part of a soldier's duty was better than another, your service was a very delicate one, just fitted for you, eh? He always does when he's cut out some hellish scrub-work for a chap. And told you, too, that as long

as you did n't go ashore, and kept to a dis-
patch-boat, or an eight-oared gig, where you
could n't deploy your men, or dress a line,
you 'd be invincible."

"He did say something like that," smiled
Calvert, with an uneasy recollection, however, that it was *the* part of his superior's
speech that particularly impressed him.

"Of course," said Kirby gravely, "*that*,
as an infantry officer, is clearly your duty."

"And don't forget, George," said Rollins
still more gravely, "that, whatever may be-
fall you, you belong to a section of that
numerically small but powerfully diversified
organization — the American Army. Remember that in the hour of peril you can address your men in any language, and be perfectly understood. And remember that when
you proudly stand before them, the eyes not
only of your own country, but of nearly all
the others, are upon you! Good-bye, Geor-
gey. I heard the major hint something
about whiskey. They say that old pirate,
Kingfisher Culpepper, had a stock of the real
thing from Robertson County laid in his
shebang on the Marsh just before he died.
Pity we are n't on terms with them, for the
cubs cannot drink it, and might be induced

to sell. Should n't wonder, by the way, **if** your friend M'Caffrey was hanging round somewhere there; he always had a keen scent. You might confiscate it as an "incitement to desertion," you know. The girl's pretty, and ought to be growing up now."

But haply at this point the sergeant stopped further raillery by reporting the detachment ready; and drawing his sword, Calvert, with a confused head, a remorseful heart, but an unfaltering step, marched off his men on his delicate mission.

It was four o'clock when he entered Jonesville. Following a matter-of-fact idea of his own, he had brought his men the greater distance by a circuitous route through the woods, thus avoiding the ostentatious exposure of his party on the open bay in a well-manned boat to an extended view from the three leagues of shore and marsh opposite. Crossing the stream, which here separated him from the Dedlow Marsh by the common ferry, he had thus been enabled to halt unperceived below the settlement and occupy the two roads by which the fugitives could escape inland. He had deemed it not impossible that, after the previous visit of the sergeant, the deserters hidden in the vicinity might return to Jonesville in the belief that the visit would not be repeated so soon. Leaving a part of his small force to patrol the road and another to deploy over the upland meadows, he entered the village. By the exercise of some boyish diplomacy and a certain prepossessing grace, which he knew when and how to employ, he became satisfied that the objects of his quest were not *there* — however, their whereabouts might have been known to the people. Dividing his party again, he concluded to take a corporal and a few men and explore the lower marshes himself.

The preoccupation of duty, exercise, and perhaps, above all, the keen stimulus of the iodine-laden salt air seemed to clear his mind and invigorate his body. He had never been in the Marsh before, and enjoyed its novelty with the zest of youth. It was the hour when the tide of its feathered life was at its flood. Clouds of duck and teal passing from the fresh water of the river to the salt pools of the marshes perpetually swept his path with flying shadows; at times it seemed as if even the uncertain ground around him itself arose and sped away on dusky wings. The vicinity of hidden pools and sloughs was betrayed by startled splashings; a few paces from their marching feet arose the sunlit pinions of a swan. The air was filled with multitudinous small cries and pipings. In this vocal confusion it was some minutes before he recognized the voice of one of his out-flankers calling to the other.

An important discovery had been made. In a long tongue of bushes that ran down to the Marsh they had found a mud-stained uniform, complete even to the cap, bearing the initial of the deserter's company.

"Is there any hut or cabin hereabouts, Schmidt?" asked Calvert.

"Dot vos schoost it, Lefdennun," replied his corporal. "Dot vos de shanty from der Kingvisher — old Gulbebber. I pet a dollar, py shimminy, dot der men haf der gekommt."

He pointed through the brake to a long, low building that now raised itself, white in the sunlight, above the many blackened piles. Calvert saw in a single reconnoitring glance that it had but one approach — the flight of steps from the Marsh. Instructing his men to fall in on the outer edge of the

brake and await his orders, he quickly made
his way across the space and ascended the
steps. Passing along the gallery he knocked
at the front door. There was no response.
He repeated his knock. Then the window
beside it opened suddenly, and he was confronted with the double-muzzle of a long
ducking-gun. Glancing instinctively along
the barrels, he saw at their other extremity
the bright eyes, brilliant color, and small set
mouth of a remarkably handsome girl. It
was the fact, and to the credit of his training, that he paid more attention to the eyes
than to the challenge of the shining tubes
before him.

" Jest stop where you are — will you!"
said the girl determinedly.

Calvert's face betrayed not the slightest
terror or surprise. Immovable as on parade,
he carried his white gloved hand to his cap,
and said gently, " With pleasure."

" Oh yes," said the girl quickly ; " but if
you move a step I 'll jest blow you and your
gloves offer that railin' inter the Marsh."

" I trust not," returned Calvert, smiling.

" And why ? "

" Because it would deprive me of the pleasure of a few moments' conversation with

you — and I've only one pair of gloves with me."

He was still watching her beautiful eyes — respectfully, admiringly, and strategically. For he was quite convinced that if he *did* move she would certainly discharge one or both barrels at him.

"Where's the rest of you?" she continued sharply.

"About three hundred yards away, in the covert, not near enough to trouble you."

"Will they come here?"

"I trust not."

"You trust not?" she repeated scornfully. "Why?"

"Because they would be disobeying orders."

She lowered her gun slightly, but kept her black brows levelled at him. "I reckon I'm a match for *you*," she said, with a slightly contemptuous glance at his slight figure, and opened the door. For a moment they stood looking at each other. He saw, besides the handsome face and eyes that had charmed him, a tall slim figure, made broader across the shoulders by an open pea-jacket that showed a man's red flannel shirt belted at the waist over a blue skirt, with

the collar knotted by a sailor's black handkerchief, and turned back over a pretty
though sunburnt throat. She saw a rather
undersized young fellow in a jaunty undress
uniform, scant of gold braid, and bearing
only the single gold shoulder-bars of his
rank, but scrupulously neat and well fitting.
Light-colored hair cropped close, the small-
est of light moustaches, clear and penetrating blue eyes, and a few freckles completed
a picture that did not prepossess her. She
was therefore the more inclined to resent the
perfect ease and self-possession with which
the stranger carried off these manifest de-
fects before her.

She laid aside the gun, put her hands
deep in the pockets of her pea-jacket, and,
slightly squaring her shoulders, said curtly,
"What do you want?"

"A very little information, which I trust
it will not trouble you to give me. My men
have just discovered the uniform belonging
to a deserter from the Fort lying in the
bushes yonder. Can you give me the slightest idea how it came there?"

"What right have you trapseing over our
property?" she said, turning upon him
sharply, with a slight paling of color.

" None whatever."

" Then what did you come for ? "

" To ask that permission, in case you would give me no information."

" Why don't you ask my brother, and not a woman? Were you afraid ? "

" He could hardly have done me the honor of placing me in more peril than you have," returned Calvert, smiling. " Then I have the pleasure of addressing Miss Culpepper ?"

" I 'm Jim Culpepper's sister."

" And, I believe, equally able to give or refuse the permission I ask."

" And what if I refuse ? "

" Then I have only to ask pardon for having troubled you, go back, and return here with the tide. You don't resist *that* with a shot-gun, do you ? " he asked pleasantly.

Maggie Culpepper was already familiar with the accepted theory of the supreme jurisdiction of the Federal Sea. She half turned her back upon him, partly to show her contempt, but partly to evade the domination of his clear, good-humored, and self-sustained little eyes.

" I don't know anythin' about your deserters, nor what rags o' theirs happen to be floated up here," she said, angrily, "and don't care to. You kin do what you like."

"Then I'm afraid I should remain here a little longer, Miss Culpepper; but my duty" —

"Your wot?" she interrupted, disdainfully.

"I suppose I *am* talking shop," he said smilingly. "Then my business" —

"Your business — pickin' up half-starved runaways!"

"And, I trust, sometimes a kind friend," he suggested, with a grave bow.

"You *trust?* Look yer, young man," she said, with her quick, fierce, little laugh, "I reckon you *trust* a heap too much!" She would like to have added, "with your freckled face, red hair, and little eyes" — but this would have obliged her to face them again, which she did not care to do.

Calvert stepped back, lifted his hand to his cap, still pleasantly, and then walked gravely along the gallery, down the steps, and towards the cover. From her window, unseen, she followed his neat little figure moving undeviatingly on, without looking to the left or right, and still less towards the house he had just quitted. Then she saw

the sunlight flash on cross-belt plates and
steel barrels, and a light blue line issued
from out the dark green bushes, round the
point, and disappeared. And then it suddenly occurred to her what she had been
doing! This, then, was her first step towards that fancy she had so lately conceived,
quarrelled over with her brother, and lay
awake last night to place anew, in spite of
all opposition! This was her brilliant idea
of dazzling and subduing Logport and the
Fort! Had she grown silly, or what had
happened? Could she have dreamed of the
coming of this whipper-snapper, with his insufferable airs, after that beggarly deserter?
I am afraid that for a few moments the
miserable fugitive had as small a place in
Maggie's sympathy as the redoubtable whipper-snapper himself. And now the cherished
dream of triumph and conquest was over!
What a "looney" she had been! Instead
of inviting him in, and outdoing him in
"company manners," and "fooling" him
about the deserter, and then blazing upon
him afterwards at Logport in the glory of
her first spent wealth and finery, she had
driven him away!

And now " he'll go and tell — tell the

Fort girls of his hairbreadth escape from the claws of the Kingfisher's daughter!"

The thought brought a few bitter tears to her eyes, but she wiped them away. The thought brought also the terrible conviction that Jim was right, that there could be nothing but open antagonism between them and the traducers of their parents, as she herself had instinctively shown! But she presently wiped that conviction away also, as she had her tears.

Half an hour later she was attracted by the appearance from the windows of certain straggling blue spots on the upland that seemed moving diagonally towards the Marsh. She did not know that it was Calvert's second "detail" joining him, but believed for a moment that he had not yet departed, and was strangely relieved. Still later the frequent disturbed cries of coot, heron, and marsh-hen, recognizing the presence of unusual invaders of their solitude, distracted her yet more, and forced her at last with increasing color and an uneasy sense of shyness to steal out to the gallery for a swift furtive survey of the Marsh. But an utterly unexpected sight met her eyes, and kept her motionless.

The birds were rising everywhere and drifting away with querulous perturbation before a small but augmented blue detachment that was moving with monotonous regularity towards the point of bushes where she had seen the young officer previously disappear. In their midst, between two soldiers with fixed bayonets, marched the man whom even at that distance she instantly recognized as the deserter of the preceding night, in the very clothes she had given him. To complete her consternation, a little to the right marched the young officer also, but accompanied by, and apparently on the most amicable terms with, Jim — her own brother!

To forget all else and dart down the steps, flying towards the point of bushes, scarcely knowing why or what she was doing, was to Maggie the impulse and work of a moment. When she had reached it the party were not twenty paces away. But here a shyness and hesitation again seized her, and she shrank back in the bushes with an instinctive cry to her brother inarticulate upon her lips. They came nearer, they were opposite to her; her brother Jim keeping step with the invader, and even conversing with him with an animation she had seldom seen upon his face — they passed ! She had been unnoticed except by one. The roving eye of the deserter had detected her handsome face among the leaves, slightly turned towards it, and poured out his whole soul in a single swift wink of eloquent but indescribable confidence.

When they had quite gone, she crept back to the house, a little reassured, but still tremulous. When her brother returned at nightfall, he found her brooding over the fire, in the same attitude as on the previous night.

"I reckon ye might hev seen me go by with the sodgers," he said, seating himself beside her, a little awkwardly, and with an unusual assumption of carelessness.

Maggie, without looking up, was languidly surprised. He had been with the soldiers — and where ?

"About two hours ago I met this yer Leftenant Calvert," he went on with increasing awkwardness, " and — oh, I say, Mag — he said he saw you, and hoped he had n't troubled ye, and — and — ye saw him, did n't ye ? "

Maggie, with all the red of the fire con-

centrated in her cheek as she gazed at the
flame, believed carelessly " that she had seen
a shrimp in uniform asking questions."

" Oh, he ain't a bit stuck up," said Jim
quickly, " that's what I like about him.
He 's ez nat'ral ez you be, and tuck my arm,
walkin' around, careless-like, laffen at what
he was doin', ez ef it was a game, and he
was n't sole commander of forty men.  He 's
only a year or two older than me — and —
and " — he stopped and looked uneasily at
Maggie.

" So ye 've bin craw-fishin' agin ? " said
Maggie, in her deepest and most scornful
contralto.

" Who 's craw-fishin' ? " he retorted, angrily.

" What 's this backen out o' what you
said yesterday ?  What 's all this trucklin'
to the Fort now ? "

" What ?  Well now, look yer," said Jim,
rising suddenly, with reproachful indignation, " darned if I don't jest tell ye every-
thin'.  I promised *him* I would n't.  He
allowed it would frighten ye."

" *Frighten me!* " repeated Maggie con-
temptuously, nevertheless with her cheek
paling again.  "Frighten me — with what ? "

"Well, since yer so cantankerous, look yer. We 've been robbed!"

"Robbed?" echoed Maggie, facing him.

"Yes, robbed by that same deserter. Robbed of a suit of my clothes, and my whiskey-flask, and the darned skunk had 'em on. And if it had n't bin for that Leftenant Calvert, and my givin' him permission to hunt him over the Marsh, we would n't have caught him."

"Robbed?" repeated Maggie again, vaguely.

"Yes, robbed! Last night, afore we came home. He must hev got in yer while we was comin' from the boat."

"Did, did that Leftenant say so?" stammered Maggie.

"Say it, of course he did! and so do I," continued Jim, impatiently. "Why, there were my very clothes on his back, and he dare n't deny it. And if you 'd hearkened to me jest now, instead of flyin' off in tantrums, you 'd see that *that 's* jest how we got him, and how me and the Leftenant joined hands in it. I did n't give him permission to hunt deserters, but *thieves*. I did n't help him to ketch the man that deserted from *him*, but the skunk that took *my* clothes. For when the Leftenant found the man's old uniform in the bush, he nat'rally kalkilated he must hev got some other duds near by in some underhand way. Don't you see? eh? Why, look, Mag. Darned if you ain't skeered after all! Who'd hev thought it? There now — sit down, dear. Why, you're white ez a gull."

He had his arm round her as she sank back in the chair again with a forced smile.

"There now," he said with fraternal superiority, "don't mind it, Mag, any more. Why, it's all over now. You bet he won't trouble us agin, for the Leftenant sez that now he's found out to be a thief, they'll jest turn him over to the police, and he's sure o' getten six months' state prison fer stealin' and burglarin' in our house. But" — he stopped suddenly and looked at his sister's contracted face; "look yer, Mag, you're sick, that's what's the matter. Take suthin'" —

"I'm better now," she said with an effort; "it's only a kind o' blind chill I must hev got on the Marsh last night. What's that?"

She had risen, and grasping her brother's arm tightly had turned quickly to the window. The casement had suddenly rattled.

" It 's only the wind gettin' up. It looked
like a sou'wester when I came in. Lot o'
scud flyin'. But *you* take some quinine,
Mag. Don't *you* go now and get down sick
like Maw."

Perhaps it was this well-meant but infelicitous reference that brought a moisture to
her dark eyes, and caused her lips to momentarily quiver. But it gave way to a quick
determined setting of her whole face as she
turned it once more to the fire, and said,
slowly :

" I reckon I 'll sleep it off, if I go to bed
now. What time does the tide fall."

" About three, unless this yer wind piles
it up on the Marsh afore then. Why ? "

" I was only wonderin' if the boat wus
safe," said Maggie, rising.

" You 'd better hoist yourself outside some
quinine, instead o' talken about those
things," said Jim, who preferred to discharge his fraternal responsibility by active
medication. " You are n't fit to read to-
night."

" Good night, Jim," she said suddenly,
stopping before him.

" Good night, Mag." He kissed her with
protecting and amiable toleration, gener-

ously referring her hot hands and feverish lips to that vague mystery of feminine complaint which man admits without indorsing.

They separated. Jim, under the stimulus of the late supposed robbery, ostentatiously fastening the doors and windows with assuring comments, calculated to inspire confidence in his sister's startled heart. Then he went to bed. He lay awake long enough to be pleasantly conscious that the wind had increased to a gale, and to be lulled again to sleep by the cosy security of the heavily timbered and tightly sealed dwelling that seemed to ride the storm like the ship it resembled. The gale swept through the piles beneath him and along the gallery as through bared spars and over wave-washed decks. The whole structure, attacked above, below, and on all sides by the fury of the wind, seemed at times to be lifted in the air. Once or twice the creaking timbers simulated the sound of opening doors and passing footsteps, and again dilated as if the gale had forced a passage through. But Jim slept on peacefully, and was at last only aroused by the brilliant sunshine staring through his window from the clear wind-swept blue arch beyond.

Dressing himself lazily, he passed into the sitting-room and proceeded to knock at his sister's door, as was his custom ; he was amazed to find it open and the room empty. Entering hurriedly, he saw that her bed was undisturbed, as if it had not been occupied, and was the more bewildered to see a note ostentatiously pinned upon the pillow, addressed in pencil, in a large school-hand, " To Jim."

Opening it impatiently, he was startled to read as follows : —

" Don't be angry, Jim dear — but it was all my fault — and I did n't tell you. I knew all about the deserter, and I gave him the clothes and things that they say he stole. It was while you was out that night, and he came and begged of me, and was mournful and hidjus to behold. I thought I was helping him, and getting our revenge on the Fort, all at the same time. Don't be mad, Jim dear, and do not be frighted fer me. I 'm going over thar to make it all right — to free *him* of stealing — to have *you* left out of it all — and take it all on myself. Don't you be a bit feared for me. I ain't skeert of the wind or of going. I 'll close reef everything, clear the creek, stretch across to Injen Island, hugg the Point, and bear up fer Logport. Dear Jim — don't get mad — but I could n't

bear this fooling of you nor *him* — and that man
being took for stealing any longer ! — Your lov-
ing sister,                              MAGGIE."

With a confused mingling of shame, anger, and sudden fear he ran out on the gallery.   The tide was well up, half the Marsh
had already vanished, and the little creek
where he had moored his skiff was now an
empty shining river.   The water was everywhere — fringing the tussocks of salt grass
with concentric curves of spume and drift,
or tumultuously tossing its white-capped
waves over the spreading expanse of the
lower bay.   The low thunder of breakers in
the farther estuary broke monotonously on
the ear.   But his eye was fascinated by a
dull shifting streak on the horizon, that,
even as he gazed, shuddered, whitened along
its whole line, and then grew ghastly gray
again.   It was the ocean bar.

## IV.

" WELL, I must say," said Cicely Preston, emphasizing the usual feminine imperative for perfectly gratuitous statement, as
she pushed back her chair from the comman-

dant's breakfast table, "I *must* really say that I don't see anything particularly heroic in doing something wrong, lying about it just to get other folks into trouble, and then rushing off to do penance in a high wind and an open boat. But she 's pretty, and wears a man's shirt and coat, and of course *that* settles anything. But why earrings and wet white stockings and slippers? And why that Gothic arch of front and a boy's hat? That 's what I simply ask ; " and the youngest daughter of Colonel Preston rose from the table, shook out the skirt of her pretty morning dress, and, placing her little thumbs in the belt of her smart waist, paused witheringly for a reply.

"You are most unfair, my child," returned Colonel Preston gravely. "Her giving food and clothes to a deserter may have been only an ordinary instinct of humanity towards a fellow-creature who appeared to be suffering, to say nothing of M'Caffrey's plausible tongue. But her periling her life to save him from an unjust accusation, and her desire to shield her brother's pride from ridicule, is altogether praiseworthy and extraordinary. And the moral influence of her kindness was strong

enough to make that scamp refuse to tell the
plain truth that might implicate her in an
indiscretion, though it saved him from state
prison."

"He knew you would n't believe him if
he had said the clothes were given to him,"
retorted Miss Cicely, "so I don't see where
the moral influence comes in. As to her
periling her life, those Marsh people are
amphibious anyway, or would be in those
clothes. And as to her motive, why, papa,
I heard you say in this very room, and
afterwards to Mr. Calvert, when you gave
him instructions, that you believed those
Culpeppers were capable of enticing away
deserters; and you forget the fuss you had
with her savage brother's lawyer about that
water front, and how you said it was such
people who kept up the irritation between
the Civil and Federal power."

The colonel coughed hurriedly. It is the
fate of all great organizers, military as well
as civil, to occasionally suffer defeat in the
family circle.

"The more reason," he said, soothingly,
"why we should correct harsh judgments
that spring from mere rumors. You should
give yourself at least the chance of over-

coming your prejudices, my child. Remember, too, that she is now the guest of the Fort."

"And she chooses to stay with Mrs. Bromley! I'm sure it's quite enough for you and mamma to do duty — and Emily, who wants to know why Mr. Calvert raves so about her — without *my* going over there to stare."

Colonel Preston shook his head reproachfully, but eventually retired, leaving the field to the enemy. The enemy, a little pink in the cheeks, slightly tossed the delicate rings of its blonde crest, settled its skirts again at the piano, but after turning over the leaves of its music book, rose, and walked pettishly to the window.

But here a spectacle presented itself that for a moment dismissed all other thoughts from the girl's rebellious mind.

Not a dozen yards away, on the wind-swept parade, a handsome young fellow, apparently halted by the sentry, had impetuously turned upon him in an attitude of indignant and haughty surprise. To the quick fancy of the girl it seemed as if some disguised rustic god had been startled by the challenge of a mortal. Under an oilskin hat, like the *petasus* of Hermes, pushed back from his white forehead, crisp black curls were knotted around a head whose beardless face was perfect as a cameo cutting. In the close-fitting blue woolen jersey under his open jacket the clear outlines and youthful grace of his upper figure were revealed as clearly as in a statue. Long fishing-boots reaching to his thighs scarcely concealed the symmetry of his lower limbs. Cricket and lawn-tennis, knickerbockers and flannels had not at that period familiarized the female eye to unfettered masculine outline, and Cicely Preston, accustomed to the artificial smartness and regularity of uniform, was perhaps the more impressed by the stranger's lawless grace.

The sentry had repeated his challenge ; an angry flush was deepening on the intruder's cheek. At this critical moment Cicely threw open the French windows and stepped upon the veranda.

The sentry saluted the familiar little figure of his colonel's daughter with an explanatory glance at the stranger. The young fellow looked up — and the god became human.

" I'm looking for my sister," he said, half awkwardly, half defiantly ; " she's here, somewhere."

" Yes — and perfectly safe, Mr. Culpepper, I think," said the arch-hypocrite with dazzling sweetness; "and we 're all so delighted. And so brave and plucky and skillful in her to come all that way — and for such a purpose."

" Then — you know — all about it " — stammered Jim, more relieved than he had imagined — " and that I " —

" That you were quite ignorant of your sister helping the deserter. Oh yes, of course," said Cicely, with bewildering promptitude. " You see, Mr. Culpepper, we girls are *so* foolish. I dare say *I* should have done the same thing in her place, only *I* should never have had the courage to do what she did afterwards. You really must forgive her. But won't you come in — *do*." She stepped back, holding the window open with the half-coaxing air of a spoiled child. " This way is quickest. *Do* come." As he still hesitated, glancing from her to the house, she added, with a demure little laugh, " Oh, I forget — this is Colonel Preston's quarters, and I 'm his daughter."

And this dainty little fairy, so natural in manner, so tasteful in attire, was one of the artificial over-dressed creatures that his sister

had inveighed against so bitterly! Was
Maggie really to be trusted? This new
revelation coming so soon after the episode
of the deserter staggered him. Nevertheless he hesitated, looking up with a certain
boyish timidity into Cicely's dangerous
eyes.

"Is — is — my sister there?"

"I'm expecting her with my mother
every moment," responded this youthful but
ingenious diplomatist sweetly; "she might
be here now; but," she added with a sudden
heart-broken flash of sympathy, "I know
*how* anxious you both must be. *I'll* take
you to her now. Only one moment, please."
The opportunity of leading this handsome
savage as it were in chains across the parade,
before everybody, her father, her mother,
her sister, and *his* — was not to be lost. She
larted into the house, and reappeared with
the daintiest imaginable straw hat on the
side of her head, and demurely took her
place at his side. "It's only over there, at
Major Bromley's," she said, pointing to one
of the vine-clad cottage quarters; but you
are a stranger here, you know, and might
get lost."

Alas! he was already that. For keeping

step with those fairy-like slippers, brushing
awkwardly against that fresh and pretty
skirt, and feeling the caress of the soft folds ;
looking down upon the brim of that berib-
boned little hat, and more often meeting the
upturned blue eyes beneath it, Jim was suddenly struck with a terrible conviction of his
own contrasting coarseness and deficiencies.
How hideous those oiled canvas fishing-
trousers and pilot jacket looked beside this
perfectly fitted and delicately gowned girl!
He loathed his collar, his jersey, his turned-
back sou'wester, even his height, which
seemed to hulk beside her — everything, in
short, that the girl had recently admired.
By the time that they had reached Major
Bromley's door he had so far succumbed to
the fair enchantress and realized her ambition of a triumphant procession, that when
she ushered him into the presence of half a
dozen ladies and gentlemen he scarcely recognized his sister as the centre of attraction,
or knew that Miss Cicely's effusive greeting
of Maggie was her first one. "I knew he
was dying to see you after all you had *both*
passed through, and I brought him straight
here," said the diminutive Machiavelli, meeting the astonished gaze of her father and the

curious eyes of her sister with perfect calmness, while Maggie, full of gratitude and admiration of her handsome brother, forgot his momentary obliviousness, and returned her greeting warmly.   Nevertheless, there was a slight movement of reserve among the gentlemen at the unlooked-for irruption of this sunburnt Adonis, until Calvert, disengaging himself from Maggie's side, came forward with his usual frank imperturbability and quiet tact, and claimed Jim as his friend and honored guest.

It then came out with that unostentatious simplicity which characterized the brother and sister, and was their secure claim to perfect equality with their entertainers, that Jim, on discovering his sister's absence, and fearing that she might be carried by the current towards the bar, had actually *swum the estuary* to Indian Island, and in an ordinary Indian canoe had braved the same tempestuous passage she had taken a few hours before.   Cicely, listening to this recital with rapt attention, nevertheless managed to convey the impression of having fully expected it from the first.   " Of course he 'd have come here ; if she 'd only waited," she said, *sotto voce*, to her sister Emily.

"He's certainly the handsomer of the two," responded that young lady.

"Of course," returned Cicely, with a superior air, "don't you see she *copies* him."

Not that this private criticism prevented either from vying with the younger officers in their attentions to Maggie, with perhaps the addition of an open eulogy of her handsome brother, more or less invidious in comparison to the officers. "I suppose it's an active out-of-door life gives him that perfect grace and freedom," said Emily, with a slight sneer at the smartly belted Calvert. "Yes; and he don't drink or keep late hours," responded Cicely significantly. "His sister says they always retire before ten o'clock, and that although his father left him some valuable whiskey he seldom takes a drop of it." "Therein," gravely concluded Captain Kirby, "lies *our* salvation. If, after such a confession, Calvert does n't make the most of his acquaintance with young Culpepper to remove that whiskey from his path and bring it here, he's not the man I take him for."

Indeed, for the moment it seemed as if he was not. During the next three or four days, in which Colonel Preston had insisted

upon detaining his guests, Calvert touched
no liquor, evaded the evening poker parties
at quarters, and even prevailed upon some
of his brother officers to give them up for
the more general entertainment of the ladies.
Colonel Preston was politician enough to
avail himself of the popularity of Maggie's
adventure to invite some of the Logport people to assist him in honoring their neighbor.
Not only was the old feud between the Fort
and the people thus bridged over, but there
was no doubt that the discipline of the Fort
had been strengthened by Maggie's extravagant reputation as a mediator among the
disaffected rank and file. Whatever characteristic license the grateful Dennis M'Caffrey — let off with a nominal punishment —
may have taken in his praise of the " Quane
of the Marshes," it is certain that the men
worshiped her, and that the band pathetically begged permission to serenade her the
last night of her stay.

At the end of that time, with a dozen
invitations, a dozen appointments, a dozen
vows of eternal friendship, much hand-shak-
ing, and accompanied by a number of the officers to their boat, Maggie and Jim departed.
They talked but little on their way home ;

by some tacit understanding they did not
discuss those projects, only recalling certain
scenes and incidents of their visit. By the
time they had reached the little creek the silence and nervous apathy which usually follow excitement in the young seemed to have
fallen upon them. It was not until after
their quiet frugal supper that, seated beside
the fire, Jim looked up somewhat self-con-
sciously in his sister's grave and thoughtful
face.

"Say, Mag, what was that idea o' yours
about selling some land, and taking a house
at Logport?"

Maggie looked up, and said passively,
"Oh, *that* idea?"

"Yes."

"Why?"

"Well," said Jim somewhat awkwardly,
"it *could* be done, you know. I'm willin'."

As she did not immediately reply, he continued uneasily, "Miss Preston says we kin
get a nice little house that is near the Fort,
until we want to build."

"Oh, then you *have* talked about it?"

"Yes — that is — why, what are ye thinkin'
of, Mag? Was n't it *your* idea all along?"
he said, suddenly facing her with querulous

embarrassment. They had been sitting in their usual evening attitudes of Assyrian frieze profile, with even more than the usual Assyrian frieze similarity of feature.

"Yes; but, Jim dear, do you think it the best thing for — for us to do?" said Maggie, with half-frightened gravity.

At this sudden and startling exhibition of female inconsistency and inconsequence, Jim was for a moment speechless. Then he recovered himself, volubly, aggrievedly, and on his legs. What *did* she mean? Was he to give up understanding girls — or was it their sole vocation in life to impede masculine processes and shipwreck masculine conclusions? Here, after all she said the other night, after they had nearly "quo'lled" over her "set idees," after she'd "gone over all that foolishness about Jael and Sisera — and there wasn't any use for it — after she'd let him run on to them officers all he was goin' to do — nay, after *she* herself, for he had heard her, had talked to Calvert about it, she wanted to know *now* if it was best." He looked at the floor and the ceiling, as if expecting the tongued and grooved planks to cry out at this crowning enormity.

The cause of it had resumed her sad gaze

at the fire. Presently, without turning her head, she reached up her long, graceful arm, and clasping her brother's neck, brought his face down in profile with her own, cheek against cheek, until they looked like the double outlines of a medallion. Then she said — to the fire :

"Jim, do you think she 's pretty?"

"Who?" said Jim, albeit his color had already answered the question.

"You know *who*. Do you like her?"

Jim here vaguely murmured to the fire that he thought her " kinder nice," and that she dressed mighty purty. "Ye know, Mag," he said with patronizing effusion, "you oughter get some gownds like hers."

"That would n't make me like her," said Maggie gravely.

"I don't know about that," said Jim politely, but with an appalling hopelessness of tone. After a pause he added slyly, "'Pears to me *somebody else* thought somebody else mighty purty — eh?"

To his discomfiture she did not solicit further information. After a pause he continued, still more archly :

"Do you like *him*, Mag?"

"I think he 's a perfect gentleman," she said calmly.

He turned his eyes quickly from the glowing fire to her face. The cheek that had been resting against his own was as cool as the night wind that came through the open door, and the whole face was as fixed and tranquil as the upper stars.

## V.

For a year the tide had ebbed and flowed on the Dedlow Marsh unheeded before the sealed and sightless windows of the "Kingfisher's Nest." Since the young birds had flown to Logport, even the Indian caretakers had abandoned the piled dwelling for their old nomadic haunts in the "bresh." The high spring tide had again made its annual visit to the little cemetery of drift-wood, and, as if recognizing another wreck in the deserted home, had hung a few memorial offerings on the blackened piles, softly laid a garland of grayish drift before it, and then sobbed itself out in the salt grass.

From time to time the faint echoes of the Culpeppers' life at Logport reached the upland, and the few neighbors who had only known them by hearsay shook their heads

over the extravagance they as yet only knew
by report. But it was in the dead ebb of
the tide and the waning daylight that the
feathered tenants of the Marsh seemed to
voice dismal prophecies of the ruin of their
old master and mistress, and to give themselves up to gloomiest lamentation and querulous foreboding. Whether the traditional
" bird of the air " had entrusted his secret
to a few ornithological friends, or whether
from a natural disposition to take gloomy
views of life, it was certain that at this hour
the vocal expression of the Marsh was hopeless and despairing. It was then that a dejected plover, addressing a mocking crew of
sandpipers on a floating log, seemed to be-
wail the fortune that was being swallowed
up by the riotous living and gambling debts
of Jim. It was then that the querulous crane
rose, and testily protested against the selling
of his favorite haunt in the sandy peninsula,
which only six months of Jim's excesses had
made imperative. It was then that a mournful curlew, who, with the preface that he had
always been really expecting it, reiterated
the story that Jim had been seen more than
once staggering home with nervous hands
and sodden features from a debauch with the

younger officers ; it was the same desponding fowl who knew that Maggie's eyes had
more than once filled with tears at Jim's
failings, and had already grown more hollow
with many watchings. It was a flock of
wrangling teal that screamingly discussed
the small scandals, jealous heart-burnings,
and curious backbitings that had attended
Maggie's advent into society. It was the
high-flying brent who, knowing how the sensitive girl, made keenly conscious at every
turn of her defective training and ingenuous
ignorance, had often watched their evening
flight with longing gaze, now " honked "
dismally at the recollection. It was at this
hour and season that the usual vague lament-
ings of Dedlow Marsh seemed to find at last
a preordained expression. And it was at
such a time, when light and water were both
fading, and the blackness of the Marsh was
once more reasserting itself, that a small
boat was creeping along one of the tortuous
inlets, at times half hiding behind the bank
like a wounded bird. As it slowly penetrated inland it seemed to be impelled by its
solitary occupant in a hesitating uncertain
way, as if to escape observation rather than
as if directed to any positive bourn. Stop-

ping beside a bank of reeds at last, the figure rose stoopingly, and drew a gun from between its feet and the bottom of the boat. As the light fell upon its face, it could be seen that it was James Culpepper! James Culpepper! hardly recognizable in the swollen features, bloodshot eyes, and tremulous hands of that ruined figure! James Culpepper, only retaining a single trace of his former self in his look of set and passionate purpose! And that purpose was to kill himself — to be found dead, as his father had been before him — in an open boat, adrift upon the Marsh!

It was not the outcome of a sudden fancy. The idea had first come to him in a taunting allusion from the drunken lips of one of his ruder companions, for which he had stricken the offender to the earth. It had since haunted his waking hours of remorse and hopeless fatuity; it had seemed to be the one relief and atonement he could make his devoted sister; and, more fatuous than all, it seemed to the miserable boy the one revenge he would take upon the faithless coquette, who for a year had played with his simplicity, and had helped to drive him to the distraction of cards and drink. Only

that morning Colonel Preston had forbidden
him the house; and now it seemed to him
the end had come.   He raised his distorted
face above the reedy bank for a last tremulous and half-frightened glance at the landscape he was leaving forever.   A glint in the
western sky lit up the front of his deserted
dwelling in the distance, abreast of which
the windings of the inlet had unwittingly
led him.   As he looked he started, and involuntarily dropped into a crouching attitude.   For, to his superstitious terror, the
sealed windows of his old home were open,
the bright panes were glittering with the
fading light, and on the outer gallery the
familiar figure of his sister stood, as of old,
awaiting his return!   Was he really going
mad, or had this last vision of his former
youth been purposely vouchsafed him?

But, even as he gazed, the appearance of
another figure in the landscape beyond the
house proved the reality of his vision, and as
suddenly distracted him from all else.   For
it was the apparition of a man on horseback
approaching the house from the upland;
and even at that distance he recognized
its well-known outlines.   It was Calvert!
Calvert the traitor!   Calvert, the man whom

he had long suspected as being the secret
lover and destined husband of Cicely Preston! Calvert, who had deceived him with
his calm equanimity and his affected preference for Maggie, to conceal his deliberate
understanding with Cicely. What was he
doing here? Was he a double traitor, and
now trying to deceive *her* — as he had him?
And Maggie here! This sudden return —
this preconcerted meeting. It was infamy!

For a moment he remained stupefied, and
then, with a mechanical instinct, plunged his
head and face in the lazy-flowing water, and
then once again rose cool and collected. The
half-mad distraction of his previous resolve
had given way to another, more deliberate,
but not less desperate determination. He
knew now *why* he came there — *why* he had
brought his gun — why his boat had stopped
when it did!

Lying flat in the bottom, he tore away
fragments of the crumbling bank to fill his
frail craft, until he had sunk it to the gun-
wale, and below the low level of the Marsh.
Then, using his hands as noiseless paddles,
he propelled this rude imitation of a floating log slowly past the line of vision, until
the tongue of bushes had hidden him from

view. With a rapid glance at the darkening
flat, he then seized his gun, and springing
to the spongy bank, half crouching half
crawling through reeds and tussocks, he
made his way to the brush. A foot and eye
less experienced would have plunged its
owner helpless in the black quagmire. At
one edge of the thicket he heard hoofs tram-
pling the dried twigs. Calvert's horse was
already there, tied to a skirting alder.

He ran to the house, but, instead of attracting attention by ascending the creaking
steps, made his way to the piles below the
rear gallery and climbed to it noiselessly.
It was the spot where the deserter had ascended a year ago, and, like him, he could
see and hear all that passed distinctly. Calvert stood near the open door as if depart-
ing. Maggie stood between him and the
window, her face in shadow, her hands
clasped tightly behind her. A profound
sadness, partly of the dying day and waning
light, and partly of some vague expiration
of their own sorrow, seemed to encompass
them. Without knowing why, a strange
trembling took the place of James Culpepper's fierce determination, and a film of
moisture stole across his staring eyes.

" When I tell you that I believe all this will pass, and that you will still win your brother back to you," said Calvert's sad but clear voice, " I will tell you why — although, perhaps, it is only a part of that confidence you command me to withhold. When I first saw you, I myself had fallen into like dissolute habits ; less excusable than he, for I had some experience of the world and its follies. When I met *you*, and fell under the influence of your pure, simple, and healthy life ; when I saw that isolation, monotony, misunderstanding, even the sense of superiority to one's surroundings could be lived down and triumphed over, without vulgar distractions or pitiful ambitions ; when I learned to love you — hear me out, Miss Culpepper, I beg you — you saved *me* — I, who was nothing to you, even as I honestly believe you will still save your brother, whom you love."

" How do you know I did n't *ruin* him ? " she said, turning upon him bitterly. " How do you know that it was n't to get rid of *our* monotony, *our* solitude that I drove him to this vulgar distraction, this pitiful — yes, you were right — pitiful ambition ? "

" Because it is n't your real nature," he said quietly.

" My real nature," she repeated with a half savage vehemence that seemed to be goaded from her by his very gentleness, " my real nature ! What did *he* — what do *you* know of it ? — My real nature ! — I 'll tell you what it was," she went on passionately. " It was to be revenged on you all for your cruelty, your heartlessness, your wickedness to me and mine in the past. It was to pay you off for your slanders of my dead father — for the selfishness that left me and Jim alone with his dead body on the Marsh. That was what sent me to Logport — to get even with you — to — to fool and flaunt you ! There, you have it now ! And now that God has punished me for it by crushing my brother — you — you expect me to let you crush *me* too."

" But," he said eagerly, advancing toward her, " you are wronging me — you are wronging yourself, cruelly."

" Stop," she said, stepping back, with her hands still locked behind her. " Stay where you are. There ! That 's enough ! " She drew herself up and let her hands fall at her side. " Now, let us speak of Jim," she said coldly.

Without seeming to hear her, he regarded her for the first time with hopeless sadness.

"Why did you let my brother believe you were his rival with Cicely Preston?" she asked impatiently.

"Because I could not undeceive him without telling him I hopelessly loved his sister. You are proud, Miss Culpepper," he said, with the first tinge of bitterness in his even voice. "Can you not understand that others may be proud too?"

"No," she said bluntly; "it is not pride but weakness. You could have told him what you knew to be true: that there could be nothing in common between her folk and such savages as we; that there was a gulf as wide as that Marsh and as black between our natures, our training and theirs, and even if they came to us across it, now and then, to suit their pleasure, light and easy as that tide — it was still there to some day ground and swamp them! And if he doubted it, you had only to tell him your own story. You had only to tell him what you have just told me — that you yourself, an officer and a gentleman, thought you loved me, a vulgar, uneducated, savage girl, and that I, kinder to you than you to me or him, made you take it back across that tide, because I could n't let you link your life with me, and drag you in the mire."

" You need not have said that, Miss Culpepper," returned Calvert with the same gentle smile, " to prove that I am your inferior
in all but one thing."

" And that ? " she said quickly.

" Is my love."

His gentle face was as set now as her own
as he moved back slowly towards the door.
There he paused.

" You tell me to speak of Jim, and Jim
only. Then hear me. I believe that Miss
Preston cares for him as far as lies in her
young and giddy nature. I could not, therefore, have crushed *his* hope without deceiving him, for there are as cruel deceits
prompted by what we call reason as by our
love. If you think that a knowledge of this
plain truth would help to save him, I beg
you to be kinder to him than you have been
to me, — or even, let me dare to hope, to
*yourself.*"

He slowly crossed the threshold, still holding his cap lightly in his hand.

" When I tell you that I am going away
to-morrow on a leave of absence, and that in
all probability we may not meet again, you
will not misunderstand why I add my prayer
to the message your friends in Logport

charged me with. They beg that you will give up your idea of returning here, and come back to them. Believe me, you have made yourself loved and respected there, in spite — I beg pardon — perhaps I should say *because* of your pride. Good-night and good-bye."

For a single instant she turned her set face to the window with a sudden convulsive movement, as if she would have called him back, but at the same moment the opposite door creaked and her brother slipped into the room. Whether a quick memory of the deserter's entrance at that door a year ago had crossed her mind, whether there was some strange suggestion in his mud-stained garments and weak deprecating smile, or whether it was the outcome of some desperate struggle within her, there was that in her face that changed his smile into a frightened cry for pardon, as he ran and fell on his knees at her feet. But even as he did so her stern look vanished, and with her arm around him she bent over him and mingled her tears with his.

"I heard it all, Mag dearest! All! Forgive me! I have been crazy! — wild! — I will reform! — I will be better! I will never disgrace you again, Mag! Never, never! I swear it!"

She reached down and kissed him. After a pause, a weak boyish smile struggled into his face.

"You heard what he said of *her*, Mag. Do you think it might be true?"

She lifted the damp curls from his forehead with a sad half-maternal smile, but did not reply.

"And Mag, dear, don't you think *you* were a little — just a little — hard on *him?* No! Don't look at me that way, for God's sake! There, I did n't mean anything. Of course you knew best. There, Maggie dear, look up. Hark there! Listen, Mag, do!"

They lifted their eyes to the dim distance seen through the open door. Borne on the fading light, and seeming to fall and die with it over marsh and river, came the last notes of the bugle from the Fort.

"There! Don't you remember what you used to say, Mag?"

The look that had frightened him had quite left her face now.

"Yes," she smiled, laying her cold cheek beside his softly. "Oh yes! It was something that came and went, 'Like a song' — 'Like a song.'"

# A KNIGHT-ERRANT OF THE FOOT-HILLS.

————◆————

## I.

As Father Felipe slowly toiled up the dusty road towards the Rancho of the Blessed Innocents, he more than once stopped under the shadow of a sycamore to rest his somewhat lazy mule and to compose his own perplexed thoughts by a few snatches from his breviary. For the good padre had some reason to be troubled. The invasion of Gentile Americans that followed the gold discovery of three years before had not confined itself to the plains of the Sacramento, but stragglers had already found their way to the Santa Cruz Valley, and the seclusion of even the mission itself was threatened. It was true that they had not brought their heathen engines to disembowel the earth in search of gold, but it was rumored that they had already speculated upon the agricultural productiveness of the land, and had espied

" the fatness thereof." As he reached the higher plateau he could see the afternoon sea-fog — presently to obliterate the fair prospect — already pulling through the gaps in the Coast Range, and on a nearer slope — no less ominously — the smoke of a recent but more permanently destructive Yankee saw-mill was slowly drifting towards the valley.

" Get up, beast ! " said the father, digging his heels into the comfortable flanks of his mule with some human impatience, " or art *thou*, too, a lazy renegade ? Thinkest thou, besotted one, that the heretic will spare thee more work than the Holy Church."

The mule, thus apostrophized in ear and flesh, shook its head obstinately as if the question was by no means clear to its mind, but nevertheless started into a little trot, which presently brought it to the low adobe wall of the courtyard of " The Innocents," and entered the gate. A few lounging *peons* in the shadow of an archway took off their broad-brimmed hats and made way for the padre, and a half dozen equally listless *vaqueros* helped him to alight. Accustomed as he was to the indolence and superfluity of his host's retainers, to-day it nevertheless seemed to strike some note of irritation in his breast.

A stout, middle-aged woman of ungirt waist and beshawled head and shoulders appeared at the gateway as if awaiting him. After a formal salutation she drew him aside into an inner passage.

"He is away again, your Reverence," she said.

"Ah — always the same?"

"Yes, your Reverence — and this time to 'a meeting' of the heretics at their *pueblo*, at Jonesville — where they will ask him of his land for a road."

"At a *meeting?*" echoed the priest uneasily.

"Ah yes! a meeting — where Tiburcio says they shout and spit on the ground, your Reverence, and only one has a chair and him they call a 'chairman' because of it, and yet he sits not but shouts and spits even as the others and keeps up a tapping with a hammer like a very *pico*. And there it is they are ever 'resolving' that which is not, and consider it even as done."

"Then he is still the same," said the priest gloomily, as the woman paused for breath.

"Only more so, your Reverence, for he reads nought but the newspaper of the *Americanos* that is brought in the ship, the 'New York 'errald' — and recites to himself the orations of their legislators. Ah! it was an evil day when the shipwrecked American sailor taught him his uncouth tongue, which, as your Reverence knows, is only fit for beasts and heathen incantation."

"Pray Heaven *that* were all he learned of him," said the priest hastily, "for I have great fear that this sailor was little better than an atheist and an emissary from Satan. But where are these newspapers and the fantasies of *publicita* that fill his mind? I would see them, my daughter."

"You shall, your Reverence, and more too," she replied eagerly, leading the way along the passage to a grated door which opened upon a small cell-like apartment, whose scant light and less air came through the deeply embayed windows in the outer wall. "Here is his *estudio*."

In spite of this open invitation, the padre entered with that air of furtive and minute inspection common to his order. His glance fell upon a rude surveyor's plan of the adjacent embryo town of Jonesville hanging on the wall, which he contemplated with a cold disfavor that even included the highly colored vignette of the projected Jonesville Hotel in the left-hand corner. He then passed to a supervisor's notice hanging near it, which he examined with a suspicion heightened by that uneasiness common to mere worldly humanity when opposed to an unknown and unfamiliar language. But an exclamation broke from his lips when he confronted an election placard immediately below it. It was printed in Spanish and English, and Father Felipe had no difficulty in reading the announcement that " Don José Sepulvida would preside at a meeting of the Board of Education in Jonesville as one of the trustees."

" This is madness," said the padre.

Observing that Dona Maria was at the moment preoccupied in examining the pictorial pages of an illustrated American weekly which had hitherto escaped his eyes, he took it gently from her hand.

" Pardon, your Reverence," she said with slightly acidulous deprecation, " but thanks to the Blessed Virgin and your Reverence's teaching, the text is but gibberish to me and I did but glance at the pictures."

"Much evil may come in with the eye," said the priest sententiously, "as I will presently show thee. We have here," he continued, pointing to an illustration of certain college athletic sports, "a number of youthful cavaliers posturing and capering in a partly nude condition before a number of shameless women, who emulate the saturnalia of heathen Rome by waving their handkerchiefs. We have here a companion picture," he said, indicating an illustration of gymnastic exercises by the students of a female academy at "Commencement," "in which, as thou seest, even the aged of both sexes unblushingly assist as spectators with every expression of immodest satisfaction."

"Have they no bull-fights or other seemly recreation that they must indulge in such wantonness?" asked Dona Maria indignantly, gazing, however, somewhat curiously at the baleful representations.

"Of all that, my daughter, has their pampered civilization long since wearied," returned the good padre, "for see, this is what they consider a moral and even a religious ceremony." He turned to an illustration of a woman's rights convention; "observe with what rapt attention the audience of that

heathen temple watch the inspired ravings
of that elderly priestess on the dais. It is
even this kind of sacrilegious performance
that I am told thy nephew Don José ex-
pounds and defends."

"May the blessed saints preserve us;
where will it lead to?" murmured the horri-
fied Dona Maria.

"I will show thee," said Father Felipe,
briskly turning the pages with the same
lofty ignoring of the text until he came to a
representation of a labor procession. "There
is one of their periodic revolutions unhappily
not unknown even in Mexico. Thou per-
ceivest those complacent artisans marching
with implements of their craft, accompanied
by the military, in the presence of their own
stricken masters. Here we see only another
instance of the instability of all communities
that are not founded on the principles of the
Holy Church."

"And what is to be done with my
nephew?"

The good father's brow darkened with the
gloomy religious zeal of two centuries ago.
"We must have a council of the family, the
alcalde, and the archbishop, at *once*," he said
ominously. To the mere heretical observer

the conclusion might have seemed lame and impotent, but it was as near the Holy Inquisition as the year of grace 1852 could offer.

A few days after this colloquy the unsuspecting subject of it, Don José Sepulvida, was sitting alone in the same apartment. The fading glow of the western sky, through the deep embrasured windows, lit up his rapt and meditative face. He was a young man of apparently twenty-five, with a colorless satin complexion, dark eyes alternating between melancholy and restless energy, a narrow high forehead, long straight hair, and a lightly penciled moustache. He was said to resemble the well-known portrait of the Marquis of Monterey in the mission church, a face that was alleged to leave a deep and lasting impression upon the observers. It was undoubtedly owing to this quality during a brief visit of the famous viceroy to a remote and married ancestress of Don José at Leon that the singular resemblance may be attributed.

A heavy and hesitating step along the passage stopped before the grating. Looking up, Don José beheld to his astonishment the slightly inflamed face of Roberto, a vagabond

American whom he had lately taken into his employment.

Roberto, a polite translation of " Bob the Bucker," cleaned out at a monte-bank in Santa Cruz, penniless and profligate, had sold his mustang to Don José and recklessly thrown himself in with the bargain. Touched by the rascal's extravagance, the quality of the mare, and observing that Bob's habits had not yet affected his seat in the saddle, but rather lent a demoniac vigor to his chase of wild cattle, Don José had retained rider and horse in his service as *vaquero.*

Bucking Bob, observing that his employer was alone, coolly opened the door without ceremony, shut it softly behind him, and then closed the wooden shutter of the grating. Don José surveyed him with mild surprise and dignified composure. The man appeared perfectly sober, — it was a peculiarity of his dissipated habits that, when not actually raving with drink, he was singularly shrewd and practical.

" Look yer, Don Kosay," he began in a brusque but guarded voice, " you and me is pards. When ye picked me and the mare up and set us on our legs again in this yer ranch, I allowed I 'd tie to ye whenever you was in trouble — and wanted me. And I reckon that's what's the matter now. For from what I see and hear on every side, although you're the boss of this consarn, you're surrounded by a gang of spies and traitors. Your comings and goings, your ins and outs, is dogged and followed and blown upon. The folks you trust is playing it on ye. It ain't for me to say why or wherefore — what's their rights and what's yourn — but I've come to tell ye that if you don't get up and get outer this ranch them d——d priests and your own flesh and blood — your aunts and your uncles and your cousins, will have you chucked outer your property, and run into a lunatic asylum."

"Me — Don José Sepulvida — a lunatico! You are yourself crazy of drink, friend Roberto."

"Yes," said Roberto grimly, "but that kind ain't *illegal*, while your makin' ducks and drakes of your property and going into 'Merikin ideas and 'Merikin speculations they reckon is. And speakin' on the square, it ain't *nat'ral*."

Don José sprang to his feet and began to pace up and down his cell-like study. "Ah, I remember now," he muttered, "I begin to comprehend: Father Felipe's homilies and discourses! My aunt's too affectionate care! My cousin's discreet consideration! The prompt attention of my servants! I see it all! And you," he said, suddenly facing Roberto, "why come you to tell me this?"

"Well, boss," said the American dryly, "I reckoned to stand by you."

"Ah," said Don José, visibly affected. "Good Roberto, come hither, child, you may kiss my hand."

"If! it's all the same to you, Don Kosay, — *that* kin slide."

"Ah, if — yes," said Don José, meditatively putting his hand to his forehead, "miserable that I am! — I remembered not you were *Americano.* Pardon, my friend — embrace me — *Conpañero y Amigo.*"

With characteristic gravity he reclined for a moment upon Robert's astonished breast. Then recovering himself with equal gravity he paused, lifted his hand with gentle warning, marched to a recess in the corner, unhooked a rapier hanging from the wall, and turned to his companion.

"We will defend ourselves, friend Roberto. It is the sword of the *Comandante* — my ancestor. The blade is of Toledo."

" An ordinary six-shooter of Colt's would lay over that," said Roberto grimly — " but that ain't your game just now, Don Kosay. You must get up and get, and at once. You must *vamose* the ranch afore they lay hold of you and have you up before the alcalde. Once away from here, they dare n't follow you where there's 'Merikin law, and when you kin fight 'em in the square."

" Good," said Don José with melancholy preciseness. " You are wise, friend Roberto. We may fight them later, as you say — on the square, or in the open Plaza. And you, *camarado, you* shall go with me — you and your mare."

Sincere as the American had been in his offer of service, he was somewhat staggered at this imperative command. But only for a moment. " Well," he said lazily, " I don't care if I do."

" But," said Don José with increased gravity, " you *shall* care, friend Roberto. We shall make an alliance, an union. It is true, my brother, you drink of whiskey, and at such times are even as a madman. It has been recounted to me that it was necessary to your existence that you are a lunatic three days of the week. Who knows? I myself, though I drink not of *aguardiente*, am accused of fantasies for all time. Necessary it becomes therefore that we should go *together*. My fantasies and speculations cannot injure you, my brother; your whiskey shall not empoison me. We shall go together in the great world of your American ideas of which I am much inflamed. We shall together breathe as one the spirit of Progress and Liberty. We shall be even as neophytes making of ourselves Apostles of Truth. I absolve and renounce myself henceforth of my family. I shall take to myself the sister and the brother, the aunt and the uncle, as we proceed. I devote myself to humanity alone. I devote *you*, my friend, and the mare — though happily she has not a Christian soul — to this glorious mission."

The few level last rays of light lit up a faint enthusiasm in the face of Don José, but without altering his imperturbable gravity. The *vaquero* eyed him curiously and half doubtfully.

"We will go to-morrow," resumed Don José with solemn decision, "for it is Wednesday. It was a Sunday that thou didst ride the mare up the steps of the Fonda and demanded that thy liquor should be served to thee in a pail. I remember it, for the landlord of the Fonda claimed twenty *pesos* for damage and the kissing of his wife. Therefore, by computation, good Roberto, thou shouldst be sober until Friday, and we shall have two clear days to fly before thy madness again seizes thee."

" They kin say what they like, Don Kosay, but *your* head is level," returned the unabashed American, grasping Don José's hand. " All right, then. *Hasta mañana*, as your folks say."

" Hasta mañana," repeated Don José gravely.

At daybreak next morning, while slumber still weighted the lazy eyelids of " the Blessed Innocents," Don José Sepulvida and his trusty squire Roberto, otherwise known as " Bucking Bob," rode forth unnoticed from the corral.

## II.

THREE days had passed. At the close of the third, Don José was seated in a cosy private apartment of the San Mateo Hotel, where they had halted for an arranged inter-

view with his lawyer before reaching San
Francisco. From his window he could see
the surrounding park-like avenues of oaks
and the level white high road, now and then
clouded with the dust of passing teams. But
his eyes were persistently fixed upon a small
copy of the American Constitution before
him. Suddenly there was a quick rap on
his door, and before he could reply to it a
man brusquely entered.

Don José raised his head slowly, and recognized the landlord. But the intruder, apparently awed by the gentle, grave, and
studious figure before him, fell back for an
instant in an attitude of surly apology.

" Enter freely, my good Jenkinson," said
Don José, with a quiet courtesy that had all
the effect of irony. " The apartment, such
as it is, is at your disposition. It is even
yours, as is the house."

" Well, I 'm darned if I know as it is,"
said the landlord, recovering himself roughly,
" and that 's jest what 's the matter. Yer 's
that man of yours smashing things right and
left in the bar-room and chuckin' my waiters
through the window."

" Softly, softly, good Jenkinson," said
Don José, putting a mark in the pages of

the volume before him. "It is necessary first that I should correct your speech. He is not my '*man*,' which I comprehend to mean a slave, a hireling, a thing obnoxious to the great American nation which *I* admire and to which *he* belongs. Therefore, good Jenkinson, say 'friend,' 'companion,' 'guide,' 'philosopher,' if you will. As to the rest, it is of no doubt as you relate. I myself have heard the breakings of glass and small dishes as I sit here; three times I have seen your waiters projected into the road with much violence and confusion. To myself I have then said, even as I say to you, good Jenkinson, 'Patience, patience, the end is not far.' In four hours," continued Don José, holding up four fingers, " he shall make a finish. Until then, not."

" Well, I 'm d——d," ejaculated Jenkinson, gasping for breath in his indignation.

" Nay, excellent Jenkinson, not dam-ned but of a possibility dam-*aged*. That I shall repay when he have make a finish."

" But, darn it all," broke in the landlord angrily.

" Ah," said Don José gravely, "you would be paid before! Good; for how much shall you value *all* you have in your bar? "

Don José's imperturbability evidently shook the landlord's faith in the soundness of his own position. He looked at his guest critically and audaciously.

" It cost me two hundred dollars to fit it up," he said curtly.

Don José rose, and, taking a buckskin purse from his saddle-bag, counted out four slugs [1] and handed them to the stupefied Jenkinson. The next moment, however, his host recovered himself, and casting the slugs back on the little table, brought his fist down with an emphasis that made them dance.

" But, look yer — suppose I want this thing stopped — you hear me — *stopped* — now."

" That would be interfering with the liberty of the subject, my good Jenkinson — which God forbid ! " said Don José calmly. " Moreover, it is the custom of the *Americanos* — a habit of my friend Roberto — a necessity of his existence — and so recognized of his friends. Patience and courage, Señor Jenkinson. Stay — ah, I comprehend ! you have — of a possibility — a wife ? "

---

[1] Hexagonal gold pieces valued at $50 each, issued by a private firm as coin in the early days.

"No, I'm a widower," said Jenkinson sharply.

"Then I congratulate you. My friend Roberto would have kissed her. It is also of his habit. Truly you have escaped much. I embrace you, Jenkinson."

He threw his arms gravely around Jenkinson, in whose astounded face at last an expression of dry humor faintly dawned. After a moment's survey of Don José's impenetrable gravity, he coolly gathered up the gold coins, and saying that he would assess the damages and return the difference, he left the room as abruptly as he had entered it.

But Don José was not destined to remain long in peaceful study of the American Constitution. He had barely taken up the book again and renewed his serious contemplation of its excellences when there was another knock at his door. This time, in obedience to his invitation to enter, the new visitor approached with more deliberation and a certain formality.

He was a young man of apparently the same age as Don José, handsomely dressed, and of a quiet self-possession and gravity almost equal to his host's.

"I believe I am addressing Don José

Sepulvida," he said with a familiar yet courteous inclination of his handsome head. Don José, who had risen in marked contrast to his reception of his former guest, answered, —

"You are truly making to him a great honor."

"Well, you're going it blind as far as *I'm* concerned certainly," said the young man, with a slight smile, "for you don't know *me.*"

"Pardon, my friend," said Don José gently, "in this book, this great Testament of your glorious nation, I have read that you are all equal, one not above, one not below the other. I salute in you the Nation! It is enough!"

"Thank you," returned the stranger, with a face that, saving the faintest twinkle in the corner of his dark eyes, was as immovable as his host's, "but for the purposes of my business I had better say I am Jack Hamlin, a gambler, and am just now dealing faro in the Florida saloon round the corner."

He paused carelessly, as if to allow Don José the protest he did not make, and then continued, —

"The matter is this. One of your *vaque-*

*ros,* who is, however, an American, was round there an hour ago bucking against faro, and put up and *lost,* not only the mare he was riding, but a horse which I have just learned is yours. Now we reckon, over there, that we can make enough money playing a square game, without being obliged to take property from a howling drunkard, to say nothing of it not belonging to him, and I 've come here, Don José, to say that if you 'll send over and bring away your man and your horse, you can have 'em both."

"If I have comprehended, honest Hamlin," said Don José slowly, "this Roberto, who was my *vaquero* and is my brother, has approached this faro game by himself unsolicited ? "

"He certainly did n't seem shy of it," said Mr. Hamlin with equal gravity. "To the best of my knowledge he looked as if he 'd been there before."

"And if he had won, excellent Hamlin, you would have given him the equal of his mare and horse ? "

"A hundred dollars for each, yes, certainly."

"Then I see not why I should send for the property which is truly no longer mine,

nor for my brother who will amuse himself
after the fashion of his country in the company of so honorable a *caballero* as yourself? Stay! oh imbecile that I am. I have
not remembered. You would possibly say
that he has no longer of horses! Play him;
play him, admirable yet prudent Hamlin. I
have two thousand horses! Of a surety he
cannot exhaust them in four hours. Therefore play him, trust to me for *recompensa,*
and have no fear."

A quick flush covered the stranger's
cheek, and his eyebrows momentarily contracted. He walked carelessly to the window, however, glanced out, and then turned
to Don José.

"May I ask, then," he said with almost
sepulchral gravity, "is anybody taking care
of you?"

"Truly," returned Don José cautiously,
"there is my brother and friend Roberto."

"Ah! Roberto, certainly," said Mr. Hamlin profoundly.

"Why do you ask, considerate friend?"

"Oh! I only thought, with your kind of
opinions, you must often feel lonely in California. Good-bye." He shook Don José's
hand heartily, took up his hat, inclined his

head with graceful seriousness, and passed out of the room. In the hall he met the landlord.

"Well," said Jenkinson, with a smile half anxious, half insinuating, "you saw him? What do you think of him?"

Mr. Hamlin paused and regarded Jenkinson with a calmly contemplative air, as if he were trying to remember first who he was, and secondly why he should speak to him at all. "Think of whom?" he repeated carelessly.

"Why him — you know — Don José."

"I did not see anything the matter with him," returned Hamlin with frigid simplicity.

"What? nothing queer?"

"Well, no — except that he's a guest in *your* house," said Hamlin with great cheerfulness. "But then, as you keep a hotel, you can't help occasionally admitting a — gentleman."

Mr. Jenkinson smiled the uneasy smile of a man who knew that his interlocutor's playfulness occasionally extended to the use of a derringer, in which he was singularly prompt and proficient, and Mr. Hamlin, equally conscious of that knowledge on the part of his companion, descended the staircase composedly.

But the day had darkened gradually into night, and Don José was at last compelled to put aside his volume. The sound of a large bell rung violently along the hall and passages admonished him that the American dinner was ready, and although the viands and the mode of cooking were not entirely to his fancy, he had, in his grave enthusiasm for the national habits, attended the *table d'hôte* regularly with Roberto. On reaching the lower hall he was informed that his henchman had early succumbed to the potency of his libations, and had already been carried by two men to bed. Receiving this information with his usual stoical composure, he entered the dining-room, but was surprised to find that a separate table had been prepared for him by the landlord, and that a rude attempt had been made to serve him with his own native dishes.

" Señores y Señoritas," said Don José, turning from it and with grave politeness addressing the assembled company, " if I seem to-day to partake alone and in a reserved fashion of certain viands that have been prepared for me, it is truly from no lack of

courtesy to your distinguished company, but
rather, I protest, to avoid the appearance of
greater discourtesy to our excellent Jenkinson, who has taken some pains and trouble
to comport his establishment to what he con-
ceives to be my desires. Wherefore, my
friends, in God's name fall to, the same as if
I were not present, and grace be with you."

A few stared at the tall, gentle, melancholy figure with some astonishment ; a few
whispered to their neighbors ; but when, at
the conclusion of his repast, Don José arose
and again saluted the company, one or two
stood up and smilingly returned the courtesy,
and Polly Jenkinson, the landlord's youngest
daughter, to the great delight of her companions, blew him a kiss.

After visiting the *vaquero* in his room,
and with his own hand applying some native
ointment to the various contusions and
scratches which recorded the late engage-
ments of the unconscious Roberto, Don José
placed a gold coin in the hands of the Irish
chamber-maid, and bidding her look after
the sleeper, he threw his *serape* over his
shoulders and passed into the road. The
loungers on the veranda gazed at him curiously, yet half acknowledged his usual se-

rious salutation, and made way for him with a certain respect. Avoiding the few narrow streets of the little town, he pursued his way meditatively along the highroad, returning to the hotel after an hour's ramble, as the evening stage-coach had deposited its passengers and departed.

"There's a lady waiting to see you upstairs," said the landlord with a peculiar smile. "She rather allowed it wasn't the proper thing to see you alone, or she wasn't quite ekal to it, I reckon, for she got my Polly to stand by her."

"Your Polly, good Jenkinson?" said Don José interrogatively.

"My darter, Don José."

"Ah, truly! I am twice blessed," said Don José, gravely ascending the staircase.

On entering the room he perceived a tall, large-featured woman with an extraordinary quantity of blond hair parted on one side of her broad forehead, sitting upon the sofa. Beside her sat Polly Jenkinson, her fresh, honest, and rather pretty face beaming with delighted expectation and mischief. Don José saluted them with a formal courtesy, which, however, had no trace of the fact that he really did not remember anything of them.

" I called," said the large-featured woman with a voice equally pronounced, " in reference to a request from you, which, though perhaps unconventional in the extreme, I have been able to meet by the intervention of this young lady's company. My name on this card may not be familiar to you — but I am ' Dorothy Dewdrop.' "

A slight movement of abstraction and surprise passed over Don José's face, but as quickly vanished as he advanced towards her and gracefully raised the tips of her fingers to his lips. " Have I then, at last, the privilege of beholding that most distressed and deeply injured of women ! Or is it but a dream ! "

It certainly was not, as far as concerned the substantial person of the woman before him, who, however, seemed somewhat uneasy under his words as well as the demure scrutiny of Miss Jenkinson. " I thought you might have forgotten," she said with slight acerbity, " that you desired an interview with the authoress of " —

" Pardon," interrupted Don José, standing before her in an attitude of the deepest sympathizing dejection, " I had not forgotten. It is now three weeks since I have

read in the journal 'Golden Gate' the eloquent and touching poem of your sufferings,
and your aspirations, and your miscompre-
hensions by those you love. I remember as
yesterday that you have said, that cruel fate
have linked you to a soulless state — that —
but I speak not well your own beautiful language — you are in tears at evenfall ' because
that you are not understood of others, and
that your soul recoiled from iron bonds, until, as in a dream, you sought succor and re-
lease in some true Knight of equal plight.' "

"I am told," said the large-featured woman with some satisfaction, "that the poem
to which you allude has been generally admired."

"Admired! Señora," said Don José, with
still darker sympathy, "it is not the word;
it is *felt*. I have felt it. When I read those
words of distress, I am touched of compas-
sion! I have said, This woman, so disconsolate, so oppressed, must be relieved, protected! I have wrote to you, at the 'Golden
Gate,' to see me here."

"And I have come, as you perceive," said
the poetess, rising with a slight smile of con-
straint; "and emboldened by your appreciation, I have brought a few trifles thrown
off " —

" Pardon, unhappy Señora," interrupted Don José, lifting his hand deprecatingly without relaxing his melancholy precision, "but to a cavalier further evidence is not required — and I have not yet make finish. I have not content myself to *write* to you. I have sent my trusty friend Roberto to inquire at the ' Golden Gate ' of your condition. I have found there, most unhappy and persecuted friend — that with truly angelic forbearance you have not told *all* — that you are *married*, and that of a necessity it is your husband that is cold and soulless and unsympathizing — and all that you describe."

" Sir ! " said the poetess, rising in angry consternation.

" I have written to him," continued Don José, with unheeding gravity ; " have appealed to him as a friend, I have conjured him as a *caballero*, I have threatened him even as a champion of the Right, I have said to him, in effect — that this must not be as it is. I have informed him that I have made an appointment with you even at this house, and I challenged him to meet you here — in this room — even at this instant, and, with God's help, we should make good our charges against him. It is yet early ; I have allowed time for the lateness of the stage and the fact that he will come by another conveyance. Therefore, O Dona Dewdrop, tremble not like thy namesake as it were on the leaf of apprehension and expectancy. I, Don José, am here to protect thee. I will take these charges " — gently withdrawing the manuscripts from her astonished grasp — " though even, as I related to thee before, I want them not, yet we will together confront him with them and make them good against him."

" Are you mad ? " demanded the lady in almost stentorious accents, " or is this an unmanly hoax ? " Suddenly she stopped in undeniable consternation. " Good heavens," she muttered, " if Abner should believe this. He is *such* a fool ! He has lately been queer and jealous. Oh dear ! " she said, turning to Polly Jenkinson with the first indication of feminine weakness, " *is* he telling the truth ? is he crazy ? what shall I do ? "

Polly Jenkinson, who had witnessed the interview with the intensest enjoyment, now rose equal to the occasion.

" You have made a mistake," she said, uplifting her demure blue eyes to Don José's dark and melancholy gaze. "This lady is a *poetess!* The sufferings she depicts, the sorrows she feels, are in the *imagination*, in her fancy only."

"Ah!" said Don José gloomily; "then it is all false."

"No," said Polly quickly, "only they are not her *own*, you know. They are somebody elses. She only describes them for another, don't you see?"

"And who, then, is this unhappy one?" asked the Don quickly.

"Well — a — friend," stammered Polly, hesitatingly.

"A friend!" repeated Don José. "Ah, I see, of possibility a dear one, even," he continued, gazing with tender melancholy into the untroubled cerulean depths of Polly's eyes, "even, but no, child, it could not be! *thou* art too young."

"Ah," said Polly, with an extraordinary gulp and a fierce nudge of the poetess, "but it *was* me."

"You, Señorita," repeated Don José, falling back in an attitude of mingled admiration and pity. "You, the child of Jenkinson!"

"Yes, yes," joined in the poetess hurriedly; "but that is n't going to stop the consequences of your wretched blunder. My husband will, be furious, and will be here at any moment. Good gracious! what is that?"

The violent slamming of a distant door at that instant, the sounds of quick scuffling on the staircase, and the uplifting of an irate voice had reached her ears and thrown her back in the arms of Polly Jenkinson. Even the young girl herself turned an anxious gaze towards the door. Don José alone was unmoved.

"Possess yourselves in peace, Señoritas," he said calmly. "We have here only the characteristic convalescence of my friend and brother, the excellent Roberto. He will ever recover himself from drink with violence, even as he precipitates himself into it with fury. He has been prematurely awakened. I will discover the cause."

With an elaborate bow to the frightened women, he left the room. Scarcely had the door closed when the poetess turned quickly to Polly. "The man's a stark staring lunatic, but, thank Heaven, Abner will see it at once. And now let's get away while we can. To think," she said, snatching up her scattered manuscripts, "that *that* was all the beast wanted."

"I'm sure he's very gentle and kind," said Polly, recovering her dimples with a demure pout; "but stop, he's coming back."

It was indeed Don José re-entering the room with the composure of a relieved and self-satisfied mind. "It is even as I said, Señora," he began, taking the poetess's hand, — "and *more*. You are *saved!*"

As the women only stared at each other, he gravely folded his arms and continued: "I will explain. For the instant I have not remember that, in imitation of your own delicacy, I have given to your husband in my letter, not the name of myself, but, as a mere *Don Fulano*, the name of my brother Roberto — 'Bucking Bob.' Your husband have this moment arrive! Penetrating the bedroom of the excellent Roberto, he has indiscreetly seize him in his bed, without explanation, without introduction, without fear! The excellent Roberto, ever ready for such distractions, have respond! In a word, to use the language of the good Jenkinson — our host, our father — who was present, he have 'wiped the floor with your husband,' and have even carried him down the staircase to the street. Believe me, he will not return. You are free!"

"Fool! Idiot! Crazy beast!" said the poetess, dashing past him and out of the door. "You shall pay for this!"

Don José did not change his imperturbable and melancholy calm. "And now, little one," he said, dropping on one knee before the half-frightened Polly, "child of Jenkinson, now that thy perhaps too excitable sponsor has, in a poet's caprice, abandoned thee for some newer fantasy, confide in me thy distress, to me, thy Knight, and tell the story of thy sorrows."

"But," said Polly, rising to her feet and struggling between a laugh and a cry. "I haven't any sorrows. Oh dear! don't you see, it's only her *fancy* to make me seem so. There's nothing the matter with me."

"Nothing the matter," repeated Don José slowly. "You have no distress? You want no succor, no relief, no protector? This, then, is but another delusion!" he said, rising sadly.

"Yes, no — that is — oh, my gracious goodness!" said Polly, hopelessly divided between a sense of the ridiculous and some strange attraction in the dark, gentle eyes that were fixed upon her half reproachfully. "You don't understand."

Don José replied only with a melancholy smile, and then going to the door, opened it with a bowed head and respectful courtesy. At the act, Polly plucked up courage again, and with it a slight dash of her old audacity.

"I 'm sure I 'm very sorry that I ain't got any love sorrows," she said demurely. "And I suppose it 's very dreadful in me not to have been raving and broken-hearted over somebody or other as that woman has said. Only," she waited till she had gained the secure vantage of the threshold, "I never knew a gentleman to *object* to it before!"

With this Parthian arrow from her blue eyes she slipped into the passage and vanished through the door of the opposite parlor. For an instant Don José remained motionless and reflecting. Then, recovering himself with grave precision, he deliberately picked up his narrow black gloves from the table, drew them on, took his hat in his hand, and solemnly striding across the passage, entered the door that had just closed behind her.

### III.

It must not be supposed that in the meantime the flight of Don José and his follower

was unattended by any commotion at the
rancho of the Blessed Innocents. At the
end of three hours' deliberation, in which the
retainers were severally examined, the corral
searched, and the well in the courtyard
sounded, scouts were dispatched in different
directions, who returned with the surprising
information that the fugitives were not in
the vicinity. A trustworthy messenger was
sent to Monterey for " custom-house paper,"
on which to draw up a formal declaration of
the affair. The archbishop was summoned
from San Luis, and Don Victor and Don
Vincente Sepulvida, with the Donas Carmen
and Inez Alvarado, and a former alcalde,
gathered at a family council the next day.
In this serious conclave the good Father
Felipe once more expounded the alienated
condition and the dangerous reading of the
absent man. In the midst of which the ordinary post brought a letter from Don José,
calmly inviting the family to dine with him
and Roberto at San Mateo on the following
Wednesday. The document was passed
gravely from hand to hand. Was it a fresh
evidence of mental aberration — an audacity
of frenzy — or a trick of the *vaquero?* The
archbishop and alcalde shook their heads

— it was without doubt a lawless, even a sacrilegious and blasphemous *fête*. But a certain curiosity of the ladies and of Father Felipe carried the day. Without formally accepting the invitation it was decided that the family should examine the afflicted man, with a view of taking active measures hereafter. On the day appointed, the traveling carriage of the Sepulvidas, an equipage coeval with the beginning of the century, drawn by two white mules gaudily caparisoned, halted before the hotel at San Mateo and disgorged Father Felipe, the Donas Carmen and Inez Alvarado and Maria Sepulvida, while Don Victor and Don Vincente Sepulvida, their attendant cavaliers on fiery mustangs, like outriders, drew rein at the same time. A slight thrill of excitement, as of the advent of a possible circus, had preceded them through the little town; a faint blending of cigarette smoke and garlic announced their presence on the veranda.

Ushered into the parlor of the hotel, apparently set apart for their reception, they were embarrassed at not finding their host present. But they were still more disconcerted when a tall full-bearded stranger, with a shrewd amused-looking face, rose from a chair by the window, and stepping forward, saluted them in fluent Spanish with a slight American accent.

"I have to ask you, gentlemen and ladies," he began, with a certain insinuating ease and frankness that alternately aroused and lulled their suspicions, "to pardon the absence of our friend Don José Sepulvida at this preliminary greeting. For to be perfectly frank with you, although the ultimate aim and object of our gathering is a social one, you are doubtless aware that certain infelicities and misunderstandings — common to most families — have occurred, and a free, dispassionate, unprejudiced discussion and disposal of them at the beginning will only tend to augment the goodwill of our gathering."

"The Señor without doubt is" — suggested the padre, with a polite interrogative pause.

"Pardon me! I forgot to introduce myself. Colonel Parker — entirely at your service and that of these charming ladies."

The ladies referred to allowed their eyes to rest with evident prepossession on the insinuating stranger. "Ah, a soldier," said Don Vincente.

"Formerly," said the American lightly; "at present a lawyer, the counsel of Don José."

A sudden rigor of suspicion stiffened the company; the ladies withdrew their eyes; the priest and the Sepulvidas exchanged glances.

"Come," said Colonel Parker, with apparent unconsciousness of the effect of his disclosure, "let us begin frankly. You have, I believe, some anxiety in regard to the mental condition of Don José."

"We believe him to be mad," said Padre Felipe promptly, "irresponsible, possessed!"

"That is your opinion; good," said the lawyer quietly.

"And ours too," clamored the party, "without doubt."

"Good," returned the lawyer with perfect cheerfulness. "As his relations, you have no doubt had superior opportunities for observing his condition. I understand also that you may think it necessary to have him legally declared *non compos*, a proceeding which, you are aware, might result in the incarceration of our distinguished friend in a mad-house."

"Pardon, Señor," interrupted Dona Maria

proudly, "you do not comprehend the family. When a Sepulvida is visited of God we do not ask the Government to confine him like a criminal. We protect him in his own house from the consequences of his frenzy."

"From the machinations of the worldly and heretical," broke in the priest, "and from the waste and dispersion of inherited possessions."

"Very true," continued Colonel Parker, with unalterable good-humor; "but I was only about to say that there might be conflicting evidence of his condition. For instance, our friend has been here three days. In that time he has had three interviews with three individuals under singular circumstances." Colonel Parker then briefly recounted the episodes of the landlord, the gambler, Miss Jenkinson and the poetess, as they had been related to him. "Yet," he continued, "all but one of these individuals are willing to swear that they not only believe Don José perfectly sane, but endowed with a singularly sound judgment. In fact, the testimony of Mr. Hamlin and Miss Jenkinson is remarkably clear on that subject."

The company exchanged a supercilious smile. "Do you not see, O Señor Advocate," said Don Vincente compassionately, "that this is but a conspiracy to avail themselves of our relative's weakness. Of a necessity they find him sane who benefits them."

"I have thought of that, and am glad to hear you say so," returned the lawyer still more cheerfully, "for your prompt opinion emboldens me to be at once perfectly frank with you. Briefly then, Don José has summoned me here to make a final disposition of his property. In the carrying out of certain theories of his, which it is not my province to question, he has resolved upon comparative poverty for himself as best fitted for his purpose, and to employ his wealth solely for others. In fact, of all his vast possessions he retains for himself only an income sufficient for the bare necessaries of life."

"And you have done this?" they asked in one voice.

"Not yet," said the lawyer.

"Blessed San Antonio, we have come in time!" ejaculated Dona Carmen. "Another day and it would have been too late; it was an inspiration of the Blessed Innocents themselves," said Dona Maria, crossing herself. "Can you longer doubt that this is the wildest madness?" said Father Felipe with flashing eyes.

"Yet," returned the lawyer, caressing his heavy beard with a meditative smile, "the ingenious fellow actually instanced the vows of *your own order*, reverend sir, as an example in support of his theory. But to be brief. Conceiving, then, that his holding of property was a mere accident of heritage, not admitted by him, unworthy his acceptance, and a relic of superstitious ignorance " —

"This is the very sacrilege of Satanic prepossession," broke in the priest indignantly.

"He therefore," continued the lawyer composedly, "makes over and reverts the whole of his possessions, with the exceptions I have stated, to his family and the Church."

A breathless and stupefying silence fell upon the company. In the dead hush the sound of Polly Jenkinson's piano, played in a distant room, could be distinctly heard. With their vacant eyes staring at him the speaker continued:

"That deed of gift I have drawn up as he dictated it. I don't mind saying that in the opinion of some he might be declared *non compos* upon the evidence of that alone. I

need not say how relieved I am to find that
your opinion coincides with my own."

"But," gasped Father Felipe hurriedly,
with a quick glance at the others, "it does
not follow that it will be necessary to resort
to these legal measures. Care, counsel, per-
suasion — "

"The general ministering of kinship —
nursing, a woman's care — the instincts of
affection," piped Dona Maria in breathless
eagerness.

"Any light social distraction — a harmless flirtation — a possible attachment," suggested Dona Carmen shyly.

"Change of scene — active exercise — ex-
periences — even as those you have related,"
broke in Don Vincente.

"I for one have ever been opposed to *legal*
measures," said Don Victor. "A mere consultation of friends — in fact, a *fête* like this
is sufficient."

"Good friends," said Father Felipe, who
had by this time recovered himself, taking
out his snuff-box portentously, "it would
seem truly, from the document which this
discreet *caballero* has spoken of, that the
errors of our dear Don José are rather of
method than intent, and that while we may
freely accept the one " —

" Pardon," interrupted Colonel Parker with bland persistence, " but I must point out to you that what we call in law ' a consideration ' is necessary to the legality of a conveyance, even though that consideration be frivolous and calculated to impair the validity of the document."

" Truly," returned the good padre insinuatingly ; " but if a discreet advocate were to suggest the substitution of some more pious and reasonable consideration " —

" But that would be making it a perfectly sane and gratuitous document, not only glaringly inconsistent with your charges, my good friends, with Don José's attitude towards you and his flight from home, but open to the gravest suspicion in law. In fact, its apparent propriety in the face of these facts would imply improper influence."

The countenances of the company fell. The lawyer's face, however, became still more good-humored and sympathizing. " The case is simply this. If in the opinion of judge and jury Don José is declared insane, the document is worthless except as a proof of that fact or a possible indication of the undue influence of his relations, which might compel the court to select his guardians and trustees elsewhere than among them."

"Friend Abogado," said Father Felipe with extraordinary deliberation, "the document thou hast just described so eloquently convinces me beyond all doubt that Don José is not only perfectly sane but endowed with a singular discretion. I consider it as a delicate and high-spirited intimation to us, his friends and kinsmen, of his unalterable and logically just devotion to his family and religion, whatever may seem to be his poetical and imaginative manner of declaring it. I think there is not one here," continued the padre, looking around him impressively, "who is not entirely satisfied of Don José's reason and competency to arrange his own affairs."

"Entirely," "truly," "perfectly," eagerly responded the others with affecting spontaneity.

"Nay, more. To prevent any misconception, we shall deem it our duty to take every opportunity of making our belief publicly known," added Father Felipe.

The padre and Colonel Parker gazed long and gravely into each other's eyes. It may have been an innocent touch of the sunlight through the window, but a faint gleam seemed to steal into the pupil of the affable

lawyer at the same moment that, probably
from the like cause, there was a slight nervous contraction of the left eyelid of the
pious father. But it passed, and the next
instant the door opened to admit Don José
Sepulvida.

He was at once seized and effusively em-
braced by the entire company with every
protest of affection and respect. Not only
Mr. Hamlin and Mr. Jenkinson, who accompanied him as invited guests, but Roberto, in a new suit of clothes and guiltless
of stain or trace of dissipation, shared in
the pronounced friendliness of the kinsmen.
Padre Felipe took snuff, Colonel Parker
blew his nose gently.

Nor were they less demonstrative of their
new convictions later at the banquet. Don
José, with Jenkinson and the padre on his
right and left, preserved his gentle and half-
melancholy dignity in the midst of the noisy
fraternization. Even Padre Felipe, in a
brief speech or exhortation proposing the
health of their host, lent himself in his own
tongue to this polite congeniality. "We
have had also, my friends and brothers," he
said in peroration, "a pleasing example of
the compliment of imitation shown by our

beloved Don José. No one who has known him during his friendly sojourn in this community but will be struck with the conviction that he has acquired that most marvelous faculty of your great American nation, the exhibition of humor and of the practical joke."

Every eye was turned upon the imperturbable face of Don José as he slowly rose to reply. " In bidding you to this *fête*, my friends and kinsmen," he began calmly, " it was with the intention of formally embracing the habits, customs, and spirit of American institutions by certain methods of renunciation of the past, as became a *caballero* of honor and resolution. Those methods may possibly be known to some of you." He paused for a moment as if to allow the members of his family to look unconscious. " Since then, in the wisdom of God, it has occurred to me that my purpose may be as honorably effected by a discreet blending of the past and the present — in a word, by the judicious combination of the interests of my native people and the American nation. In consideration of that purpose, friends and kinsmen, I ask you to join me in drinking the good health of my host Señor Jenkinson, my future father-in-law, from whom I have to-day had the honor to demand the hand of the peerless Polly, his daughter, as the future mistress of the Rancho of the Blessed Innocents."

The marriage took place shortly after. Nor was the free will and independence of Don José Sepulvida in the least opposed by his relations. Whether they felt they had already committed themselves, or had hopes in the future, did not transpire. Enough that the escapade of a week was tacitly forgotten. The only allusion ever made to the bridegroom's peculiarities was drawn from the demure lips of the bride herself on her installation at the " Blessed Innocents."

" And what, little one, didst thou find in me to admire ? " Don José had asked tenderly.

" Oh, you seemed to be so much like that dear old Don Quixote, you know," she answered demurely.

" Don Quixote," repeated Don José with gentle gravity. " But, my child, that was only a mere fiction — a romance, of one Cervantes. Believe me, of a truth there never was any such person ! "

# A SECRET OF TELEGRAPH HILL.

## I.

As Mr. Herbert Bly glanced for the first
time at the house which was to be his future
abode in San Francisco, he was somewhat
startled. In that early period of feverish
civic improvement the street before it had
been repeatedly graded and lowered until
the dwelling — originally a pioneer suburban
villa perched upon a slope of Telegraph Hill
— now stood sixty feet above the sidewalk,
superposed like some Swiss châlet on successive galleries built in the sand-hill, and connected by a half-dozen distinct zigzag flights
of wooden staircase. Stimulated, however,
by the thought that the view from the top
would be a fine one, and that existence there
would have all the quaint originality of Rob-
inson Crusoe's tree-dwelling, Mr. Bly began
cheerfully to mount the steps. It should be
premised that, although a recently appointed
clerk in a large banking house, Mr. Bly was

somewhat youthful and imaginative, and regarded the ascent as part of that "Excelsior" climbing pointed out by a great poet as a praiseworthy function of ambitious youth.

Reaching at last the level of the veranda, he turned to the view. The distant wooded shore of Contra Costa, the tossing white-caps and dancing sails of the bay between, and the foreground at his feet of wharves and piers, with their reed-like jungles of masts and cordage, made up a bright, if somewhat material, picture. To his right rose the crest of the hill, historic and memorable as the site of the old semaphoric telegraph, the tossing of whose gaunt arms formerly thrilled the citizens with tidings from the sea. Turning to the house, he recognized the prevailing style of light cottage architecture, although incongruously confined to narrow building plots and the civic regularity of a precise street frontage. Thus a dozen other villas, formerly scattered over the slope, had been laboriously displaced and moved to the rigorous parade line drawn by the street surveyor, no matter how irregular and independent their design and structure. Happily, the few scrub-oaks and low bushes which formed the scant vegetation of this vast sand dune offered no obstacle and suggested no incongruity. Beside the house before which Mr. Bly now stood, a prolific Madeira vine, quickened by the six months' sunshine, had alone survived the displacement of its foundations, and in its untrimmed luxuriance half hid the upper veranda from his view.

Still glowing with his exertion, the young man rang the bell and was admitted into a fair-sized drawing-room, whose tasteful and well-arranged furniture at once prepossessed him. An open piano, a sheet of music carelessly left on the stool, a novel lying face downwards on the table beside a skein of silk, and the distant rustle of a vanished skirt through an inner door, gave a suggestion of refined domesticity to the room that touched the fancy of the homeless and nomadic Bly. He was still enjoying, in half embarrassment, that vague and indescribable atmosphere of a refined woman's habitual presence, when the door opened and the mistress of the house formally presented herself.

She was a faded but still handsome woman. Yet she wore that peculiar long, limp, formless house-shawl which in certain phases of Anglo-Saxon spinster and widowhood assumes the functions of the recluse's veil and

announces the renunciation of worldly vanities and a resigned indifference to external
feminine contour. The most audacious masculine arm would shrink from clasping that
shapeless void in which the flatness of ascet-
icism or the heavings of passion might alike
lie buried. She had also in some mysterious
way imported into the fresh and pleasant
room a certain bombaziny shadow of the
past, and a suggestion of that appalling reminiscence known as "better days." Though
why it should be always represented by ashen
memories, or why better days in the past
should be supposed to fix their fitting symbol
in depression in the present, Mr. Bly was too
young and too preoccupied at the moment to
determine. He only knew that he was a little frightened of her, and fixed his gaze with
a hopeless fascination on a letter which she
somewhat portentously carried under the
shawl, and which seemed already to have
yellowed in its arctic shade.

"Mr. Carstone has written to me that
you would call," said Mrs. Brooks with languid formality. "Mr. Carstone was a valued friend of my late husband, and I suppose
has told you the circumstances — the only
circumstances — which admit of my enter-

taining his proposition of taking anybody, even temporarily, under my roof. The absence of my dear son for six months at Portland, Oregon, enables me to place his room at the disposal of Mr. Carstone's young protégé, who, Mr. Carstone tells me, and I have every reason to believe, is, if perhaps not so seriously inclined nor yet a church communicant, still of a character and reputation not unworthy to follow my dear Tappington in our little family circle as he has at his desk in the bank.".

The sensitive Bly, struggling painfully out of an abstraction as to how he was ever to offer the weekly rent of his lodgings to such a remote and respectable person, and also somewhat embarrassed at being appealed to in the third person, here started and bowed.

"The name of Bly is not unfamiliar to me," continued Mrs. Brooks, pointing to a chair and sinking resignedly into another, where her baleful shawl at once assumed the appearance of a dust-cover; "some of my dearest friends were intimate with the Blys of Philadelphia. They were a branch of the Maryland Blys of the eastern shore, one of whom my Uncle James married. Perhaps you are distantly related?"

Mrs. Brooks was perfectly aware that her visitor was of unknown Western origin, and a poor but clever protégé of the rich banker; but she was one of a certain class of American women who, in the midst of a fierce democracy, are more or less cat-like conservators of family pride and lineage, and more or less felinely inconsistent and treacherous to republican principles. Bly, who had just settled in his mind to send her the rent anonymously — as a weekly valentine — recovered himself and his spirits in his usual boyish fashion.

"I am afraid, Mrs. Brooks," he said gayly, "I cannot lay claim to any distinguished relationship, even to that ' Nelly Bly ' who, you remember, ' winked her eye when she went to sleep.' " He stopped in consternation. The terrible conviction flashed upon him that this quotation from a popular negro-minstrel song could not possibly be remembered by a lady as refined as his hostess, or even known to her superior son. The conviction was intensified by Mrs. Brooks rising with a smileless face, slightly shedding the possible vulgarity with a shake of her shawl, and remarking that she would show him her son's room, led the way upstairs to the apartment recently vacated by the perfect Tappington.

Preceded by the same distant flutter of unseen skirts in the passage which he had first noticed on entering the drawing-room, and which evidently did not proceed from his companion, whose self-composed cerements would have repressed any such indecorous agitation, Mr. Bly stepped timidly into the room. It was a very pretty apartment, suggesting the same touches of tasteful refinement in its furniture and appointments, and withal so feminine in its neatness and regularity, that, conscious of his frontier habits and experience, he felt at once repulsively incongruous. " I cannot expect, Mr. Bly," said Mrs. Brooks resignedly, " that you can share my son's extreme sensitiveness to disorder and irregularity; but I must beg you to avoid as much as possible disturbing the arrangement of the book-shelves, which, you observe, comprise his books of serious reference, the Biblical commentaries, and the sermons which were his habitual study. I must beg you to exercise the same care in reference to the valuable offerings from his Sabbath-school scholars which are upon the mantel. The embroi-

dered book-marker, the gift of the young ladies of his Bible-class in Dr. Stout's church,
is also, you perceive, kept for ornament and
affectionate remembrance. The harmonium
— even if you are not yourself given to sacred song — I trust you will not find in your
way, nor object to my daughter continuing
her practice during your daily absence.
Thank you. The door you are looking at
leads by a flight of steps to the side street."

"A very convenient arrangement," said
Bly hopefully, who saw a chance for an
occasional unostentatious escape from a too
protracted contemplation of Tappington's
perfections. "I mean," he added hurriedly,
"to avoid disturbing you at night."

"I believe my son had neither the necessity nor desire to use it for that purpose,"
returned Mrs. Brooks severely; "although
he found it sometimes a convenient short cut
to church on Sabbath when he was late."

Bly, who in his boyish sensitiveness to
external impressions had by this time concluded that a life divided between the past
perfections of Tappington and the present
renunciations of Mrs. Brooks would be intolerable, and was again abstractedly invent-
ing some delicate excuse for withdrawing

without committing himself further, was here suddenly attracted by a repetition of the rustling of the unseen skirt. This time it was nearer, and this time it seemed to strike even Mrs. Brooks's remote preoccupation. " My daughter, who is deeply devoted to her brother," she said, slightly raising her voice, " will take upon herself the care of looking after Tappington's precious mementoes, and spare you the trouble. Cherry, dear! this way. This is the young gentleman spoken of by Mr. Carstone, your papa's friend. My daughter Cherubina, Mr. Bly."

The fair owner of the rustling skirt, which turned out to be a pretty French print, had appeared at the doorway. She was a tall, slim blonde, with a shy, startled manner, as of a penitent nun who was suffering for some conventual transgression — a resemblance that was heightened by her short-cut hair, that might have been cropped as if for punishment. A certain likeness to her mother suggested that she was qualifying for that saint's ascetic shawl — subject, however, to rebellious intervals, indicated in the occasional sidelong fires of her gray eyes. Yet the vague impression that she knew more of the world than her mother, and that she did not look at all as if her name was Cherubina, struck Bly in the same momentary glance.

" Mr. Bly is naturally pleased with what he has seen of our dear Tappington's appointments; and as I gather from Mr. Carstone's letter that he is anxious to enter at once and make the most of the dear boy's absence, you will see, my dear Cherry, that Ellen has everything ready for him ? "

Before the unfortunate Bly could explain or protest, the young girl lifted her gray eyes to his. Whether she had perceived and understood his perplexity he could not tell ; but the swift shy glance was at once appealing, assuring, and intelligent. She was certainly unlike her mother and brother. Acting with his usual impulsiveness, he forgot his previous resolution, and before he left had engaged to begin his occupation of the room on the following day.

The next afternoon found him installed. Yet, after he had unpacked his modest possessions and put them away, after he had placed his few books on the shelves, where they looked glaringly trivial and frivolous beside the late tenant's severe studies ; after he had set out his scanty treasures in the way of photographs and some curious me-

mentoes of his wandering life, and then
quickly put them back again with a sudden
angry pride at exposing them to the unsym-
pathetic incongruity of the other ornaments,
he, nevertheless, felt ill at ease. He glanced
in vain around the pretty room. It was not
the delicately flowered wall-paper; it was
not the white and blue muslin window-cur-
tains gracefully tied up with blue and white
ribbons; it was not the spotless bed, with its
blue and white festooned mosquito-net and
flounced valances, and its medallion portrait
of an unknown bishop at the back; it was
not the few tastefully framed engravings of
certain cardinal virtues, "The Rock of
Ages," and "The Guardian Angel"; it was
not the casts in relief of "Night" and
"Morning"; it was certainly not the cosy
dimity-covered arm-chairs and sofa, nor yet
the clean-swept polished grate with its cheerful fire sparkling against the chill afternoon
sea-fogs without; neither was it the mere
feminine suggestion, for that touched a sympathetic chord in his impulsive nature; nor
the religious and ascetic influence, for he
had occupied a monastic cell in a school of
the padres at an old mission, and slept profoundly; — it was none of those, and yet a

part of all. Most habitations retain a cast
or shell of their previous tenant that, fitting
tightly or loosely, is still able to adjust itself
to the newcomer; in most occupied apartments there is still a shadowy suggestion of
the owner's individuality; there was nothing
here that fitted Bly — nor was there either,
strange to say, any evidence of the past proprietor in this inhospitality of sensation. It
did not strike him at the time that it was
this very *lack* of individuality which made it
weird and unreal, that it was strange only
because it was *artificial*, and that a *real*
Tappington had never inhabited it.

He walked to the window — that never-
failing resource of the unquiet mind — and
looked out. He was a little surprised to
find, that, owing to the grading of the house,
the scrub-oaks and bushes of the hill were
nearly on the level of his window, as also
was the adjoining side street on which his
second door actually gave. Opening this,
the sudden invasion of the sea-fog and the
figure of a pedestrian casually passing along
the disused and abandoned pavement not a
dozen feet from where he had been comfortably seated, presented such a striking contrast to the studious quiet and cosiness of his

secluded apartment that he hurriedly closed the door again with a sense of indiscreet exposure. Returning to the window, he glanced to the left, and found that he was overlooked by the side veranda of another villa in the rear, evidently on its way to take position on the line of the street. Although in actual and deliberate transit on rollers across the backyard and still occulting a part of the view, it remained, after the reckless fashion of the period, inhabited. Certainly, with a door fronting a thoroughfare, and a neighbor gradually approaching him, he would not feel lonely or lack excitement.

He drew his arm-chair to the fire and tried to realize the all-pervading yet evasive Tappington. There was no portrait of him in the house, and although Mrs. Brooks had said that he "favored" his sister, Bly had, without knowing why, instinctively resented it. He had even timidly asked his employer, and had received the vague reply that he was "good-looking enough," and the practical but discomposing retort, "What do you want to know for?" As he really did not know why, the inquiry had dropped. He stared at the monumental crystal inkstand half full of ink, yet spotless and free from stains, that stood on the table, and tried to picture Tappington daintily dipping into it to thank the fair donors — " daughters of Rebecca." Who were they? and what sort of man would they naturally feel grateful to?

What was that?

He turned to the window, which had just resounded to a slight tap or blow, as if something soft had struck it. With an instinctive suspicion of the propinquity of the adjoining street he rose, but a single glance from the window satisfied him that no missile would have reached it from thence. He scanned the low bushes on the level before him; certainly no one could be hiding there. He lifted his eyes toward the house on the left; the curtains of the nearest window appeared to be drawn suddenly at the same moment. Could it have come from there? Looking down upon the window-ledge, there lay the mysterious missile — a little misshapen ball. He opened the window and took it up. It was a small handkerchief tied into a soft knot, and dampened with water to give it the necessary weight as a projectile.

Was it apparently the trick of a mischievous child? or —

But here a faint knock on the door leading into the hall checked his inquiry. He opened it sharply in his excitement, and was embarrassed to find the daughter of his hostess standing there, shy, startled, and evidently equally embarrassed by his abrupt response.

" Mother only wanted me to ask you if Ellen had put everything to rights," she said, making a step backwards.

" Oh, thank you. Perfectly," said Herbert with effusion. " Nothing could be better done. In fact " —

" You 're quite sure she has n't forgotten anything ? or that there is n't anything you would like changed ? " she continued, with her eyes leveled on the floor.

" Nothing, I assure you," he said, looking at her downcast lashes. As she still remained motionless, he continued cheerfully, " Would you — would you — care to look round and see ? "

" No ; I thank you."

There was an awkward pause. He still continued to hold the door open. Suddenly she moved forward with a school-girl stride, entered the room, and going to the harmonium, sat down upon the music-stool beside it, slightly bending forward, with one long, slim, white hand on top of the other, resting over her crossed knees.

Herbert was a little puzzled. It was the awkward and brusque act of a very young person, and yet nothing now could be more gentle and self-composed than her figure and attitude.

" Yes," he continued, smilingly; " I am only afraid that I may not be able to live quite up to the neatness and regularity of the example I find here everywhere. You know I am dreadfully careless and not at all orderly. I shudder to think what may happen ; but you and your mother, Miss Brooks, I trust, will make up your minds to overlook and forgive a good deal. I shall do my best to be worthy of Mr. Tap — of my predecessor — but even then I am afraid you 'll find me a great bother."

She raised her shy eyelids. The faintest ghost of a long-buried dimple came into her pale cheek as she said softly, to his utter consternation :

" Rats ! "

Had she uttered an oath he could not have been more startled than he was by this choice gem of Western saloon-slang from the pure lips of this Evangeline-like figure before him. He sat gazing at her with a wild hysteric desire to laugh. She lifted her eyes again, swept him with a slightly terrified glance, and said:

"Tap says you all say that when any one makes-believe politeness to you."

"Oh, your *brother* says that, does he?" said Herbert, laughing.

"Yes, and sometimes 'Old rats.' But," she continued hurriedly, "*he* does n't say it; he says *you* all do. My brother is very particular, and very good. Doctor Stout loves him. He is thought very much of in all Christian circles. That book-mark was given to him by one of his classes."

Every trace of her dimples had vanished. She looked so sweetly grave, and withal so maidenly, sitting there slightly smoothing the lengths of her pink fingers, that Herbert was somewhat embarrassed.

"But I assure you, Miss Brooks, I was not making-believe. I am really very careless, and everything is so proper — I mean so neat and pretty — here, that I" — he stopped, and, observing the same backward wandering of her eye as of a filly about to shy, quickly changed the subject. "You have, or are about to have, neighbors?" he said, glancing towards the windows as he recalled the incident of a moment before.

"Yes; and they're not at all nice people. They are from Pike County, and very queer. They came across the plains in '50. They say 'Stranger'; the men are vulgar, and the girls very forward. Tap forbids my ever going to the window and looking at them. They're quite what you would call 'off color.'"

Herbert, who did not dare to say that he never would have dreamed of using such an expression in any young girl's presence, was plunged in silent consternation.

"Then your brother doesn't approve of them?" he said, at last, awkwardly.

"Oh, not at all. He even talked of having ground-glass put in all these windows, only it would make the light bad."

Herbert felt very embarrassed. If the mysterious missile came from these objectionable young persons, it was evidently because they thought they had detected a more accessible and sympathizing individual in the stranger who now occupied the room. He concluded he had better not say anything about it.

Miss Brooks's golden eyelashes were bent towards the floor. "Do you play sacred music, Mr. Bly?" she said, without raising them.

"I am afraid not."

"Perhaps you know only negro-minstrel songs?"

"I am afraid — yes."

"I know one." The dimples faintly came back again. "It's called 'The Ham-fat Man.' Some day when mother isn't in I'll play it for you."

Then the dimples fled again, and she immediately looked so distressed that Herbert came to her assistance.

"I suppose your brother taught you that too?"

"Oh dear, no!" she returned, with her frightened glance; "I only heard him say some people preferred that kind of thing to sacred music, and one day I saw a copy of it in a music-store window in Clay Street, and bought it. Oh no! Tappington didn't teach it to me."

In the pleasant discovery that she was at times independent of her brother's perfections, Herbert smiled, and sympathetically drew a step nearer to her. She rose at once, somewhat primly holding back the sides of her skirt, school-girl fashion, with thumb and finger, and her eyes cast down.

"Good afternoon, Mr. Bly."

"Must you go? Good afternoon."

She walked directly to the open door, looking very tall and stately as she did so, but without turning towards him. When she reached it she lifted her eyes; there was the slightest suggestion of a return of her dimples in the relaxation of her grave little mouth. Then she said, "Good-bye, Mr. Bly," and departed.

The skirt of her dress rustled for an instant in the passage. Herbert looked after her. "I wonder if she skipped then — she looks like a girl that might skip at such a time," he said to himself. "How very odd she is — and how simple! But I must pull her up in that slang when I know her better. Fancy her brother telling her *that!* What a pair they must be!" Nevertheless, when he turned back into the room again he forbore going to the window to indulge further curiosity in regard to his wicked neighbors. A certain new feeling of respect to his late companion — and possibly to himself — held him in check. Much as he resented Tappington's perfections, he resented quite as warmly the presumption that he was not quite as perfect, which was implied in that mysterious overture. He glanced at the stool on which she had been sitting with a half-brotherly smile, and put it reverently on one side with a very vivid recollection of her shy maidenly figure. In some mysterious way too the room seemed to have lost its formal strangeness; perhaps it was the touch of individuality — *hers* — that had been wanting? He began thoughtfully to dress himself for his regular dinner at the Poodle Dog Restaurant, and when he left the room he turned back to look once more at the stool where she had sat. Even on his way to that fast and famous café of the period he felt, for the first time in his thoughtless but lonely life, the gentle security of the home he had left behind him.

## II.

It was three or four days before he became firmly adjusted to his new quarters. During this time he had met Cherry casually on the staircase, in going or coming, and received her shy greetings; but she had not

repeated her visit, nor again alluded to it.
He had spent part of a formal evening in
the parlor in company with a calling deacon,
who, unappalled by the Indian shawl for
which the widow had exchanged her household cerements on such occasions, appeared
to Herbert to have remote matrimonial de-
signs, as far at least as a sympathetic deprecation of the vanities of the present, an
echoing of her sighs like a modest encore, a
preternatural gentility of manner, a vague
allusion to the necessity of bearing " one another's burdens," and an everlasting " promise " in store, would seem to imply. To
Herbert's vivid imagination, a discussion on
the doctrinal points of last Sabbath's ser-
mon was fraught with delicate suggestion ;
and an acceptance by the widow of an appointment to attend the Wednesday evening
" Lectures " had all the shy reluctant yielding of a granted rendezvous. Oddly enough,
the more formal attitude seemed to be reserved for the young people, who, in the suggestive atmosphere of this spiritual flirtation, alone appeared to preserve the propri-
eties and, to some extent, decorously chaperon their elders. Herbert gravely turned
the leaves of Cherry's music while she played

and sang one or two discreet but depressing songs expressive of her unalterable but proper devotion to her mother's clock, her father's arm-chair, and her aunt's Bible; and Herbert joined somewhat boyishly in the soul-subduing refrain. Only once he ventured to suggest in a whisper that he would like to add *her* music-stool to the adorable inventory; but he was met by such a disturbed and terrified look that he desisted. "Another night of this wild and reckless dissipation will finish me," he said lugubriously to himself when he reached the solitude of his room. "I wonder how many times a week I'd have to help the girl play the spiritual gooseberry downstairs before we could have any fun ourselves?"

Here the sound of distant laughter, interspersed with vivacious feminine shrieks, came through the open window. He glanced between the curtains. His neighbor's house was brilliantly lit, and the shadows of a few romping figures were chasing each other across the muslin shades of the windows. The objectionable young women were evidently enjoying themselves. In some conditions of the mind there is a certain exasperation in the spectacle of unmeaning enjoyment, and he shut the window sharply. At the same moment some one knocked at his door.

It was Miss Brooks, who had just come upstairs.

"Will you please let me have my music-stool?"

He stared at her a moment in surprise, then recovering himself, said, "Yes, certainly," and brought the stool. For an instant he was tempted to ask why she wanted it, but his pride forbade him.

"Thank you. Good-night."

"Good-night!"

"I hope it was n't in your way?"

"Not at all."

"Good-night!"

"Good-night."

She vanished. Herbert was perplexed. Between young ladies whose naïve exuberance impelled them to throw handkerchiefs at his window and young ladies whose equally naïve modesty demanded the withdrawal from his bedroom of a chair on which they had once sat, his lot seemed to have fallen in a troubled locality. Yet a day or two later he heard Cherry practising on the harmonium as he was ascending the stairs on his return from business; she had departed

before he entered the room, but had left the
music-stool behind her. It was not again
removed.

One Sunday, the second or third of his
tenancy, when Cherry and her mother were
at church, and he had finished some work
that he had brought from the bank, his former restlessness and sense of strangeness
returned. The regular afternoon fog had
thickened early, and, driving him back from
a cheerless, chilly ramble on the hill, had left
him still more depressed and solitary. In
sheer desperation he moved some of the furniture, and changed the disposition of several smaller ornaments. Growing bolder, he
even attacked the sacred shelf devoted to
Tappington's serious literature and moral
studies. At first glance the book of sermons
looked suspiciously fresh and new for a volume of habitual reference, but its leaves
were carefully cut, and contained one or two
book-marks. It was only another evidence
of that perfect youth's care and neatness.
As he was replacing it he noticed a small
object folded in white paper at the back
of the shelf. To put the book back into
its former position it was necessary to take
this out. He did so, but its contents slid

from his fingers and the paper to the floor.
To his utter consternation, looking down he
saw a pack of playing-cards strewn at his
feet!

He hurriedly picked them up. They were
worn and slippery from use, and exhaled a
faint odor of tobacco. Had they been left
there by some temporary visitor unknown to
Tappington and his family, or had they been
hastily hidden by a servant? Yet they were
of a make and texture superior to those that
a servant would possess; looking at them
carefully, he recognized them to be of a quality used by the better-class gamblers. Restoring them carefully to their former position, he was tempted to take out the other
volumes, and was rewarded with the further
discovery of a small box of ivory counters,
known as "poker-chips." It was really
very extraordinary! It was quite the *cache*
of some habitual gambler. Herbert smiled
grimly at the irreverent incongruity of the
hiding-place selected by its unknown and
mysterious owner, and amused himself by
fancying the horror of his sainted predecessor had *he* made the discovery. He determined to replace them, and to put some mark
upon the volumes before them in order to

detect any future disturbance of them in his absence.

Ought he not to take Miss Brooks in his confidence? Or should he say nothing about it at present, and trust to chance to discover the sacrilegious hider? Could it possibly be Cherry herself, guilty of the same innocent curiosity that had impelled her to buy the " Ham-fat Man " ? Preposterous! Besides, the cards had been used, and she could not play poker alone!

He watched the rolling fog extinguish the line of Russian Hill, the last bit of far perspective from his window. He glanced at his neighbor's veranda, already dripping with moisture; the windows were blank; he remembered to have heard the girls giggling in passing down the side street on their way to church, and had noticed from behind his own curtains that one was rather pretty. This led him to think of Cherry again, and to recall the quaint yet melancholy grace of her figure as she sat on the stool opposite. Why had she withdrawn it so abruptly; did she consider his jesting allusion to it indecorous and presuming? Had he really meant it seriously; and was he beginning to think too much about her? Would she

ever come again? How nice it would be if
she returned from church alone early, and
they could have a comfortable chat together
here! Would she sing the "Ham-fat Man"
for him? Would the dimples come back if
she did? Should he ever know more of this
quaint repressed side of her nature? After
all, what a dear, graceful, tantalizing, lova-
ble creature she was! Ought he not at all
hazards try to know her better? Might it
not be here that he would find a perfect realization of his boyish dreams, and in *her* all
that — what nonsense he was thinking!

Suddenly Herbert was startled by the
sound of a light but hurried foot upon the
wooden outer step of his second door, and
the quick but ineffective turning of the door-
handle. He started to his feet, his mind still
filled with a vision of Cherry. Then he as
suddenly remembered that he had locked the
door on going out, putting the key in his
overcoat pocket. He had returned by the
front door, and his overcoat was now hanging in the lower hall.

The door again rattled impetuously. Then
it was supplemented by a female voice in a
hurried whisper: "Open quick, can't you?
do hurry!"

He was confounded. The voice was authoritative, not unmusical; but it was *not* Cherry's. Nevertheless he called out quickly, " One moment, please, and I 'll get the key ! " dashed downstairs and up again, breathlessly unlocked the door and threw it open.

Nobody was there !

He ran out into the street. On one side it terminated abruptly on the cliff on which his dwelling was perched ; on the other, it descended more gradually into the next thoroughfare ; but up and down the street, on either hand, no one was to be seen. A slightly superstitious feeling for an instant crept over him. Then he reflected that the mysterious visitor could in the interval of his getting the key have easily slipped down the steps of the cliff or entered the shrubbery of one of the adjacent houses. But why had she not waited ? And what did she want ? As he reëntered his door he mechanically raised his eyes to the windows of his neighbor's. This time he certainly was not mistaken. The two amused, mischievous faces that suddenly disappeared behind the curtain as he looked up showed that the incident had not been unwitnessed. Yet it was impossible that it could have been either of *them.* Their house was only accessible by a long détour. It might have been the trick of a confederate; but the tone of half familiarity and half entreaty in the unseen visitor's voice dispelled the idea of any collusion. He entered the room and closed the door angrily. A grim smile stole over his face as he glanced around at the dainty saint-like appointments of the absent Tappington, and thought what that irreproachable young man would have said to the indecorous intrusion, even though it had been a mistake. Would those shameless Pike County girls have dared to laugh at *him?*

But he was again puzzled to know why he himself should have been selected for this singular experience. Why was *he* considered fair game for these girls? And, for the matter of that, now that he reflected upon it, why had even this gentle, refined, and melancholy Cherry thought it necessary to talk slang to *him* on their first acquaintance, and offer to sing him the "Ham-fat Man"? It was true he had been a little gay, but never dissipated. Of course he was not a saint, like Tappington — oh, *that* was it! He believed he understood it now. He was suffering from that extravagant con-

ception of what worldliness consists of, so
common to very good people with no knowledge of the world. Compared to Tappington he was in their eyes, of course, a rake
and a roué. The explanation pleased him.
He would not keep it to himself. He would
gain Cherry's confidence and enlist her sympathies. Her gentle nature would revolt at
this injustice to their lonely lodger. She
would see that there were degrees of goodness besides her brother's. She would perhaps sit on that stool again and *not* sing the
" Ham-fat Man."

A day or two afterwards the opportunity
seemed offered to him. As he was coming
home and ascending the long hilly street, his
eye was taken by a tall graceful figure just
preceding him. It was she. He had never
before seen her in the street, and was now
struck with her ladylike bearing and the
grave superiority of her perfectly simple
attire. In a thoroughfare haunted by handsome women and striking toilettes, the refined grace of her mourning costume, and a
certain stateliness that gave her the look of a
young widow, was a contrast that evidently
attracted others than himself. It was with
an odd mingling of pride and jealousy that

he watched the admiring yet respectful
glances of the passers-by, some of whom
turned to look again, and one or two to re-
trace their steps and follow her at a decorous distance. This caused him to quicken
his own pace, with a new anxiety and a remorseful sense of wasted opportunity. What
a booby he had been, not to have made more
of his contiguity to this charming girl — to
have been frightened at the naïve decorum
of her maidenly instincts! He reached her
side, and raised his hat with a trepidation at
her new-found graces — with a boldness that
was defiant of her other admirers. She
blushed slightly.

" I thought you 'd overtake me before,"
she said naïvely. "*I* saw *you* ever so long
ago."

He stammered, with an equal simplicity,
that he had not dared to.

She looked a little frightened again, and
then said hurriedly : " I only thought that
I would meet you on Montgomery Street,
and we would walk home together. I don't
like to go out alone, and mother cannot always go with me. Tappington never cared
to take me out — I don't know why. I think
he did n't like the people staring and stop-

ping us. But they stare more — don't you
think? — when one is alone. So I thought
if you were coming straight home we might
come together — unless you have something
else to do?"

Herbert impulsively reiterated his joy at
meeting her, and averred that no other engagement, either of business or pleasure,
could or would stand in his way. Looking
up, however, it was with some consternation
that he saw they were already within a block
of the house.

"Suppose we take a turn around the hill
and come back by the old street down the
steps?" he suggested earnestly.

The next moment he regretted it. The
frightened look returned to her eyes; her
face became melancholy and formal again.

"No!" she said quickly. "That would
be taking a walk with you like these young
girls and their young men on Saturdays.
That's what Ellen does with the butcher's
boy on Sundays. Tappington often used to
meet them. Doing the 'Come, Philanders,'
as he says you call it."

It struck Herbert that the didactic Tappington's method of inculcating a horror of
slang in his sister's breast was open to some

objection; but they were already on the steps of their house, and he was too much mortified at the reception of his last unhappy suggestion to make the confidential disclosure he had intended, even if there had still been time.

"There's mother waiting for me," she said, after an awkward pause, pointing to the figure of Mrs. Brooks dimly outlined on the veranda. "I suppose she was beginning to be worried about my being out alone. She 'll be so glad I met you." It did n't appear to Herbert, however, that Mrs. Brooks exhibited any extravagant joy over the occurrence, and she almost instantly retired with her daughter into the sitting-room, linking her arm in Cherry's, and, as it were, empanoplying her with her own invulnerable shawl. Herbert went to his room more dissatisfied with himself than ever.

Two or three days elapsed without his seeing Cherry; even the well-known rustle of her skirt in the passage was missing. On the third evening he resolved to bear the formal terrors of the drawing-room again, and stumbled upon a decorous party consisting of Mrs. Brooks, the deacon, and the pastor's wife — but not Cherry. It struck him

on entering that the momentary awkwardness of the company and the formal beginning of a new topic indicated that *he* had
been the subject of their previous conversation. In this idea he continued, through that
vague spirit of opposition which attacks impulsive people in such circumstances, to generally disagree with them on all subjects,
and to exaggerate what he chose to believe
they thought objectionable in him. He did
not remain long; but learned in that brief
interval that Cherry had gone to visit a
friend in Contra Costa, and would be absent
a fortnight; and he was conscious that the
information was conveyed to him with a
peculiar significance.

The result of which was only to intensify
his interest in the absent Cherry, and for a
week to plunge him in a sea of conflicting
doubts and resolutions. At one time he
thought seriously of demanding an explanation from Mrs. Brooks, and of confiding to
her — as he had intended to do to Cherry —
his fears that his character had been misinterpreted, and his reasons for believing so.
But here he was met by the difficulty of
formulating what he wished to have explained, and some doubts as to whether his

confidences were prudent. At another time
he contemplated a serious imitation of Tappington's perfections, a renunciation of the
world, and an entire change in his habits.
He would go regularly to church — *her*
church, and take up Tappington's desolate
Bible-class. But here the torturing doubt
arose whether a young lady who betrayed a
certain secular curiosity, and who had evidently depended upon her brother for a
knowledge of the world, would entirely like
it. At times he thought of giving up the
room and abandoning for ever this doubly
dangerous proximity ; but here again he was
deterred by the difficulty of giving a satisfactory reason to his employer, who had procured it as a favor. His passion — for such
he began to fear it to be — led him once to
the extravagance of asking a day's holiday
from the bank, which he vaguely spent in
the streets of Oakland in the hope of accidentally meeting the exiled Cherry.

### III.

THE fortnight slowly passed. She returned, but he did not see her. She was always out or engaged in her room with some

female friend when Herbert was at home. This was singular, as she had never appeared to him as a young girl who was fond of visiting or had ever affected female friendships. In fact, there was little doubt now that, wittingly or unwittingly, she was avoiding him.

He was moodily sitting by the fire one evening, having returned early from dinner. In reply to his habitual but affectedly careless inquiry, Ellen had told him that Mrs. Brooks was confined to her room by a slight headache, and that Miss Brooks was out. He was trying to read, and listening to the wind that occasionally rattled the casement and caused the solitary gas-lamp that was visible in the side street to flicker and leap wildly. Suddenly he heard the same footfall upon his outer step and a light tap at the door. Determined this time to solve the mystery, he sprang to his feet and ran to the door; but to his anger and astonishment it was locked and the key was gone. Yet he was positive that *he* had not taken it out.

The tap was timidly repeated. In desperation he called out, "Please don't go away yet. The key is gone; but I'll find it in a moment." Nevertheless he was at his wits' end.

There was a hesitating pause and then the sound of a key cautiously thrust into the lock. It turned; the door opened, and a tall figure, whose face and form were completely hidden in a veil and long gray shawl, quickly glided into the room and closed the door behind it. Then it suddenly raised its arms, the shawl was parted, the veil fell aside, and Cherry stood before him!

Her face was quite pale. Her eyes, usually downcast, frightened, or coldly clear, were bright and beautiful with excitement. The dimples were faintly there, although the smile was sad and half hysterical. She remained standing, erect and tall, her arms dropped at her side, holding the veil and shawl that still depended from her shoulders.

"So — I've caught you!" she said, with a strange little laugh. "Oh yes. 'Please don't go away yet. I'll get the key in a moment,'" she continued, mimicking his recent utterance.

He could only stammer, " Miss Brooks — then it was *you?* "

"Yes; and you thought it was *she*, didn't you? Well, and you're caught! I didn't believe it; I wouldn't believe it when they said it. I determined to find it out myself. And I have; and it's true."

Unable to determine whether she was serious or jesting, and conscious only of his delight at seeing her again, he advanced impulsively. But her expression instantly changed : she became at once stiff and school-girlishly formal, and stepped back towards the door.

"Don't come near me, or I'll go," she said quickly, with her hand upon the lock.

"But not before you tell me what you mean," he said half laughingly half earnestly. "Who is *she?* and what would n't you have believed? For upon my honor, Miss Brooks, I don't know what you are talking about."

His evident frankness and truthful manner appeared to puzzle her. "You mean to say you were expecting no one?" she said sharply.

"I assure you I was not."

"And — and no woman was ever here — at that door?"

He hesitated. "Not to-night — not for a long time; not since you returned from Oakland."

"Then there *was* one?"

"I believe so."

"You *believe* — you don't *know?*"

"I believed it was a woman from her voice; for the door was locked, and the key was downstairs. When I fetched it and opened the door, she — or whoever it was — was gone."

"And that's why you said so imploringly, just now, 'Please don't go away yet'? You see I've caught you. Ah! I don't wonder you blush!"

If he had, his cheeks had caught fire from her brilliant eyes and the extravagantly affected sternness — as of a school-girl monitor — in her animated face. Certainly he had never seen such a transformation.

"Yes; but, you see, I wanted to know who the intruder was," he said, smiling at his own embarrassment.

"You did — well, perhaps *that* will tell you? It was found under your door before I went away." She suddenly produced from her pocket a folded paper and handed it to him. It was a misspelt scrawl, and ran as follows: —

"Why are you so cruel? Why do you keep me dansing on the stepps before them gurls at the windows? Was it that stuck-up Saint, Miss Brooks, that you were afraid

of, my deer? Oh, you faithless trater!
Wait till I ketch you! I 'll tear your eyes
out and hern!"

It did not require great penetration for
Herbert to be instantly convinced that the
writer of this vulgar epistle and the owner
of the unknown voice were two very different individuals. The note was evidently a
trick. A suspicion of its perpetrators flashed
upon him.

"Whoever the woman was, it was not she
who wrote the note," he said positively.
"Somebody must have seen her at the door.
I remember now that those girls — your
neighbors — were watching me from their
window when I came out. Depend upon it,
that letter comes from them."

Cherry's eyes opened widely with a sudden childlike perception, and then shyly
dropped. "Yes," she said slowly; "they *did*
watch you. They know it, for it was they
who made it the talk of the neighborhood,
and that 's how it came to mother's ears."
She stopped, and, with a frightened look,
stepped back towards the door again.

"Then *that* was why your mother" —

"Oh yes," interrupted Cherry quickly.
"That was why I went over to Oakland, and

why mother forbade my walking with you
again, and why she had a talk with friends
about your conduct, and why she came near
telling Mr. Carstone all about it until I
stopped her." She checked herself — he
could hardly believe his eyes — the pale,
nun-like girl was absolutely blushing.

"I thank you, Miss Brooks," he said
gravely, "for your thoughtfulness, although
I hope I could have still proven my innocence to Mr. Carstone, even if some unknown
woman tried my door by mistake, and was
seen doing it. But I am pained to think
that *you* could have believed me capable of
so wanton and absurd an impropriety — and
such a gross disrespect to your mother's
house."

"But," said Cherry with childlike naïveté,
"you know *you* don't think anything of such
things, and that's what I told mother."

"You told your mother *that?*"

"Oh yes — I told her Tappington says
it's quite common with young men. Please
don't laugh — for it's very dreadful. Tappington did n't laugh when he told it to me
as a warning. He was shocked."

"But, my dear Miss Brooks" —

"There — now you're angry — and that's

as bad. Are you sure you did n't know that woman?"

"Positive!"

"Yet you seemed very anxious just now that she should wait till you opened the door."

"That was perfectly natural."

"I don't think it was natural at all."

"But — according to Tappington"—

"Because my brother is very good you need not make fun of him."

"I assure you I have no such intention. But what more can I say? I give you my word that I don't know who that unlucky woman was. No doubt she may have been some nearsighted neighbor who had mistaken the house, and I dare say was as thoroughly astonished at my voice as I was at hers. Can I say more? Is it necessary for me to swear that since I have been here no woman has ever entered that door — but"—

"But who?"

"Yourself."

"I know what you mean," she said hurriedly, with her old frightened look, gliding to the outer door. "It's shameful what I've done. But I only did it because — because I had faith in you, and did n't believe what they said was true." She had already turned the lock. There were tears in her pretty eyes.

"Stop," said Herbert gently. He walked slowly towards her, and within reach of her frightened figure stopped with the timid respect of a mature and genuine passion. "You must not be seen going out of that door," he said gravely. "You must let me go first, and, when I am gone, lock the door again and go through the hall to your own room. No one must know that I was in the house when you came in at that door. Goodnight."

Without offering his hand he lifted his eyes to her face. The dimples were all there — and something else. He bowed and passed out.

Ten minutes later he ostentatiously returned to the house by the front door, and proceeded up the stairs to his own room. As he cast a glance around he saw that the music-stool had been moved before the fire, evidently with the view of attracting his attention. Lying upon it, carefully folded, was the veil that she had worn. There could be no doubt that it was left there purposely. With a smile at this strange girl's last characteristic act of timid but compromising recklessness, after all his precautions, he raised it tenderly to his lips, and then hastened to hide it from the reach of vulgar eyes. But had Cherry known that its temporary resting-place that night was under his pillow she might have doubted his superior caution.

When he returned from the bank the next afternoon, Cherry rapped ostentatiously at his door. "Mother wishes me to ask you," she began with a certain prim formality, which nevertheless did not preclude dimples, "if you would give us the pleasure of your company at our Church Festival to-night? There will be a concert and a collation. You could accompany us there if you cared. Our friends and Tappington's would be so glad to see you, and Dr. Stout would be delighted to make your acquaintance."

"Certainly!" said Herbert, delighted and yet astounded. "Then," he added in a lower voice, "your mother no longer believes me so dreadfully culpable?"

"Oh no," said Cherry in a hurried whisper, glancing up and down the passage; "I've been talking to her about it, and she is satisfied that it is all a jealous trick and slander of these neighbors. Why, I told her that they had even said that *I* was that mysterious woman; that I came that way to you because she had forbidden my seeing you openly."

" What! You dared say that?"

" Yes; don't you see? Suppose they said they *had* seen me coming in last night — *that* answers it," she said triumphantly.

" Oh, it does?" he said vacantly.

" Perfectly. So you see she's convinced that she ought to put you on the same footing as Tappington, before everybody; and then there won't be any trouble. You'll come, won't you? It won't be so *very* good. And then, I've told mother that as there have been so many street-fights, and so much talk about the Vigilance Committee lately, I ought to have somebody for an escort when I am coming home. And if you're known, you see, as one of *us*, there'll be no harm in your meeting me."

" Thank you," he said, extending his hand gratefully.

Her fingers rested a moment in his. " Where did you put it?" she said demurely.

" It? Oh! *it's* all safe," he said quickly, but somewhat vaguely.

" But I don't call the upper drawer of your bureau safe," she returned poutingly, " where *everybody* can go. So you'll find it *now* inside the harmonium, on the keyboard."

" Oh, thank you."

" It's quite natural to have left it there *accidentally* — is n't it ? " she said imploringly, assisted by all her dimples. Alas ! she had forgotten that he was still holding her hand. Consequently, she had not time to snatch it away and vanish, with a stifled little cry, before it had been pressed two or three times to his lips. A little ashamed of his own boldness, Herbert remained for a few moments in the doorway listening, and looking uneasily down the dark passage. Presently a slight sound came over the fanlight of Cherry's room. Could he believe his ears ? The saint-like Cherry — no doubt tutored, for example's sake, by the perfect Tappington — was softly whistling.

In this simple fashion the first pages of this little idyl were quietly turned. The book might have been closed or laid aside even then. But it so chanced that Cherry was an unconscious prophet; and presently it actually became a prudential necessity for

her to have a masculine escort when she
walked out. For a growing state of lawless-
ness and crime culminated one day the deep
tocsin of the Vigilance Committee, and at
its stroke fifty thousand peaceful men, re-
verting to the first principles of social safety,
sprang to arms, assembled at their quarters,
or patrolled the streets. In another hour
the city of San Francisco was in the hands
of a mob — the most peaceful, orderly, well
organized, and temperate the world had ever
known, and yet in conception as lawless,
autocratic, and imperious as the conditions
it opposed.

## IV.

HERBERT, enrolled in the same section
with his employer and one or two fellow-
clerks, had participated in the meetings of
the committee with the light-heartedness and
irresponsibility of youth, regretting only the
loss of his usual walk with Cherry and the
hours that kept him from her house. He
was returning from a protracted meeting
one night, when the number of arrests and
searching for proscribed and suspected characters had been so large as to induce fears
of organized resistance and rescue, and on

reaching the foot of the hill found it already so late, that to avoid disturbing the family he resolved to enter his room directly by the door in the side street. On inserting his key in the lock it met with some resisting obstacle, which, however, yielded and apparently dropped on the mat inside. Opening the door and stepping into the perfectly dark apartment, he trod upon this object, which proved to be another key. The family must have procured it for their convenience during his absence, and after locking the door had carelessly left it in the lock. It was lucky that it had yielded so readily.

The fire had gone out. He closed the door and lit the gas, and after taking off his overcoat moved to the door leading into the passage to listen if anybody was still stirring. To his utter astonishment he found it locked. What was more remarkable — the key was also *inside!* An inexplicable feeling took possession of him. He glanced suddenly around the room, and then his eye fell upon the bed. Lying there, stretched at full length, was the recumbent figure of a man.

He was apparently in the profound sleep of utter exhaustion. The attitude of his limbs and the order of his dress — of which

only his collar and cravat had been loosened
— showed that sleep must have overtaken
him almost instantly. In fact, the bed was
scarcely disturbed beyond the actual impress
of his figure. He seemed to be a handsome,
matured man of about forty; his dark
straight hair was a little thinned over the
temples, although his long heavy moustache
was still youthful and virgin. His clothes,
which were elegantly cut and of finer material than that in ordinary use, the delicacy
and neatness of his linen, the whiteness of
his hands, and, more particularly, a certain
dissipated pallor of complexion and lines of
recklessness on the brow and cheek, indicated to Herbert that the man before him
was one of that desperate and suspected
class — some of whose proscribed members
he had been hunting — the professional
gambler!

Possibly the magnetism of Herbert's intent
and astonished gaze affected him. He moved
slightly, half opened his eyes, said "Halloo,
Tap," rubbed them again, wholly opened
them, fixed them with a lazy stare on Herbert, and said:

"Now, who the devil are you?"

"I think *I* have the right to ask that

question, considering that this is my room," said Herbert sharply.

" *Your* room ? "

" Yes ! "

The stranger half raised himself on his elbow, glanced round the room, settled himself slowly back on the pillows, with his hands clasped lightly behind his head, dropped his eyelids, smiled, and said :

" Rats ! "

" What ? " demanded Herbert, with a resentful sense of sacrilege to Cherry's virgin slang.

" Well, old rats then ! D' ye think I don't know this shebang ? Look here, Johnny, what are you putting on all this side for, eh ? What 's your little game ? Where 's Tappington ? "

" If you mean Mr. Brooks, the son of this house, who formerly lived in this room," replied Herbert, with a formal precision intended to show a doubt of the stranger's knowledge of Tappington, " you ought to know that he has left town."

" Left town ! " echoed the stranger, raising himself again. " Oh, I see ! getting rather too warm for him here ? Humph ! I ought to have thought of that. Well, you know, he *did* take mighty big risks, anyway!" He was silent a moment, with his brows knit and a rather dangerous expression in his handsome face. "So some d—d hound gave him away — eh?"

"I hadn't the pleasure of knowing Mr. Brooks except by reputation, as the respected son of the lady upon whose house you have just intruded," said Herbert frigidly, yet with a creeping consciousness of some unpleasant revelation.

The stranger stared at him for a moment, again looked carefully round the room, and then suddenly dropped his head back on the pillow, and with his white hands over his eyes and mouth tried to restrain a spasm of silent laughter. After an effort he succeeded, wiped his moist eyes, and sat up.

"So you didn't know Tappington, eh?" he said, lazily buttoning his collar.

"No."

"No more do I."

He retied his cravat, yawned, rose, shook himself perfectly neat again, and going to Herbert's dressing-table quietly took up a brush and began to lightly brush himself, occasionally turning to the window to glance out. Presently he turned to Herbert and said:

"Well, Johnny, what's your name?"

"I am Herbert Bly, of Carstone's Bank."

"So, and a member of this same Vigilance Committee, I reckon," he continued.

"Yes."

"Well, Mr. Bly, I owe you an apology for coming here, and some thanks for the only sleep I've had in forty-eight hours. I struck this old shebang at about ten o'clock, and it's now two, so I reckon I've put in about four hours' square sleep. Now, look here." He beckoned Herbert towards the window. "Do you see those three men standing under that gaslight? Well, they're part of a gang of Vigilantes who've hunted me to the hill, and are waiting to see me come out of the bushes, where they reckon I'm hiding. Go to them and say that I'm here! Tell them you've got Gentleman George — George Dornton, the man they've been hunting for a week — in this room. I promise you I won't stir, nor kick up a row, when they've come. Do it, and Carstone, if he's a square man, will raise your salary for it, and promote you." He yawned slightly, and then slowly looking around him, drew the easy-chair towards him and dropped comfortably in it, gazing at the astounded and motionless Herbert with a lazy smile.

"You're wondering what my little game is, Johnny, ain't you? Well, I'll tell you. What with being hunted from pillar to post, putting my old pards to no end of trouble, and then slipping up on it whenever I think I've got a sure thing like this," — he cast an almost affectionate glance at the bed, — "I've come to the conclusion that it's played out, and I might as well hand in my checks. It's only a question of my being *run out* of 'Frisco, or hiding until I can *slip out* myself; and I've reckoned I might as well give them the trouble and expense of transportation. And if I can put a good thing in your way in doing it — why, it will sort of make things square with you for the fuss I've given you."

Even in the stupefaction and helplessness of knowing that the man before him was the notorious duellist and gambler George Dornton, one of the first marked for deportation by the Vigilance Committee, Herbert recognized all he had heard of his invincible coolness, courage, and almost philosophic fatalism. For an instant his youthful imagination checked even his indignation. When he recovered himself, he said, with rising color and boyish vehemence :

" Whoever *you* may be, I am neither a police officer nor a spy. You have no right to insult me by supposing that I would profit by the mistake that made you my guest, or that I would refuse you the sanctuary of the roof that covers your insult as well as your blunder."

The stranger gazed at him with an amused expression, and then rose and stretched out his hand.

" Shake, Mr. Bly! You 're the only man that ever kicked George Dornton when he deserved it. Good-night!" He took his hat and walked to the door.

" Stop! " said Herbert impulsively; " the night is already far gone; go back and finish your sleep."

" You mean it ? "

" I do."

The stranger turned, walked back to the bed, unfastening his coat and collar as he did so, and laid himself down in the attitude of a moment before.

" I will call you in the morning," continued Herbert. " By that time," — he hesitated, — " by that time your pursuers may have given up their search. One word more. You will be frank with me ? "

" Go on."

" Tappington and you are — friends ? "

" Well — yes."

" His mother and sister know nothing of this ? "

" I reckon he did n't boast of it. *I* did n't. Is that all ? " sleepily.

" Yes."

" Don't *you* worry about *him*. Goodnight."

" Good-night."

But even at that moment George Dornton had dropped off in a quiet, peaceful sleep.

Bly turned down the light, and, drawing his easy-chair to the window, dropped into it in bewildering reflection. This then was the secret — unknown to mother and daughter — unsuspected by all! This was the double life of Tappington, half revealed in his flirtation with the neighbors, in the hidden cards behind the books, in the mysterious visitor — still unaccounted for — and now wholly exploded by this sleeping confederate, for whom, somehow, Herbert felt the greatest sympathy! What was to be done ? What should he say to Cherry — to her mother — to Mr. Carstone ? Yet he had felt he had done right. From time to time he turned to the motionless recumbent shadow on the bed and listened to its slow and peaceful respiration. Apart from that undefinable attraction which all original natures have for each other, the thrice-blessed mystery of protection of the helpless, for the first time in his life, seemed to dawn upon him through that night.

Nevertheless, the actual dawn came slowly. Twice he nodded and awoke quickly with a start. The third time it was day. The street-lamps were extinguished, and with them the moving, restless watchers seemed also to have vanished. Suddenly a formal deliberate rapping at the door leading to the hall startled him to his feet.

It must be Ellen. So much the better; he could quickly get rid of her. He glanced at the bed; Dornton slept on undisturbed. He unlocked the door cautiously, and instinctively fell back before the erect, shawled, and decorous figure of Mrs. Brooks. But an utterly new resolution and excitement had supplanted the habitual resignation of her handsome features, and given them an angry sparkle of expression.

Recollecting himself, he instantly stepped forward into the passage, drawing to the door behind him, as she, with equal celerity, opposed it with her hand.

"Mr. Bly," she said deliberately, "Ellen has just told me that your voice has been heard in conversation with some one in this room late last night. Up to this moment I have foolishly allowed my daughter to persuade me that certain infamous scandals regarding your conduct here were false. I must ask you as a gentleman to let me pass now and satisfy myself."

"But, my dear madam, one moment. Let me first explain — I beg " — stammered Herbert with a half-hysterical laugh. "I assure you a gentleman friend " —

But she had pushed him aside and entered precipitately. With a quick feminine glance round the room she turned to the bed, and then halted in overwhelming confusion.

"It's a friend," said Herbert in a hasty whisper. "A friend of mine who returned with me late, and whom, on account of the disturbed state of the streets, I induced to stay here all night. He was so tired that I have not had the heart to disturb him yet."

"Oh, pray don't! — I beg " — said Mrs. Brooks with a certain youthful vivacity, but still gazing at the stranger's handsome features as she slowly retreated. "Not for worlds!"

Herbert was relieved; she was actually blushing.

"You see, it was quite unpremeditated, I assure you. We came in together," whispered Herbert, leading her to the door, "and I"—

"Don't believe a word of it, madam," said a lazy voice from the bed, as the stranger leisurely raised himself upright, putting the last finishing touch to his cravat as he shook himself neat again. "I'm an utter stranger to him, and he knows it. He found me here, hiding from the Vigilantes, who were chasing me on the hill. I got in at that door, which happened to be unlocked. He let me stay because he was a gentleman — and — I was n't. I beg your pardon, madam, for having interrupted him before you; but it was a little rough to have him lie on *my* account when he was n't the kind of man to lie on his *own*. You 'll forgive him — won't you, please? — and, as I'm taking myself off now, perhaps you 'll overlook *my* intrusion too."

It was impossible to convey the lazy

frankness of this speech, the charming smile with which it was accompanied, or the easy yet deferential manner with which, taking up his hat, he bowed to Mrs. Brooks as he advanced toward the door.

"But," said Mrs. Brooks, hurriedly glancing from Herbert to the stranger, "it must be the Vigilantes who are now hanging about the street. Ellen saw them from her window, and thought they were *your* friends, Mr. Bly. This gentleman — your friend" — she had become a little confused in her novel excitement — "really ought not to go out now. It would be madness."

"If you would n't mind his remaining a little longer, it certainly would be safer," said Herbert, with wondering gratitude.

"I certainly should n't consent to his leaving my house now," said Mrs. Brooks with dignity; "and if you would n't mind' calling Cherry here, Mr. Bly — she's in the dining-room — and then showing yourself for a moment in the street and finding out what they wanted, it would be the best thing to do."

Herbert flew downstairs; in a few hurried words he gave the same explanation to the astounded Cherry that he had given to

her mother, with the mischievous addition
that Mrs. Brooks's unjust suspicions had
precipitated her into becoming an amicable
accomplice, and then ran out into the street.
Here he ascertained from one of the Vigilantes, whom he knew, that they were really
seeking Dornton ; but that, concluding that
the fugitive had already escaped to the
wharves, they expected to withdraw their
surveillance at noon. Somewhat relieved,
he hastened back, to find the stranger
calmly seated on the sofa in the parlor with
the same air of frank indifference, lazily
relating the incidents of his flight to the
two women, who were listening with every
expression of sympathy and interest. "Poor
fellow !" said Cherry, taking the astonished
Bly aside into the hall, "I don't believe he's
half as bad as *they* said he is — or as even
*he* makes himself out to be. But *did* you
notice mother ?"

Herbert, a little dazed, and, it must be
confessed, a trifle uneasy at this ready acceptance of the stranger, abstractedly said
he had not.

"Why, it's the most ridiculous thing.
She's actually going round *without her
shawl*, and does n't seem to know it."

## V.

When Herbert finally reached the bank that morning he was still in a state of doubt and perplexity. He had parted with his grateful visitor, whose safety in a few hours seemed assured, but without the least further revelation or actual allusion to anything antecedent to his selecting Tappington's room as refuge. More than that, Herbert was convinced from his manner that he had no intention of making a confidant of Mrs. Brooks, and this convinced him that Dornton's previous relations with Tappington were not only utterly inconsistent with that young man's decorous reputation, but were unsuspected by the family. The stranger's familiar knowledge of the room, his mysterious allusions to the "risks" Tappington had taken, and his sudden silence on the discovery of Bly's ignorance of the whole affair — all pointed to some secret that, innocent or not, was more or less perilous, not only to the son but to the mother and sister. Of the latter's ignorance he had no doubt — but had he any right to enlighten them? Admitting that Tappington had deceived

them with the others, would they thank him
for opening their eyes to it? If they had already a suspicion, would they care to know
that it was shared by him? Halting between his frankness and his delicacy, the
final thought that in his budding relations
with the daughter it might seem a cruel bid
for her confidence, or a revenge for their distrust of him, inclined him to silence. But
an unforeseen occurrence took the matter
from his hands. At noon he was told that
Mr. Carstone wished to see him in his private room!

Satisfied that his complicity with Dornton's escape was discovered, the unfortunate
Herbert presented himself, pale but self-pos-
sessed, before his employer. That brief man
of business bade him be seated, and standing
himself before the fireplace, looked down curiously, but not unkindly, upon his employee.

"Mr. Bly, the bank does not usually interfere with the private affairs of its em-
ployees, but for certain reasons which I prefer to explain to you later, I must ask you
to give me a straightforward answer to one
or two questions. I may say that they have
nothing to do with your relations to the bank,
which are to us perfectly satisfactory."

More than ever convinced that Mr. Carstone was about to speak of his visitor, Herbert signified his willingness to reply.

"You have been seen a great deal with
Miss Brooks lately — on the street and elsewhere — acting as her escort, and evidently
on terms of intimacy. To do you both justice, neither of you seemed to have made it
a secret or avoided observation; but I must
ask you directly if it is with her mother's
permission?"

Considerably relieved, but wondering what
was coming, Herbert answered, with boyish
frankness, that it was.

"Are you — engaged to the young lady?"

"No, sir."

"Are you — well, Mr. Bly — briefly, are
you what is called 'in love' with her?"
asked the banker, with a certain brusque
hurrying over of a sentiment evidently in-
compatible with their present business surroundings.

Herbert blushed. It was the first time he
had heard the question voiced, even by himself.

"I am," he said resolutely.

"And you wish to marry her?"

"If I dared ask her to accept a young

man with no position as yet," stammered
Herbert.

" People don't usually consider a young
man in Carstone's Bank of no position," said
the banker dryly ; " and I wish for your sake
*that* were the only impediment.  For I am
compelled to reveal to you a secret."  He
paused, and folding his arms, looked fixedly
down upon his clerk.  " Mr. Bly, Tappington Brooks, the brother of your sweetheart,
was a defaulter and embezzler from this
bank ! "

Herbert sat dumfounded and motionless.

" Understand two things," continued Mr.
Carstone quickly.  " First, that no purer or
better women exist than Miss Brooks and
her mother.   Secondly, that they know nothing of this, and that only myself and one
other man are in possession of the secret."

He slightly changed his position, and went
on more deliberately.   " Six weeks ago Tappington sat in that chair where you are sitting now, a convicted hypocrite and thief.
Luckily for him, although his guilt was
plain, and the whole secret of his double life
revealed to me, a sum of money advanced in
pity by one of his gambling confederates had
made his accounts good and saved him from

suspicion in the eyes of his fellow-clerks and
my partners. At first he tried to fight me
on that point; then he blustered and said
his mother could have refunded the money;
and asked me what was a paltry five thousand dollars! I told him, Mr. Bly, that it
might be five years of his youth in state
prison; that it might be five years of sorrow
and shame for his mother and sister; that it
might be an everlasting stain on the name
of his dead father — my friend. He talked
of killing himself: I told him he was a cow-
ardly fool. He asked me to give him up
to the authorities: I told him I intended to
take the law in my own hands and give him
another chance; and then he broke down. I
transferred him that very day, without giving him time to communicate with anybody,
to our branch office at Portland, with a
letter explaining his position to our agent,
and the injunction that for six months he
should be under strict surveillance. I myself undertook to explain his sudden departure to Mrs. Brooks, and obliged him to write
to her from time to time." He paused, and
then continued: " So far I believe my plan
has been successful: the secret has been
kept; he has broken with the evil associates

that ruined him here — to the best of my knowledge he has had no communication with them since; even a certain woman here who shared his vicious hidden life has abandoned him."

" Are you sure?" asked Herbert involuntarily, as he recalled his mysterious visitor.

" I believe the Vigilance Committee has considered it a public duty to deport her and her confederates beyond the State," returned Carstone dryly.

Another idea flashed upon Herbert. " And the gambler who advanced the money to save Tappington?" he said breathlessly.

" Was n't such a hound as the rest of his kind, if report says true," answered Carstone. " He was well known here as George Dornton — Gentleman George — a man capable of better things. But he was before your time, Mr. Bly — *you* don't know him."

Herbert did n't deem it a felicitous moment to correct his employer, and Mr. Carstone continued: "I have now told you what I thought it was my duty to tell you. I must leave *you* to judge how far it affects your relations with Miss Brooks."

Herbert did not hesitate. " I should be very sorry, sir, to seem to undervalue your

consideration or disregard your warning ;
but I am afraid that even if you had been
less merciful to Tappington, and he were
now a convicted felon, I should change
neither my feelings nor my intentions to his
sister."

" And you would still marry her ? " said
Carstone sternly ; " *you*, an employee of the
bank, would set the example of allying yourself with one who had robbed it ? "

"I — am afraid I would, sir," said Herbert slowly.

" Even if it were a question of your remaining here ? " said Carstone grimly.

Poor Herbert already saw himself dismissed and again taking up his weary quest
for employment; but, nevertheless, he answered stoutly :

" Yes, sir."

" And nothing will prevent you marrying
Miss Brooks ? "

" Nothing — save my inability to support
her."

" Then," said Mr. Carstone, with a peculiar light in his eyes, " it only remains for
the bank to mark its opinion of your conduct by *increasing your salary to enable
you to do so !* Shake hands, Mr. Bly," he

said, laughing. " I think you 'll do to tie
to — and I believe the young lady will be of
the same opinion. But not a word to either
her or her mother in regard to what you
have heard. And now I may tell you something more. I am not without hope of Tappington's future, nor — d—n it ! — without
some excuse for his fault, sir. He was arti-
ficially brought up. When my old friend
died, Mrs. Brooks, still a handsome woman,
like all her sex would n't rest until she had
another devotion, and wrapped herself and
her children up in the Church. Theology
may be all right for grown people, but it 's
apt to make children artificial ; and Tappington was pious before he was fairly good.
He drew on a religious credit before he had
a moral capital behind it. He was brought
up with no knowledge of the world, and
when he went into it — it captured him. I
don't say there are not saints born into the
world occasionally ; but for every one you 'll
find a lot of promiscuous human nature.
My old friend Josh Brooks had a heap of
it, and it would n't be strange if some was
left in his children, and burst through their
straight-lacing in a queer way. That 's all !
Good-morning, Mr. Bly. Forget what I 've

told you for six months, and then I should n't
wonder if Tappington was on hand to give
his sister away."

.    .    .    .    .    .    .

Mr. Carstone's prophecy was but half
realized. At the end of six months Herbert Bly's discretion and devotion were duly
rewarded by Cherry's hand. But Tappington did *not* give her away. That saintly
prodigal passed his period of probation with
exemplary rectitude, but, either from a dread
of old temptation, or some unexplained reason, he preferred to remain in Portland, and
his fastidious nest on Telegraph Hill knew
him no more. The key of the little door
on the side street passed, naturally, into the
keeping of Mrs. Bly.

Whether the secret of Tappington's
double life was ever revealed to the two
women is not known to the chronicler. Mrs.
Bly is reported to have said that the climate
of Oregon was more suited to her brother's
delicate constitution than the damp fogs of
San Francisco, and that his tastes were always opposed to the mere frivolity of metropolitan society. The only possible reason for
supposing that the mother may have become
cognizant of her son's youthful errors was in

the occasional visits to the house of the handsome George Dornton, who, in the social revolution that followed the brief reign of the Vigilance Committee, characteristically returned as a dashing stockbroker, and the fact that Mrs. Brooks seemed to have discarded her ascetic shawl forever. But as all this was contemporaneous with the absurd rumor, that owing to the loneliness induced by the marriage of her daughter she contemplated a similar change in her own condition, it is deemed unworthy the serious consideration of this veracious chronicle.

# CAPTAIN JIM'S FRIEND.

---

## I.

HARDLY one of us, I think, really believed in the auriferous probabilities of Eureka Gulch. Following a little stream, we had had one day drifted into it, very much as we imagined the river gold might have done in remoter ages, with the difference that *we* remained there, while the river gold to all appearances had not. At first it was tacitly agreed to ignore this fact, and we made the most of the charming locality, with its rare watercourse that lost itself in tangled depths of manzanita and alder, its laurel-choked pass, its flower-strewn hillside, and its summit crested with rocking pines.

"You see," said the optimistic Rowley, "water 's the main thing after all. If we happen to strike river gold, thar 's the stream for washing it; if we happen to drop into quartz — and that thar rock looks mighty

likely — thar ain't a more natural-born site
for a mill than that right bank, with water
enough to run fifty stamps. That hillside
is an original dump for your tailings, and
a ready found inclined road for your trucks,
fresh from the hands of Providence; and that
road we 're kalkilatin' to build to the turn-
pike will run just easy along that ridge."

Later, when we were forced to accept the
fact that finding gold was really the primary
object of a gold-mining company, we still remained there, excusing our youthful laziness
and incertitude by brilliant and effective sar-
casms upon the unremunerative attractions of
the gulch. Nevertheless, when Captain Jim,
returning one day from the nearest settlement and post-office, twenty miles away,
burst upon us with " Well, the hull thing 'll
be settled now, boys ; Lacy Bassett is coming
down yer to look round," we felt considerably relieved.

And yet, perhaps, we had as little reason
for it as we had for remaining there. There
was no warrant for any belief in the special
divining power of the unknown Lacy Bassett, except Captain Jim's extravagant faith
in his general superiority, and even that had
always been a source of amused skepticism

to the camp. We were already impatiently familiar with the opinions of this unseen oracle ; he was always impending in Captain Jim's speech as a fragrant memory or an unquestioned authority. When Captain Jim began, " Ez Lacy was one day tellin' me," or, " Ez Lacy Bassett allows," or more formally, when strangers were present, " Ez a partick- ler friend o' mine, Lacy Bassett — maybe ez you know him — sez," the youthful and lighter members of the Eureka Mining Company glanced at each other in furtive enjoyment. Nevertheless no one looked more eagerly forward to the arrival of this apocryphal sage than these indolent skeptics. It was at least an excitement ; they were equally ready to accept his condemnation of the locality or his justification of their original selection.

He came. He was received by the Eureka Mining Company lying on their backs on the grassy site of the prospective quartz mill, not far from the equally hypothetical " slide " to the gulch. He came by the future stage road — at present a thickset jungle of scrub- oaks and ferns. He was accompanied by Captain Jim, who had gone to meet him on the trail, and for a few moments all critical inspection of himself was withheld by the extraordinary effect he seemed to have upon the faculties of his introducer.

Anything like the absolute prepossession of Captain Jim by this stranger we had never imagined. He approached us running a little ahead of his guest, and now and then returning assuringly to his side with the expression of a devoted Newfoundland dog, which in fluffiness he generally resembled. And now, even after the introduction was over, when he made a point of standing aside in an affectation of carelessness, with his hands in his pockets, the simulation was so apparent, and his consciousness and absorption in his friend so obvious, that it was a relief to us to recall him into the conversation.

As to our own first impressions of the stranger, they were probably correct. We all disliked him; we thought him conceited, self-opinionated, selfish, and untrustworthy. But later, reflecting that this was possibly the result of Captain Jim's over-praise, and finding none of these qualities as yet offensively opposed to our own selfishness and conceit, we were induced, like many others, to forget our first impressions. We could easily correct him if he attempted to impose upon *us*, as he evidently had upon Captain Jim. Believing, after the fashion of most humanity, that there was something about *us* particularly awe-inspiring and edifying to vice or weakness of any kind, we good-humoredly yielded to the cheap fascination of this showy, self-saturated, over-dressed, and underbred stranger. Even the epithet of " blower " as applied to him by Rowley had its mitigations ; in that Trajan community a bully was not necessarily a coward, nor florid demonstration always a weakness.

His condemnation of the gulch was sweeping, original, and striking. He laughed to scorn our half-hearted theory of a gold deposit in the bed and bars of our favorite stream. We were not to look for auriferous alluvium in the bed of any present existing stream, but in the " cement " or dried-up bed of the original prehistoric rivers that formerly ran parallel with the present bed, and which — he demonstrated with the stem of Pickney's pipe in the red dust — could be found by sinking shafts at right angles with the stream. The theory was to us, at that time, novel and attractive. It was true that the scientific explanation, although full and gratuitous, sounded vague and incoherent. It was true that the geological terms were not always correct, and their pronunciation defective, but we accepted such extraordinary discoveries as " ignus fatuus rock," " splendiferous drift," " mica twist " (recalling a popular species of tobacco), " iron pirates," and " discomposed quartz " as part of what he not inaptly called a " tautological formation," and were happy. Nor was our contentment marred by the fact that the well-known scientific authority with whom the stranger had been intimate, — to the point of " sleeping together " during a survey, — and whom he described as a bent old man with spectacles, must have aged considerably since one of our party saw him three years before as a keen young fellow of twenty-five. Inaccuracies like those were only the carelessness of genius. " That's my opinion, gentlemen," he concluded, negligently rising, and with pointed preoccupation whipping the dust of Eureka Gulch from his clothes with his handkerchief, " but of course it ain't nothin' to me."

Captain Jim, who had followed every word with deep and trustful absorption, here repeated, " It ain't nothing to him, boys," with a confidential implication of the gratuitous blessing we had received, and then added, with loyal encouragement to him, " It ain't nothing to you, Lacy, in course," and laid his hand on his shoulder with infinite tenderness.

We, however, endeavored to make it something to Mr. Lacy Bassett. He was spontaneously offered a share in the company and a part of Captain Jim's tent. He accepted both after a few deprecating and muttered asides to Captain Jim, which the latter afterwards explained to us was the giving up of several other important enterprises for our sake. When he finally strolled away with Rowley to look over the gulch, Captain Jim reluctantly tore himself away from him only for the pleasure of reiterating his praise to us as if in strictest confidence and as an entirely novel proceeding.

"You see, boys, I did n't like to say it afore *him*, we bein' old friends; but, between us, that young feller ez worth thousands to the camp. Mebbee," he continued with grave naïveté, " I ain't said much about him afore, mebbee, bein' old friends and accustomed to him — you know how it is, boys, — I have n't appreciated him as much ez

I ought, and ez you do. In fact, I don't ezakly remember how I kem to ask him down yer. It came to me suddent, one day only a week ago Friday night, thar under that buck-eye; I was thinkin' o' one of his sayins, and sez I — thar's Lacy, if he was here he'd set the hull thing right. It was the ghost of a chance my findin' him free, but I did. And there *he* is, and yer *we* are settled! Ye noticed how he just knocked the bottom outer our plans to work. Ye noticed that quick sort o' sneerin' smile o' his, didn't ye — that's Lacy! I've seen him knock over a heap o' things without sayin' any-thin' — with jist that smile."

It occurred to us that we might have some difficulty in utilizing this smile in our pres-ent affairs, and that we should have prob-ably preferred something more assuring, but Captain Jim's faith was contagious.

"What is he, anyway?" asked Joe Walker lazily.

"Eh!" echoed Captain Jim in astonish-ment. "What is Lacy Bassett?"

"Yes, what is he?" repeated Walker.

"Wot *is* — he?"

"Yes."

"I've knowed him now goin' as four

year," said Captain Jim with slow reflective contentment. "Let's see. It was in the fall o' '54 I first met him, and he's allus been the same ez you see him now."

"But what is his business or profession? What does he do?"

Captain Jim looked reproachfully at his questioner.

"Do?" he repeated, turning to the rest of us as if disdaining a direct reply. "Do? — why, wot he's doin' now. He's allus the same, allus Lacy Bassett."

Howbeit, we went to work the next day under the superintendence of the stranger with youthful and enthusiastic energy, and began the sinking of a shaft at once. To do Captain Jim's friend justice, for the first few weeks he did not shirk a fair share of the actual labor, replacing his objectionable and unsuitable finery with a suit of serviceable working clothes got together by general contribution of the camp, and assuring us of a fact we afterwards had cause to remember, that "he brought nothing but himself into Eureka Gulch." It may be added that he certainly had not brought money there, as Captain Jim advanced the small amounts necessary for his purchases in the distant settlement, and for the still smaller sums he lost at cards, which he played with characteristic self-sufficiency.

Meantime the work in the shaft progressed slowly but regularly. Even when the novelty had worn off and the excitement of anticipation grew fainter, I am afraid that we clung to this new form of occupation as an apology for remaining there; for the fascinations of our vagabond and unconventional life were more potent than we dreamed of. We were slowly fettered by our very freedom; there was a strange spell in this very boundlessness of our license that kept us from even the desire of change; in the wild and lawless arms of nature herself we found an embrace as clinging, as hopeless and restraining, as the civilization from which we had fled. We were quite content after a few hours' work in the shaft to lie on our backs on the hillside staring at the unwinking sky, or to wander with a gun through the virgin forest in search of game scarcely less vagabond than ourselves. We indulged in the most extravagant and dreamy speculations of the fortune we should eventually discover in the shaft, and believed that we were practical. We broke our "saleratus

bread " with appetites unimpaired by restlessness or anxiety; we went to sleep under
the grave and sedate stars with a serene consciousness of having fairly earned our rest;
we awoke the next morning with unabated
trustfulness, and a sweet obliviousness of
even the hypothetical fortunes we had perhaps won or lost at cards overnight. We
paid no heed to the fact that our little capital was slowly sinking with the shaft, and
that the rainy season — wherein not only
" no man could work," but even such play
as ours was impossible — was momentarily
impending.

In the midst of this, one day Lacy Bassett
suddenly emerged from the shaft before his
" shift " of labor was over with every sign of
disgust and rage in his face and inarticulate
with apparent passion. In vain we gathered
round him in concern; in vain Captain Jim
regarded him with almost feminine sympathy, as he flung away his pick and dashed
his hat to the ground.

" What's up, Lacy, old pard? What's
gone o' you?" said Captain Jim tenderly.

" Look!" gasped Lacy at last, when every
eye was on him, holding up a small fragment of rock before us and the next moment

grinding it under his heel in rage. "Look! To think that I've been fooled agin by this blanked fossiliferous trap — blank it! To think that after me and Professor Parker was once caught jist in this way up on the Stanislaus at the bottom of a hundred-foot shaft by this rotten trap — that yer I am — bluffed agin!"

There was a dead silence; we looked at each other blankly.

"But, Bassett," said Walker, picking up a part of the fragment, "we've been finding this kind of stuff for the last two weeks."

"But how?" returned Lacy, turning upon him almost fiercely. "Did ye find it super-posed on quartz, or did you find it *not* super-posed on quartz? Did you find it in volcanic drift, or did ye find it in old red-sand-stone or coarse illuvion? Tell me that, and then ye kin talk. But this yer blank fossil-iferous trap, instead o' being superposed on top, is superposed on the bottom. And that means" —

"What?" we all asked eagerly.

"Why — blank it all — that this yer con-vulsion of nature, this prehistoric volcanic earthquake, instead of acting laterally and chuckin' the stream to one side, has been revolutionary and turned the old river-bed bottom-side up, and yer d—d cement hez got half the globe atop of it! Ye might strike it from China, but nowhere else."

We continued to look at one another, the older members with darkening faces, the younger with a strong inclination to laugh. Captain Jim, who had been concerned only in his friend's emotion, and who was hanging with undisguised satisfaction on these final convincing proofs of his superior geological knowledge, murmured approvingly and confidingly, "He's right, boys! Thar ain't another man livin' ez could give you the law and gospil like that! Ye can tie to what he says. That's Lacy all over."

Two weeks passed. We had gathered, damp and disconsolate, in the only available shelter of the camp. For the long summer had ended unexpectedly to us; we had one day found ourselves caught like the improvident insect of the child's fable with gauzy and unseasonable wings wet and bedraggled in the first rains, homeless and hopeless. The scientific Lacy, who lately spent most of his time as a bar-room oracle in the settlement, was away, and from our dripping canvas we could see Captain Jim returning

from a visit to him, slowly plodding along
the trail towards us.

"It's no use, boys," said Rowley, sum-
marizing the result of our conference, "we
must speak out to him, and if nobody else
cares to do it I will. I don't know why we
should be more mealy-mouthed than they are
at the settlement. They don't hesitate to
call Bassett a dead-beat, whatever Captain
Jim says to the contrary."

The unfortunate Captain Jim had halted
irresolutely before the gloomy faces in the
shelter. Whether he felt instinctively some
forewarning of what was coming I cannot
say. There was a certain dog-like consciousness in his eye and a half-backward glance
over his shoulder as if he were not quite certain that Lacy was not following. The rain
had somewhat subdued his characteristic
fluffiness, and he cowered with a kind of
sleek storm-beaten despondency over the
smoking fire of green wood before our tent.

Nevertheless, Rowley opened upon him
with a directness and decision that astonished us. He pointed out briefly that Lacy
Bassett had been known to us only through
Captain Jim's introduction. That he had
been originally invited there on Captain

Jim's own account, and that his later connection with the company had been wholly the result of Captain Jim's statements. That, far from being any aid or assistance to them, Bassett had beguiled them by apocryphal knowledge and sham scientific theories into an expensive and gigantic piece of folly. That, in addition to this, they had just discovered that he had also been using the credit of the company for his own individual expenses at the settlement while they were working on his d—d fool shaft — all of which had brought them to the verge of bankruptcy. That, as a result, they were forced now to demand his resignation — not only on their general account, but for Captain Jim's sake — believing firmly, as they did, that he had been as grossly deceived in his friendship for Lacy Bassett as *they* were in their business relations with him.

Instead of being mollified by this, Captain Jim, to our greater astonishment, suddenly turned upon the speaker, bristling with his old canine suggestion.

"There! I said so! Go on! I'd have sworn to it afore you opened your lips. I knowed it the day you sneaked around and wanted to know wot his business was! I

said to myself, Cap, look out for that sneakin'
hound Rowley, he's no friend o' Lacy's.
And the day Lacy so far demeaned himself as to give ye that splendid explanation
o' things, I watched ye; ye didn't think
it, but I watched ye. Ye can't fool me! I
saw ye lookin' at Walker there, and I said
to myself, Wot's the use, Lacy, wot's the
use o' your slingin' them words to such as
*them?* Wot do *they* know? It's just their
pure jealousy and ignorance. Ef you'd
come down yer, and lazed around with us
and fallen into our common ways, you'd ha'
been ez good a man ez the next. But no, it
ain't your style, Lacy, you're accustomed to
high-toned men like Professor Parker, and
you can't help showing it. No wonder you
took to avoidin' us; no wonder I've had to
foller you over the Burnt Wood Crossin'
time and again, to get to see ye. I see it
all now; ye can't stand the kempany I
brought ye to! Ye had to wipe the slum
gullion of Eureka Gulch off your hands,
Lacy" — He stopped, gasped for breath, and
then lifted his voice more savagely, " And
now, what's this? Wot's this hogwash?
this yer lyin' slander about his gettin' things
on the kempany's credit? Eh, speak up,
some of ye!"

We were so utterly shocked and stupefied
at the degradation of this sudden and unexpected outburst from a man usually so honorable, gentle, self-sacrificing, and forgiving,
that we forgot the cause of it and could only
stare at each other. What was this cheap
stranger, with his shallow swindling tricks,
to the ignoble change he had worked upon
the man before us. Rowley and Walker,
both fearless fighters and quick to resent an
insult, only averted their saddened faces and
turned aside without a word.

"Ye dussen't say it! Well, hark to me
then," he continued with white and feverish lips. "*I* put him up to helpin' himself.
*I* told him to use the kempany's name for
credit. Ye kin put that down to *me*. And
when ye talk of *his* resigning, I want ye to
understand that *I* resign outer this rotten
kempany and *take him with me!* Ef all
the gold yer lookin' for was piled up in that
shaft from its bottom in hell to its top in the
gulch, it ain't enough to keep me here away
from him! Ye kin take all my share — all
*my* rights yer above ground and below it —
all I carry," — he threw his buckskin purse
and revolver on the ground, — "and pay
yourselves what you reckon you've lost

through *him.* But you and me is quits from to-day."

He strode away before a restraining voice or hand could reach him. His dripping figure seemed to melt into the rain beneath the thickening shadows of the pines, and the next moment he was gone. From that day forward Eureka Gulch knew him no more. And the camp itself somehow melted away during the rainy season, even as he had done.

## II.

THREE years had passed. The pioneer stage-coach was sweeping down the long descent to the pastoral valley of Gilead, and I was looking towards the village with some pardonable interest and anxiety. For I carried in my pocket my letters of promotion from the box seat of the coach — where I had performed the functions of treasure messenger for the Excelsior Express Company — to the resident agency of that company in the bucolic hamlet before me. The few dusty right-angled streets, with their rigid and staringly new shops and dwellings, the stern formality of one or two obelisk-like meeting-house spires, the illimitable out-

lying plains of wheat and wild oats beyond,
with their monotony scarcely broken by
skeleton stockades, corrals, and barrack-
looking farm buildings, were all certainly
unlike the unkempt freedom of the mountain
fastnesses in which I had lately lived and
moved. Yuba Bill, the driver, whose usual
expression of humorous discontent deepened
into scorn as he gathered up his reins as if
to charge the village and recklessly sweep it
from his path, indicated a huge, rambling,
obtrusively glazed, and capital-lettered building with a contemptuous flick of his whip as
we passed. "Ef you're kalkilatin' we 'll
get our partin' drink there you're mistaken.
That 's wot they call a *temperance house* —
wot means a place where the licker ye get
underhand is only a trifle worse than the
hash ye get above - board. I suppose it 's
part o' one o' the mysteries o' Providence
that wharever you find a dusty hole like this
— that 's naturally *thirsty* — ye run agin a
'temperance' house. But never *you* mind!
I should n't wonder if thar was a demijohn
o' whiskey in the closet of your back office,
kept thar by the feller you 're relievin' —
who was a white man and knew the ropes."

A few minutes later, when my brief in-

stallation was over, we *did* find the demijohn in the place indicated.  As Yuba Bill
wiped his mouth with the back of his heavy
buckskin glove, he turned to me not unkindly.  "I don't like to set ye agin Gil-
e-ad, which is a scrip-too-rural place, and a
God-fearin' place, and a nice dry place, and
a place ez I've heard tell whar they grow
beans and pertatoes and garden sass; but
afore three weeks is over, old pard, you'll
be howlin' to get back on that box seat with
me, whar you uster sit, and be ready to take
your chances agin, like a little man, to get
drilled through with buckshot from road
agents.  You hear me!  I'll give you three
weeks, sonny, just three weeks, to get your
butes full o' hayseed and straws in yer har;
and I'll find ye wadin' the North Fork at
high water to get out o' this."  He shook
my hand with grim tenderness, removing his
glove — a rare favor — to give me the pres-
sure of his large, soft, protecting palm, and
strode away.  The next moment he was
shaking the white dust of Gilead from his
scornful chariot-wheels.

In the hope of familiarizing myself with
the local interests of the community, I took
up a copy of the "Gilead Guardian" which

lay on my desk, forgetting for the moment
the usual custom of the country press to dis-
place local news for long editorials on foreign subjects and national politics. I found,
to my disappointment, that the " Guardian "
exhibited more than the usual dearth of domestic intelligence, although it was singularly oracular on "The State of Europe,"
and " Jeffersonian Democracy." A certain
cheap assurance, a copy-book dogmatism, a
colloquial familiarity, even in the impersonal
plural, and a series of inaccuracies and blunders here and there, struck some old chord
in my memory. I was mutely wondering
where and when I had become personally
familiar with rhetoric like that, when the
door of the office opened and a man entered.
I was surprised to recognize Captain Jim.

I had not seen him since he had indignantly left us, three years before, in Eureka
Gulch. The circumstances of his defection
were certainly not conducive to any volun-
tary renewal of friendship on either side ;
and although, even as a former member of
the Eureka Mining Company, I was not conscious of retaining any sense of injury, yet
the whole occurrence flashed back upon me
with awkward distinctness. To my relief,

however, he greeted me with his old cordiality; to my amusement he added to it a
suggestion of the large forgiveness of conscious rectitude and amiable toleration. I
thought, however, I detected, as he glanced
at the paper which was still in my hand and
then back again at my face, the same uneasy
canine resemblance I remembered of old. He
had changed but little in appearance; perhaps he was a trifle stouter, more mature,
and slower in his movements. If I may
return to my canine illustration, his grayer,
dustier, and more wiry *ensemble* gave me
the impression that certain pastoral and agricultural conditions had varied his type, and
he looked more like a shepherd's dog in
whose brown eyes there was an abiding consciousness of the care of straying sheep, and
possibly of one black one in particular.

He had, he told me, abandoned mining
and taken up farming on a rather large
scale. He had prospered. He had other
interests at stake, " A flour-mill with some
improvements — and — and "— here his eyes
wandered to the " Guardian " again, and
he asked me somewhat abruptly what I
thought of the paper. Something impelled
me to restrain my previous fuller criticism,

and I contented myself by saying briefly that I thought it rather ambitious for the locality. "That's the word," he said with a look of gratified relief, "'ambitious' — you've just hit it. And what's the matter with thet? Ye kan't expect a high-toned man to write down to the level of every karpin' hound, ken ye now? That's what he says to me" — He stopped half confused, and then added abruptly: "That's one o' my investments."

"Why, Captain Jim, I never suspected that you" —

"Oh, I don't *write* it," he interrupted hastily. "I only furnish the money and the advertising, and run it gin'rally, you know; and I'm responsible for it. And I select the eddyter — and" — he continued, with a return of the same uneasy wistful look — "thar's suthin' in thet, you know, eh?"

I was beginning to be perplexed. The memory evoked by the style of the editorial writing and the presence of Captain Jim was assuming a suspicious relationship to each other. "And who's your editor?" I asked.

"Oh, he's — he's — er — Lacy Bassett," he replied, blinking his eyes with a hopeless

assumption of carelessness. "Let's see!
Oh yes! You knowed Lacy down there at
Eureka. I disremembered it till now. Yes,
sir!" he repeated suddenly and almost rudely,
as if to preclude any adverse criticism, "he's
the eddyter!"

To my surprise he was quite white and
tremulous with nervousness. I was very
sorry for him, and as I really cared very
little for the half-forgotten escapade of his
friend except so far as it seemed to render
*him* sensitive, I shook his hand again heartily
and began to talk of our old life in the gulch
— avoiding as far as possible any allusion to
Lacy Bassett. His face brightened; his old
simple cordiality and trustfulness returned,
but unfortunately with it his old disposition
to refer to Bassett. "Yes, they waz high
old times, and ez I waz sayin' to Lacy on'y
yesterday, there is a kind o' freedom 'bout
that sort o' life that runs civilization and
noospapers mighty hard, however high-toned
they is. Not but what Lacy ain't right,"
he added quickly, "when he sez that the
opposition the 'Guardian' gets here comes
from ignorant low-down fellers ez wos
brought up in played-out camps, and can't
tell a gentleman and a scholar and a scien-

tific man when they sees him. No! So I sez to Lacy, ' Never you mind, it 's high time they did, and they 've got to do it and to swaller the "Guardian," if I sink double the money I 've already put into the paper.' "

I was not long in discovering from other sources that the " Guardian " was not popular with the more intelligent readers of Gilead, and that Captain Jim's extravagant estimate of his friend was by no means indorsed by the community. But criticism took a humorous turn even in that practical settlement, and it appeared that Lacy Bassett's vanity, assumption, and ignorance were an unfailing and weekly joy to the critical, in spite of the vague distrust they induced in the more homely-witted, and the dull acquiescence of that minority who accepted the paper for its respectable exterior and advertisements. I was somewhat grieved, however, to find that Captain Jim shared equally with his friend in this general verdict of incompetency, and that some of the most outrageous blunders were put down to *him.* But I was not prepared to believe that Lacy had directly or by innuendo helped the public to this opinion.

Whether through accident or design on

his part, Lacy Bassett did not personally obtrude himself upon my remembrance until a month later. One dazzling afternoon, when the dust and heat had driven the pride of Gilead's manhood into the surreptitious shadows of the temperance hotel's back room, and had even cleared the express office of its loungers, and left me alone with darkened windows in the private office, the outer door opened and Captain Jim's friend entered as part of that garish glitter I had shut out. To do the scamp strict justice, however, he was somewhat subdued in his dress and manner, and, possibly through some gentle chastening of epigram and revolver since I had seen him last, was less aggressive and exaggerated. I had the impression, from certain odors wafted through the apartment and a peculiar physical exaltation that was inconsistent with his evident moral hesitancy, that he had prepared himself for the interview by a previous visit to the hidden fountains of the temperance hotel.

"We don't seem to have run agin each other since you've been here," he said with an assurance that was nevertheless a trifle forced, " but I reckon we're both busy men,

and there's a heap too much loafing goin' on
in Gilead. Captain Jim told me he met you
the day you arrived; said you just cottoned
to the 'Guardian' at once and thought
it a deal too good for Gilead; eh? Oh,
well, jest ez likely he *did n't* say it — it was
only his gassin'. He's a queer man — is
Captain Jim."

I replied somewhat sharply that I considered him a very honest man, a very simple
man, and a very loyal man.

"That's all very well," said Bassett, twirling his cane with a patronizing smile, "but,
as his friend, don't you find him considerable of a darned fool?"

I could not help retorting that I thought
*he* had found that hardly an objection.

"*You* think so," he said querulously, apparently ignoring everything but the practical
fact, — "and maybe others do; but that's
where you're mistaken. It don't pay. It
may pay *him* to be runnin' me as his particular friend, to be quotin' me here and there,
to be gettin' credit of knowin' me and my
friends and ownin' me — by Gosh! but I
don't see where the benefit to *me* comes in.
Eh? Take your own case down there at
Eureka Gulch; did n't he send for me just to

show me up to you fellers? Did I want to
have anything to do with the Eureka Company? Did n't he set me up to give my opinion about that shaft just to show off what
I knew about science and all that? And
what did he get me to join the company for?
Was it for you? No! Was it for me?
No! It was just to keep me there for *himself*, and kinder pit me agin you fellers and
crow over you! Now that ain't my style!
It may be *his* — it may be honest and simple and loyal, as you say, and it may be all
right for him to get me to run up accounts
at the settlement and then throw off on me
— but it ain't my style. I suppose he let
on that I did that. No? He did n't?
Well then, why did he want to run me off
with him, and cut the whole concern in an
underhand way and make me leave with
nary a character behind me, eh? Now, I
never said anything about this before — did
I? It ain't like me. I would n't have
said anything about it now, only you talked
about *my* being benefited by his darned
foolishness. Much I 've made outer *him*."

Despicable, false, and disloyal as this
was, perhaps it was the crowning meanness
of such confidences that his very weakness

seemed only a reflection of Captain Jim's own, and appeared in some strange way to degrade his friend as much as himself. The simplicity of his vanity and selfishness was only equalled by the simplicity of Captain Jim's admiration of it. It was a part of my youthful inexperience of humanity that I was not above the common fallacy of believing that a man is " known by the company he keeps," and that he is in a manner responsible for its weakness; it was a part of that humanity that I felt no surprise in being more amused than shocked by this revelation. It seemed a good joke on Captain Jim !

" Of course *you* kin laugh at his darned foolishness; but, by Gosh, it ain't a laughing matter to me ! "

" But surely he 's given you a good position on the ' Guardian,' " I urged. " That was disinterested, certainly."

" Was it ? I call that the cheekiest thing yet. When he found he could n't make enough of me in private life, he totes me out in public as *his* editor — the man who runs *his* paper ! And has his name in print as the proprietor, the only chance he 'd ever get of being before the public. And don't know the whole town is laughing at him J "

"That may be because they think *he* writes some of the articles," I suggested.

Again the insinuation glanced harmlessly from his vanity. "That couldn't be, because *I* do all the work, and it ain't his style," he said with naïve discontent. "And it's always the highest style, done to please him, though between you and me it's sorter castin' pearls before swine — this 'Frisco editing — and the public would be just as satisfied with anything I could rattle off that was peart and sassy, — something spicy or personal. I'm willing to climb down and do it, for there's nothin' stuck-up about me, you know; but that darned fool Captain Jim has got the big head about the style of the paper, and darned if I don't think he's afraid if there's a lettin' down, people may think it's him! Ez if! Why, you know as well as me that there's a sort of snap *I* could give these things that would show it was me and no slouch did them, in a minute."

I had my doubts about the elegance or playfulness of Mr. Bassett's trifling, but from some paragraphs that appeared in the next issue of the "Guardian" I judged that he had won over Captain Jim — if indeed that gentleman's alleged objections were not

entirely the outcome of Bassett's fancy. The
social paragraphs themselves were clumsy
and vulgar. A dull-witted account of a
select party at Parson Baxter's, with a point-
blank compliment to Polly Baxter his daughter, might have made her pretty cheek burn
but for her evident prepossession for the
meretricious scamp, its writer. But even
this horse-play seemed more natural than
the utterly artificial editorials with their
pinchbeck glitter and cheap erudition; and
thus far it appeared harmless.

I grieve to say that these appearances
were deceptive. One afternoon, as I was returning from a business visit to the outskirts
of the village, I was amazed on reëntering
the main street to find a crowd collected
around the "Guardian" office, gazing at the
broken glass of its windows and a quantity
of type scattered on the ground. But my
attention was at that moment more urgently
attracted by a similar group around my own
office, who, however, seemed more cautious,
and were holding timorously aloof from the
entrance. As I ran rapidly towards them, a
few called out, "Look out — he's in there!"
while others made way to let me pass. With
the impression of fire or robbery in my mind,

I entered precipitately, only to find Yuba Bill calmly leaning back in an arm-chair with his feet on the back of another, a glass of whiskey from my demijohn in one hand and a huge cigar in his mouth. Across his lap lay a stumpy shotgun which I at once recognized as "the Left Bower," whose usual place was at his feet on the box during his journeys. He looked cool and collected, although there were one or two splashes of printer's ink on his shirt and trousers, and from the appearance of my lavatory and towel he had evidently been removing similar stains from his hands. Putting his gun aside and grasping my hand warmly without rising, he began with even more than his usual lazy imperturbability :

"Well, how's Gilead lookin' to-day?"

It struck me as looking rather disturbed, but, as I was still too bewildered to reply, he continued lazily :

"Ez you did n't hunt me up, I allowed you might hev got kinder petrified and dried up down yer, and I reckoned to run down and rattle round a bit and make things lively for ye. I've jist cleared out a newspaper office over thar. They call it the 'Guardi-an,' though it did n't seem to offer much

pertection to them fellers ez was in it. In
fact, it was n't ez much a fight ez it orter hev
been. It was rather monotonous for me."

"But what's the row, Bill? What has
happened?" I asked excitedly.

"Nothin' to speak of, I tell ye," replied
Yuba Bill reflectively. "I jest meandered
into that shop over there, and I sez, 'I
want ter see the man ez runs this yer mill
o' literatoor an' progress.' Thar waz two
infants sittin' on high chairs havin' some
innocent little game o' pickin' pieces o' lead
outer pill-boxes like, and as soon ez they
seed me one of 'em crawled under his
desk and the other scooted outer the back
door. Bimeby the door opens again, and a
fluffy coyote-lookin' feller comes in and allows that *he* is responsible for that yer
paper. When I saw the kind of animal he
was, and that he had n't any weppings, I
jist laid the Left Bower down on the floor.
Then I sez, 'You allowed in your paper
that I oughter hev a little sevility knocked
inter me, and I'm here to hev it done. You
ken begin it now.' With that I reached
for him, and we waltzed oncet or twicet
around the room, and then I put him up
on the mantelpiece and on them desks and

little boxes, and took him down again, and kinder wiped the floor with him gin'rally, until the first thing I knowed he was outside the winder on the sidewalk. On'y blamed if I did n't forget to open the winder. Ef it had n't been for that, it would hev been all quiet and peaceful-like, and nobody hev knowed it. But the sash being in the way, it sorter created a disturbance and unpleasantness *outside*."

"But what was it all about?" I repeated. "What had he done to you?"

"Ye 'll find it in that paper," he said, indicating a copy of the "Guardian" that lay on my table with a lazy nod of his head. "P'r'aps you don't read it? No more do I. But Joe Bilson sez to me yesterday : ' Bill,' sez he, ' they 're goin' for ye in the " Guardian." ' ' Wot 's that?' sez I. ' Hark to this,' sez he, and reads out that bit that you 'll find there."

I had opened the paper, and he pointed to a paragraph. "There it is. Pooty, ain't it?" I read with amazement as follows : —

"If the Pioneer Stage Company want to keep up with the times, and not degenerate into the old style ' one hoss ' road-wagon business, they 'd better make some reform on the line.

They might begin by shipping off some of the old-time whiskey-guzzling drivers who are too high and mighty to do anything but handle the ribbons, and are above speaking to a passenger unless he's a favorite or one of their set. Over-praise for an occasional scrimmage with road agents, and flattery from Eastern greenhorns, have given them the big head. If the fool-killer were let loose on the line with a big club, and knocked a little civility into their heads, it would n't be a bad thing, and would be a parti-cular relief to the passengers for Gilead who have to take the stage from Simpson's Bar."

"That's my stage," said Yuba Bill quietly, when I had ended; "and that's *me.*"

"But it's impossible," I said eagerly. "That insult was never written by Captain Jim."

"Captain Jim," repeated Yuba Bill re-flectively. "Captain Jim, —yes, that was the name o' the man I was playin' with. Shortish hairy feller, suthin' between a big coyote and the old-style hair-trunk. Fought pretty well for a hay - footed man from Gil-e-ad."

"But you 've whipped the wrong man, Bill," I said. "Think again! Have you had any quarrel lately?— run against any

newspaper man ? " The recollection had
flashed upon me that Lacy Bassett had
lately returned from a visit to Stockton.

Yuba Bill regarded his boots on the other
arm-chair for a few moments in profound
meditation. " There was a sort o' gaudy
insect," he began presently, " suthin' halfway betwixt a hoss-fly and a devil's darnin'-
needle, ez crawled up onter the box seat with
me last week, and buzzed! Now I think on
it, he talked high-faluten' o' the inflooence
of the press and sech. I may hev said
'shoo' to him when he was hummin' the
loudest. I mout hev flicked him off oncet
or twicet with my whip. It must be him.
Gosh ! " he said suddenly, rising and lifting
his heavy hand to his forehead, " now I
think agin *he was the feller ez crawled
under the desk when the fight was goin' on,
and stayed there.* Yes, sir, that was *him.*
His face looked sorter familiar, but I did n't
know him moultin' with his feathers off."
He turned upon me with the first expression
of trouble and anxiety I had ever seen him
wear. "Yes, sir, that 's him. And I 've
kem — me, Yuba Bill ! — kem *myself,* a
matter of twenty miles, totin' a *gun* — a
gun, by Gosh ! — to fight that — that — that

potatar-bug!" He walked to the window, turned, walked back again, finished his whiskey with a single gulp, and laid his hand almost despondingly on my shoulder. "Look ye, old — old fell, you and me 's ole friends. Don't give me away. Don't let on a word o' this to any one! Say I kem down yer howlin' drunk on a gen'ral tear! Say I mistook that newspaper office for a cigar-shop, and — got licked by the boss! Say anythin' you like, 'cept that I took a gun down yer to chase a fly that had settled onter me. Keep the Left Bower in yer back office till I send for it. Ef you 've got a back door somewhere handy where I can slip outer this without bein' seen I 'd be thankful."

As this desponding suggestion appeared to me as the wisest thing for him to do in the then threatening state of affairs outside, — which, had he suspected it, he would have stayed to face, — I quickly opened a door into a courtyard that communicated through an alley with a side street. Here we shook hands and parted; his last dejected ejaculation being, "That potatobug!" Later I ascertained that Captain Jim had retired to his ranch some four miles distant. He was not seriously hurt, but looked, to use the words of my informant, "ez ef he 'd been hugged by a playful b'ar." As the "Guardian" made its appearance the next week without the slightest allusion to the fracas, I did not deem it necessary to divulge the real facts. When I called to inquire about Captain Jim's condition, he himself, however, volunteered an explanation.

"I don't mind tellin' you, ez an old friend o' mine and Lacy's, that the secret of that there attack on me and the 'Guardian' was perlitikal. Yes, sir! There was a powerful orginization in the interest o' Halkins for assemblyman ez did n't like our high-toned editorials on caucus corruption, and hired a bully to kem down here and suppress us. Why, this yer Lacy spotted the idea to oncet; yer know how keen he is."

"Was Lacy present?" I asked as carelessly as I could.

Captain Jim glanced his eyes over his shoulder quite in his old furtive canine fashion, and then blinked them at me rapidly. "He war! And if it warn't for *his* pluck and *his* science and *his* strength, I don't know whar *I'd* hev been now! Howsom-

ever, it's all right. I've had a fair offer to
sell the 'Guardian' over at Simpson's Bar,
and it's time I quit throwin' away the work
of a man like Lacy Bassett upon it. And
between you and me, I've got an idea and
suthin' better to put his talens into."

### III.

IT was not long before it became evident
that the "talens" of Mr. Lacy Bassett, as
indicated by Captain Jim, were to grasp at
a seat in the state legislature. An editorial in the "Simpson's Bar Clarion" boldly
advocated his pretensions. At first it was
believed that the article emanated from the
gifted pen of Lacy himself, but the style
was so unmistakably that of Colonel Star-
bottle, an eminent political "war-horse" of
the district, that a graver truth was at once
suggested, namely, that the "Guardian"
had simply been transferred to Simpson's
Bar, and merged into the "Clarion" solely
on this condition. At least it was recognized that it was the hand of Captain Jim
which guided the editorial fingers of the
colonel, and Captain Jim's money that dis-
tended the pockets of that gallant political
**leader.**

Howbeit Lacy Bassett was never elected;
in fact he was only for one brief moment a
candidate.    It was related that upon his first
ascending the platform at Simpson's Bar a
voice in the audience said lazily, " Come
down ! " That voice was Yuba Bill's.    A
slight confusion ensued, in which Yuba Bill
whispered a few words in the colonel's ear.
After a moment's hesitation the " war-horse "
came forward, and in his loftiest manner regretted that the candidate had withdrawn.
The next issue of the " Clarion " proclaimed
with no uncertain sound that a base conspiracy gotten up by the former proprietor of
the " Guardian " to undermine the prestige
of the Great Express Company had been
ruthlessly exposed, and the candidate on
learning it *himself* for the first time, withdrew his name from the canvass, as became
a high - toned gentleman.    Public opinion,
ignoring Lacy Bassett completely, unhesitat-
ingly denounced Captain Jim.

During this period I had paid but little
heed to Lacy Bassett's social movements, or
the successes which would naturally attend
such a character with the susceptible sex.    I
had heard that he was engaged to Polly Baxter, but that they had quarrelled in conse-

quence of his flirtations with others, especially a Mrs. Sweeny, a profusely ornamented
but reputationless widow. Captain Jim had
often alluded with a certain respectful pride
and delicacy to Polly's ardent appreciation
of his friend, and had more than half hinted
with the same reverential mystery to their
matrimonial union later, and his intention
of "doing the square thing" for the young
couple. But it was presently noticed that
these allusions became less frequent during
Lacy's amorous aberrations, and an occasional depression and unusual reticence
marked Captain Jim's manner when the
subject was discussed in his presence. He
seemed to endeavor to make up for his
friend's defection by a kind of personal homage to Polly, and not unfrequently accompanied her to church or to singing-class. I
have a vivid recollection of meeting him one
afternoon crossing the fields with her, and
looking into her face with that same wistful,
absorbed, and uneasy canine expression that
I had hitherto supposed he had reserved for
Lacy alone. I do not know whether Polly
was averse to the speechless devotion of these
yearning brown eyes; her manner was animated and the pretty cheek that was nearest

me mantled as I passed ; but I was struck
for the first time with the idea that Captain
Jim loved her ! I was surprised to have that
fancy corroborated in the remark of another
wayfarer whom I met, to the effect, "That
now that Bassett was out o' the running it
looked ez if Captain Jim was makin' up for
time ! " Was it possible that Captain Jim
had always loved her ? I did not at first
know whether to be pained or pleased for
his sake. But I concluded that whether the
unworthy Bassett had at last found a *rival*
in Captain Jim or in the girl herself, it was
a displacement that was for Captain Jim's
welfare. But as I was about leaving Gilead
for a month's transfer to the San Francisco
office, I had no opportunity to learn more
from the confidences of Captain Jim.

I was ascending the principal staircase of
my San Francisco hotel one rainy afternoon,
when I was pointedly recalled to Gilead by
the passing glitter of Mrs. Sweeny's jewelry
and the sudden vanishing behind her of a
gentleman who seemed to be accompanying
her. A few moments after I had entered
my room I heard a tap at my door, and
opened it upon Lacy Bassett. I thought
he looked a little confused and agitated.

Nevertheless, with an assumption of cordiality and ease he said, " It appears we 're neighbors. That 's my room next to yours." He pointed to the next room, which I then remembered was a sitting-room *en suite* with my own, and communicating with it by a second door, which was always locked. It had not been occupied since my tenancy. As I suppose my face did not show any extravagant delight at the news of his contiguity, he added, hastily, " There 's a transom over the door, and I thought I 'd tell you you kin hear everything from the one room to the other."

I thanked him, and told him dryly that, as I had no secrets to divulge and none that I cared to hear, it made no difference to me. As this seemed to increase his confusion and he still hesitated before the door, I asked him if Captain Jim was with him.

" No," he said quickly. " I have n't seen him for a month, and don't want to. Look here, I want to talk to you a bit about him." He walked into the room, and closed the door behind him. " I want to tell you that me and Captain Jim is played! All this runnin' o' me and interferin' with me is played! I 'm tired of it. You kin tell him so from me."

" Then you have quarrelled ? "

" Yes.  As much as any man can quarrel with a darned fool who can't take a hint."

" One moment.  Have you quarrelled about Polly Baxter ? "

" Yes," he answered querulously.  " Of course I have.  What does he mean by interfering ? "

" Now listen to me, Mr. Bassett," I interrupted.  " I have no desire to concern myself in your association with Captain Jim, but since you persist in dragging me into it, you must allow me to speak plainly.  From all that I can ascertain you have no serious intentions of marrying Polly Baxter.  You have come here from Gilead to follow Mrs. Sweeny, whom I saw you with a moment ago.  Now, why do you not frankly give up Miss Baxter to Captain Jim, who will make her a good husband, and go your own way with Mrs. Sweeny?  If you really wish to break off your connection with Captain Jim, that's the only way to do it."

His face, which had exhibited the weakest and most pitiable consciousness at the mention of Mrs. Sweeny, changed to an expression of absolute stupefaction as I concluded.

" Wot stuff are you tryin' to fool me with ? " he said at last roughly.

"I mean," I replied sharply, "that this double game of yours is disgraceful. Your association with Mrs. Sweeny demands the withdrawal of any claim you have upon Miss Baxter at once. If you have no respect for Captain Jim's friendship, you must at least show common decency to her."

He burst into a half-relieved, half-hysteric laugh. "Are you crazy?" gasped he. "Why, Captain Jim's just huntin' *me* down to make *me* marry Polly. That's just what the row's about. That's just what he's interferin' for — just to carry out his darned fool ideas o' gettin' a wife for me; just his vanity to say *he's* made the match. It's *me* that he wants to marry to that Baxter girl — not himself. He's too cursed selfish for that."

I suppose I was not different from ordinary humanity, for in my unexpected discomfiture I despised Captain Jim quite as much as I did the man before me. Reiterating my remark that I had no desire to mix myself further in their quarrels, I got rid of him with as little ceremony as possible. But a few minutes later, when the farcical side of the situation struck me, my irritation was somewhat mollified, without however increasing my respect for either of the actors.

The whole affair had assumed a triviality that was simply amusing, nothing more, and I even looked forward to a meeting with Captain Jim and *his* exposition of the matter — which I knew would follow — with pleasurable anticipation. But I was mistaken.

One afternoon, when I was watching the slanting volleys of rain driven by a strong southwester against the windows of the hotel reading-room, I was struck by the erratic movements of a dripping figure outside that seemed to be hesitating over the entrance to the hotel. At times furtively penetrating the porch as far as the vestibule, and again shyly recoiling from it, its manner was so strongly suggestive of some timid animal that I found myself suddenly reminded of Captain Jim and the memorable evening of his exodus from Eureka Gulch. As the figure chanced to glance up to the window where I stood I saw to my astonishment that it *was* Captain Jim himself, but so changed and haggard that I scarcely knew him. I instantly ran out into the hall and vestibule, but when I reached the porch he had disappeared. Either he had seen me and wished to avoid me, or he had encountered the object of his quest, which I at once concluded must be Lacy Bassett. I was so much impressed and worried by his appearance and manner, that, in this belief, I overcame my aversion to meeting Bassett, and even sought him through the public rooms and lobbies in the hope of finding Captain Jim with him. But in vain; possibly he had succeeded in escaping his relentless friend.

As the wind and rain increased at nightfall and grew into a tempestuous night, with deserted streets and swollen waterways, I did not go out again, but retired early, inexplicably haunted by the changed and brooding face of Captain Jim. Even in my dreams he pursued me in his favorite likeness of a wistful, anxious, and uneasy hound, who, on my turning to caress him familiarly, snapped at me viciously, and appeared to have suddenly developed a snarling rabid fury. I seemed to be awakened at last by the sound of his voice. For an instant I believed the delusion a part of my dream. But I was mistaken; I was lying broad awake, and the voice clearly had come from the next room, and was distinctly audible over the transom.

"I've had enough of it," he said, "and

I'm givin' ye now — this night — yer last
chance. Quit this hotel and that woman, and
go back to Gilead and marry Polly. Don't do
it and I'll kill ye, ez sure ez you sit there
gapin' in that chair. If I can't get ye to
fight me like a man, — and I'll spit in yer
face or put some insult onto you afore that
woman, afore everybody, ez would make a
bigger skunk nor you turn, — I'll hunt ye
down and kill ye in your tracks."

There was a querulous murmur of interruption in Lacy's voice, but whether of defiance or appeal I could not distinguish.
Captain Jim's voice again rose, dogged and
distinct.

"Ef *you* kill me it's all the same, and I
don't say that I won't thank ye. This yer
world is too crowded for yer and me, Lacy
Bassett. I've believed in ye, trusted in ye,
lied for ye, and fought for ye. From the
time I took ye up — a feller-passenger to
'Fresco — believin' there wor the makin's
of a man in ye, to now, you fooled me, —
fooled me afore the Eureka boys; fooled me
afore Gilead; fooled me afore *her*; fooled
me afore God! It's got to end here. Ye've
got to take the curse of that foolishness off
o' me! You've got to do one single thing

that's like the man I took ye for, or you've got to die. Times waz when I'd have wished it for your account — that's gone, Lacy Bassett! You've got to do it for *me*. You've got to do it so I don't see 'd—d fool' writ in the eyes of every man ez looks at me."

He had apparently risen and walked towards the door. His voice sounded from another part of the room.

"I'll give ye till to-morrow mornin' to do suthin' to lift this curse off o' me. Ef you refoose, then, by the living God, I'll slap yer face in the dinin'-room, or in the office afore them all! You hear me!"

There was a pause, and then a quick sharp explosion that seemed to fill and expand both rooms until the windows were almost lifted from their casements, a hysterical inarticulate cry from Lacy, the violent opening of a door, hurried voices, and the tramping of many feet in the passage. I sprang out of bed, partly dressed myself, and ran into the hall. But by that time I found a crowd of guests and servants around the next door, some grasping Bassett, who was white and trembling, and others kneeling by Captain Jim, who was half lying in the doorway against the wall.

"He heard it all," Bassett gasped hysterically, pointing to me. " *He* knows that this man wanted to kill me."

Before I could reply, Captain Jim partly raised himself with a convulsive effort. Wiping away the blood that, oozing from his lips, already showed the desperate character of his internal wound, he said in a husky and hurried voice : "It's all right, boys! It's my fault. It was *me* who done it. I went for him in a mean underhanded way jest now, when he had n't a weppin nor any show to defend himself. We gripped. He got a holt o' my derringer — you see that 's *my* pistol there, I swear it — and turned it agin me in self - defense, and sarved me right. I swear to God, gentlemen, it's so !" Catching sight of my face, he looked at me, I fancied half imploringly and half triumphantly, and added, " I might hev knowed it ! I allers allowed Lacy Bassett was game ! — game, gentlemen — and he was. If it's my last word, I say it — he was game ! "

And with this devoted falsehood upon his lips and something of the old canine instinct in his failing heart, as his head sank back he seemed to turn it towards Bassett, as if to stretch himself out at his feet. Then the light failed from his yearning upward glance, and the curse of foolishness was lifted from him forever.

So conclusive were the facts, that the coroner's jury did not deem it necessary to detain Mr. Bassett for a single moment after the inquest. But he returned to Gilead, married Polly Baxter, and probably on the strength of having "killed his man," was unopposed on the platform next year, and triumphantly elected to the legislature!